Praise for T

'Intriguing, subtle and brimful of subterranean sadness, *The Spill* sucked me in from the first page. A thoughtful, sensitive look at the lies we tell ourselves and the stories we tell each other, and the ways we help piece together the people closest to us.' **Jane Rawson**

'Brilliantly comic and tender, this is a sharp and intimate portrayal of that most mystifying of things: family. Neeme gives us a real world; of chaotic fragments drawn with charm and compassion. These are people, like us, making lives of their messes.' **Robert Lukins**

'This compelling, beautifully crafted story introduces us to a pair of sisters, and then peels back the layers of their history to reveal the complexities and contradictions at the heart of love. Reading *The Spill* feels like being welcomed into a new family and gradually making sense of their complicated dynamics. The sisters and their troubled mother are flawed, frustrating, and at times infuriating, yet relatable and deeply endearing. Imbi Neeme is a hugely talented writer with an eye for the nuances that inform relationships. The family and their history will linger on in your mind long after you've finished the book.' **Kerri Sackville**

'Imbi Neeme's prose thrums, and her characters are so deep and richly imagined that it's astounding to think *The Spill* is her first novel. This is the story of sisters coming to terms with their mother's alcoholism and their father's shortcomings as a husband and a parent, but it's also a study of generational cause and effect and the ways we hurt the ones we most want to protect. I was hooked at first by the writing, but I soon found myself so invested in the characters that I didn't come up for air until I'd finished.' **J. P. Pomare**

About the author

IMBI NEEME IS a recovering blogger, impending novelist and compulsive short story writer. Her manuscript *The Spill* was awarded the 2019 Penguin Literary Prize.

She was also the recipient of the 2019 Henry Handel Richardson Fellowship at Varuna for excellence in short story writing. Her short fiction has won prizes in the 2019 Newcastle Short Story Awards, the 2018 Boroondara Literary Awards, and has been shortlisted for the 2018 Peter Carey Short Story Award.

Her first manuscript, *The Hidden Drawer*, made the judges' commended list in the 2015 Victorian Premier's Award for an Unpublished Manuscript and was selected for the 2015 Hachette/Queensland Writers Centre Manuscript Development Program.

She blogged for many years at *Not Drowning, Mothering*, which won the 2010 Bloggies award for best Australian/New Zealand Weblog.

She lives in Melbourne with her partner, kids and largely indifferent pets.

IMBI
NEEME

the spill

VIKING
an imprint of
PENGUIN BOOKS

For my sisters

VIKING

UK | USA | Canada | Ireland | Australia
India | New Zealand | South Africa | China

Viking Australia is part of the Penguin Random House group of companies whose
addresses can be found at global.penguinrandomhouse.com.

Penguin
Random House
Australia

First published by Viking Australia in 2020

Cover image by Klaus Vedfelt/Getty Images
Cover design by Alex Ross © Penguin Random House Australia Pty Ltd
Typeset in 13/17 pt Adobe Garamond by Post Pre-press, Brisbane
Printed and bound in Australia by Griffin Press, part of Ovato, an accredited
ISO AS/NZS 14001 Environmental Management Systems printer

A catalogue record for this
book is available from the
National Library of Australia

ISBN 978 1 76089 376 7

penguin.com.au

After the spill

1982

THE TWO GIRLS waited for their mother on the verandah of the Bruce Rock pub, which offered shade but little relief from the heat of the late afternoon. They swung their legs while they waited, slowly stirring the hot air and red dust, while the dogs around their feet lay panting, waiting patiently for their owners inside.

The girls' mother, Tina, was also inside, matching the locals middy for middy. It was the medicine she needed after the shock of the accident and the morning that had led up to it. The locals, in turn, were amused to have a lady from the city sitting alongside them in the front bar, like she belonged there.

'My bloody husband is driving from bloody Perth,' she told them all. 'Because of the bloody accident.'

One of the old guys raised his glass. 'To the bloody accident!' he shouted.

'To the bloody accident!' the rest of the front bar echoed, shoving their glasses in the air.

Tina laughed and raised her glass too, like the accident was something worth celebrating.

Occasionally, the publican would bring a couple of lemonades out to the girls, which ended up being more water than anything because the ice melted so quickly.

The third time, Tina came out with him to give them a packet of salt and vinegar Samboys.

Samantha jumped to her feet the moment she saw her mother. 'Is Daddy coming?' she asked, but Tina's focus was on the publican.

'Isn't Bevan looking after us *marvellously*,' she remarked, her consonants all soggy with the drink.

'Evan,' the publican corrected her.

'Evan. What do you say, girls?'

The girls thanked the publican in unison, diverging only when one called him Bevan and the other called him Evan.

Evan/Bevan gave a cursory nod and disappeared inside. Tina went to follow him but Samantha grabbed her hand.

'Mum?' she asked. The question about her father was still hanging in the air.

'Yes, Sammy,' Tina replied, with a sigh, as she gently removed her hand from her daughter's grasp. 'Your father is on his way . . . for whatever *that's* worth.'

As she pushed the doors to the front bar open, the crowd inside cheered at her return.

'Do you think he'll be here soon?' Samantha asked Nicole.

'Yes,' Nicole replied. As the older sister, she often felt obliged to sound more certain than she felt.

'Why do you think the car flipped like that?'

'I think Mum was going too fast around the corner.'

'Did you ask Mum to go fast?'

'No!' Nicole was outraged. 'Why would I ask Mum to do that?'

'Because you wanted to watch *Young Talent Time*.'

'Don't be silly,' Nicole said, with a frown.

The two girls continued to swing their legs. On Samantha's thigh, just above the knee, a bruise was already swelling.

'It's going to go a good colour,' she remarked, pleased. 'I'm going to show everyone at school on Monday.'

Nicole was too busy frowning. Samantha reached up to touch the bandage over her sister's left eyebrow. 'Does it hurt?' she asked.

Nicole shrugged. 'A bit.'

'Your cut's not as big as my bruise,' Samantha concluded, before noticing something poking out of the pocket on the front of Nicole's dress. 'Hey, what's that in your pocket?'

'It's nothing,' Nicole said, in a way that suggested it was definitely something.

'It's a lollipop. No fair!' Samantha cried. 'How come you got a lollipop and I didn't?'

'Because I got stitches,' Nicole told her.

After the crash, some strangers had stopped and wrapped the three of them in blankets and taken them to the Bruce Rock Memorial Hospital in the back of a station wagon. They'd had to wait for two hours in Emergency alongside the Saturday morning sports injuries but in the end, only Nicole had needed medical attention. The nurse had offered her the lollipop for her bravery and Nicole had accepted it, even though she was now in Year Seven and much too old for lollipops.

'My bruise is bigger and I didn't get anything,' Samantha was whining. 'Come on, we can share it. Lick for lick.'

'That's gross.'

Samantha tried to grab the lollipop out of her sister's pocket. 'Give it to me. You don't like them anyway.' Her voice was rising, like a kettle starting to boil.

Nicole sighed and handed her sister the sweet. It was always best to give in when her sister got like this.

Samantha put the lollipop in the pocket of her dress and immediately went back to swinging her legs, like nothing had happened.

'WHERE'S YOUR MOTHER?'

It was the first question that Craig asked his daughters, before he had even said hello or asked whether they were okay.

Nicole tipped her head towards the inside of the pub. 'She's inside.'

'Was she inside before?'

'Before?'

'Before the accident.'

Even though only a few hours had passed, the accident already felt like a lifetime ago to both girls. And the time before the accident, the breakfast of cold toast at the motel, felt like it had happened to other people altogether, to two other girls and their mum.

Nicole scratched her head. 'I saw her with a—' she started to say, but then stopped herself. 'No, she wasn't drinking.'

'Are you sure?' Craig asked.

'We were going too fast,' Samantha said.

'No, we weren't,' Nicole snapped.

'You said we were.'

'No, I didn't.'

'Girls . . .' Craig warned. He reached out and gently touched

4

Nicole's face, just near the bandage, and he softened a little, like butter in the heat. 'You okay, Nic?'

'Yeah. I got six stitches. But it didn't hurt. Not much.'

'You were in the front?'

'I was,' Samantha piped up. 'I made Nicole swap.'

'No, you didn't,' Nicole said. 'Mum made us swap.'

'No, she didn't.'

'It doesn't matter,' Craig said, laying a hand on each girl's shoulder. 'It's just good that Sammy was in the front. She's too little to be sitting in the back where there's no seatbelt.'

'I got a bruise on my leg,' Samantha continued, enjoying the spotlight. She lifted the hem of her dress to show the side of her leg. 'We reckon it's going to go a good colour. And I got a lollipop, too.'

Samantha didn't look at Nicole when she said that.

'You deserve it,' Craig said. 'Now, you girls just wait here while I go get your mother and then we'll head back home.'

'But what about Mum's car?' Nicole asked. 'And all our stuff?'

'That's all sorted,' Craig reassured her. 'That was the easy part.'

INSIDE THE PUB, Craig's entrance was met with a shriek from Tina.

'It's my bloody husband from bloody Perth!'

'To the bloody husband from bloody Perth!' The crowd roared and lifted their glasses in the air.

Craig ignored the raucous greeting and marched over to his wife. 'Let's go.'

'Piss off, I'm having a drink,' Tina said. One of her bra straps had slipped down her arm and was hanging limply, like a flag at half-mast.

Craig grabbed her by the elbow and firmly guided her out

of the pub, amidst the cheering and jeering of the crowd in the front bar.

'You're hurting me,' Tina was shouting as they stepped out onto the verandah, even though she was laughing.

'You're hurting Mum!' Nicole pulled at her father's sleeve, while Samantha began to cry and all the dogs on the porch started barking.

Tina kept laughing, as Craig's grip tightened on her elbow. 'Ladies and gentlemen! The circus is leaving town!'

IT WASN'T UNTIL they were all seated in Craig's parked car that anyone realised Tina was still holding her middy of Swan Lager. She held it to her lips and started to drink it in huge gulps.

The girls gasped. They weren't allowed to drink or eat in Craig's Mazda RX7.

'Jesus, Tina,' Craig said. 'Haven't you had enough?'

'No. Never.'

'Well, I have.'

'Actually, I don't think you have, Craig.' Tina turned to him and looked him squarely in the eye.

Craig paused for the briefest of moments and then reached over to wrestle the glass off his wife, spilling its remaining contents all over her and his precious upholstery in the process.

'No more,' he said, as he threw the now-empty glass out the car window, where it smashed into pieces on the hot bitumen.

'More,' Tina said, now sullen.

Craig ignored her and revved the engine loudly, like a metal lion warning its prey. Tina slumped down in her seat.

After a few more roars, the car took off, with only Samantha's sniffling in the back seat and the stench of spilt beer to score the long, red road back to Perth.

Nicole

AFTER THE BURIAL, I found myself separated from the rest of the family. The sudden rain had sent everyone scattering and I quickly lost sight of Dad and Celine, who were supposed to be giving me a lift to the house.

I took shelter under a large tree next to a group of people I didn't recognise. From the way they were talking about my mother, they clearly didn't recognise me either.

'Pissing down for an old pisshead,' a man in a wrinkled linen jacket remarked.

'I don't know why they're bothering to bury her. Surely her body is so soaked in the sauce, it will never decompose,' another man said.

The women tittered, but then one of them noticed me and, nudging the others, hissed the word *daughter*.

'Nicole, isn't it?' the woman said, sidling over to me. I felt my hackles rise. 'You gave a lovely speech. We all knew your mum from school.'

'Such a shame,' said the man with the linen jacket.

'You spoke so beautifully at the service,' said the other. 'Sorry for your loss.'

Sorry my arse, I thought. I nodded at the group and stepped out from the shelter of the tree, preferring to get wet than listen to their false platitudes.

As I walked through the cemetery, I marvelled at the Perth summer rain. The heavy, fat drops were falling so far from each other that it almost seemed possible to walk between them without getting wet.

But I was getting wet.

I thought back to a day from my childhood where we'd lingered too long on the beach and the afternoon sea breeze had whipped the sand up into our eyes. There had been a storm coming in off the Indian Ocean and lightning had fired up the horizon. Samantha and I had run to the car to take shelter, but Mum had stood at the top of the dunes, looking out at the sea, greeting the storm.

I stopped walking and looked back over at the hole where my mother's body now lay.

The storm has finally passed, Mum, I thought.

WHEN MY FATHER saw how wet I was, he jumped out of his Lexus ES 350 and grabbed a towel from the boot.

'Thanks, Dad,' I said.

But the towel wasn't for me, it was for the back seat of his car.

Celine was in the passenger seat, busy reapplying her make-up using the rear-view mirror. 'Got to get my face back on,' she said brightly, as I climbed carefully into the back seat. 'Where's that lovely Prince Charming of yours?'

'Jethro's gone ahead to deal with the caterers,' I said, trying to straighten the towel underneath me.

'He's a keeper, that one. You can thank me at your wedding for getting you two together.'

I clenched my teeth and smiled politely. Jethro and I had been happily together for ten years and yet Celine was still trying to push us down the aisle like it was 1955.

'Sure,' I said.

Even under all that make-up, Celine's face was looking pale and puffy in the reflection of the rear-view mirror. I remembered Samantha's theory that Celine was trying to get pregnant. Maybe she was right, after all.

'Finished,' Celine announced, twisting the mirror back around to face the driver's side. Dad immediately readjusted it, and then moved on to fussing with the powered wing mirrors.

We were never going to leave at this rate. I had an urge to shake myself off like a dog over Dad's precious upholstery.

'Was that Meg I saw at the funeral?' Dad asked, as he continued to fiddle with even more mirror-related knobs.

'Yeah,' I said.

'I haven't seen her in more than thirty years.'

'Who's Meg?' Celine asked, now brushing her hair, in long decisive strokes.

'Tina's sister,' Dad replied.

'Was she the one doing the ugly crying? The one that looked like Tina, but, um, much younger?'

'There's only two years between them, would you believe.'

'Really? Meg must have a great skin care routine.'

'Not to mention a fully-functioning liver,' I piped up and then immediately regretted it. It felt far too soon to be making light of Mum's drinking. 'I thought it was good of Aunt Meg to come.'

To tell the truth, I'd been surprised she'd flown over from Melbourne for the funeral; she'd barely seen Mum over the past three decades. But then, I knew from my own experiences that sisters were sisters, no matter the time or distance. She had as much of a right to grieve as any of us.

'I'm so sorry for your loss,' Celine said. She had now turned in her seat to give me her full attention. 'Of course, I only met Tina a few times, but I do know this: she loved you and Samantha very much.'

It wasn't much consolation, being told by my father's third wife that my dead mother loved me, especially when accompanied by the whirr of the powered wing mirrors. But I knew Celine meant well.

'She wasn't the easiest person to know,' I admitted. I could see the back of my father's head nod slightly, perhaps in agreement. Or maybe he was still looking at the bloody mirrors.

GIVEN HOW MANY career drunks were in attendance at Tina's wake, precious little alcohol was being served. All around our large front living room, people were nursing empty glasses, their eyes occasionally darting towards the kitchen.

'What's going on with the drinks?' Jethro whispered to me.

'I think we both know what's going on with the drinks. Or rather, *who*.'

Jethro rolled his eyes. 'I should have known. Do you want me sort it out?'

'No, I'll do it.'

I hated confrontation but it wasn't fair on Jethro to make him deal with another situation of my sister's making. I headed towards the kitchen with my empty glass, but was intercepted by Aunt Meg.

'Nicky,' she said, clutching my arm tightly, her eyes wide and red. 'Can we talk? There's some things I really need to tell you and Sammy before I fly back to Melbourne tomorrow.'

I knew I should speak to her but I was on a mission.

'Sure thing, Aunt Meg,' I said, freeing myself from her grip. 'But later, okay? I just have to attend to something first.'

In the kitchen, I asked the caterer what was going on with the drinks service.

'Your sister told us to slow it down,' she confessed, with a sheepish look. 'She was, uh, scary.'

I looked back through the open kitchen door at Samantha, who was glaring across the crowd at me, and swallowed.

'Yes, she is scary,' I said, as I raised my empty glass to Samantha. I knew this was a battle I wasn't going to win. I turned back to the caterer. 'Now, get me a teacup full of vodka. *Stat.*'

OF COURSE, THE great benefit of not serving much alcohol at the wake was that all the guests were gone by seven-thirty, even Aunt Meg, who, as she was being ushered out the door, was still insisting that she needed to talk to Samantha and me before she flew home.

'I'll ring you in the morning to make a plan,' I told her, patting her on the arm. I had barely spoken to the woman in decades, so I was fairly confident it could wait another day.

Once the last guest had left, I kicked off my shoes and sank into the lounge next to Samantha who was sitting upright, her hands in her lap and her shoes still on.

For a long time, we sat in silence. This was the first time we had been alone since Mum had died. I had made sure of it, ignoring the entreaties Samantha had made in her texts and phone calls, all of which had come too late, after Mum had already gone. Even now, I could only handle her being here because I had enough vodka in my system to dull my grief.

After a while, I got sick of the silence and pulled a jigsaw puzzle out from under the coffee table.

'I saved this for after the wake,' I said, putting it on the table. 'It's one of Mum's. I thought it would be a good way to honour her.'

I didn't add that I had planned to do the jigsaw with Jethro, who was now making himself scarce somewhere else in the house. He wasn't exactly one of Samantha's greatest fans.

'Oh god.' Samantha was looking at the box with barely disguised horror. 'If it's one of Tina's, there'll be pieces missing.'

'So?'

'There's not much point doing it if it's not complete.'

'Life is like a jigsaw puzzle without all the pieces,' I reminded her, as I pulled the lid off. 'And we still do life.'

'Some of us do it better than others.'

I didn't respond. Instead, I started to separate out the edge pieces, while Samantha sat beside me, looking anywhere except at the puzzle.

'I haven't seen that photo in years,' she said, after a few minutes. She was staring at a framed photo of our mother on top of a corner cabinet, surrounded by red roses. It had been taken in 1968, the year she met our father. 'She looks so beautiful.'

'That's the nicest thing you've said about Mum in decades,' I couldn't help remarking. 'I'm obviously not counting the time you called her a fucking bitch at my fortieth.'

'I think we both know whose fault that was,' she said, her lips pursed.

'Well, I know you think it was *this* fucking bitch's fault.' As the words fell out of my mouth, I realised that drinking all that vodka had definitely been a mistake.

Samantha shifted in her seat. 'I still don't know why you invited her,' she said, primly.

I returned to the puzzle, trying my best to shrug off the conversation.

'Is that new?' Samantha asked me, now focusing on the cabinet on top of which the photo sat.

'No, it's just one we moved from the yellow room. It's a heavy bugger.' I shot her a sideways glance before adding, 'As heavy as a Pritikin scone, one might say.'

I had been hoping to raise a smile, but all Samantha could muster was a grimace. A million years ago, one of her schoolfriends had brought a batch of Pritikin scones to our house. Mum had tried to eat one and had used Pritikin scones as a point of reference for anything heavy ever since. Samantha never appreciated the joke but I'd always found it hilarious.

'Oh come on, Sam. Try to see the *lighter* side of life,' I said, elbowing her gently. 'Get it? Lighter?'

I held the open jigsaw box out to her as a peace offering. Samantha gave a small, tight smile.

'Okay, I'll help you,' she said, accepting the box. 'Do you have a board or a puzzle mat that we should be using?'

'It's fine here on the table.'

'But what if the puzzle gets in the way?'

'We'll just use the other lounge room.'

And as quickly as I'd won her over, I lost her again by reminding her that I lived in a house with more than one living area. She pressed her lips together so hard I thought her face was going to implode. For reasons I had never understood, she had a big bee in her bonnet about 'Jethro's millions', as she liked to refer to Jethro's wealth. She always said it like I'd deliberately found a rich boyfriend just to piss her off.

Samantha held position for a few seconds, and then her face suddenly relaxed. 'You start putting the edge pieces together,' she told me, now focusing entirely on the box. 'I'll keep looking for them.'

As I started to connect the pieces, my mind turned back to the funeral service and I realised Samantha hadn't said anything about my eulogy.

'What did you think of my speech?' I asked her. Hot damn, this vodka was making me bold. I'd normally wait five years to get up the courage to ask this kind of question. At this rate, my next question would be why the hell she never visited Mum in hospital.

'It was fine,' Samantha said with the tiniest of shrugs as she carefully picked through the pieces.

'Fine?'

'It was good.'

'*Good?*' I was annoyed. I had spent too many hours on the eulogy for it to be just 'good'.

'Yes, good.'

'You think you could have done better?' I asked her. 'Remember that speech you gave at my twenty-first?'

'I didn't give a speech at your twenty-first.'

'Yes, you did. You said this big naff thing about us sisters being like seatbelts for each other.'

'No, I didn't. I would never say something like that.'

'Mum and I always used to make jokes about it behind your back.'

'Mum wasn't even there.'

'Yes, she was.'

'No, she wasn't,' Samantha said firmly. 'I should know. I was the one who did the invitation list and I didn't invite her.'

I was sure Mum had been there. I remembered her being there, sitting with me on the love seat in the backyard in Mount Lawley.

'And look,' Samantha continued, 'even if she *was* there, and even if I *had* given a speech, she wouldn't have remembered it. God knows, she was pissed almost every day back then.'

'Actually, Sam, she always remembered,' I replied, the anger rising from deep within my gut. I hated the way she exaggerated Mum's drinking, like it was the only thing she ever did with her life. 'She remembered more things than Dad. He was always so focused on his wives.'

I knew I was using the word 'wives' like it was thirty wives and not just three. I also knew that Samantha was trying to drag me back into the ghost of an unfinished argument.

'At least he loved his *wives*. Tina just loved the bottle,' she said, picking out another edge piece from the puzzle box.

'Who's being a fucking bitch now?'

'You're drunk.'

'No, I'm not. I'm "tired and emotional". We buried Mum today.'

'I can't believe you're drunk.'

Suddenly, I felt overwhelmed by the full weight of my tiredness. And the vodka.

'Let's not do this,' I said.

'Okay.' Samantha stood up and started picking up empty glasses. 'Let's not.'

'And don't do that either. The caterers are coming back to do that tomorrow. That's why we pay them the big bucks.'

'Just let me do my thing.'

'As long as your thing doesn't involve Jethro's record collection again,' I said.

'What kind of a person arranges records in the order that they bought them,' Samantha muttered.

'Um, someone who values his own memories?'

Samantha gave a small *hmmph* and continued picking up glasses. I abandoned the puzzle and swung my body around to lie along the length of the couch. Samantha continued to clean up.

'Just like old times!' I exclaimed, but she ignored me.

I looked back at the photo of my mother, her dark hair swept up in a way that seemed to defy gravity, her eyes clear and her smile wide. It was such a stark contrast to the Tina who had lain in her bed at Mount Hospital, hooked up to machines, her skin yellow under the strip lighting.

The waste of it all.

I closed my eyes again and gave in to the fatigue. And the vodka.

'I'M OFF HOME.'

Samantha was standing over me, holding a large bunch of white lilies in a ceramic vase.

I had no idea how much time had passed. It could have been minutes or it could have been days. And for some reason, I was on the floor, a cushion under my head. Embarrassed, I pulled myself back up onto the couch.

'You fell,' Samantha informed me, her jaw tight. 'But you didn't wake up.'

'I'm pretty tired,' I said. '*And* emotional, don't forget.'

'No, I hadn't forgotten,' she said and I knew she wouldn't have. She nodded at the vase in her arms. 'Is this your vase?'

'I don't know. Probably?' I guessed.

'You honestly don't know if it's your vase or not?' Samantha was incredulous.

'Why? Do you do a nightly inventory of your kitchen cupboards?' I shot back. 'It might have come with the flowers.'

Samantha took a deep breath and then continued. 'I'm taking these flowers home, if you don't mind. Trent really likes lilies.'

Even though my sister had been married to him for over twenty years, I had no idea that Trent was the kind of guy to have a strong preference for lilies.

'Take more flowers, if you want. There's so many of them,' I told her. 'Seriously, what are we supposed to do with so many fucking flowers?'

'Maybe you'll think about that the next time you're buying flowers for somebody else,' Samantha snapped.

'What is that supposed to mean?'

'Aunt Meg rang,' Samantha said, ignoring my question. 'She wants to talk to us both before she leaves.'

I let the conversation move on, although I still wanted to know what problem she had with me and flowers. 'Yeah, I know. Maybe the Ghost Aunt will finally tell us why we haven't seen her in over thirty years.'

'Maybe. I've told her we'll meet her at the Blue Duck tomorrow at noon.'

'Noon? You couldn't have checked with me first? I might have something on.' I didn't have anything on. Living with Jethro had turned me into a professional Lady of Leisure, much to Samantha's eternal disgust.

'When do you ever have anything on?' she said.

I just shut my eyes and waited for the front door to finally slam shut. And the minute it did, I realised that, despite everything, I missed her almost as much as I now missed my mother.

'Has she gone?'

It was Jethro, peeking around the doorway.

'Yes, she's gone.'

'Thank god for that,' he said, walking in with a bottle of red and two glasses. 'I hope she didn't touch my record collection.'

'I told her not to.'

'As if that would make any difference,' Jethro muttered. 'Anyway, enough about Samantha. I think we should raise a toast.' He poured out some wine and thrust a glass into my hand. 'To Tina,' he said, holding his glass up high. 'Whose light shone bright but burnt out way too fast.'

'To Tina.'

As I clinked my glass against Jethro's, I noticed how the light hit the wine and made it look like a bright and beautiful jewel and nothing like the poison Samantha was always claiming it was.

'To Tina,' I said again, bringing the glass to my lips and drinking.

I felt the warmth of the wine travel down through my body and thought of how no amount of wine could bring any warmth back to my mother, lying in that dark hole in the cemetery. I turned to tell Jethro this and, in doing so, my knee knocked the edge of the jigsaw puzzle box, sending the pieces scattering everywhere.

And then the tears finally came.

Piece #1: 1984

'WHAT ARE YOU doing?'

Samantha did her best to ignore Nicole, who was looming over her while she tried to tuck a sheet in between her single mattress and the bed base.

'No, seriously, Sam,' Nicole persisted. 'What the hell are you doing?'

'I'm trying to make it look nice,' Samantha replied. 'Helen Millet has a valance on her bed that matches the curtains.'

'Well, that just looks stupid.'

'You look stupid.'

Samantha knew without looking that Nicole was rolling her eyes, but she decided not to engage. There was too much to do before Helen Millet arrived. Everything needed to be perfect. Since she and Helen Millet had been put in the same Year Seven class, they had been hanging out more, and this sleepover was going to make them best friends. Samantha was sure of it.

'There,' she said, stepping back from the bed, finally satisfied. She turned her attention back to her sister, who was now lying on her own bed. 'Can you at least make your bed?' she asked.

'I thought we would just pull a sheet over it,' Nicole replied slyly. 'You know, to make it look "nice".'

As Samantha felt the sharp sting of tears in her eyes, she quickly turned away so Nicole couldn't see.

TO HER CREDIT, Tina made a real effort to get the house ready for Helen Millet. She pulled out the old upright vacuum cleaner, which Samantha had forgotten they even had, and pushed it across the worn carpets. She fluffed up the pillows on the sofa and opened all the windows to let the fresh air in, all the while singing along to the radio.

Nicole put her hands over her ears and pretended to be embarrassed.

'Oh, *Mum*,' she said, but she was laughing.

Samantha would have laughed too, but she'd already seen Tina drinking pale liquid from a tall tumbler full of ice. Ever since the car accident three years ago, she'd felt uneasy whenever she saw Tina with a drink of any kind, even if it looked like a glass of water.

Helen Millet arrived at five o'clock, wearing a pink backpack and holding her own pillow. Her mother, dressed in neat white slacks with a pastel yellow jumper draped around her shoulders, accompanied her to the front door.

'We're so pleased you can join us, Helen,' Tina said, her voice as smooth as glass.

'Here's some Pritikin scones for dessert,' Helen Millet's mother said, handing over a Tupperware container. 'I'm trying to keep Helen away from refined grains.' She fished a small white card from her purse. 'And here's my number if there are any problems.'

The minute the front door was closed, Tina made a big point of tucking the card into her bra. Luckily, Helen Millet was too busy taking off her pink backpack to notice.

'We're having pasta for tea,' Samantha whispered to Helen Millet, hoping that pasta didn't contain too many refined grains.

'I love pasta,' Helen Millet whispered back and Samantha felt glad.

While Tina cooked dinner, Samantha and Helen worked on Tina's jigsaw puzzle at the kitchen table. Nicole was reading one of her books in the corner. Samantha didn't know why Nicole couldn't read in bed like she normally did, but she tried not to let it bother her.

The puzzle had loads of very small pieces, most of which were sky. Samantha never had much luck putting pieces together, but she loved sorting them into different colours. She kept glancing over at Helen to see if she was having fun, but Helen wasn't giving much away. In any case, Samantha was finding it hard to concentrate. The rattle of ice as Tina took each sip of her drink was making her anxious. Eventually, she stood and picked up Tina's glass from the kitchen bench.

'Can I have a sip?' she asked, thinking that this would make Tina realise that she knew it was alcohol.

But Tina only laughed. 'When you're eighteen,' she replied, and took back the glass. 'You can have ice in your cordial if you want something fancy.'

'Gee, thanks, Tina. Frozen water and cordial,' Nicole said, looking up from her book. 'Yummy.'

'Suit yourselves,' Tina said. 'Now, if you'll excuse me, I have a phone call to make.'

As she left the room, she banged her hip really hard on the side of the table, knocking the box of unsorted puzzle pieces onto the floor, but she didn't appear to notice.

Samantha immediately leapt from her chair and started picking them up.

'You call your mum "Tina"?' Helen Millet asked Nicole. She didn't seem to be bothered by the pieces on the floor.

'Well, it *is* her name,' Nicole replied. 'Sometimes we even call her "Teensy".'

'That's what *Dad* used to call her. Nicole's only showing off because I have a friend here.' Samantha wanted Helen Millet's attention back on her.

'Don't be a dick,' Nicole said.

'Mum!' Samantha shouted. She immediately regretted this automatic response because she knew it would bring Tina back into the room and back to her glass.

But Tina was still in the hall. 'I'm just leaving Aunty Meg a message for her birthday,' she shouted back.

'Didn't we do that yesterday?' Nicole asked Samantha.

Samantha nodded. She remembered they'd all sung 'Happy Birthday' into Aunt Meg's answering machine.

'I know we did that yesterday,' Tina said, re-entering the room. 'That's the fourth message I've left. Hopefully she'll ring back this time.'

She stepped around all the jigsaw pieces – and Samantha – on the floor and picked up her drink.

Samantha watched her, biting her lip hard.

INSTEAD OF EATING dinner on their laps like they usually did when Tina had a jigsaw puzzle on the table, Tina spread a tablecloth over the pieces. Samantha didn't like it when Tina did that. She always worried that the tablecloth would disrupt her careful colour sorting, and that when they removed the tablecloth at the end of the meal, the pieces would fly everywhere. Missing pieces never bothered Tina or Nicole the way they bothered Samantha.

Over dinner, Tina told them stories from her own childhood, including the time her sister Meg had peed her pants in primary school.

'She was so upset, I gave her my own undies to wear. But then I forgot about it and did a cartwheel in front of a bunch of Grade Six boys at play lunch.'

'Oh, Mum,' Nicole said. 'You're embarrassing Sam.'

But Samantha had barely been listening to the stories. She'd been too busy worrying about the number of times Tina had refilled her tumbler with whatever it was in the bottle on top of the fridge. Since Helen had arrived, there had been six. Six glasses of whatever.

'Who wants dessert?' Tina asked, her words sticking to each other. She'd clearly forgotten about the Pritikin scones Helen Millet's mother had given her because she pulled the ice cream out of the freezer and gave them each a spoon.

'Dig in, girls!' she said. 'I'm going to . . .'

And then she left the room without finishing her sentence.

'My mum would never let us eat from the container,' Helen told Samantha.

'I'm so sorry,' Samantha said. 'Do you want a bowl? Or a Pritikin scone instead?'

'No, it's kind of cool.'

'Mum is a true bohemian,' Nicole said.

Samantha had no idea what a bohemian was but she knew that if it involved eating ice cream straight from the container she didn't want to be one.

Helen Millet probably didn't know what a bohemian was either, but she was now looking at Nicole, encouraging her to say more. And Nicole was more than happy to oblige.

'Last weekend, she gave us Twisties and apple slices for dinner,' she said. 'And she once let us cut her hair. Not just a little bit, but a whole heap.'

Helen leaned in, still wanting more. Samantha gave Nicole the dirtiest look she could muster, but Nicole kept going.

'And then there was the time that Sam had no clean socks for school,' she said. 'Mum washed some in the kitchen sink with all the dishes and then put them in the oven to dry. They came out like cardboard and she called them *Socks à la mode*.'

'Your mum is so funny,' Helen said, and in that moment, Samantha saw how brightly both Nicole and Tina were shining in Helen Millet's eyes and she became filled with fury.

Suddenly, it felt like she was up on the ceiling, looking down on herself and everyone else.

'Tina's not funny, she's drunk,' she heard herself saying as she slammed her spoon on the table. 'Here, come with me.'

'What are you doing?' Nicole was sounding concerned.

But Samantha couldn't stop this other version of herself. This Other Samantha was filled with furious regret for having invited Helen Millet into her house. This Other Samantha wanted to punish Tina, to punish Nicole for spilling their secrets, and even to punish Helen Millet simply for being there.

She led Helen Millet firmly by the hand to Tina's bedroom and showed her the two Coolabah casks and a large, almost empty bottle of whisky on her bedside table, where normal people might have books or photos or ornaments.

'See this? This isn't funny or cool.'

'Don't be such a bitch, Sam,' Nicole was hissing from the doorway. 'Get out of Mum's room.'

'Settle, my petals,' Tina said, appearing next to Nicole in the doorway. She was laughing.

Helen looked on, her mouth open. Samantha couldn't tell what was more shocking to Helen Millet: the stash of alcohol, Nicole's use of the word 'bitch' or Tina's laughter.

THE THREE GIRLS brushed their teeth in silence and got into bed just before ten. Helen was sleeping on a mattress on the floor in between Samantha and Nicole's beds.

'Why is there a sheet tucked under your mattress like that?' Helen asked Samantha.

'It's a valance,' Nicole informed her. Samantha couldn't tell if she was being sarcastic or not.

'My mum did it. She must have been drunk,' Samantha replied. She quickly turned off the light so that Helen Millet and Nicole couldn't see her lying face or the fake valance. She hoped that in the dark they could forget everything that had happened and they could start whispering and giggling, like girls were supposed to do at sleepovers.

But instead of whispering and giggling, Helen just said in a small voice, 'I want to go home.'

'Okay,' Samantha said with a small sigh, switching the light back on. 'Let's get my mum to ring your mum.'

AFTER HELEN MILLET'S mum, still dressed in her white slacks and yellow jumper, picked her daughter up, Samantha and Nicole returned to their room and to their beds, stepping around the empty mattress on the floor like it was a corpse.

'I think your bed looks nice like that,' Nicole remarked but Samantha knew she was just being kind. The bed looked stupid.

Even she could see that now.

Nicole fell asleep quickly, but Samantha lay awake for ages, unable to sleep. Eventually, she heard the TV go off in the lounge room and the sound of Tina gently bouncing from wall to wall down the hallway and then picking up the phone.

'I miss you, Meg,' Tina said. But she must have said it to nobody at all, because Samantha didn't hear her dial Meg's number. There were a few seconds of silence and then Samantha heard the clunk of the receiver being replaced and Tina going into her room.

Samantha thought about Aunt Meg and how long it had been since she had visited them. And then she thought of how she, herself, would one day live in a different house from her own sister and how weird that would be. Even though Nicole made her mad sometimes, she knew that she would miss her as much as Tina must miss Meg.

'Nicole,' she whispered into the semi-darkness, but Nicole didn't wake up. She thought about climbing into her sister's bed like she used to do when she was smaller, but she was worried Nicole would get grumpy with her. She decided to go to Tina's bed, instead. She knew that Tina would be awake, reading her book late into the night.

Tina was awake, but she wasn't reading. Instead, she was lying on top of her bed, fully clothed and sniffing. The minute she saw Samantha, however, she sat up, all smiles.

'Hello, my little love,' she exclaimed, patting the empty space on the bed beside her. 'Did you have a bad dream?'

Samantha shook her head as she climbed onto the bed. 'I can't sleep,' she said.

'I'm sorry your friend left. Sleeping over in a strange house can be really hard for some kids,' Tina offered.

Samantha tried to say something in response but surprised herself by bursting into tears instead.

'It's okay,' Tina said, putting her arm around her.

'No, it's not okay!' Samantha sobbed, as she sunk into her mother's arms. 'Mum, what if nobody ever likes me? What if nobody ever wants to be my friend?'

'Oh, now,' Tina said softly. 'Sometimes it just takes time to find real friends. And *I* like you. I like you a lot. Also Nicole likes you. And your dad likes you. And I'm pretty certain that Helen likes you, too.'

'Not anymore.'

'Don't be too sure about that. Anyway, I just tried to eat one of those Pritikin scones and I almost broke a tooth.'

Samantha giggled and snuggled even closer into her mother's embrace. As she closed her eyes and drifted off to sleep, she thought of Helen Millet's bed with its clean white sheets and its ruffled valance, but she knew that it wasn't any better than the place she was now. She wished that it would always feel this way.

Piece #2: 1991

THE DAY OF Nicole's twenty-first party started like any other in a long, blurry chain of identical days living with Tom and Kim in Inverness Crescent. Bongs at noon, followed by Frosties and Coco Pops – this time without milk because someone, probably Tom, had put the empty carton back in the fridge. Then *Days of Our Lives*, *The Bold and the Beautiful* and *Fraggle Rock*. All punctuated with more bongs.

And then Samantha turned up.

Samantha turning up was not an unusual event. Sometimes she would drop by in her tan-coloured Datsun 180B on her way to TAFE to warn Nicole of the evils of marijuana. On those occasions, Nicole would often tell her sister to *fuck-the-fuck-off*, but her words would then turn into crystals and fall onto the ground, and she would laugh as she tried to pick all those *fuck-the-fuck-off*-ing crystals up. Samantha would purse her lips, get back in her Datsun 180B and drive off.

Samantha's love for that car drove Nicole nuts. Samantha spent more time cleaning and vacuuming it than their father did with his new Jaguar XJ Series 3. Nicole could never understand how people could love cars that much. She didn't even have one. Didn't need one. The only place she ever had to go was the Mirrabooka CES every second Thursday to hand in her dole form, and even then, she was able to take the Green Mercedes there. The Green Mercedes was what Kim called the MTT buses because they were all 'fucking Mercs', even the ones that went to Mirrabooka. Nicole found those Thursdays exhausting. She had no idea how anybody managed to hold down a full-time job. Still, going to Mirrabooka every second Thursday gave her life some semblance of shape. If it wasn't for the dole, Nicole would have given up on the concept of time altogether.

As it was, she had completely forgotten it was the day of her twenty-first party until Samantha arrived.

'Choose Life is here to see you,' Kim informed Nicole. 'And she's brought her play things.'

'What?' Nicole had been napping on the couch and hadn't even heard the doorbell.

'Time to get ready!' Samantha announced brightly as she pushed past Kim and headed straight for the kitchen. She was carrying her hairdryer, electric curler set and make-up case. Nicole dragged herself up from the couch and followed her.

'Do you want a classic updo or do you want Big Hair like Cindy Crawford?' Samantha asked, as she started setting everything up on the table. 'I could even do a beauty spot, if you like.'

'Do whatever you like,' Nicole said. She knew she probably

wanted an updo but she'd long since surrendered all control of the party to her sister.

'Big Hair it is!' Samantha said, plugging in her curler set.

Nicole swallowed her disappointment.

'You guys playing dress-ups?' Tom asked as he got ready for his shift at the Dog Swamp video store. He was the only member of the household with a job but it was only because of the easy access to new releases and porn.

'It's my party tonight,' Nicole said, pointing at the invitation she'd stuck to the door of the fridge weeks ago, right next to the handle so he'd notice it.

'Oh, yeah. That thing. Have a good time.'

'You're not coming?' Samantha asked, incredulous.

'Maybe after my shift.' He pulled an almost-finished container of orange juice from the fridge door, chugged it and then put the empty container back. 'Later days.'

'I thought he was your boyfriend,' Samantha whispered, once Tom had left the room.

Nicole shrugged. She'd never tried to label her relationship with Tom. They just slept together when they felt like it, which actually wasn't that often.

'Hey, you still have a scar,' Samantha said, tentatively touching the spot on Nicole's eyebrow where she'd had stitches almost ten years before. 'I wonder what struck you in the car crash to make such a deep cut.'

'My own razor-sharp wit,' Nicole replied.

'I've been thinking about that crash a lot lately,' Samantha said as she started to put the hot curlers in Nicole's hair.

'I never think about it.'

'About how drunk Mum was.'

'She says she wasn't.'

'We both know that's not true.'

But Nicole wasn't sure if she really did know that. It didn't matter how many times she told Samantha she'd only seen their mother *holding* the bottle of alcohol in the motel parking lot and not actually *drinking* from it, Samantha always chose to believe the worst of Tina.

Nicole didn't want to fight, so she concentrated on the heat of the curlers against her scalp and let the moment pass.

THANKS TO SAMANTHA, Nicole arrived at her party at Craig and Donna-Louise's Mount Lawley home on time and completely straight. She'd tried to convince Kim to come with them but Kim said she would come later, which was probably her way of saying 'I'm going to get baked and watch *Cannonball Run II* instead'.

Nicole grabbed a West Coast wine cooler from one of the eskies in the laundry, hoping it would take the edge off, or at least partially deflate the Big Hair that Samantha had given her.

As she stepped out into the backyard, she was struck by how much effort Samantha had made. She'd decorated the trees with fairy lights and carefully placed tea light candles inside coloured glasses all around the garden beds. Along the back fence, she'd even spelt Nicole's name with large letters cut out from bright red cardboard.

'Do you like what we've done for you?' Samantha said, appearing out of nowhere, with her boyfriend, Trent, beside her like a faithful hound. 'Trent and I worked all afternoon.'

Trent bowed his head. 'Sammy did most of the work.'

'I love it,' Nicole told them, and found that she actually meant it.

Samantha beamed at them both. 'Anything for my biggest and only-est sister!'

*

31

THE NIGHT WORE on, in a long blur of lukewarm wine coolers and inane small talk. At one point, Nicole found herself blissfully alone and finally able to get a good look at the rest of the party. She saw Craig and Donna-Louise holding court with some of the older relatives from the Cooper side of the family, probably talking about tax breaks and real estate. She saw her cousins, spoilt private school brats now doing Commerce–Law or Law–Commerce at UWA, drinking irresponsibly in the corner. She saw people from school, most of whom she'd already forgotten. She even saw some of Craig's business associates, sweating in their sports jackets and nylon trousers.

No sign of Kim, of course. Or Tom.

And no Tina.

She went to look for Samantha to ask where Tina was but found herself face-to-face with Ben Porter, her Year Ten boyfriend.

'Hey, Nicky,' he said. 'Thanks for the invite.'

Nicole tried not to grimace. She hated it when anyone outside the immediate family called her Nicky.

'You're welcome, *Benny*,' she said, wondering why on earth Samantha had invited him. There was no way Nicole wanted him here, not after the way he'd dropped her at the Year Ten River Rock and she'd spent the entire boat trip crying in the toilets.

If Ben remembered any of that, he gave no sign. Instead, he launched into a long story about the trip he'd just taken to Bali with his fiancée. Nicole could tell he thought he was an exciting world adventurer like Alby Mangels, instead of just a guy wearing a 96FM sweatshirt, drinking XXXX in someone's backyard.

'You should go, Nicky. It's so exotic,' Ben said. 'And surprisingly affordable. I mean, Kuta is practically an outer suburb of Perth these days.'

Nicole smiled and nodded and then someone put 'Eternal Flame' on the stereo and Ben asked her to dance and she knew this was probably going to be the worst night of her life.

AT THE FIRST opportunity, she broke away from Ben and sought out Samantha. She found her in a corner of the garden with Trent, away from the rest of the party.

'Are you having the best time?' Samantha asked brightly.

'Where's Mum?'

There was an awkward pause while Samantha looked at the ground and Trent turned red.

'I'll get us another Pepsi,' Trent said, and quickly disappeared.

'Well?' Nicole demanded.

'She . . . I didn't invite her,' Samantha replied, before adding, 'I invited Aunt Meg, but. She couldn't make it, but she said happy birthday!'

She smiled at Nicole as if that made up for everything. But Nicole didn't give a shit about Aunt Meg's birthday wishes. She hadn't seen the woman in years.

'That's fucked up,' she told Samantha. 'You invited our Ghost Aunt and Ben-Fucking-Porter but you didn't invite Mum?'

'Dad said Donna-Louise wasn't comfortable having her in the house.' Samantha shrugged, still looking at the ground.

I didn't realise it was Donna-Louise's party, Nicole wanted to say but she knew it wasn't really her party either. She looked over to where Craig and Donna-Louise were fussing over the cushions on their wrought-iron love seat. Someone had probably made the mistake of sitting on it.

'Anyway, I saw you dancing with Ben Porter. You looked like you were having fun,' Samantha said in that voice of hers that always felt like a mosquito in Nicole's ear.

'Yeah, I've been pretending to have fun all night,' Nicole replied far too quickly and instantly regretted it. Samantha was now looking like she was going to cry.

'I thought you were having a good time,' she said, her voice trembling slightly.

'I'm having the *best* time,' Nicole quickly reassured her sister. 'I really am. Anyway, I'm sure Mum wouldn't have come even if you had invited her.'

Samantha nodded, eagerly swallowing the lie. Nicole felt even worse about Tina's absence than ever.

THE SPEECHES WERE mercifully short. Craig said a few words about his first-born and how proud she made him.

'Look how beautiful she is,' he said, gesturing at her and her Big Hair. Everyone clapped and Nicole's Big Hair took a bow.

Samantha then got up and made a short speech about how, in 1981, Nicole had swapped seats with her just before they were in a car accident and how that simple act had probably saved her life.

'There was no seatbelt in the back seat and, as the younger and smaller sister, I might have been thrown from the car and killed, had I been sitting there. As sisters,' Samantha continued, 'I like to think we will always be each other's seatbelt.'

Someone at the back of the crowd made a *nawwww* sound and Samantha beamed, evidently pleased with her metaphor. Nicole looked around again to see if Kim had arrived but there was still no sign of her.

'Speech!' shouted a cousin, who was wearing a pink pinstriped shirt and braces, like he was Michael Douglas in *Wall Street*.

Nicole stood up, thanked everyone for coming and sat down. Then she stood up again and thanked Samantha and Trent for all the work they'd done, and Craig and Donna-Louise for hosting. And then she sat down. And then she stood up one last time, wanting to say something about how she wished Tina was there, but someone had already put the stereo back on and everyone had turned away from her.

Nicole couldn't remember a time when she'd ever felt more alone.

AFTER ANOTHER HOUR of meaningless chatter, the guests finally seemed to be getting ready to leave and Nicole began to relax. The ordeal was almost over. But then Samantha and Trent made a big point of covering Nicole's eyes and leading her around to the front of the house.

'Surprise!' they both exclaimed, as they took away their hands, revealing the Gobbles party bus, ready to take all the guests to the Gobbles nightclub in the city.

Nicole really was surprised. She'd had her sarcasm dial turned up to eleven when she'd told Samantha that she'd always wanted to ride on the Gobbles party bus. She should have known better; Samantha had never been good at picking up on sarcasm.

Following the big reveal, there was a maelstrom of activity, as people piled onto the bus and into cars. Nicole even saw Craig and Donna-Louise ushering some of the pinstriped cousins into their Jaguar, which was particularly brave of Craig, considering how drunk the cousins all were.

'Come on, Nic. Jump aboard!' Samantha shouted from the steps of the bus.

'Johnno wants me to ride with him!' Nicole shouted back. 'Johnno' was a safe choice for the lie as there were at least three guests who answered to the name.

'But the Gobbles party bus!' Samantha exclaimed.

Nicole shrugged, as if to say, *But Johnno insists!* and then went and hid around the side of the house.

When she was sure everyone had gone, she went and sat on the love seat in the backyard. She picked at the nail polish Samantha had insisted on applying and wondered if Tom might turn up after his shift after all and if he might kiss her. She had a sudden urge to feel close to someone.

She lay down on the love seat and closed her eyes.

She was woken some time later by a voice ringing out. 'My baby is turning twenty-one! Am I too late to make a speech?'

It was Tina, teetering down the side path in a ridiculous pair of heels, triumphantly holding up a bottle of Lambrusco and two plastic champagne glasses.

'You're far too late,' Nicole told her.

'Good. I hate all that shit,' Tina said, setting the glasses and the Lambrusco on a table. The glasses had little star stickers on them, like the kind that Nicole used to get on her work in primary school. 'Jesus,' Tina continued, 'what happened to your hair?'

'Samantha.'

'Enough said.'

Tina unscrewed the bottle, pausing to make a popping noise with her mouth, and poured two generous glasses, the Lambrusco slopping all over the place.

She handed one to Nicole and then held hers up high above her head like a torch. 'To you getting the key to the door. Or whatever,' Tina said. 'I wish you many things, my darling Nicole. But mostly, I wish you a full life. Don't do what I've done. Don't piss most of it away.'

Nicole went to speak but Tina stopped her, the smile now completely gone from her face. 'I know you think the bongs are different, but they're not. They're really not.'

They remained on the love seat in silence, drinking the sickeningly sweet Lambrusco as the fairy lights flickered and, one by one, the tea lights burnt out. When the Lambrusco was finished, Tina foraged around until she found a bottle of Tia Maria stashed under one of the trestle tables.

'*Tia Maria, golden brown,*' she sang, as she poured some into their plastic glasses. '*Drink it while everyone else is in town.*'

Not everyone was in town, though. Nicole thought of Kim and Tom on the couch in Inverness Crescent and knew she didn't want to be there with them. Not when they hadn't bothered to travel the two kilometres to come to her party.

'I've really missed this place,' Tina said, after a pause. Nicole looked at her mother, surprised. It had been so long since they had all lived there together – her, Samantha, Tina and Craig – she'd kind of forgotten that it had ever been Tina's home. Certainly, since Donna-Louise had moved in and beige-ified it, it was hard to imagine Tina having ever lived there at all.

'There's some stuff,' Tina said, but then paused to drink her Tia Maria. She started again. 'There's some stuff I've been waiting until you were old enough to tell you. And now—' She paused again for another sip. 'Now you're old enough.'

'Like what?' Nicole leant in, afraid and slightly excited at the same time.

'Like your stepmother is a cunt.'

'Mum!'

'Oh come on, Nicole. It's always been the Pritikin scone in the room. I've tried to be polite about her all these years and Samantha probably loves her better than she loves me, but it's true. She's a cunt.'

'Donna-Louise is not that bad,' Nicole said, but even as she said it, she knew it wasn't necessarily true. Donna-Louise was generally as warm towards Nicole as the iceberg that struck the *Titanic*.

'And there's other stuff. Lots of stuff. But not stuff for tonight. Tonight, my beautiful child, is a party night.'

'I'll drink to that!' Nicole said, bringing her glass to her lips and then grimacing. The Tia Maria tasted like coffee-flavoured cough mixture.

'There you are,' Craig said from behind them as he stepped out from the house through the sliding doors. Nicole felt Tina stiffen next to her. 'Samantha was looking for you everywhere at the club. Everyone missed you.'

Nicole noticed that even though he was talking to her, he was looking at Tina.

'I just wasn't in the mood for a nightclub,' Nicole said, placing her Tia Maria on the table. 'Where's Donna-Louise?'

'DL went to bed with a headache. I was turning off the lights when I heard your voices out here and I realised the party was still going.'

He was still looking at Tina. Nicole couldn't remember the last time she'd been alone with both her parents like this.

Tina grabbed Nicole's glass of Tia Maria and slugged it back. Nicole could feel a storm brewing.

'We should go, Mum.'

'I'll drop you both home,' Craig said.

Nicole frowned. 'But we live in opposite directions.'

'It's okay, you're just down the road, Nic. I'll drop you first and then take Tina to Bassendean. It's too late for you to be walking. Especially in those heels, Teensy.'

His use of the old nickname thankfully made Tina smile, like the sun breaking through dark clouds.

'"Teensy",' she repeated and then took another slug, this time directly from the bottle. 'Nobody's called me that for years. What was that thing I used to call you? Other than "arsehole", that is.'

Thankfully, Craig laughed, although Nicole felt it really could have gone either way. 'You used to call me "Craggy".'

'Ah, yes. Craggy,' Tina said. 'Well, *Craggy*, I would love a lift home.'

'This way, *Teensy*,' Craig said, offering her his arm. Tina took it and the two of them headed off down the side path.

Nicole hung back, observing the two of them walking arm in arm, like they were heading down the aisle. She couldn't wait to tell Samantha about this strange moment of truce – if Samantha ever forgave her for not going to Gobbles nightclub, that was.

Samantha

EVERYONE AT THE wake kept going on about how *tasteful* everything was. The house. The furnishings. The catering. Normally, it would be driving me nuts because I knew it had nothing to do with Nicole's amazing taste and everything to do with her boyfriend's money. But today, there was something else that was bothering me even more.

After all my phone calls and texts and emails telling Nicole not to serve alcohol at the wake, she'd completely ignored me and now, here we were, with the wine flowing freely. At Tina's wake, of all places.

I stood in Nicole's living room, sipping mineral water from a wine glass and trying to remain calm. Next to me, Trent was having a conversation with some man he'd met, a distant cousin of Tina's, but my focus kept drifting over to the large group in the corner.

Back at the funeral home and the cemetery, the group had been quiet enough, introducing themselves as Tina's 'friends from the pub'. But now at the house, the more they drank, the louder they became. They had started squawking and flapping like a flock of geese about to either take flight or peck each other to death. Watching them now, I couldn't help but imagine Tina among them, the squawkiest and flappiest of them all. I felt my chest constrict.

Trent nudged me.

'Huh?' I looked at him, and he directed my attention to Tina's cousin, standing beside us.

'I said, you have a nice house,' the cousin said. 'Very tasteful.'

Even though he'd introduced himself to us less than ten minutes ago, I had already forgotten his name.

'It's not—' I started to say.

'Thank you,' Trent butted in. 'We're very proud of it.'

He grinned at me, pleased with himself.

'Yes, we are. Very, very proud,' I said, playing along. Trent's grin grew even wider.

'I'm more of a boat person myself,' the cousin said. 'I took Tina out on the river a few years back. Not on the boat I have now. My old boat. She was an interesting beast.'

'Who, Tina?' Trent asked, clearly having the time of his life.

'No, no, my boat,' the cousin said. 'I have a new one these days. I've called it *Second Wind*. You know, after that Billy Joel song . . .'

But he had lost my attention again. Now I was busy watching one of the catering staff approach us with a full tray of drinks. The cousin took a glass of champagne but Trent just shook his head. He knew better, today of all days, than to drink in front of me. I kept watching the tray-bearer as he made his way to the couch behind us, where my daughter Rosemary was sitting, immersed in her phone, the great love of her life. He offered her a glass of wine and even though she didn't accept it, I almost imploded.

'Did you see that?' I hissed to Trent, the minute the cousin had stepped away to re-fill his plate. 'That waiter just offered Rose a drink.'

'She's twenty, Sam,' Trent said through a mouth full of food. 'Geez, this foie gras is good. Have you tried it?'

'But she *looks* seventeen,' I told him. Trent was obviously going to be no help, so I left him to his fancy food and headed to the kitchen.

'Who's in charge?' I demanded.

A flustered woman wearing a striped apron over a loud floral dress hesitantly stepped forward. 'I am?'

'Can you please slow down the drinks service,' I said using the same voice I use whenever I get cold calls on my mobile.

'We're just doing what Nico—'

'Nicole's mother – *my* mother – was an alcoholic who died of acute liver failure. Plying the guests with alcohol at her wake, particularly my underage daughter, is inappropriate. I'd hate to have to make a complaint.'

The caterer swallowed my small yet necessary lie about Rosemary's age and nodded.

'Good,' I said. 'We understand each other.'

I returned to Trent and his new friend, my heart thumping hard.

Trent gave me an enquiring look. 'Are you all right?' he asked, laying his hand on my arm.

'Yeah,' I said, breathing out. There was something about the feeling of his skin against mine that always grounded me. 'I just had to deal with something in the kitchen.'

Rosemary came over, her coat in her hand. 'It's time to go, Dad,' she said to Trent, not even looking at me. We'd had a fight before the funeral about her outfit and she still hadn't forgiven me.

'Why are you taking Rose?' I asked Trent, confused. Rose had come in her own car, which, after our argument, had been a bit of a relief.

'I'm dropping her off at her shift and then taking her piece-of-shit car to Simon. He said he'd look at it as a favour.' Trent turned back to the cousin. 'Sorry, Rick, mate, I've got to bail. Rose has work.'

'Today?' Rick, whose name I finally remembered was actually Nick, was clearly surprised.

'She couldn't get out of it,' I rushed in to explain on Rosemary's behalf. 'And really, she and Tina weren't exactly *close*.'

Rosemary looked away, embarrassed, and I suddenly found myself wanting to let this complete stranger know that it wasn't Rosemary's fault. It had been my decision to let Tina see her granddaughter only a handful of times in the last decade and, I'd have this Nick/Rick know, I'd done it for good reasons.

But Rosemary and Trent were already leaving, and the cousin had gone back to talking about his boat.

'You should come out on the river some time. Your husband and daughter, too,' the cousin was saying, but I was watching Rosemary as she waited for Trent to grab some more foie gras. I was wondering how she would feel at my funeral. Would she cry like Aunt Meg when my coffin was lowered? Or would she feel numb like I did now?

My attention shifted from Rosemary over to the kitchen, where I could see Nicole through the open door, talking to the caterer. I felt my body tense up in anticipation of a further battle, but then she turned to look at me and raised her empty glass.

I nodded, relieved and yet strangely disappointed that she had surrendered. All my outrage about the wine had at least given me something to feel.

AS NICOLE WAS seeing the last guest out, I tried to make myself comfortable on the white suede couch. The whiteness and obvious expense of the couch always made it hard for me to relax on it. Only someone without kids could buy such an impractical thing.

I also couldn't relax because Nicole was slurring her words a little as she tried to push the ridiculous jigsaw puzzle with its inevitably missing pieces on me.

At first, I tried to put it down to tiredness. After all, Nicole had only had tea all afternoon. But then the conversation started to career out of control and I realised that Nicole was actually drunk. I stood up and started tidying away the empty glasses, turning my anger into order like Donna-Louise had taught me.

'Just like old times,' Nicole said, lying back on the white suede monstrosity.

I thought of the hundreds of times I'd cleaned the brick townhouse on Railway Parade while Tina lay drunk and Nicole read her books.

Now Tina was dead and Nicole lay drunk.

It wasn't like old times at all.

AS I WORKED my way around the room, stacking glasses on a tray, I did my best to ignore my sister, who was now snoring gently on the couch. I also did my best not to think of my dead mother, back in that cold cemetery. I hadn't properly said goodbye to her and, when I allowed myself to feel my shame, it felt as sharp as pressing glass into my flesh.

After a few minutes of actively doing my best, I abandoned the tray and decided to have a look around the ground floor of the house. I hadn't really had a chance to do so in years, not since that disastrous dinner Nicole had hosted for her fortieth birthday – another memory that stung, like glass into flesh.

I pushed it all aside and concentrated on the house. I had never admitted this to anyone, not even Trent, but I really loved this place. It was everything that our dark, narrow townhouse in Maylands was not. It had high ceilings. It had natural light. It had spacious rooms and spectacular views of the river. It also had millions and millions of dollars of equity behind it.

I wandered into my favourite room, the front living room, with its large windows overlooking the river. I sat on one of the large Chesterfields, bolstered by cushions fluffed up like colourful clouds, and gazed out at the view. During the day, the river shone like a jewel, and even in the fading light, it was still spectacular. As I leaned back against one of the cushions, it gave a small sigh and I realised it was filled with feathers, probably from some rare, endangered bird.

Tentatively, I put my feet up on the coffee table, which I suspected was worth more than my car. I'd seen Nicole do this once and had envied her ease in such an opulent setting.

Somewhere upstairs, I heard a door close and I immediately put my feet back on the floor. It was probably Jethro. He'd been pretty much hiding from me ever since Nicole's disastrous fortieth. It had been the longest game of hide and seek ever, although it was all hiding and no seeking

As I picked up the tray of glasses, the photos on display on the sideboard caught my eye. Most of them, I noted, were of Jethro's family. There were a few photos of Jethro and Nicole together in exotic-looking places and some photos of Jethro when he was younger, wearing a tie and blazer from a private school. Then I spotted something familiar near the back – a framed photo of the whole family taken on my wedding day, which I had given to Nicole one Christmas. It was the only photo I had of Dad, Donna-Louise, Nicole and me together.

I examined it closer and saw a passport-sized photo of Tina tucked into the top corner of the frame. My chest tightened again. All these years, I had felt only relief that Tina's appearance at my wedding had been fleeting. The day had been stressful enough without Tina's particular brand of chaos. But the fact that Nicole had done the analogue version of photoshopping her into the family photo told me she felt differently. And the knot in my chest made me think that maybe, now that Tina was gone, I did too.

I grabbed the tray and made my way past Nicole, still asleep on the couch. When I walked into the kitchen, I saw it immediately: the bottle of vodka in the corner with its lid off. The source of Nicole's sogginess.

Before I could stop myself, I had gone to take a big, lovely swig. But my arm froze halfway to my mouth and I put it down again. I remembered that I was driving, and that was one of my rules: never drink and drive.

But I wanted the vodka. I needed it.

I quickly tried to turn my attention to something else, and found myself picking up the cookie jar shaped like Cookie Monster's head from the kitchen bench instead. It was a leftover from Nicole's previous life in that one-bedroom unit in Inglewood with the mould on the walls and the fridge in the lounge room. I'd always assumed the jar had been a gift from Darren, her awful ex-boyfriend. Why she'd brought it here, I'd never been able to work out, especially when it looked so incongruous with the rest of the 'tasteful' kitchen.

It still had a price tag on the back of it. It was typical of Nicole to have never removed it in the twenty years she'd owned the jar. $4.99 from Red Spot. I shook my head. Darren sure knew how to spoil a lady.

I poured a bit of dishwashing liquid onto a Chux to get the price tag off. As I scrubbed, I thought about Darren. There were many reasons Trent should never have set him up with Nicole, and the continued presence of this awful jar, still tainting all of our lives, was one of them.

I was almost done scrubbing when a text came through from Rosemary.

Shift finishing early @ 9. Dad and car still with Simon.

It was a direct command to pick her up. Rosemary wasn't the type to add 'please' or 'thank you', not when it came to me. I was only her mother. I had only almost *died* giving birth to her, after all. When I'd told her that once in an argument, she'd said 'I wish you *had* died.' I'd known it was a throwaway line but it had hurt far more than I could admit.

Nine o'clock was still an hour away – not enough time to go home before heading into the city, but too much time to be left alone with an open bottle of vodka. I considered waking up Nicole. Reigniting another argument with her would be one way of filling the time.

As if on cue, I heard a gentle thud from the back living room. I ran to check on her and found that she had rolled off the couch. The vodka in her system combined with the soft rug on the floor had obviously cushioned the fall, because she was still asleep. I gently lifted her head and slipped one of the throw cushions under it so she would be more comfortable. Then I stood back and looked at her for a while, watching her chest gently rise and fall.

With her manicured nails and her stylish haircut and her expensive clothes, she was so different from the Nicole that used to lie, stoned out of her skull, on that filthy corduroy couch in Menora. Or the Nicole who used to work in the sandwich bar and break up with Darren every other week. Or the Nicole who used to work from home in her pyjamas amidst a sea of unwashed coffee cups.

I imagined lying next to her on the soft rug, the way we used to when we were little girls when one of us – usually me – had a bad dream. For so many years, she had been the most constant thing in my life, but these days we were practically strangers. I left her to her sleep and wandered around the room, studying the cards on the flowers. I recognised some of the names. Old family friends. Distant relatives. The nurses at the private hospital where Tina had spent her last days, thanks to Jethro's millions.

And then I came to a big bunch of white lilies on top of a small round table. The card read *To Nicole and Samantha and families, our condolences. Tina was the life of our party. From the gang at The Ambassador Tavern.*

For a moment, all the emotions I had been doing my very best not to feel, all that grief that I'd pushed down, threatened to rise back up and take me over completely. It was alcohol that had made her the life of their party and it was alcohol that had killed her. How could they be so insensitive? I wanted to throw the flowers onto Nicole's expensive cream carpet and jump up and down on them. Instead, I found myself, as if on autopilot, heading back into the kitchen to that bottle of vodka, as if that was the only thing in the world that could help me.

I grabbed it with both hands, like a baby holding a bottle, and was just about to bring it to my lips when my phone rang. It was a call from an unknown number.

'Hello?' I answered the phone, placing the vodka gently back on the bench.

'Sammy, it's Meg. Your aunty Meg. Sorry to ring so late, but I've been trying to ring Nicole and haven't got through.'

'She's asleep,' I said.

'Well, um, this is a bit awkward. I'm still hoping to talk to you girls before I head home tomorrow. There's some things . . .' Her voice trailed off into uncertainty.

'Aunt Meg?'

'There's some things I need to tell you both. About your parents' divorce,' she said, the strength in her voice returning. 'Things I should have talked about years ago.'

I glanced again at the cookie jar. The Meg situation was like that price tag. If left to Nicole, it was never going to be resolved. It was up to me to sort it out.

'Okay,' I said, and arranged to meet Aunt Meg the following day at noon.

After I ended the call I looked at the vodka bottle on the bench and then through the open door to the lilies from 'The Gang' in the next room and I had an idea. Cradling the whole lot – the flowers, the vase and the vodka – in my arms like a sleeping child, I went to say goodbye to my sister.

'I'm off home,' I told Nicole, as she emerged from her drunken stupor.

Even as I told her about the meeting with Aunt Meg the next day, I knew she would try to find a way to get out of it. I'd have to work extra hard to make her come.

As I turned to go, my eye caught the photo of Tina on top of the cabinet and a thousand feelings filled my chest: regret, sadness, despair. Fury.

Outside, it took me a few moments to locate the bins, but I finally found them, neatly stored away in their own wooden structure, like a little house Jethro and Nicole had built especially for their precious rubbish. Opening one up, I dumped the flowers, vase and all, inside and then I emptied the remaining vodka over the lot. It was a waste of the flowers and the vase, and an even bigger waste of the vodka, but it made me feel better. It was proof that I still had control.

Kind of.

Piece #3: 1995

'BRIDE OR GROOM?' the usher asked Nicole and Tina.

'Neither,' Tina said with a wink. 'I'm not getting married.'

'Sorry?'

'Bride,' Nicole stepped in to clarify, and the usher duly directed them to the left-hand side of the church.

'For someone in such a hideous suit, he really lacked a sense of humour,' Tina said, as she settled in a pew near the back.

Nicole hesitated. 'Don't you want to sit closer to the front?'

'What? Near your father and Donna-Louise?'

'Fair enough,' Nicole said, sitting next to her. As she did, she took care to smooth out the back of her Angel Hearts floral dress and adjust the Perfecto biker leather jacket she'd bought from Orphans. The jacket was the most expensive item of clothing she'd ever bought in her twenty-five years on the planet and she wanted it to look its best at all times.

'Troy doesn't look well, even at this distance,' Tina observed.

'You mean Trent.'

'Who's Trent?' Tina joked.

Tina was right. Trent really didn't look well. Pachelbel's 'Canon in D' had started up, and he was standing at the front of the church, all pale and blinking as the bridesmaids, who were wearing butter-yellow dresses, made their way down the aisle.

'His face is the same colour as their dresses,' Nicole whispered to Tina.

'I bet you're glad you decided not to be in the bridal party,' Tina whispered back and Nicole nodded.

Tina didn't know that Samantha hadn't even asked Nicole to be in the bridal party but now wasn't the time to explain. Not that Nicole was upset about it. Not really. Well, not much.

The music changed to Mendelssohn's 'Wedding March' and Tina swivelled around in her seat. 'Oh, my. She looks beautiful.'

Nicole turned too. There was Samantha, on Craig's arm, in all her white meringued glory. Nicole wanted to catch her eye, but Samantha's gaze was fixed straight ahead on her future husband.

'My baby,' Tina said and her eyes filled with tears. Nicole took her hand and squeezed it tight.

When they reached the front of the church, Craig handed his daughter over to Trent and sat down next to a large yellow feathered hat that Nicole could only assume was Donna-Louise.

'Looks like Donna-Louise's come dressed as Big Bird,' Tina said, her tears now gone, and Nicole felt glad she hadn't insisted that they sit closer to the front.

*

AFTER THE CEREMONY, while everyone milled around on the steps of the church, Tina pulled Nicole aside.

'Nic, I'm not feeling the best. I think I might give the reception a miss and go home.'

Nicole was confused. Tina had seemed perfectly healthy during the ceremony. 'Are you sure, Mum? Trent's mum might have a Panadol.'

'No, darling. I think I just need to have a lie-down,' Tina replied, a faint tremolo in her voice.

'Let me at least call you a cab.' Nicole was now worried. She pulled her Motorola out of her handbag.

'No, no, I'll just hail one on Beaufort Street,' Tina insisted. 'Please tell Sammy and Troy I'm sorry and that I hope they have a lovely day.'

Nicole went to argue but one of Trent's brothers spotted her and came over to shake her hand. By the time she was able to turn around again, Tina had gone.

'Family of the bride!' the photographer shouted.

Nicole found herself being swallowed by the crowd and spat out at the foot of the church steps. She took a deep breath and walked up to join Samantha and Trent.

'Sammy, you look beautiful!' she said.

Samantha gave the same pinched smiled she always gave when she was wearing expensive lipstick. 'Thanks, Nic.'

'Listen, Mum felt sick and had to go,' Nicole told her in a low voice. 'But she sends all her love.'

Samantha didn't even blink. 'We've seated you next to that guy Darren I was telling you about,' she whispered back. 'You know, the guy from Trent's work. He's single at the moment.'

Nicole stared at her. 'Did you hear what I said about Mum?'

'Yes, I heard,' Samantha said, her attention now on Craig and Donna-Louise, who were climbing the steps towards them.

'Congratulations, darling,' Craig said, kissing Samantha's cheek.

'Father of the bride, stand here.' The photographer pointed to a spot next to Trent. 'And you must be the mother,' she said to Donna-Louise. Nobody corrected her. 'You stand here, on the other side of your lovely daughter.'

'Hello, Nicole,' Donna-Louise said, as she stepped in between Samantha and Nicole, her yellow feathers poking Nicole in the neck.

'You the sister?' the photographer asked Nicole. 'You're even taller than they said. Do you mind going down a step?'

Nicole's cheeks grew hot as she did what she was told. When she'd put on her wedding outfit that morning, she'd felt elegant and pretty. Now she felt like André the Giant.

'Great. Okay. Family of the bride, say cheese!' the photographer barked and everyone smiled, except Nicole.

AT THE RECEPTION, Nicole checked the seating plan and discovered that she was on Table Eleven, right at the back, with nobody she knew or had even heard of, except this guy Darren that Samantha had been talking to her about for months, like he was the Chosen One. She scanned the plan to see where Tina would have been seated if she hadn't disappeared, but she couldn't see her mother's name anywhere.

It didn't take long for Nicole to discover why Darren was single. He had recently come back from four years of teaching English in Japan and spoke like he was the only person in the world to have experienced another culture.

'In Japan, the bride changes dress and hairstyle a number of times over the course of the wedding day,' Darren told her over the entree, in a strange Australian–American hybrid accent, each word carefully enunciated like he was afraid they might shatter in his mouth. 'Your sister would have changed at least twice by now.'

'My sister will never change,' Nicole quipped but the joke was lost on Darren.

'Also, the newlywed couple gives presents to their guests, not the other way around. In Japan, the tradition is for the guests to give the couple money, not kitchen appliances or vazes.' He used the American pronunciation of 'vase'. 'It's a much more practical gift, if you think about it.'

'*Vaze?*' Nicole asked, echoing his pronunciation.

'You know, the vessel that you put cut flowers in.' Darren seemed to think she didn't know what a vase was.

They ate in silence for a while. Nicole looked around the room at all the other guests, dressed up in their finery, so many of them complete strangers to her. She wondered how Samantha could possibly know so many people Nicole had never met.

'What do you do for a living?' Darren asked.

'I'm a card-carrying member of the Comancheros,' Nicole joked, with a nod at the jacket she'd carefully hung over the back of her chair. Darren looked at her blankly. He was a tough crowd. 'But seriously, I work as a sandwich hand, although I prefer to call myself a "bread artist".'

'You'd struggle to find a job in Japan,' Darren replied. 'They don't eat a lot of sandwiches.'

'Perhaps I could retrain as a sushi chef?'

'Perhaps,' Darren replied. 'Samantha said you're single. How old are you?'

'Twenty-five,' she replied, somewhat surprised by the bluntness of his question.

'Ah,' he said, with a small smile.

'What do you mean by "ah"?'

'Next year, you'll be Christmas Cake.'

'I'll be what?'

'Christmas Cake. In Japan, they have a tradition of eating fruitcake on Christmas Day. After the twenty-sixth, the cake is no good to anyone.'

Nicole sat with that for a moment and then made a big point of turning away from Darren. She tried to join the conversation about superannuation between the two older men seated to her right, who had introduced themselves earlier as Trent's father's friends from the Rotary Club. After a few minutes of smiling and nodding, she returned to her meal. As she shoved small chunks of tough steak into her mouth, she thought longingly of her copy of *The Bridges of Madison County* at home by her bedside, with its promise of a gentler world far removed from this one, with its tedious superannuation talk and its even more tedious Darren. She took a big sip of her wine and reluctantly turned back to Darren, who was picking at his food.

'How's the chicken?' she asked him.

'Dry,' he replied. 'In Japan, the wedding feasts are amazing. None of this alternating chicken or steak shit.'

'How many Japanese weddings have you actually been to, Darren?'

'Um, one.'

Nicole drained her glass. 'You're a bit of a prick, you know that, right?' she said.

Darren shrugged. 'In Japan, the girls say I look like Michael J. Fox.'

Nicole laughed and reached for more wine. She was going to need it to get through to dessert.

The problem was, of course, that after a few more wines, Darren really did start to look like Michael J. Fox, and then he asked her to dance and revealed himself to be a great dancer. Nicole started to relax and have fun, despite herself.

'How are you liking Darren?' Trent asked her at one point, as she passed him on the way back from the bathroom. His face was flushed and his tie was loose.

'He's fun!' Nicole replied, the awkward Christmas Cake conversation now hours behind them. She and Trent both turned to watch Darren, who was dancing with one of Trent's elderly aunts, patiently showing her how to do the Chicken Dance.

'Hey, I'm sorry you weren't sitting up with us at the bridal table,' he told her. 'But Sammy really wanted you to sit next to Darren.'

Nicole turned to Trent, incredulous. 'More than she wanted me to be a bridesmaid?'

Trent shrugged. 'I guess. You know Sammy, she's always got her reasons. Like with Tina. She had big reasons there.'

'What do you m—' Nicole began to say, but then Darren appeared.

'There you are!' he said, grabbing Nicole's hand. 'In Japan, I made it my mission to teach as many people the Chicken Dance as I could. Don't think you can get out of it.'

Nicole tried to resist his pull and return to her conversation, but Trent was gone.

AFTER A WHOLE lot of Chicken Dancing and the Nutbush, Nicole and Darren stepped outside onto the terrace and found themselves alone. Nicole was dizzy with the dancing and the drink and was glad to get some cool air into her lungs.

'You're so much prettier than your sister,' Darren told her.

'You really don't have a filter, do you?'

'After four years of living in a place where very few people understood what I was saying, no, I don't.'

'Well, this is my sister's special day, and today she's the most beautiful girl on the planet.'

'Whatever you say,' Darren said, leaning forward to kiss her.

The softness of his lips surprised her and she found herself melting into him. After a few minutes of silent surrender, he pulled back and looked at her.

'You're so big and tall and solid,' he said. 'In Japan, the girls are all tiny, like little birds that might snap in two if you hold them too tight.'

'Less of the "in Japan" and more of the kissing,' Nicole said, her voice not her own, while back inside 'Achy Breaky Heart' started up on the dance floor.

Piece #4: 1997

EVEN THOUGH SAMANTHA'S waters had broken, she and Trent were still standing on the footpath outside their block of flats arguing about who was going to drive to the hospital.

'Seriously, Sam, give me the keys,' Trent pleaded.

'I'll be fine.'

'You're in labour. I think there are rules against driving a car when you're in labour.'

Samantha went to disagree but another contraction took hold and she had to lean on the car while she found her way through it.

'See? You can't be driving when this happens,' Trent said in a soothing tone, as he rubbed her back.

'We'll just have to pull over ever ten minutes when the contraction hits,' Samantha gasped through the pain.

'Every five and a half minutes,' Trent corrected her. 'I've been timing you.'

Even though she was now on the other side of the contraction, Samantha knew she'd lost the fight. She handed him the keys. 'Don't become my Most Hated,' she warned.

In their antenatal classes, the midwife had told them that there was always a 'Most Hated' person who became the focus of all the birthing mother's anger and frustration, and that all the husbands should hope and pray it wouldn't be them.

At the hospital, the orderlies immediately sat her in a wheelchair.

'I'm perfectly fine to walk,' Samantha was protesting when the midwife showed up.

'You might be able to walk, Mrs Chapman, but you're not going to,' she said, in a clipped British accent.

'Give her a copy of my birth plan,' Samantha told Trent. 'I'm sure it says something about no wheelchairs in there.'

'Save it for the birthing suite, Mrs Chapman,' the midwife said, before setting off with a purposeful stride. 'Come along now.'

'Who calls people by their surnames these days?' Trent whispered. 'Mrs Chapman is my mother.'

'She's calling me Mrs Chapman and yet talking to me like I'm three,' Samantha whispered back. 'I'm twenty-five, for god's sake.'

As Trent started to push her in the wheelchair, Samantha looked up at him and they exchanged a conspiratorial smile. They'd found their Most Hated.

UP IN THE birthing suite, nobody else was interested in her birth plan either, least of all the baby, who appeared to be choosing his or her own path into the world.

Even Samantha, having emerged on the other side of yet another powerful contraction, was losing faith in her plan. The drug-free birth she'd been imagining was feeling more and more like a fairy story.

'Get me an epidural,' she said, gripping Trent's hand. 'I want an epidural.'

'Can she, uh, have an epidural?' Trent asked the British midwife, who was currently the only medical professional in the room. Things between Samantha and the midwife had grown so tense that Trent was now forced to mediate every single exchange between them.

'It's too late for an epidural, Mrs Chapman. You're too dilated,' the midwife told Samantha. 'But you can have gas.'

'You can have gas,' Trent repeated.

'I don't want gas, I want a fucking epidural!' Samantha was seeing red now.

The midwife just shook her head.

'It's too late, Sammy,' Trent translated and Samantha screwed her face up into a small tight ball in response.

After what seemed like a decade's worth of contractions, the midwife checked again to see how dilated Samantha was.

'Still at nine centimetres,' she said, disapprovingly, like Samantha had the ability to dilate her cervix at will and was keeping it at nine centimetres simply to be difficult.

They had Samantha hooked up to a machine to monitor both the baby's and her heart rate. The monitor had become the soundtrack for her labour, very different to the Bach cello suite she'd specified in her birth plan.

A man, presumably a doctor, arrived, had a look at her chart and at the heart monitor, and then walked out without saying a word.

'Nice to meet you, too,' Samantha called out after him, between clenched teeth.

A minute or two later, the same man returned. 'We don't like the way the baby's responding to labour, so we're taking you in for surgery,' he informed her.

Samantha wanted to tell him that she didn't like the way *he* was responding to her labour, but another contraction consumed her.

After the contraction had finished, the nurses started to prep Samantha for surgery.

'At least you're getting your epidural now,' Trent told her.

'It's a spinal block, not an epidural,' Samantha snapped. 'Didn't you read the birthing book I gave you?'

Trent was fast becoming her Most Hated, but thankfully, at that moment, the British midwife reappeared. 'Come along, Mr Chapman,' she said. 'We need to get you prepped for the operating room!'

'No, wait,' Trent said, holding his hand out towards the midwife, as if fending her off with some wizard's spell. 'I need to tell my wife that I love her.'

The midwife tutted while Trent leant back towards Samantha.

'I love you, Sammy,' he whispered. 'I think you're amazing.'

He kissed her softly on her forehead and for a moment, everything felt okay. But then the Most Hated ushered Trent away and the nightmare continued.

As she sat on the edge of her bed, waiting for the anaesthetist to slide a needle into her spinal column, Samantha considered what was about to happen. Yes, she had read that birthing book she gave Trent – she'd read it cover to cover – but she'd glossed over the chapter on Caesareans.

'This wasn't part of my birth plan,' Samantha told the anaesthetist.

'It never is,' the anaesthetist sighed. She seemed quite sad about it.

'Not in the details, no,' Samantha's favourite midwife said, now back in the room. 'But we're going to get your baby out, happy, healthy and alive. And *that* was the goal of your birth plan, was it not?'

Put that way, Samantha had to agree. But she still just wanted to punch her Most Hated in her Most Hated mouth.

'Now, stay very still,' the anaesthetist said.

Samantha felt a short intense burn as the needled entered her spine, and then a warm nothingness spread through her legs. *This must be what it feels like to be erased*, she thought.

When the spinal block had taken full hold, she was wheeled into the operating theatre, like an item inside a shopping trolley. There, many people were rushing around, looking incredibly busy, except Trent, who was standing to the side, looking frightened.

'Where's the machine that goes *ping*?' he asked her, trying to make a joke, and Samantha found herself thinking, *Please, don't let me die and have a Monty Python quote be the very last thing I hear.* But then she saw how worried he was.

She held out her hand to him. 'It's going to be okay,' she said, wishing he would say the same to her. He just squeezed her hand and tried to smile.

Samantha closed her eyes. She knew she and her baby were currently the focus of every single person in that busy room, and yet she had never felt more invisible.

'They're starting now,' the midwife told them, in a hushed, reverent tone, as if a classical music recital were about to commence.

After the sensation of some distant tugging that felt like it was happening to a version of herself in a dream within a dream within another dream being had by the real Samantha, the baby was pulled out, healthy and alive but perhaps not happy, from the sound it was making.

'It's a girl,' the surgeon announced.

'She's haemorrhaging,' someone else said.

'The baby?' Samantha turned to the midwife.

'No, you. You're haemorrhaging. Your uterus has turned boggy and they need to stop the bleeding,' the midwife told her.

'Boggy?'

Samantha was still trying to get her head around what was happening, when the baby, a red ball of anger, was quickly presented to her and then whisked out of the room, with Trent following haplessly behind.

'We won't be long,' the surgeon told her, peering over the curtain again.

Samantha closed her eyes. Women with boggy uteruses obviously didn't deserve their babies.

AFTER AN HOUR and a half alone in recovery, she was finally wheeled up to the ward where she found Trent holding the small, shouting creature.

'She's perfect,' he said.

'She's loud.'

'Do you want to hold her?'

Samantha wanted to say no. Ninety minutes hadn't been long enough for her to recover. She needed more time to try to understand what had gone wrong, what she might have done differently to have not ended up in surgery, cut open and bleeding all over the place like an animal in an abattoir.

But she nodded and held out her arms. She knew that was what was expected of her. She needed to be a mother now.

Trent handed her the bawling bundle. 'How's your uterus?'

'Behaving itself again, apparently.' Samantha was frowning at her angry baby. 'What do you think is wrong with her? Why is she crying?'

'They told me she's hungry.'

Samantha tried to rock the baby in her arms, like they did in the movies, but it made no difference. She felt panic rising inside her chest. What if this thing that she had always assumed would be easy, as natural as breathing, was something she couldn't do?

'I called Mum and Dad and they're on their way,' Trent said, trying to make himself heard over the baby's cries. 'Do you want me to ring Tina and your dad?'

'Call Nicole. She can tell Tina.' Samantha and Tina hadn't really spoken in the past three years, not since Samantha asked her not to come to her wedding reception. 'But tell her I don't want Tina here.'

Trent nodded. 'And your dad?'

'You can try, but I think he and Donna-Louise are in Busselton for a golf tournament. I'm sure they'll visit when they get back.'

'Okay, I'll go ring Nicole and then I'll wait for Mum and Dad at reception.' He went to leave but then paused in the doorway. 'Are you okay?'

'I'm okay,' Samantha said.

But she wasn't okay. She couldn't move her legs. She didn't know what would happen if she needed to go to the toilet. There was a tube attached to her hand and she didn't know why. She was thirsty but she couldn't reach the water jug or the glass on the side table. And she was holding an angry baby.

Another midwife, slightly less face-punchworthy than the first, bustled into the room.

'Time to get that baby on the boob,' she said, lifting up one side of Samantha's gown to expose her breast. As she took the baby's head and mashed it against Samantha's nipple, Samantha silently dubbed her the Moderately Hated.

'There.' The Moderately Hated stood back, obviously pleased with her handiwork. 'I'll just go get some paperwork and I'll be back.'

Samantha was experiencing the same kind of cold shock she felt after the accident out at Bruce Rock. She remembered the people who had stopped and helped them out of the car, and how they had wrapped them in kind words and blankets. She wished someone would wrap her in kind words and blankets now.

'Is the baby feeding?' The Moderately Hated had returned, clipboard in hand.

'I'm not sure,' Samantha admitted.

The midwife peered at the baby on Samantha's boob. 'She looks like she's feeding,' she said, in a vaguely accusatory tone, as if Samantha were lying. Then she noticed the full jug of water. 'Why haven't you drunk anything?' she scolded.

Samantha wanted to tell her that she couldn't bloody reach the jug and, actually, she'd been in the room for less than ten minutes, but she couldn't find the strength or the words. Instead she sat there, clutching her baby on her breast, helpless and immobile while the midwife completed her paperwork

A few minutes later, Trent and his parents, Barb and Brian, burst in. Brian was waving a bottle of Veuve Clicquot.

'To wet the baby's head!' he said.

'None for the new mother. She's feeding,' the Moderately Hated said, delivering her parting shot before she and her clipboard left the room.

'Who invited that party pooper?' Brian said, rolling his eyes.

'How's my little princess?' Barb swooped in uncomfortably close to Samantha's exposed breast to look at the baby, who was still feeding. Luckily, Brian was more interested in popping the cork and pouring the champagne into four plastic cups.

'Samantha doesn't drink,' Trent reminded Brian when he went to hand Samantha a cup.

'But this is an important occasion!' Brian protested. 'Can't we entice you to one little glass, Sammy?'

'I will have a glass.' Samantha had found her voice again. *After all*, she thought, *it's not every day I get to bring a new life into the world and almost die at the same time.*

Ignoring Trent's shocked expression, she accepted the plastic cup and took a tentative sip before anyone had actually made a toast. The tiny little bubbles of star-shine slid down her throat, as light as air, hitting a spot inside her that had never been hit before and she felt her body properly relax.

It was the first drink she'd had since she was thirteen.

She looked at the baby and felt the love come, now that the knot in her chest had loosened.

'Hello, baby,' she said, before knocking back the rest of the champagne. It went down easily.

Nicole

I WOKE JUST AFTER eleven, my mouth dry and my head all soupy with vodka, red wine and grief. On my bedside table, Jethro had left a glass of water and two Panadol, which I duly swallowed.

I picked my phone up to distract myself from my hangover, only to find a series of texts from Samantha.

Blue Duck @ noon. Don't forget!

Meg has important information about Mum. She wants to tell us both.

You're coming, right?

Please text me to tell me you're coming.

Hello?

I pushed the phone away from me with a groan. Now Samantha was being as bad as Aunt Meg. Her sudden keenness could only mean that Meg's 'important information' was something I wasn't ready to hear, something that might vindicate Samantha's decision not to visit Mum in hospital before she died.

I rolled onto my back and looked up at the shadows dancing on the ceiling. The patterns of light reminded me of the ceiling rose in my bedroom in Mount Lawley, when Dad's house was still the family home and we had all lived there together with Mum. While my parents were shouting at each other in the next room, I would stare at the ceiling for hours, imagining friendly faces in the plasterwork, smiling down on me. Protecting me.

I thought of Mum lying in her hospital bed, staring at the panelled ceiling and strip lighting, and felt a wave of grief wash over me. There had been no comfort or protection for her – not then, and not in the months beforehand where nobody had been watching her and nobody had noticed her dying, not even me.

There was a soft knock and Jethro came in with some coffee. 'Hello, sleepyhead,' he said. 'How are you feeling?'

'Ordinary,' I admitted, as I sat up in bed. 'It's hard to know which is worse: the grief or the hangover.'

I knew, of course, that the grief was worse. Much, much worse.

'Food is a good way to ease both,' Jethro said. 'I'll make you a proper breakfast once the caterers have been. But here's some coffee to tide you over. And, um, some light reading material.'

He sheepishly handed over the architectural plans he'd had drawn up for the renovation just before Mum went into hospital.

'There's no pressure to look at them immediately,' he added quickly. 'I just wanted to put them back on your radar.'

A year previously, Jethro had decided that it was time for us to either renovate and redecorate this house or to move to another house altogether. 'I'm sick of us living in Suzette's shadow,' he'd said, referring to his cow of an ex-wife who had taken almost fifty per cent of his net worth and an even higher percentage of their mutual friends. In the year before they separated, Suzette had renovated and redecorated the whole house. Not personally, of course – I'm sure she wouldn't have wanted to spoil her manicure – but with the help of a large team of designers and overpriced tradies. Jethro had told me that he had only just seen the last tradie out the front door when Suzette told him she was leaving him.

I carefully placed the plans on my bedside table. Even though I was haunted by the ghosts of Suzette and her design team in every room of this house, whenever Jethro tried to talk about renovating or moving, I found myself changing the subject.

Luckily, this time Jethro did it for me.

'Hey, here's something weird for you,' he said, as he picked up a pillow from the floor and fluffed it up. 'When I went outside to get the paper this morning, I noticed someone had pulled the bin out of its housing and dumped a whole vase of flowers in it.'

I immediately thought of the vase of flowers that Samantha had left with the previous night. 'White lilies?'

'Got it in one. Hang about . . . is this your handiwork?'

I shook my head. 'Sam took some lilies with her, but she wouldn't have put them in the bin. She was taking them home for Trent or something.'

'Maybe,' Jethro said, putting the fluffed pillow behind my back. 'The thing is, the whole mess stank of booze.'

'That really is weird.' I reached for my coffee.

Had Samantha put the flowers in the bin? She seemed so determined to take them home, and she wasn't the type to change her mind between the front door and her car. It didn't make sense, particularly if there was also alcohol involved.

Another memory flashed into my head, like an image thrown briefly onto a screen. Samantha in the kitchen of that small Shenton Park flat on the eve of the millennium. The bottle of tequila beside her, its red hat bottle-top to the side. The shot glass at her lips. Rosemary crying in the room down the hall.

I pushed the thought aside and finished the last of my coffee. Some memories were like dark, empty rooms I didn't like to go into, especially when I was feeling fragile.

'So what do you want to do today?' Jethro asked.

'Nothing. Just be with you.'

'Well, that's worked out well, because I just want to be with you.'

We smiled at each other and I felt that satisfying click that I always felt when I was with Jethro, like two pieces of jigsaw that connect to each other. In that moment, all my guilt and grief disappeared. That was Jethro's special kind of magic.

'Let's go out for lunch. Somewhere fancy near some water,' Jethro suggested. 'How about the place that does the roast vegetable salad that you love?'

'Sounds great. I'll make us a booking,' I said, reaching for my phone. But then I remembered Samantha's text and my stomach clenched. 'First, though, I've just got to tell Sam I can't do the thing she wants me to do.'

Jethro raised an eyebrow. 'As if Samantha would ever let you not do the thing she wants you to do.'

'This time, she's going to have to.'

I texted: *Soz Sam. Woke up with a terrible headache. Please give Meg my apologies.*

The second I pressed 'Send', the doorbell rang.

'Must be the caterers,' I said.

'You stay in bed, I'll go,' Jethro offered, but I had already jumped out of bed and was putting on my slippers.

'No, I'll deal with it. I need to apologise for Sam's scariness last night.'

But when I opened the front door, instead of the caterers,

I found my sister standing there, with a full face of make-up, wearing heels and holding her phone.

'I just got your text,' she said, one eyebrow raised.

'I thought we were meeting at the cafe,' I replied.

'We were, but I knew you'd try to get out of this,' she said, before adding, 'You look well.'

I looked at my feet. 'I'm just not ready to talk about Mum. Not with Meg.' *Or with you*, I added silently. Always silently. Even if the words had managed to bubble almost all the way to the surface, I'd have found a way to submerge them again.

'Well, you'll have to tell Meg herself that you're not coming. She's in the car.'

Sure enough, there was Meg, waving at me from the front seat of Sam's car. I waved back half-heartedly and started to walk sheepishly over to her.

'You don't want to disappoint a little old lady,' Samantha called out after me, but I ignored her.

'Hi, Aunt Meg,' I said, as she wound down the window. 'I'm . . . well, I've got a bit of a headache.' Even as I spoke, I knew I wasn't convincing anyone.

Luckily, Aunt Meg didn't embarrass us both and call me out on the lie. She just folded her hands on her lap and said, 'I wouldn't have asked to meet with you girls if I didn't think it was important.'

She then looked up at me with her blue eyes, so much like Mum's, and I felt any resolve I might have had slip away, like booze into a wheelie bin.

'It won't take long. My flight's at three, anyway,' she said. 'We could even stop for coffee here if you're not feeling well.'

I thought of how Jethro would feel about Samantha being in our house two days in a row.

'No, it's okay,' I said, with an inward sigh. 'The sea air will do my head good. I'll just get out of my pyjamas.'

'Oh, they're your pyjamas, are they? I find it so hard to tell with the fashions these days,' Meg said with a little laugh. This time, I sighed out loud as I headed back to the house. As if a grown woman would ever wear a T-shirt with 'I ♥ sleep' emblazoned across it as daywear.

Samantha was still standing on the doorstep.

'Are you coming now?' she said, not bothering to hide her smile.

'You're pretty happy with yourself,' I mumbled, as I passed her.

'What can I say? I'm very persuasive,' she called down the hall after me.

'WELL?' JETHRO HAD stayed upstairs in the bedroom. He'd obviously worked out that it was Sam at the door.

'The situation's hopeless,' I told him. 'She's got Meg in the car. And now they're both out there waiting for me.'

'I told you she wouldn't let you not do the thing she wanted you to do.'

I stepped into my walk-in wardrobe and started throwing some clothes on. 'Look, I'll just go for as long as I can stand it, and then I'll come back and we can get on with our day. She can't take the whole day away from us.'

'I bet she'll try. Remember how she turned your fortieth into a shitstorm? There's still a mark on my grandmother's sideboard from where she threw that fork.' The look on his face was so sad.

'Oh Jethro,' I said. 'I'm not saying my fortieth was the best night of my life. But really, I should have told her I was inviting Mum. She must have felt under siege.'

'Why do you defend her when she upsets you all the time? You're always telling me about things she says and things she does that hurt you. And yet you do everything she tells you. I just don't get it.'

Of course he didn't. Jethro was an only child who had never experienced the eternal push–pull dance of siblings.

'She's my sister. And we just lost our mum, remember?' I said. Aware that I'd just played the grief card, I quickly added, 'But listen, I'll be back as soon as I can. I'll pick up some takeaway from that Thai place you like. We can eat out of the containers and watch crap TV.'

Jethro smiled again and sunlight re-entered the room. 'Sounds like a plan.'

SAMANTHA WAS STILL standing on the doorstep, while Aunt Meg waited patiently in the car.

'I'm going to take my car because I've got to run some errands on the way home,' I told Samantha, wresting back as much control of the situation as I dared.

Samantha just shrugged. 'Suit yourself.'

I passed the bin house on the way to my car and remembered the flowers.

'Hey, Sam,' I said, turning back, using the last of the bravery that the previous night's vodka had given me. 'Jethro said he found a whole vase of flowers in the bin this morning.' There wasn't enough bravery in the tank to mention the stink of booze, however. 'They weren't the ones you took with you, were they?'

Samantha stared at me, unblinkingly. 'No,' she said, after a beat. 'I took those flowers home with me.'

'Oh, okay.'

'What, you don't believe me?'

'I didn't say I didn't believe you.'

Samantha shifted her weight from one foot to the other.

'That's the problem with you, Nic. You never say what you believe or don't believe. You never say anything.'

She spun on her high heel and strode off to her car in a huff, leaving me behind. I stood for a moment in the brightness of the day to consider what had just happened. Something told me I'd caught Samantha in a lie much bigger than a vase of flowers in a bin, and it sat heavily in my empty stomach.

Piece #5: 2010

THE PAVLOVA HAD failed in all the ways a pavlova could possibly fail. Samantha had over-beaten the egg whites and set the oven temperature too high. And now she was left with a frisbee made of meringue that had still managed to sink in the middle.

'That's Nicole's birthday ruined,' Trent joked, when he saw the mess.

'Maybe it's a sign that we shouldn't go,' Samantha grumbled.

She had been feeling cross with Nicole for insisting on hosting them for lunch when she couldn't even cook. Samantha had offered to host a number of times but Nicole had refused. At least, Samantha told herself, they didn't have to go out to some fancy restaurant they couldn't afford and suffer the humiliation of Jethro paying for it all like they were children.

Trent stuck a small bit of broken meringue into his mouth. 'Hey, this actually tastes great. I bet it will be the best thing at the lunch.'

'Well, that's not hard,' Samantha said, thinking of the last time Nicole had hosted a special lunch. 'Remember that Christmas she served us frozen ham and potato gems?'

'I wasn't there, remember,' Trent said pointedly. Their eyes met briefly and then Samantha looked away. She didn't know why she'd brought up that Christmas. She knew neither of them wanted to think of the fight they'd had and how she'd gone to Nicole's without him. It was all water under a very distant bridge now.

'This is the worst pavlova I've ever made,' she announced, returning her attention to the meringue frisbee. 'I'm going to have to turn it into Eton Mess.'

'Careful now. Jethro probably went to Eton,' Trent joked and Samantha laughed, grateful that the conversation had moved on. If it weren't for Trent's Teflon-like relationship with the past, they would have broken up years ago. Samantha, in stark contrast, always let the past crust over her like an extra skin.

'Is Rose ready?' she asked him.

'Yeah. She must have taken her headphones off long enough to get her clothes over her head because she's fully dressed.'

Samantha sighed. Either the iPod or the Nintendo DSi always seemed to be in between Rosemary and the rest of the world. Someone at work had sent Samantha an article about kids and screen addiction and Samantha had been thinking they should try to reduce Rose's screen time. But then, screens kept her happy. And if Rosemary was happy, then Samantha was happy. And if Samantha was happy, she was less likely to reach for the bottle.

Put that way, it was best that the screens won.

*

AS SHE STEPPED through the front door of Nicole and Jethro's house, Samantha realised that her pavlova and Rosemary's screen time were the last things she needed to worry about.

First, she heard Tina's voice ahead of her somewhere in the house.

And then, she heard her father's voice behind her as he and Celine made their way up the path.

Samantha's world was collapsing in on itself, just like her failed pavlova. She turned to look at Trent, whose face mirrored her alarm.

'Oh shit,' he said.

Samantha immediately leapt into action. She turned around and, as her father approached the front door, she grabbed the bottles of wine he was carrying.

'I don't think we should be having these.'

'Why not?' Craig looked confused.

'Nicole can tell you why,' she replied, quickly stashing the wine behind a pot plant.

'Surprise!' Tina said, appearing in the hallway.

'Well, this really *is* a surprise,' said Craig, although the look on his face suggested it was much more of a shock.

TRENT, BRAVE TO the very last, jumped straight into facilitating the small talk between Craig, Jethro and Tina, while Celine offered to take Rosemary outside to see the fishpond at the bottom of the garden.

Samantha felt a small knot tighten inside her chest as she watched Rosemary willingly shed herself of her iPod's earphones for the first time in days and take Celine's hand.

'You look so pretty today, Aunty Celine,' Rosemary said, as the two of them headed into the garden through the French doors.

Samantha quickly excused herself, saying she was going to help Nicole in the kitchen. There, she found Nicole carefully arranging a mound of king prawns on a giant platter.

'Why didn't you tell me Mum was coming?' Samantha hissed, as she sat on one of the leather stools at the end of the huge island bench.

'Would you have come if you'd known?'

'I don't know. But I would have liked the choice.'

'Tina rang me yesterday. She told me she was sober and, actually, I believed her. She sounded the most sober she'd been forever.'

'I'm surprised you could remember what that even sounded like.'

'Be nice,' Nicole pleaded, looking up from the prawns. 'It's my birthday.'

Samantha sighed and, twisting on her stool, looked around Nicole's beautiful kitchen. It was roughly three times the size of Samantha's, even though Nicole did about a third of the cooking that Samantha did. Among its many fancy features was a double oven ('One for savoury, one for sweets,' Nicole had once explained to her, as if she would ever attempt both at once), a coffeemaker the size of an industrial washing machine, and a whole wall of fridges and freezers, including a dedicated wine fridge with a clear glass door, and one with an ice and soda water dispenser. According to Nicole, one of the drawer-like freezers was filled entirely with different flavours of ice cream.

Samantha found herself standing by the wine fridge, wishing she could open one of the bottles. She didn't even like wine.

In the middle of the island bench, lit up by a giant chandelier, was a large pile of discarded packaging.

Nicole saw her looking at the pile. 'I outsourced the catering,' she explained, gesturing to the large foil containers heating up in one of the ovens (the savoury one, Samantha presumed). '*Simply heat and serve.*'

'Like the frozen ham of 2001?'

'Why are you still going on about that?'

'Why do you still have that hideous jar?' Samantha retorted. She had caught sight of the Cookie Monster jar on the bench behind Nicole.

'It's not hideous,' Nicole said. Her face was now a closed shop and she continued her work in silence, while Samantha looked on, wondering how the hell that jar could still mean so much to her sister.

TINA HAD BEEN sober for five months. At least, that was what she said as they started to eat their lunch. Everyone sipped their mineral water and smiled politely, except for Rosemary, who had her iPod back on and was oblivious. Under normal circumstances, Samantha would have insisted (or at least tried to insist) that Rosemary take the earphones off. But these weren't normal circumstances. It was better for Rosemary if she stayed inside her music bubble.

'I've even got a job,' Tina said. 'Working at the Bassendean Coles as a night filler. I go in overnight when the supermarket is closed and I restock the shelves. And then I sleep all day.'

No difference there, thought Samantha.

'That's great, Mum,' Nicole said.

'And I'm thinking of going back to study. I just picked up some forms to enrol at TAFE. Maybe interior design.'

'Really great,' Nicole echoed. But Tina was looking at Craig, who, in turn, was looking at his hands.

'What do you think, Craig?' she asked him.

'I think it's, um, great, too.'

'Really? Because I seem to remember you telling me I was going to die drunk, penniless and alone in a ditch.'

'I never said that,' Craig spluttered.

'Yes, you did. You know you did.'

'Well, if I did, I regret it,' Craig said, lifting his chin a little. 'You've done things you've regretted, haven't you?'

'More than you'll ever know,' Tina replied, every word like a punch. Craig bowed his head again and Samantha considered stabbing her own hand with her fork.

'This beef is lovely, Nicole,' said Celine.

Tina turned to look at her as if she had just realised she was there. 'And what are you doing these days, *Celeste*? Are you still modelling?'

'No, those days are behind me,' Celine laughed. As far as Samantha knew, Celine had only ever had one modelling gig that she did as a favour for a friend and yet Tina always liked to claim that Craig had married 'a model half his age'. Technically, she wasn't actually half his age. But at thirty-five, she was two years younger than Samantha.

'These days, I'm an MUA for a start-up cosmetics company.'

'A what?'

'An MUA. A make-up artist.'

'We like to pronounce it "mwah!", like a kiss,' Craig said, almost relaxing into the conversation for a second. But then he remembered where he was and who he was talking to and he put his head back down.

'Mwah! Like a kiss!' Tina exclaimed, clapping her hands together like a small child. 'How adorable!'

Celine, her eyes wide, pressed her napkin to her mouth while Craig continued to look at his hands.

'She's very good,' Jethro piped up. 'I've recommended her

to many people. You've even done some TV work, haven't you, Celine?'

'Yes, I worked on last year's Channel 7 Telethon. I did hair and make-up for Sally Stanton and Jack Yabsley. You know, from *Saturday Disney*?'

'I have no idea what language you are speaking right now,' Tina said. 'But I'm sure it's all very impressive.'

Nicole stood up. 'I'll just go check on dessert,' she said.

'Let me help you,' Samantha was quick to offer.

'I'm fine.'

'I'm happy to help,' Samantha insisted with the smile of a saint about to slay some pagans.

HER SMILE DISAPPEARED the minute they stepped back into the kitchen.

'This is a disaster,' Samantha told her sister. 'You've got to get her out of here.'

'What are you talking about? It's going fine.'

'Dad has barely eaten anything.'

'Celine probably has him on another diet.'

'Tina keeps calling Celine "Celeste".'

'So what? Mum always calls Trent "Troy". It's her way of showing affection.'

'Yeah, and we all know how much Trent really loves that.'

Samantha watched as Nicole checked the apple crumble in the sweets oven and then turned the temperature up. She was probably ruining it.

'You always do this, you know,' Samantha observed.

'Do what?'

'Sabotage your own events. You missed the Gobbles party bus at your own twenty-first. And you completely stuffed up lunch the one year you hosted Christmas.'

'I'm not sure two examples count as "always",' Nicole said in a small voice.

'And now you invite Tina *and* Dad to your fortieth? What were you thinking?'

'That they're both my parents.' Nicole's voice was now even smaller.

'Well, good for you. Tina stopped being my parent twenty-five years ago,' Samantha said, marching out of the room. She stood in the hallway and breathed in and out for a minute to try to get her anger levels back under control. She could do this. She knew she could. Her reward at the end of the day would be the hidden vodka, waiting for her at home.

But the minute she stepped into the dining room, she realised the situation had worsened. Rosemary was nowhere to be seen. And now Celine and Jethro were looking down at their hands, too, and Trent had the wild eyes of a drowning man. Only Tina was smiling and tucking into her meal.

'Where's Rose?' Samantha asked the room.

'I just showed her where the Xbox is,' Jethro said.

'Her iPod battery had run out,' Trent explained.

'It was like her i-Thingy was a person who had died, it was such a huge drama,' Tina piped up. 'She was demanding to go home to recharge it. Imagine wanting to leave a party because of a battery!'

'I can't see why it's so hard to imagine,' Samantha retorted. 'You always leave the party when the wine runs out.'

'Touché,' Tina said, with a laugh that sounded like a peal of tiny bells. 'Although these days, I'm all about the food. The sauce on this beef has such complexity of flavour! Who would have thought that Nic would become such a great cook!'

'She didn't cook it, *Tina*,' Samantha said. She usually avoided calling Tina anything, so the name came out barbed.

'Well, she's got great taste in caterers. God knows where she got her great taste. The rest of us have no clue, wouldn't you say, Sam?'

Samantha could taste the bile in her mouth. 'It's not taste she has, it's money.'

'Maybe it is. But she certainly knows how to spend it,' Tina replied, all matter-of-fact, before turning to Trent. 'How's it going at the Bunnings? You never really struck me as the handyman type.'

'It's, uh, Home Hardware,' Trent corrected her. He'd recently taken a systems support job there, joking that he was expanding his knowledge of 'hardware'. It was true that he'd never picked up a power tool in his life, but then again, neither had Tina.

'Oh, really? That's not as big, is it? You weren't tempted to take one of those FIFO jobs? I heard that's where the real money is,' Tina said, going in for her next forkful of food.

'We decided that it was better for me to be home with Sam and Rose,' Trent replied. He smiled over at Samantha and she did her best to smile back, but she didn't like where Tina was going with all this.

'But imagine, you could have had a much nicer home to return to every six weeks if you had. Oh well.'

'I don't think you can talk.' Samantha was starting to see red now. 'You can't say "Oh well" about our house and Trent's job when you live in a Housing Authority flat and stack shelves for a living.'

Tina stared at Samantha for a moment. There was something in her eyes that was setting hard, like concrete. 'Now, now,' she said. 'I didn't mean anything by "Oh well". It's just a little expression of mine. I'm sorry if it caused any offence, Troy.'

'*Trent*,' Samantha muttered under her breath.

'Anyway, I'm actually delighted to see you made it along today,' Tina continued. 'I guess you two didn't break up this time . . .'

Now Trent was looking down at his hands, too. Before she knew what she was doing, Samantha had leapt up and hurled her fork like a warning shot at the empty spot next to Tina, hitting the mahogany sideboard in the corner of the room with great force.

Jethro gasped. 'That's my grandmother's sideboard,' he said.

'I don't give a flying fuck about your grandmother or her sideboard,' Samantha told him. She had now fully become the Other Samantha, the one from her childhood, the one Donna-Louise tried to help her control, the one she drank to placate. And she had no idea how she could stop herself. 'You can go out and buy another hundred sideboards with the change in your pocket.'

Ashen-faced, Jethro got up and left the room, but Samantha was past caring.

'As for you,' she said turning back to Tina. 'Stop being such a fucking bitch. I had no idea being sober made you this fucking *mean*.'

'Sam! What are you doing?' Nicole was standing at the doorway.

'I'm not doing anything,' Samantha said, her tantrum still in full swing. 'It's all Tina's fault.'

'What did I say?' Tina set down her fork and looked at all of them with the wide-eyed innocence of a wolf wearing the severed head of a sheep as a hat.

Craig exchanged urgent looks with Celine and muttered, 'We should go.'

'No, I should go,' Tina said. 'I'm obviously not welcome. And if I stay any longer, Samantha might start throwing *knives* at me.'

'You *are* welcome here, Mum, of course you are. You're all welcome,' Nicole said desperately. 'Please, it's my birthday.'

But Tina was already on her feet. 'I'm sorry if I said anything to offend you or Trent, Samantha,' she said, primly, before turning to Nicole. 'Happy birthday, my beautiful girl.'

And with that, she left the room, Nicole at her heel.

Samantha sat down, now deflated.

'We really should go, too,' Craig said. 'Cee-Cee's got an early job tomorrow morning.'

'I'm doing a client's make-up in Peppermint Grove,' Celine said brightly. 'She's going to an assembly at her kids' school and she wants to look her best. Full on, huh?'

And after a flurry of air kisses and firm handshakes, they were gone.

The minute they were alone, Samantha looked over at Trent for support, but he wouldn't meet her eye.

'Why won't you tell your family the truth about that Christmas?' he said quietly. 'I'm sick of looking like the villain.'

'With all that just happened, *that's* the thing that bothers you? Not Tina being such a bitch about our house and our life?' Samantha asked. She was struggling to keep herself from shouting again. 'Anyway, we all know that Nicole was the real villain that Christmas, with that frozen ham.'

'Jesus, Samantha.' Trent still couldn't look at her. 'Sometimes you're very hard to love.'

Trent's words winded her. Struggling to breathe, she pushed through the large double doors into the piano room and, sitting on the piano stool, she closed her eyes and concentrated on her breathing. In and out. In and out. As all her anger – at Tina, at Nicole, at Trent – rose up in her chest, she pushed it out with each breath. And when the shame at having behaved so very badly rose as high as her throat, she pushed that out, too.

When she finally felt like an empty shell again, she opened her eyes and looked around the room. Other than the piano, there was only a painting of a girl at a piano that she was pretty certain was by a famous artist, and a huge chandelier. It was so typical of Jethro and Nicole to have a whole room dedicated to an instrument neither of them played.

She heard Jethro returning to the dining room. 'Where's everyone gone?' he asked, his voice muffled. She crept closer to the doors so she could hear better.

'They, uh, had to go,' Trent said.

'Samantha, too?' asked Jethro. He sounded hopeful.

'No, she's . . . somewhere.'

There was a slight pause while Jethro obviously did his best to swallow his disappointment. 'Well, now that Tina's gone,' he finally said, 'can we at least open some wine?'

'Hell yeah,' said Trent, suddenly sounding happier.

'Which would you prefer: a Henry James Pinot Noir or a Man O' War Syrah?'

'I really don't mind,' Trent replied.

'Okay, well, let's start with the Man O' War. It feels somewhat fitting,' Jethro said, and the two men laughed.

'I'm sorry about my wife,' Trent said. 'She's complicated.'

There was the sound of Jethro pouring the wine. '*People* are complicated, mate,' Jethro said. 'A glass of this will make everything simpler.'

'Sure will.'

Listening to this conversation, Samantha felt small and sad. All this time, she'd thought Trent drank because he was weak, like she was. Like Tina was. The thought that he might drink just to cope with her – or worse yet, to escape from her altogether – was too much to bear. Unable to listen anymore, she crept out the other door only to immediately run into

Nicole, who seemed to be doing her own creeping about in the hall.

'Which room is Rose in?' Samantha asked, avoiding her sister's eyes. She knew she should apologise for what had happened, but she still felt too embarrassed.

'In the yellow room,' Nicole replied, gesturing down the hallway behind her. She wasn't looking at Samantha, either.

'Thanks,' Samantha mumbled and set off to find her daughter.

Eventually she found Rosemary frantically manipulating an Xbox controller in a room whose yellow walls perfectly matched the yellow throw cushions on the leather couches.

'How are you doing, darling?' Samantha asked, sitting on one of the couches. She picked up a perfect yellow cushion and hugged it. 'Did you eat enough food?'

'Yep!'

Samantha closed her eyes and tried not to think of her husband drinking wine back in the dining room, or of the wine itself. But after a few seconds, the sound of rapid gunfire on the television made her open her eyes again.

'What on earth are you playing?' she asked in horror, as she watched her twelve-year-old daughter gun down a man wearing a bandana and army fatigues.

'*Call of Duty: Black Ops*,' Rosemary said, taking another man down with a single headshot. 'I found it in the cupboard.'

'Turn it off.'

'Why?'

'Because it's not age-appropriate.'

'Jethro said I could play any game I wanted. It's his house and his rules,' Rosemary said, reloading her weapon.

'Well, I'm your mother.'

'Biologically, yes,' she said, taking another shot at someone's head.

Samantha didn't have the energy to stop her daughter, but nor could she watch. She stood up and walked over to the other side of the room, to the large set of shelves full of records.

'Typical that Jethro still owns vinyl,' she said, although she knew Rosemary wasn't listening.

As she pulled each record out, she automatically began to order them alphabetically by artist. The Beach Boys before the Beatles. The Jam before Billy Joel. Tom Waits before the White Stripes . . .

Slowly but surely, the Other Samantha and the clamour of rapid gunfire faded completely away, leaving only the sound of her heart beating.

Piece #6: 1999

'YOU CAN'T SPEND New Year's by yourself! Come to ours! Trent and I are making paella.'

'Um . . .' Nicole hesitated. The thought of spending New Year's stone cold sober, listening to Samantha tell Trent that he was doing everything wrong was hardly appealing. But then again, as she and Darren were on another 'break', she wasn't exactly looking forward to seeing the new millennium in on her own.

'You have to come. I insist!' Samantha said.

'Okay, okay,' Nicole replied, although she knew she'd regret it. 'But only if you can tell me what the hell paella is.'

'It's Spanish rice,' Samantha explained. 'Bring half a kilo of prawns. Fresh ones, not frozen. Oh, and some lemons and limes. Trent is making mocktails!'

Nicole sighed. She was twenty-nine years old and she was

going to spend New Year's drinking soft drink from a margarita glass.

TWO DAYS LATER, she dutifully showed up at Samantha and Trent's small flat in Shenton Park with half a kilo of prawns in one hand and a bag full of limes and lemons in the other. Trent greeted her at the front door, wearing a sombrero and holding what Nicole presumed was a non-alcoholic margarita.

'*Hola, gringo!*'

'*Gringa*,' she corrected him. 'Anyway, I thought paella was Spanish, not Mexican.'

'Spanish. Mexican. What's the difference?'

'Uh, the North Atlantic Ocean?'

'A mere pond,' Trent said with a grin. 'No Darren tonight?'

'Didn't Sam tell you? We're on a break.'

'Oh, that's a shame,' Trent said, although he clearly meant the opposite. Now that the two of them didn't work together anymore, Trent barely bothered to hide his dislike of Darren. 'Where's he at tonight?'

'I have no idea,' she replied, although she knew he was probably down at Club Rumours hoping to shove his tongue down a twenty-year-old's throat. He'd told her a number of times that he could get a younger, more petite girlfriend, like it was a matter of him just trading Nicole in like a used car.

'Trent, you got the wrong rice!' Samantha shouted from the kitchen. She was standing at the small island bench with a copy of *The Barefoot Contessa Cookbook* in front of her, along with a thousand different ingredients, each in their own little bowl, like she was on a cooking show.

'The literal translation of "paella" is "a shit load of washing up",' Trent told Nicole.

'The recipe says medium-grain. You got long-grain,' Samantha said.

Trent ignored her. He was good at ignoring Samantha in a way Nicole never could.

'Would you like a non-alcoholic margarita, Nic?'

'Sure. Thanks.'

Trent moved around to a corner of the kitchen where he'd set up a small bar, with glasses, juice, ice and, to Nicole's surprise, a large unopened bottle of tequila with a red plastic hat for a lid.

'Is that actual alcohol I see before me?' she asked.

'Sam and I agreed that we can make a boozy one a little closer to midnight,' Trent said, as he salted the rim of a glass. Nicole looked over at Samantha, who gave a small nod.

It's a Millennium Miracle, Nicole thought.

Down the hall, Rosemary started to wail. 'Mummy! Daddy!' she cried.

'Not again,' Trent said. 'It's been so hard to settle her tonight.'

'It's going to be even harder when the aeroplanes start dropping out of the sky at midnight,' Nicole replied.

Trent, who'd been working for a Y2K consultancy for the past twelve months, laughed. 'Not on my watch.'

'I'll see to Rosemary, will I?' Samantha said with the air of a martyr, as she looked up from the recipe book.

'No, no. You're cooking. I'll go.'

He handed Nicole her mocktail and disappeared off down the hall.

Nicole stood and watched her sister frown at the recipe book for a few moments.

'Can I help?'

'I'm fine.'

After a few more moments of watching Samantha continue to frown, Nicole decided to drink her mocktail out on the balcony, which offered the scenic view of the block of flats across the street. From the lack of lights, Nicole guessed everyone was out at some party or another tonight. Only the flat on the end of the second floor seemed to show any signs of life. There, Nicole could see a woman, silhouetted by the fluorescent light in the room behind her, sitting alone on the balcony. Nicole couldn't tell from her shadow what age the woman was, but there was something very peaceful about her.

'Are these prawns frozen?' Samantha shouted from the kitchen.

Nicole sighed.

BY THE TIME Rosemary was settled and then re-settled in her cot and dinner was finally cooked, served and eaten, it was almost ten o'clock. The three of them were out on the balcony, sitting on fold-out chairs with their plates on their laps.

'That was delicious,' Nicole said to Samantha, as she finished her last forkful.

'The rice was too sticky.'

'That's not because it wasn't medium-grain,' Trent was quick to add.

'Maybe not,' Samantha replied in a tone of voice that suggested it was exactly the reason the rice was too sticky.

'Great flavours,' Nicole said, hoping to side-step the argument.

'I reckon it's time to open that tequila,' Trent said, rubbing his hands together.

Samantha's eyes darted to her watch. 'It's a bit early. Midnight's still two hours away.'

'But it's New Year's Eve, Sammy,' Trent pleaded.

'One cocktail,' Samantha replied. She stood up and started

to collect the dirty plates. Nicole saw Trent trying to hide a smile and Samantha must have too, because she added, 'That's what we agreed.'

'Yes, one cocktail. And we'll sip it really, really slowly, we promise.'

The minute Samantha disappeared inside with the plates, Trent leant over to Nicole and said, in an arch whisper, 'She said one cocktail, but she didn't say anything about how strong it was allowed to be.'

Nicole had to laugh.

WHILE TRENT WENT inside to mix the drinks, Nicole looked back over at the lone woman's flat. The balcony was now empty and the light was off. Maybe she'd gone to a party. Or maybe she'd gone to bed. Nicole really hoped it was the latter. She liked the idea of the woman feeling so comfortable in her solitude that she had no problem turning in two hours' shy of the new millennium.

'Get this into you.' Trent was back beside her, holding out a margarita glass filled to the brim with a pale liquid.

Nicole took a sip. The cocktail was so strong, she spluttered a little.

'Jesus, Trent. This is ninety-nine parts tequila, one part everything else.'

'I know,' he said with a wide smile. 'Chug-a-lug, pooh bear.'

Nicole took another small sip and put the drink down.

'What's Sam doing?' she asked.

'The dishes. She insisted.' Trent didn't need to explain any further.

'Who lives at the end there?' Nicole asked Trent, pointing at the lone woman's flat.

'The local cat lady. None of her cats seem to like her, though, because they're always running away. She's forever sticking MISSING CAT posters up around the place,' Trent replied, just as Rosemary's mournful cry started up again from inside the flat.

'Mummy! Daddy!'

'Shit,' Trent said.

'I'll go this time,' Nicole offered.

'Are you sure?' Trent was already getting up.

'Yeah, it can be my New Year's gift to both of you.' She put her cocktail down and went inside.

'Sam, I'm checking on Rose,' she said as she passed the kitchen on the way to Rosemary's bedroom.

'Oh, is she crying?' Samantha's voice sounded a million miles away.

'You can't hear her?'

Samantha returned to scrubbing a large pot.

Nicole started off down the hall but then with each step grew increasingly uncertain. She couldn't remember what the rule was for re-settling Rosemary before midnight. Was she supposed to keep her in the cot or was she allowed to pick her up? Samantha was always very particular when it came to these things.

As she returned to the kitchen, she saw Samantha moving a small glass away from her lips to the kitchen bench, but the action was so quick and fluid that she immediately thought she must have imagined it.

'What now?' Samantha's tone was short.

'Should I pick her up or should I pat her in the cot?'

'Do whatever you want. It's a new millennium, after all,' Samantha said, turning back to the dishes, not looking at Nicole. The tequila bottle was open beside her on the bench, its red plastic hat sitting beside it.

Nicole headed back down the hall, confused. She wasn't sure what was more unsettling: the open bottle of tequila or Samantha's complete lack of instruction.

By the time she got to Rosemary's door, however, the crying had stopped. She stood there, a long time, waiting. Listening. Wondering about what she saw. But when she passed the kitchen again, neither Samantha nor the tequila and its little red hat were there.

She found Trent alone on the balcony.

'Where's Sam?'

'Brushing her teeth.'

'What? There's only an hour to go. She can't give up so close to the finishing line.'

'Try telling her that.'

Nicole picked up her cocktail and winced as she sipped it again. She imagined this was what it was like to drink methylated spirits.

Sam appeared at the doorway. 'Goodnight,' she said.

'See you next millennium,' Nicole replied.

'Yeah, see you next millennium,' Trent echoed, getting up to give Samantha a kiss, but she had already stepped back into the shadows of the flat.

TRENT AND NICOLE sat in silence on the balcony. In the distance, they could hear the parties in the neighbourhood picking up volume as the city began the downhill slide to midnight. She thought again of that woman in the other block of flats and she wondered what Tina was doing tonight, if she was alone or if she was at the pub.

'You have to forgive Sam,' Trent said. 'She's been a bit upset since the accident the other day.'

'What accident?' Nicole said, sitting up straight in her seat. 'She didn't tell me about any accident.'

'Well, it wasn't really an accident. It was a near miss, but Sam was really shaken up by it. She was driving back from the shops with Rose and she took a corner too fast and the car went into a spin and she ended up facing the wrong way. There wasn't any damage to anyone or even to the car. But the way Sam went on about it—'

'She took a corner too fast?'

'I know, right? She normally drives slower than my nanna.'

Nicole thought of how Samantha, when she was younger, had cried when she thought Craig or Tina was driving too fast. That was after that car accident when the car had spun and then flipped like a pancake.

They sat in silence and finished their cocktails.

'Fifteen minutes to go,' Trent said, looking at his watch. 'What do you say about a cheeky shot of tequila for the stroke of midnight? We could even do the whole lick, sip, suck thing.'

'Sure. Why not.'

Trent went back inside and Nicole looked again at the dark flats and thought of Darren dancing like a dickhead at Club Rumours with all the teenagers. She wondered if he was thinking of her. Probably not.

'I can't find the tequila,' Trent said, as he came back out onto the balcony, empty-handed. 'Sam must have hidden it. Or poured it down the sink.'

'Or down her throat.'

Trent laughed. He thought Nicole was joking, but Nicole wasn't sure if she was. She thought again of that swift arm movement. Glass from lips.

They sat in silence until finally the sky above them exploded into colour and the streets around them erupted into a chorus of cheers and car horns.

'Happy new millennium,' Trent said quietly.

'Happy new millennium,' Nicole replied. But she was still thinking of Samantha taking that corner too fast, tyres screeching and car spinning out of control, like Tina's car had on that dusty red road almost twenty years ago at Bruce Rock.

Samantha

'I HAD AN AFFAIR with your father,' Aunt Meg said over the din of the Blue Duck Cafe. She said it in such a matter-of-fact way that it took a few moments for her words to properly land in my brain.

I opened my own mouth to reply but no words came out. I looked at Nicole beside me to see her reaction, but she was leaning in towards Meg and I couldn't see her face.

'When?' she asked.

'In the year leading up to your parents' separation,' Meg replied. At least she had the decency to look away from us at this point. 'I'm not proud of myself and what I did, but, well . . . your father was persuasive.'

'Did Mum know?' Nicole asked.

Aunt Meg shook her head. 'No. Tina knew that Craig was

being unfaithful but she didn't know I was the one he was being unfaithful with. Once, we almost got caught out, but then . . .'

'Then what?' My voice had managed to come back and the words came out much louder and heavier than I expected.

'Then Tina got drunk and crashed the car with you girls in it and, uh, the rest is history.'

'So, what you're saying is that Tina crashed the car because you were fucking Dad?'

Aunt Meg flinched when I said this. 'No, no,' she said hurriedly. Then she added, 'Not really. When she crashed the car, she was on her way to our parents' place. Later, she told me she'd been trying to leave him.'

Nicole and I must have been looking at her blankly, because she changed tack. 'Didn't you ever wonder why you were on the way to Kalgoorlie and not heading back to Perth to start school?'

'We *were* on our way back to Perth,' I told her. She hadn't been there. How would she know?

'No,' she said patiently. 'You were on your way to Kalgoorlie.'

By this stage, I was ready to call it. 'This is bullshit,' I declared. 'You've barely had anything to do with us or Tina for years and now you've popped up out of nowhere with these terrible lies. I can tell you this much: Dad wasn't unfaithful to Tina, not with you, not with anyone else. Dad left Tina because she was a drunk. End of story.'

I glanced over at Nicole for support, but she was regarding Aunt Meg thoughtfully. She clearly didn't share my outrage, and that just fuelled it even further. 'Don't tell me you believe this, Nic?'

'I'm not believing or disbelieving anything at this stage, Sam. I'm just listening to what Meg has to say.'

'Well, I don't believe it.' I was aware that I was now slouching in my chair like a sullen teenager. I looked back at Meg. 'And even if what you're saying is true, why the fuck are you telling us now? You've basically had nothing to do with our lives for thirty-five years. You made yourself so scarce we used to call you "The Ghost Aunt". Why do you even care?'

Meg cleared her throat. 'After the accident, I broke it off with your dad immediately and moved to Melbourne. But as you know, things between your parents rapidly fell apart. I pretended to myself that I moved to get away from Craig, but really, I think it was to get away from all the guilt I felt.'

As she spoke, she started to swirl the froth on the top of her latte with a spoon. I found myself watching that instead of her.

'Tina always tried. Always sent gifts and cards and called me on my birthday. She was always drunk when she rang. And I found myself withdrawing from the whole situation. Then, after our parents died, I dropped out of Tina's life altogether. It was easier than watching her drink herself to death, knowing the part I played in it. Of course, I always told myself I would find a chance to come clean with her, that I would tell her about the affair, but then Nicole got in contact with me to say Tina was dead and I finally felt the full weight of everything.' She placed her fist against her breast. 'I thought I was going to explode. Telling you both felt like the only thing that was left for me to do.'

'But why?' I demanded, looking back up at her. 'It's not like you ever gave two fucks about what happened to me and Nic, anyway.'

'I know it must seem that way,' Meg said, eyes down again. 'I was too young and silly to have thought about the impact the separation would have on you two. It was only much later after I'd actually lived some life and seen what divorce can do to kids that I realised you might have needed me in your lives. But by then, it all felt too late to do anything.'

'But why now? Tina's dead. What difference does it make, except maybe to you?' I asked.

'Because it's the truth. Surely that counts for something. Your parents' divorce wasn't all Tina's fault. It was mine, too. And Craig's.'

'Things are very rarely one person's fault,' Nicole observed, which just angered me even further.

'Except when it came to Tina and drinking,' I said. 'Then it really was all Tina's fault.'

'Don't be like that,' Nicole said, putting her hand on my arm, but I shook it off.

'At least I'm being like *something*, not just soaking up this bullshit like a sponge.' I pushed away my half-finished coffee and stood up. 'Nicole can give you a lift to the airport, Aunt Meg. I've got to go.'

'But where?' Meg said, suddenly old and feeble again, but I couldn't respond. Instead, I threw a twenty dollar note on the table and walked out as quickly as I could without running.

I DIDN'T GO to my car. Instead, I took off my shoes and walked to the near-empty beach. The Fremantle Doctor, the afternoon sea breeze, had already come in and cleared away most of the swimmers, surfers and sunbathers. Only those who didn't mind the occasional mouthful of sand remained. And at that moment, a mouthful of sand felt like the best option I had.

The day was hot and even though I knew I hadn't put enough sunscreen on and that my dress wasn't giving me much cover, I was past caring. I was too angry at Meg and Nicole. I was angry with Tina, too. I'd never had a mother, not properly, not in the way people were supposed to have a mother. How dare they try to take my father away from me as well?

I thought of the vodka bottle from Nicole's kitchen; the smell of it as I emptied it onto those flowers. The waste. The release.

I sat on the beach for as long as I could but I desperately needed something to push Meg's words out of my head. I stood up and walked back to the road, up towards the Ocean Beach Hotel.

The Sunday Session at the OBH was in full swing. It was heaving with young people, drinking and laughing and being young. I couldn't help but hate them all.

My heart tightened a little when I spotted one couple through the open windows: a short dark-haired girl talking to a tall guy with square shoulders and shaggy hair with what looked like a jug of Coke between them. They struck me as a younger version of Trent and me, a sober nation of two amidst a sea of drinkers. I remembered how relieved I'd been to find someone like me, someone who didn't see the point in erasing themselves with alcohol every weekend.

The booze had managed to find us both, in the end.

I bought a hipflask-sized bottle of vodka from the bottle shop and then slunk over to the park across the road, the sea breeze whipping my long hair around my face. I wanted to go back to the car to get one of the scrunchies I kept in the glove box, but I didn't want to risk seeing Nicole or Aunt Meg again.

Just then, a stretch limousine pulled up in front of me, distracting me. Now I was faced with another couple – a woman wearing a boned satin gown she'd been vacuum-sealed into, and a man, considerably older than she was, looking hot and bothered in his suit.

The groom began to remove his jacket but the bride was quick to intervene.

'You'll ruin the photos!' she said to him, as the wind lifted up her veil so that it was like a plume of smoke around her head.

'But this jacket is ruining my day,' he protested. 'It's so hot!'

'The photos are more important,' she replied.

She was right, of course. I only really remembered the bits of my wedding that had been captured in the photos. Everything that had fallen outside the camera's neat rectangular frame had been easier to forget.

A second stretch limousine pulled up and three lavender-coloured bridesmaids and three groomsmen tumbled out. They were all a similar age to the bride and I found myself wondering if they were the bride's friends or the groom's children. At Celine and Dad's wedding, now almost a decade ago, Nicole and I had been forced to wear pale pink organza, even though we were both in our thirties. I had been petite enough to (almost) carry it off but Nicole had looked ready for Las Vegas in those ridiculous heels and all that make-up. And yet, that had been the day she had met Jethro and the two of them had ridden off into the sunset to Dalkeith.

And what had I managed to do in those ten years? I had stayed in the same dank townhouse, ignoring Trent, arguing with Rosemary and drinking in the shadows.

As the bride began screeching at the groomsmen to keep their jackets on, I decided to head back to the beach, despite the wind.

I sat a few metres from the water, looking out at the clear blue horizon and then down at the vodka bottle, still in its brown paper bag, beside me on the ever-shifting sand. Hardly an 'Instaworthy' moment, as Rosemary would call it, but this was my moment.

I pulled the bottle out of the bag and read the label. It contained eleven standard drinks, which was eleven points in the system I'd developed. Each day I didn't drink gave me five points and each standard drink I consumed cost me one point.

I hadn't had a single drink since Tina died and out of habit I started to calculate how many days had passed so I could work out how many points I'd earned. Then I stopped myself.

'Fuck the points,' I said, as I opened the bottle and, turning my head away from the wind to avoid getting sand in my mouth, took my first sip.

Fuck the points was exactly the kind of thing Tina would have said. But in that moment, I knew I wasn't like Tina. I was entirely like myself. This was who I was. I was Samantha, and I was drinking as much as it took to forget I was Samantha at all.

Piece #7: 2007

A S NICOLE STEPPED into the cafe, she felt her stomach tighten, as if in anticipation of a punch.

It had been four months since she'd last caught up with Samantha and, if left to Nicole, she'd have gladly waited another four months. She always felt better about herself when she was away from Samantha and her barbed comments.

However, Samantha had phoned, insisting that they do the dress fittings together, and Nicole had found herself surrendering once again.

'Hello, stranger,' Samantha said when she saw Nicole. She stood up to give her the ghost of a kiss on her cheek and Nicole got the usual strong whiff of peppermint. She had a private theory that Samantha brushed her teeth in the car while she drove.

Nicole stood back to look at her sister. Judging from her clothes – a pencil skirt and neatly pressed blouse – she had come straight from work. Nicole, in contrast, had come straight from home and was still wearing the clothes she'd slept in. It had taken her half an hour to find her shoes amidst the mess of her dark ground-floor flat, which was more cave than human dwelling.

Samantha sat back down, smoothing out her skirt as she did so. 'How are you?'

'Fine. Although I'm not exactly looking forward to this dress fitting.'

'Why not?'

'Don't you think there should be some international law that protects women over thirty-five from being forced to wear organza?'

'Really? That's your only objection to Dad marrying Celine? Having to wear a bridesmaid's dress?' Samantha said, her mouth forming a thin line. 'I keep thinking of poor Donna-Louise.'

Nicole wanted to say something like, *I think poor Donna-Louise is quite happy with her huge settlement and her ultra-white house in Busselton.* Instead, she said, 'Dad and Donna-Louise divorced almost two years ago. Dad's allowed to move on, isn't he?'

Samantha raised an eyebrow and then glanced at the menu, leaving Nicole to shift uncomfortably in her seat. 'What do you think about the whole church wedding thing?' she asked.

'I had a church wedding,' Samantha snapped. 'There's nothing wrong with that.'

From the pan into the flames, Nicole thought. This conversation was not going well. 'I'm not saying there is. I was just a bit surprised, that's all. Dad has always said he's an atheist.'

'Maybe he's doing it to make Celine happy.' Samantha

shrugged. 'Anyway, he said you have a new job.'

The change of subject was welcome. Any further talk about Craig's wives, ex- and imminent, would only lead them into even more treacherous waters.

'Yeah, I'm doing data entry for this big company. They courier me boxes of files and I work my own hours in my pyjamas,' Nicole explained. 'It means I can keep on top of my demanding TV schedule.'

'Ah, right,' Samantha said. 'What are you watching these days?'

Nicole reeled off a list of shows, leaving off a few of the trashier reality TV ones.

'And any men on the scene?'

'No. It's just me and the TV,' Nicole said, trying to keep the tone light. Five years after Darren had finally broken up with her for good, she was still in recovery. He'd left her when she'd really needed him and she couldn't imagine trusting anyone again. Not that she'd ever really trusted Darren.

'How's Trent?' Nicole asked. If she hadn't seen Samantha in a long time, it had been even longer since she'd seen Trent. She actually missed him.

'Good,' Samantha replied. 'He's been offered a tech support job up in Newman, one of those fly-in-fly-out things for ridiculous amounts of money.'

'Is he going to take it?'

Samantha gave a little shrug. 'We're talking about it. Six weeks feels like a long time for him to be away.'

Nicole couldn't imagine Samantha surviving six weeks without Trent. They'd been joined at the hip for so long now, it was hard to think of one without the other. She wondered if she would ever have a relationship as solid as theirs.

She turned her attention to the menu and baulked. 'Why

is everything so expensive?' Her electricity bill was due any day now and she'd already maxed her credit card. 'I got charged $8 for a latte the other day.'

'That's Boomtown for you. This is my shout.'

'You don't have to do that.'

'But I want to.'

'Thanks,' Nicole said, grateful and embarrassed. But mostly grateful.

'HERE THEY ARE! My bridies!' Celine exclaimed, throwing her arms out to embrace Nicole and Samantha as they entered the bridal shop.

While the dressmaker started measuring Samantha, Celine handed Nicole a glass of champagne and a sheet of paper.

'I've printed this schedule for the wedding day so you know when and where to go for make-up and hair.' She paused to give Nicole a coy look. 'We need you to look nice! There's a certain someone I've invited to the wedding who I think you're really going to like.'

'I've heard that line before,' Nicole said, giving Samantha a pointed look, but typically, Samantha ignored it. These days, Samantha didn't like to take credit for having match-made Nicole and Darren at her own wedding. Her revisionist version of history placed the blame squarely on Trent's shoulders.

'This one is a real keeper. He's an Anderson. You know, of the *Anderson* Andersons?' Nicole didn't know. 'He's the CEO of this social enterprise venture that trains baristas in remote communities. Craig knows him through his networks and he's letting us use his Rolls Royce as the bridal car. Of course, when he offered that, we had to invite him. And then I found out he was single!'

'Oh, okay.'

Celine lowered her voice and leant forward. 'Rumour has it that his wife left him for the pool boy but still managed to get half his money in the settlement.'

Nicole hadn't had a boyfriend for almost five years, but some half-rich loser with a caffeine addiction and a broken heart didn't exactly sound like a good candidate. But she put on a bright smile and nodded. 'He sounds great. I can't wait to meet him.'

ON THE DAY of the wedding, Nicole dragged herself out of her bed and made it to her 9 am make-up call at the beauty parlour only half an hour late. Samantha was already there, her hair in curlers. Rosie, her hair already done, was sitting in the corner playing on her ever-present Nintendo DS, her bridesmaid dress hung up on the wall beside her. Nicole couldn't remember the last time she'd seen Rosie unattached to a device. If it wasn't the DS, it was the television or the iPod or the computer, or she was playing Snake on Trent's phone.

'Where's Celine?' Nicole asked Samantha.

'In the back room. She's been here since 6am. Françoise and F'nelle are doing some serious things to her hair.'

'Françoise and who?'

'F'nelle! F-apostrophe-N-E-double-L-E!' said a woman, dressed entirely in purple, as she emerged from the back room. 'You must be Nicole! I'm F'nelle and I'm getting you ready for the ball, Cinders!'

She guided Nicole to a chair and then took her face in her hands. She considered it for a long time.

'Yes. Yes. Yes,' she said, and then, 'Yes.'

Nicole shifted uncomfortably in her seat. 'Yes?'

'Yes,' F'nelle repeated and then let go of Nicole's face. 'Let's get started! Françoise? I think we're going to use a mid-autumn palette with a number three foundation with this one.'

A small, orange-tinted woman, presumably Françoise, emerged from the back room. She, too, held Nicole's face in her hands.

'Yessss,' she said, after a moment, in a heavy accent. 'What moisturiser do you use? You have za skin of, how you say, a *zombi*.'

Nicole sighed. 'It's the same word in English. Zombie.'

Hours – maybe years – later, she was finally ready, her hair curled and set with some kind of superglue and her pores struggling for air under all that contouring, foundation and powder. She felt even less like herself than she had when Samantha had dressed her up like Cindy Crawford at her twenty-first.

'There,' F'nelle said, admiring her handiwork. 'We've sure made those features of yours work a little harder for you. Particularly your eyes. We've got those baby blues popping!'

'Not sure how I feel about using the word "popping" when it comes to eyeballs,' Nicole whispered to Rosie when F'nelle disappeared into the back room at the mysterious Françoise's bidding.

'Don't worry, Aunty Nic. Your eyeballs are still in your head,' Rosie whispered back, looking up briefly from her DS. 'You look really pretty. Aunty Celine says you're going to meet your new boyfriend today.'

'Did she now?' Nicole turned to Samantha and mouthed the question '*Aunty* Celine?' but Samantha just shrugged. As Celine was younger than both of them, Nicole guessed it wouldn't do anyone any good for Rosemary to call her 'Nanna'.

F'nelle re-emerged from the back room.

'Did someone say Celine?' she said, dramatically, before stepping back for Celine's big entrance in her long satin dress.

Her hair was a geyser of ringlets. Françoise followed, fussing with the train of the dress.

'Ta da!' Celine said.

'Aunty Celine, you look like a princess!' Rosemary said, jumping up and rushing forward to hug her.

'Careful of Aunty Celine's dress, Rose,' Samantha warned, but Celine didn't seem to mind.

'Thank you, darling girl,' Celine said, hugging Rosemary back. 'Now where's *your* little princess dress? The car is leaving here in ten minutes.'

Samantha looked up at the clock on the wall and frowned. 'But it's not even eleven. The schedule said the car would be here at eleven-thirty.'

'Oh, that clock's wrong,' said F'nelle. 'We set it half an hour slow on purpose to stop people from getting too nervous. It's all part of our process.'

'What about people who are only nervous about being on time?' Samantha wanted to know. 'Have you considered them in your process?'

'Um, I'll wait outside,' Nicole said, eager to get away from the fight.

Carefully gathering a handful of her pink organza skirt, she stepped out onto the street.

An enormous white car was parked directly outside, with a driver in a black suit standing stiffly by the back passenger door. The driver smiled when he saw her.

'Are you part of the wedding party?' he asked.

'No, I'm off to play a spot of tennis,' she replied, and the driver laughed.

'I should have known from the shoes,' he said. 'You can always tell a tennis pro from their shoes.'

'These are the highest heels I've ever worn,' Nicole admitted.

Samantha had argued long and hard with Celine about the folly of putting a tall woman in such tall shoes, but Celine had insisted that Nicole should 'celebrate her height'.

'I can see all the way to Rottnest Island from up here. Well, I could, if I wasn't wearing these false eyelashes. Every time I blink, I think I'm being attacked by a large black insect.'

The driver laughed again. He was the best audience she'd had in years. He was also good-looking, in a quiet 'your friendly accountant' kind of way, with undertones of George Clooney. The fact she was getting his attention, even for a moment, made her a little giddy. She quickly turned her focus to the car he was driving. 'So this is the Rolls Celine's been banging on about. Why on earth would anyone own such a monstrously large thing? Looks like someone's got penis issues.'

'Not into cars, then?'

'Not really. My small pile of shit probably cost a fraction of this one and it still gets me from A to B.'

'I totally agree.'

'But you drive it for a living.'

'I actually don't drive it for a living. I, um, own it.'

'You own it?' Nicole blinked hard.

'Well, I inherited it. I'd never buy a car like this.'

Nicole was mortified. This was the guy Celine had been talking about. One of the *Anderson* Andersons, whatever that meant.

'Oh,' she said, her cheeks growing hotter than the sun. 'Sorry, your car really is very nice. I was just . . .'

'Being honest? I don't get a lot of people being honest around me, so it's very welcome,' he reassured her. 'I'd love to get rid of it but my mother would kill me. It was her father's, and once a year I take her out for her birthday in it. The gears are shot and it takes a certain touch. Thus, I'm your driver today. Jethro Anderson, at your service.'

He took a little bow and her heart skipped a couple of beats. *Oh god,* she thought. *I'm in trouble.*

'I'm Nicole Cooper.'

'You're one of Craig's daughters, right? We've been doing business for years and he always talks glowingly about his girls.'

Nicole couldn't imagine what her father could say about her that could be glowing. *My daughter works at home in her pyjamas and once binge-watched the entire first season of* Lost *in one long weekend.*

'Nice to meet you.' Nicole put on her best smile and held out her hand to shake his. His hand felt soft and warm.

'It's really nice to meet you too, Nicole.'

There was something nice about the way he said her name, like it was a delicate and beautiful object he was holding very carefully.

'Oh! You've met Jethro already! Isn't he just the darlingest thing?' Celine said, as she stepped out of the parlour and onto the street, with Françoise and F'nelle fluttering around her and Samantha and Rosemary trailing behind. Rosemary was still glued to her DS.

Jethro seemed embarrassed, like a little boy being made to perform in front of his parents' friends.

'Here comes the bride!' Nicole exclaimed, to take the pressure off Jethro. 'You look magnificent.'

'Six hours in hair and make-up, you'd sure hope I look magnificent.' Celine laughed.

Jethro opened the back door of the car. 'Your carriage awaits,' he said.

'Samantha and Rose, you come in the back with me. Nicole, you go in the front, next to Jethro,' Celine said, with a wink that Nicole hoped Jethro didn't see.

'Where's your dad?' Samantha asked. 'Isn't he supposed to travel with us to the church?'

'He's meeting us there with the rest of the guests,' Celine said. 'I'm my own woman. I'm giving myself away.'

Nicole had to admire Celine in that moment.

F'nelle stepped forward to take charge. 'Small princess, you in first,' she said. Rosemary went to climb into the car, but Samantha stopped her.

'Rose, I thought I told you to put the DS away.'

'Why? I want to play it in the car.' Rosemary scowled. Nicole could see Samantha stiffen.

'Oh, come on, small princess,' Celine said. 'You'll need your hands free so we can wave at all our royal subjects!'

Rosemary's scowl immediately disappeared. 'Okay!' she said beaming, as she handed over the DS to Samantha without looking at her.

Nicole glanced sympathetically at her sister, but she had turned away to pack the DS in the small backpack she was holding. She seemed to be having trouble with the zip.

'Let me help you with that,' Jethro said, extending his hand towards her.

'I can do it myself,' Samantha snapped and Jethro stepped back, surprised.

Once F'nelle had finally stopped fussing with the skirt of Celine's dress in the back of the car and everyone was in place, Jethro started the engine and, with a crunch of metal, got the car into gear.

'I told you it took a certain touch,' he said to Nicole.

'We'll follow behind,' said F'nelle through the window.

'They're coming to the church?' Nicole asked, surprised.

'So they can touch up our make-up after the service and during the reception,' Celine said. 'Perfection like this requires upkeep!'

Nicole let out a little groan. Jethro shot her a quick glance before he started to pull out into the traffic.

'I've got a tennis racquet in the boot to ward off those black insects,' he said in a low voice and Nicole smiled at him, both grateful and wary at the same time.

Piece #8: 1990

SAMANTHA HADN'T REALLY wanted to go to Rottnest Island after the TAE. She knew that her way of celebrating the end of exams was markedly different from all the other Year Twelve students. However, Kerstin had promised her that the week wouldn't be all about drinking.

'We can ride to the West End and look out for whales and seals,' she'd said. 'I'll even play Scrabble with you!'

On their first night, Samantha slipped on her Snoopy pyjamas and put the kettle on. She was looking forward to the bike ride the next morning.

Kerstin's cousin, Christine, who had gone to another school, was outraged when she saw Samantha. 'What! You're not coming to the pub?'

'I don't drink,' Samantha explained.

Christine shook her head in disbelief. 'Why the fuck not?'

'She just doesn't,' Kerstin said, as she stepped out of the bathroom. Samantha was dismayed to see her all dressed up, ready to go out with the others to the Quokka Arms.

'I thought you were going to stay here with me,' she whispered to Kerstin as the others started to head out the door. 'You said!'

'I know, I know, but it's our first night,' Kerstin said, without quite looking at her as she walked out the door in a cloud of cheap perfume and hair gel. 'I'll stay back with you tomorrow, I promise!'

'And our bike ride?' Samantha called after her. 'Don't forget our bike ride!'

Kerstin didn't respond.

Samantha stood with her disappointment in the empty chalet for a few moments and then set to work. She spent the next half-hour picking up wet towels and washing cereal-encrusted bowls. Life with Donna-Louise had made it impossible to relax in a messy room.

'There. That's better,' she said to no one at all, when the room was tidy. She picked up her copy of *Circle of Friends* and took it with her to bed where she read until she fell asleep.

She was woken hours later by the other girls returning home.

'Sshhh,' Kerstin was saying, in a sandpaper whisper.

'Why?'

'Samantha.'

'Why do you care about that frigid bitch?' Samantha was pretty certain that was Christine, the cousin. She was using her outdoor voice.

'You're right.' Kerstin giggled. 'She's pretty uptight.'

Samantha pulled her sleeping bag up around her ears and did her best not to listen to any more of their conversation.

The next morning, she woke early and, as the other girls softly snored, she thought of what she'd heard in the night. Christine's words had hurt a little, but Kerstin's had landed a punch right in her guts. She knew Kerstin had been drunk, but in her limited experience, alcohol had a way of pushing the truth out. Did Kerstin really think she was uptight? They'd been best friends since Year Seven and Samantha had assumed Kerstin accepted her quirks just as she accepted Kerstin's, but maybe Kerstin had just been tolerating them all this time.

She looked over at Kerstin, shrouded in her sleeping bag, and wondered if she should wake her. The two of them could leave all the others behind and ride off to the West End for the day, like Kerstin had promised. But what if Kerstin was too hungover to go and complained about being woken up? Then she'd be even more of a frigid bitch in everyone's eyes.

She decided to take a walk along Thomson Bay to the bakery. Buying fresh bread for everyone could be the gesture of goodwill that would prove she was all right after all. But when the others finally got up around noon, they just scoffed down the bread without any thanks and then complained about Samantha having moved their towels.

Only Kerstin showed any appreciation. 'Thanks for getting a tank loaf,' she said to Sam while they did the dishes together. 'You remembered that's my favourite.'

Samantha saw this as an opening. 'So are you ready for our bike ride?' she asked Kerstin. 'We could go swimming at the Basin instead, if you want?'

'Maybe later,' Kerstin said.

But later, the others started drinking beers with some of the guys in the next chalet and Kerstin joined them, so Samantha went for a swim by herself and then cycled to Parakeet Bay. By the time she got back, everyone had gone out, Kerstin included. They hadn't even left a note.

Samantha picked up her book. She told herself that she'd prefer to read about a group of friends in distant Ireland rather than spend time with actual friends, but even she knew that the veneer on the lie was starting to wear thin.

AS SAMANTHA QUEUED for the bakery the next morning, she noticed a tall, slightly gangly guy looking over at her. After she'd bought her bread and croissants, she found him waiting for her outside.

'Hi,' the guy said. 'I saw you here yesterday morning.'

'So?' Samantha felt wary, despite the guy's open face and likeable grin.

'I guess all your friends are like mine and are too hungover to go buy their own bread?'

Samantha nodded. 'Yeah. By the time they've got up, it's after lunch and the bakery's run out.'

'Do you, um, mind if I walk with you for a bit?'

Samantha shrugged. They walked together in silence past the tourist information centre and down along the bay.

'I'm Trent, by the way,' the guy said after a while. He held out his hand and Samantha shook it.

'I'm Samantha.'

'So where are you staying, Samantha?'

'In one of the chalets at the far end of Thomson's Bay,' she replied, pointing in the distance.

'You got a chalet? Mint! We left it too late to book and could only get a couple of spots at Tent City.'

'How's Tent City working out for you?'

'It's gross,' Trent said. 'Full of topless guys drinking Emu Bitter for breakfast. I don't really get it.'

'Me neither,' Samantha admitted. 'I don't really drink.'

'Snap!' Trent smiled. 'At first, I thought I was the only one under forty on the whole island who wasn't drinking, but when I saw you going to the bakery so early two mornings in a row, I grew hopeful. So what do you do when everyone's at the pub?'

'I read. What do you do?'

'The first couple of nights I went with them and drank lemonade, but it just seemed to annoy people. And then the last two nights, I've stayed in the tent and read by torchlight until the battery's run out. Tonight's my last night. I've completely run out of batteries and will probably have to just sit in the dark, until one of the Jackos comes back and steps on my head.'

'You share a tent with more than one Jacko?'

'One has Jackson as a surname and the other has Jack as a first name. We call them Jacko One and Jacko Two, and sometimes just "One" and "Two". It gets a bit confusing.'

'I can imagine,' Samantha said. 'We have a Kerstin, a Chrissy and a Christine in our chalet and that gets pretty confusing too.'

They'd arrived at the chalet, which was still as silent as the drunken sailor's grave. Samantha wished she'd taken a longer route home so she could talk with Trent more. She hadn't realised quite how lonely she'd been feeling until they'd started chatting.

'This is me,' she said, shyly.

'Um, thanks for the conversation,' Trent replied, drawing out each word. His apparent reluctance to stop talking made Samantha feel bold.

'Well, if you don't want to sit in the dark or get despised at the pub tonight, you could always come here. We have electricity and stuff.'

Trent smiled. 'Electricity and stuff would be great.'

'Great,' replied Samantha, happy at last to be at Rottnest.

She stepped into the chalet. Wet clothing and towels were

spread over the tiled living space from the night before. Remnants from a drunken midnight swim, perhaps.

She pottered in the kitchen as quietly as she could manage (Christine had shouted at her the day before for running the water too loudly) and then, after carefully brushing the sand off the couch, she sat down to eat a slice of bread with butter and honey while she read her book.

Kerstin was first to emerge, an hour later.

'Hey there,' she said, cutting herself a slice of bread and spreading it thickly with jam. 'I'm sorry I didn't stay with you last night. Christine was being pretty insistent. And we ended up having quite a night, as you probably can tell from the mess.'

As Kerstin launched into a long story involving swimming out fully clothed to someone's boat to join a party, Samantha wondered if she should tell her about Trent.

'I got so shit-faced they had to drag me back to shore on an inflatable banana lounge shaped like a dragon,' Kerstin was saying. 'Although I'm not sure it's technically a banana lounge if it's not shaped like an actual banana.' She paused and looked awkwardly at her feet. 'I can stay home tonight with you if want me to.'

'It's okay,' Samantha said. 'You should go with the others. I'm in the middle of a really good book.'

'Well, if you're sure,' Kerstin said. She didn't even bother to hide her relief, and that made Samantha resolve not to mention Trent. The chasm between the two friends was now as much of her making as it was Kerstin's and that made her feel like she had some control.

THAT NIGHT, AFTER everybody went off to the pub, Trent showed up with a bottle of Coke and some candles.

'So you don't think I'm just here for your electricity,' he said. 'I'm also here for your table and your well-defined toilet. In Tent City, pretty much anywhere that isn't distinctly a person or a tent is a potential toilet. It's disgusting.'

They drank Coke, chatted and played Scrabble by candlelight. As Trent reached over to set out a word, Samantha noticed a small scar along his jawline, accentuated by the shadows cast by the candles.

'Where did you get that scar?' she asked.

'A car accident when I was seven. We were on holiday in Melbourne and a drunk driver ran into the side of our car. Luckily, I had just swapped sides because I wanted to look out the window at Luna Park. But I still ended up with a bit of glass in my face.'

Samantha felt a little thrill at this moment of commonality.

'I was in a car accident, too,' she said. 'When I was nine. Except in my case, my mum was the drunk driver.'

'Wow. Was anyone hurt?'

'Not really. My older sister had to have a few stitches, just near her eye. She was in the back where there was no seatbelt. My dad always said I was lucky because we'd swapped places so that I was sitting in the front where the seatbelt was.'

'It makes you think, doesn't it?' Trent said.

'What?'

'That every decision we make could be leading us towards or away from our death.'

'Yeah.' Samantha stared at the board in front her and at her neat row of tiles along the rack. 'Or towards complete and utter defeat.'

She leant over and turned TIN into TINE by adding an E, and then laid the rest of her tiles on the board to form the word EXCITED.

Trent slow-clapped her. 'Impressive.'

After the game was finished, they packed up the board and went for a walk. There were parties happening all over the island, but amidst the chaos, there were still a few families trying to holiday.

'I reckon they're from overseas and they now think this is the Australian way of life,' Trent observed of one couple sitting out on their porch, anxiously clutching small children to their chests while drunken teenagers careened all over the pathway.

They stopped to watch one drunk girl attempting to carry a bicycle down a set of stone steps. Trent ran over and tried to help her.

'Don't touch me or my fucking bike, you fucking letch,' she said, before falling down the remaining steps. Trent waited to see that she was okay and then shrugged and returned to Samantha's side.

'Some people,' he muttered.

'Look,' Samantha said, a few minutes later, pointing at the lit-up window of a cabin. 'There's some kids our age playing Scrabble.'

'With their parents,' Trent laughed.

Behind them, a guy was vomiting in the bushes. 'Carrot! So much carrot!' he was shouting. Trent and Samantha exchanged looks and stifled their laughter.

'Are you okay, mate?' Trent said, venturing a little closer.

'Yeah, I'm good,' the guy said cheerily. 'I didn't even eat any carrot today. Weird, hey?'

'Yep, it's weird all right,' Trent said. As the guy started vomiting again, Trent took Samantha by the hand and pulled her away, still laughing.

In the semi-darkness, with all the stuff going on around them, all Samantha could feel was the warmth of Trent's hand. She hoped he'd never let go.

Eventually, though, they arrived at the chalet and Trent released his hold.

'Do you want to play another game of Scrabble?' she asked him.

'I do, but I'd better not. We're booked on the early ferry back,' he said. 'I have a feeling that I'm the only one who's going to make it. But then, I'm the only one who can't afford to buy another ticket.' He pushed some sand around with his shoe. 'Do you think I could get your number? It might be fun to hang out when we're back in Perth.'

'Sure,' Samantha said. She ran inside to write her phone number on a piece of paper. The bedroom was a mess and it took more than a few seconds for her to locate a pen. She ripped a corner off a brown paper bag and, as she wrote the numbers down, she thought, *These are the most important numbers I'll ever write.*

Outside, Trent was waiting patiently, his hands stuffed in his pockets. 'Thanks,' he said, reaching out for the slip of paper. He paused for a moment and then leant down and kissed her gently on the cheek. 'It was really nice to not drink with you, Samantha.'

'It was really nice to not drink with you, Trent.'

Samantha watched him walk away and then slowly went back into the chalet.

When she went to bed that night, she held the cheek that he'd kissed and smiled. Her smile didn't disappear all night, not even after Kerstin – or was it Christine? – threw a wet towel on her head when they got back from the pub. She thought of Trent over in Tent City, having his head stepped on by a Jacko or two, and she knew she wasn't alone.

Nicole

WHEN TRENT ASKED me to come over, I almost said no. I was still angry with Samantha for storming off. But then I remembered Meg's parting words as I had dropped her off at the airport.

'Promise me you two will look after each other,' she'd said. 'Promise me you won't let things slide so badly that they can't be fixed or, like me, leave it too late.'

And so I got in my car and drove to Trent and Samantha's townhouse.

Trent met me at the front door, his face pale. 'Thank you for coming over. I've been so worried.'

'Where's her car?' I had automatically looked for it as I'd driven up the street.

'She came home in a taxi last night. I have no idea where

the car is and she won't tell me. Do you know where she went?'

'No clue.' I shrugged. 'She wasn't with us that long before she left. I went looking, but couldn't find her.'

I didn't tell Trent – or Aunt Meg, for that matter – that I hadn't actually looked that hard for Samantha. I'd been too angry. But nor did Trent ask why she'd left in the first place.

'Where is she now?'

'In the spare room. I've tried to get her to come out a few times, but the door is locked and she says she's not ready. I've got this big thing at work that starts at nine and leaving Rose to deal with it is a bit like pouring gasoline on the fire . . .'

'Does she sleep in the spare room often?'

'What is this, the Spanish Inquisition?' Trent joked and I hoped Samantha couldn't hear him. I knew she hated it when Trent quoted Monty Python. 'To be honest, she sleeps in there once or twice a week, usually because she has a headache or I'm snoring too loudly. But lately it's been almost every night.'

I felt sad thinking of the two of them sleeping separately. I'd been with Jethro for ten years now and waking up next to him was still one of my greatest pleasures.

'What do you think is going on with her?' I asked. None of this was sitting well with me.

'People grieve in different ways, I guess,' Trent said, with a small shrug. It was like a line he had read in a funeral home's brochure. I wondered if he knew more but was choosing not to tell me.

'Well, it's okay. You can go now. I'll look after her.'

'Thanks.' Trent hugged me awkwardly. It was an uncharacteristic move, but a strangely welcome one.

After he'd gone, I walked up the narrow staircase and carefully knocked on the door of the spare room.

No answer. I knocked again.

'Sammy? It's me. Nic.'

'Has Trent gone?'

'Yes.'

'I'll be out in a minute.'

Once I could hear sounds that confirmed Sam was actually getting up, I went back down to the front room. Outside the townhouse, I could see Trent carefully reversing his car out from their tiny garage onto the street. Even from this distance, I could see the worry on his face. He was a good man. A good man who loved my sister, even when my sister was at her hardest to love. I just wished I understood what was going on between them.

Finally Samantha appeared, her face scrubbed free of make-up and any discernible expression. She gave me a quick hug, briefly enclosing me in a cloud of perfume and mouthwash.

'Do you want a coffee?' she asked.

'Sure.'

'Rose?' Samantha shouted out. 'Do you want a coffee?'

She was met with silence. 'I guess she's still asleep. Or not here. She's like a cat these days. Comes and goes as she pleases.'

While the coffee machine whirred, I wandered over to the small dining area and picked up a photo taken at Rosemary's high school graduation from the sideboard. Trent and Rosemary were both beaming but Samantha looked like she had swallowed a lemon.

'Proud mama,' I joked, holding up the photo to Samantha.

'Yeah, well, I didn't have much to be proud of at that time,' she replied.

Ouch, I thought, putting the photo down. I now remembered the whole drama of Rosemary getting drunk on the last day of school and Samantha going ballistic, as if Rose had been the first Year Twelve student to ever get drunk on muck-up day.

I picked up the next photo, a soft-focus portrait of Trent and Samantha at their wedding. It was a photo that I'd seen a billion times, but never looked at properly. Now I could see that Trent was smiling down at Samantha but Samantha was only looking *towards* Trent, but not directly at him. And the more I looked at her, the more I realised how forced her smile was.

'You don't take sugar, do you?' Samantha asked.

I shook my head, not taking my eyes off the photo in my hand. 'You look so beautiful.' *And sad,* I wanted to add. *You look so sad.*

Samantha handed me a coffee and sat down heavily in one of the armchairs. 'I'm guessing you haven't come here to do an audit of my photos.'

'No, actually, I'm here because your husband was worried about you,' I said, settling down opposite her.

'He has no need to worry,' Samantha said breezily. 'I just needed some space. People grieve in different ways.'

She'd obviously read the same brochure as Trent.

'Meg was worried about you too,' I said. I seemed to be listing everyone who was worried about her except myself.

'She should be worried, telling such lies. I mean, think about it: all those years and Tina, pissed as pissed can be, never let slip that Dad cheated on her? Not once? It's hard to believe.' She took a sip of her black coffee. 'She didn't exactly hide her dislike of him. I don't believe for a moment that she wouldn't have used it as ammunition, especially when she was in one of her mean moods.'

'Actually, I asked Meg about that, after you . . . left us.' I wanted to say *after you spat the dummy.* 'She said she didn't know why Mum never talked about it. It was something she always wondered about, but was also quite glad about, considering her part in it.'

'I still don't buy it.' Samantha gave a little pout.

'Well, I was thinking about it and maybe she did kind of tell us,' I said slowly. 'But maybe we weren't listening properly or we just didn't know what to listen out for. I remember her saying a couple of times that there was a promise she and Dad made each other, that she'd kept her part of it and he didn't keep his. Do you remember anything like that, Sam?'

'No, I don't.' Samantha's face was a closed door.

By this stage, all my concern for Samantha had been shelved and I was left wondering why she was being so mulish about the whole Aunt Meg thing. I tried a different tack.

'I looked up Bruce Rock on Google Maps last night. Look here,' I said, showing Samantha the screen on my phone. 'See where the dropped pin is? That's Bruce Rock. That's where we ended up at that pub, waiting for Dad to drive from Perth to pick us up. Even with Mum's driving, there's no way Bruce Rock is on the way to Perth if you're coming from Hyden. That's where we always stayed on the way back from Esperance, remember?'

Samantha shook her head. She'd only been ten the last time we'd holidayed in Esperance so her memories of the brown-bricked motel we used to stop at near Hyden were probably not as vivid as mine.

'The more I think about it, the more I kind of remember something about a change of plan, but I can't remember what the change was from or to. It's all a bit hazy.'

The past felt like something hidden behind a backlit curtain – I could see its silhouette but none of the details.

Samantha pushed my phone away.

'Okay, so Meg was right and we were on our way to Kalgoorlie. But so what? That doesn't prove a thing. Maybe she just wanted to visit Nanna and Poppa.'

'We should talk to Dad,' I said, but then, out of habit,

immediately backed down and added, 'If you think that's a good idea, that is.'

'Oh, yeah, I think it's a *great* idea. Let's barge in on Dad and make accusations based on nothing but something the Ghost Aunt made up.'

'For one thing, I don't think she made it up. Why would she do such a thing? In any case, we wouldn't just "barge in and make accusations". We would just talk to him. We would ask him what happened.'

Even as I said it, I tried to imagine how we could possibly bring up such a topic casually in conversation. *Hey, Dad, can you please pass the salt and, while you're at it, can you tell me whether you fucked around with Mum's sister?*

Samantha drained the rest of her coffee. 'Let's not be hasty. It's been thirty-six years. We don't have to go rushing in like bulls in a glass factory.'

'I think it's "bulls in a china shop".'

'Whatever. Either way, bulls have no business being there. In any case, we need to focus on other things, like sorting out Mum's flat,' Samantha continued. 'I reckon we go through everything and divide it into things to keep, things to give to charity and things to chuck.'

'I'll start the sorting if you organise the skip,' I said quickly. I could imagine Samantha emptying all of Mum's life directly into the bin, given half a chance.

As she reached over to place her empty coffee cup on the table, I noticed a nasty bruise on her upper arm.

'Where did you get that bruise?' I asked.

Samantha looked at her arm, surprised. 'I guess I must have knocked it against something. Clumsy me.'

Her answer reminded me of a similar conversation I'd had with Mum, just before we found out she was sick. While Mum had been brushing off a different problem altogether, I couldn't help but think this bruise was hiding something too. It looked exactly the kind of bruise you might get from being grabbed very hard.

I HADN'T BEEN inside Mum's flat since she first went into hospital and I'd gone to pick up some of her belongings. Now, as it had then, it felt like a moment trapped in time: a cup of tea on the counter, this time with a healthy layer of mould growing on its surface; an open book lying facedown on the coffee table, waiting to be picked up again; an open copy of *TV Week* with programs that were never watched circled in red pen; an unfinished jigsaw puzzle on the dining table. I could feel the grief bubbling up into the base of my throat like percolating coffee but before it took me over completely I rolled up my sleeves and set to work.

The first thing I did was go into the kitchen and remove all the empty bottles and wine casks. I wanted to clear them away before Samantha arrived and made the face she usually made when presented with evidence of Mum's drinking.

Then I cleared the fridge out. There was depressingly little in there, most of it in jars or open cans. The crisper held a single stick of celery which, judging from the half-empty carton of tomato juice and the almost-empty bottle of Tabasco sauce, had probably only been purchased as a garnish for a Bloody Mary.

I threw everything into a garbage bag and lugged it out to the bins. After the morning's weirdness with Samantha, it felt good having something to distract me.

One of Mum's neighbours, a small beige-coloured woman, was also taking out her rubbish.

'You Tina's girl?'

'Yes, one of them.'

'Sorry for your loss. It was our loss, too. All of us here in the flats. She was a good woman, your mum. Always willing to lend a hand. Always ready for a laugh.'

'Thank you.'

I'd always hated this place and thought it a horrible place for Mum to live. But as I watched the beige-coloured lady scuttle away, I realised it had probably given Mum a stronger sense of family than Samantha and I had ever managed to.

BACK IN THE flat, I decided to tackle the bedroom next. The bed was unmade, and the bottom sheet had come loose from the base, exposing the badly stained mattress. There was clothing on the floor, some of which was from when I had been frantically trying to find clean pyjamas for Mum to wear in hospital, and some from the last time Mum had got dressed in this room. I wondered if she had known that that day would be the last time she would ever dress herself.

I opened the built-in wardrobe and ran my hand along the dresses. Mum had always loved dresses, the brighter the better. I pulled out one of my favourites, a 1950s-style dress patterned with large red roses, and wished, not for the first time, that I'd been petite like my mother and Samantha so I could carry off dresses like that. I put the dress aside for Rosemary. Maybe she would like it.

As I worked my way through the wardrobe, I discovered a box in the corner full of Mum's diaries. They were all the same type: a Collins slimline pocket diary, one week to view, black, with small gold lettering on the front page. There were about thirty of them. Mum was always carrying one around in her handbag when I was a child. I had sneaked a look at them a few times but had never found anything of interest.

I picked one up. 1986.

Each entry was like a haiku. A few dot points about the weather, appointments, what we ate for dinner, shopping lists.

Monday 20 January
Dentist 4 N
Rain.
Binbags, white socks, bra for S.
Dinner – toasted cheese sandwiches with pickle!

Saturday 29 March
S too much party. Stayed with C & DL.
32° but stormy.
Martinis without olives.

Thursday 22 May
S stayed for dinner. Pizza with middle still frozen.
24° cloudy sky, felt like rain but there was no rain.
Wanted rain.

Tuesday 9 December
Uncomfortable lunch with S & N.
S surly. Wouldn't eat veg.
No rain. Pot plants on balcony dying.

I put the diary back and took the whole box out to my car. I didn't want to risk Samantha dumping them all in the recycling, not when there might be something, some small seed of truth, somewhere in one of those slim little books.

Piece #9: 2015

I**T WAS MUCK-UP** Day and all over the city, Year Twelve students were getting dressed up, drunk and sick. But when Trent had driven Rosemary to a champagne breakfast in Bedford that morning, Samantha hadn't been worried at all. She knew Rosemary understood the dangers of alcohol – they'd talked about it many times over the years, particularly when she'd hit fifteen and all her friends had started drinking. Samantha would pick Rosemary up from parties with teenagers vomiting in the front garden and be relieved and grateful to find her daughter sober and smiling every single time. She'd come to believe that Rosemary had been spared the urge to drink that consumed both Tina and her. So when she got the call from the school, her heart broke a little.

The school nurse greeted her at the school office and took

her around to a small room where Rosemary was sitting, dressed in a clown costume and holding a bucket. Her clown make-up had been badly smudged, resulting in something truly, yet unintentionally, horrifying. Slumped alongside her in the sick bay was a naughty nurse, a gorilla and a boy in a nun costume, all holding similar buckets.

Samantha greeted her daughter wordlessly, her lips pressed firmly together, then led her out to the car. They drove home in silence, the air in the car as thick and cloying as the smell of alcohol and vomit on Rosemary's breath.

Samantha's head was still fuzzy from her own vodka intake the night before. The vodka had been hidden in the super-sized slushy she'd bought from the 7-Eleven on her way home from work. Trent and Rosemary had teased her about the slushy but she'd drunk it anyway.

At the first set of lights, she pulled a chewy mint out of her bag to clean away the bitter taste in her mouth.

Eventually, Rosemary had to break the silence.

'Just say something, Mum!' she said. 'I know I've disappointed you, so can you please just go ahead and say it!'

Samantha was surprised by Rosemary's tone. She was used to her being demanding, but this was a different kind of demand. It was a demand for love.

She swallowed the rest of her mint. 'Yes, I'm disappointed,' she said. 'I'm sure your teachers are disappointed, too. Let's just hope they're willing to overlook this incident.'

As she spoke, she didn't look at Rosemary. She was trying hard to keep any emotion out of her voice, but really, all she wanted was to shake her daughter and shout a lot. She remembered Tina's face just before Tina slapped her, all those years ago, and she wondered if her own face looked like Tina's had then.

'I guess since it's my last day, they can't expel me,' Rosemary attempted to joke, but then leant forward into the bucket she was still holding. After a few moments of heavy breathing and spitting, she leant back. 'I feel terrible. Why do people even like alcohol when it makes you feel this bad?'

It was a fair question. Any feelings that drinking alleviated for Samantha only seemed to come back even stronger once the alcohol had worn off. And yet, she still drank. She wondered if Tina felt the same.

They drove in silence.

When the car stopped at the next lights, Rosemary grabbed Samantha's arm. 'Talk to me, Mum.'

'Just concentrate on not being sick in the car, Rose,' was all Samantha could muster.

'But I want you to talk to me, Mum. Dad likes to talk but you don't. You're all buttoned up, like . . . like one of those Victorian ladies who never show their ankles, and I never ever know what you're thinking. What are you thinking? I want to know what you're thinking.'

'I'm thinking that I need to get you home and let you sleep this off.'

'I'm sorry I'm not perfect,' Rosemary said, leaning forward and throwing up in the bucket.

'None of us are,' Samantha said, knowing Rosemary wouldn't hear her over the sound of her retching.

THE NEXT MORNING, Rosemary, pale and sheepish, emerged briefly from her bedroom to get a glass of water.

'How's your head?' Trent called out to her, as she disappeared back up the stairs.

'Horrible,' Rosemary called back.

Samantha waited until she heard the bedroom door close before she leant into Trent.

'What do you think her punishment should be?' she asked.

'I think being sick and hungover is punishment enough,' Trent replied.

'But she needs to learn,' Samantha said. 'I really thought I'd taught her.'

'Yes, well, we all enjoyed your twelve-part lecture series about the perils of alcohol,' Trent remarked drily. 'But the truth is that she's eighteen now. You can't really tell her what to do any more.'

It was then Samantha realised exactly what she needed to do.

'I have an idea,' she said, leaning even closer to Trent. 'It's Tina's birthday this weekend and Nicole's asked me to check in on her while she's away because of that fall she had.'

Nicole had said Tina had been bruised pretty badly by the fall, which Samantha had no doubt was alcohol-related and probably happened all the time. She imagined Tina was like one of those toys that collapses and then springs up again when you press and release its base. But Nicole had sounded worried when she'd rung to ask Samantha the favour. She and Jethro had been about to fly in someone's private jet to someone else's private island off the coast of Queensland, just for dinner. So obviously she wasn't *that* worried.

'And?' Trent wanted to know.

'And it might be good for Rose to come with me to Tina's house. To see.'

Trent didn't need to ask what she thought Rosemary would see.

'DO I HAVE to come with you?' Rosemary was lying on the couch next to Trent. It was the Sunday afternoon and she'd already forgotten she was still in the doghouse.

'Yes, you do. She's your grandmother and it's her birthday,' she told Rosemary with much more conviction than she felt.

'It's not like she really wants to see me. She doesn't even know me,' Rosemary moaned. 'And Dad and I were about to watch *Game of Thrones*.'

'It can wait until we come back, can't it, Trent? We'll only be gone for an hour.'

'Sure, I can wait,' Trent said. 'Anyway, it's about time you learnt that the true meaning of life is family obligation.'

'Then why aren't you coming?' Rosemary said, poking him in the stomach.

'Because, young lady, after almost twenty years of being married to your mother, your grandmother still can't manage to get my name right. I'm not sure she and I really categorise each other as "family".'

Samantha gave Trent a warning look.

'It's true,' Trent muttered, under his breath, as he picked up the remote.

'We'll be back before you know it,' Samantha said, holding out her hand to help Rosemary up from the couch.

'I FORGOT GRAMMY Tina lived so close,' Rosemary observed, as they pulled into Tina's street. The drive had taken them less than five minutes. 'I can't remember the last time we came to visit her here. For ages, I thought she actually lived with Aunty Nic.'

'They used to live together, but Aunty Nic moved out about twenty-five years ago. Tina has been alone ever since.'

'Wow. Twenty-five years of living by herself. She must get lonely.'

'I guess she sometimes does,' Samantha said. 'Anyway, we

shouldn't feel too sorry for her. She hasn't exactly made good life choices.'

'What do you mean?'

'Well, she's mostly put drinking before everything and everyone else,' Samantha told her. 'I haven't told you this before, but your grandmother is an alcoholic.'

Rosemary looked completely underwhelmed by this big reveal. 'Yeah, I kind of worked that out from all the things I've heard you and Dad say.'

Samantha was disappointed that her words hadn't carried the weight she'd wanted, but she persisted. 'Okay, so you knew. But it's one thing knowing and another thing seeing.'

She reached into the back seat for the chocolates and flowers she'd bought from Coles, both heavily discounted. As she got out of the car, she braced herself for the reality of Tina's birthday. The drinking before midday. The sagging couch and the broken blinds. The total loneliness.

She knew that Rosemary needed to see this. She needed to know what a life spent in the arms of alcohol looked like.

She also knew that she, herself, needed to be reminded.

As they walked up the stairs towards Tina's flat, they heard music.

'Someone's having a party,' Rosemary remarked. As they turned onto the first floor walkway, Samantha realised that it was Tina.

The door to her flat was wide open. Inside, there were about fifteen people squashed in, all laughing and drinking, like drunken sardines. An elderly guy wearing a bow tie was mixing cocktails in the kitchen.

'Happy birthday to me!' Tina exclaimed when she saw Samantha and Rosemary standing awkwardly at the door. She was dressed in a 1950s-style dress with big red roses and holding a martini glass. 'Everyone, this is my daughter Samantha and my granddaughter Rosemary.'

Everyone cheered.

'Would you like a drink?' Tina asked them, but she was looking at Rosemary, who, in turn, was looking at the bartender with wide eyes.

'No,' Samantha said, a little too fiercely. 'We just came to give you these.'

As she held out the flowers and the chocolates, she realised she hadn't taken the discount stickers off them.

'You shouldn't have!' Tina said, in a tone that suggested she'd seen the stickers, too.

Someone turned the volume of the music up and a couple of people started to dance.

'Who are all these people?' Samantha shouted over the music. Tina ushered them back out to the walkway so they could hear each other.

'Just the gang from the Admiral's Tavern,' Tina said. 'When I told them Nicole was away and I was all alone on my birthday, they came over to throw me a party.'

Samantha felt a slight sting. She'd rung Tina to tell her that she would come by on her birthday, but she obviously didn't count.

Now that Tina was standing outside, Samantha could see the huge, dark-purple bruises on her left arm that Nicole had told her about.

'How did you do that?'

'No idea,' Tina replied brightly. 'Clumsy me, I guess.'

'Tina! We're going to do the limbo,' someone shouted from inside. 'We're using Thommo's walking stick.'

'Always so inventive,' Tina remarked. 'Do you want to play?'

Again, she was looking at Rosemary.

'No,' Samantha replied for the two of them. 'We have to get back home.'

'How's Troy?'

'Fine.' She didn't even bother to play her game and correct her.

'Give him my love!'

Samantha and Rosemary watched her go back into the flat and effortlessly limbo under Thommo's walking stick.

'It would have actually been fun to stay,' Rosemary said, as they got back into the car.

Samantha didn't reply. As she pulled the car back out onto the street, she realised that maybe her real problem with Tina was not so much that she drank, but that she always made drinking look like so much fun.

Piece #10: 2018

THE FIRST NICOLE knew of Tina's illness was when the hospital rang.

'Leave it,' Jethro said. They'd only just sat down to dinner, but Nicole had a feeling she should answer it.

'Am I speaking to Nicole Cooper?' a woman's voice asked.

'Yes. Who is this?'

'My name is Maeve Roland and I'm ringing from the Royal Perth Hospital. I'm sorry to tell you that your mother, Tina, collapsed while taking the garbage out at her home and is now in a critical condition.'

All the warmth vanished from Nicole's body. 'Critical condition? Why? What's happened?'

'The doctors will be able to give you more information. Are you able to come in straight away?'

'Yes. We can be there in about fifteen minutes.'

'Is it Tina?' Jethro asked, when Nicole hung up. He had obviously read the situation as he was already putting his shoes on.

She nodded.

'Right. Let's go.'

'Let me just ring Samantha first,' Nicole said.

'Okay,' Jethro said, although Nicole could see he wasn't really that okay with it. He always thought Samantha added unnecessary stress when it came to anything to do with Tina. He was right, but she was Tina's daughter, too, and Nicole needed her.

Samantha answered after just two rings.

'Mum's in the Royal Perth,' Nicole told her. 'She collapsed and they're saying it's serious. Jethro and I are heading in there now. Can you meet us?'

There was a long pause on the other end of the phone.

'I'm . . .' Samantha started.

'You're what?'

'Yes, I'll be there.' And then she hung up.

AT THE HOSPITAL, they found Tina in a stable condition and asleep. But any relief Nicole might have felt was instantly negated by the stern tone of the doctor.

'The situation is very serious,' she said, peering over the top of her glasses at Nicole. 'Essentially, your mother is experiencing acute liver failure. Her liver's cells are being destroyed faster than the liver can replace them and we may be past the stage where we can save her. How long has she been sick?'

'I . . .' Nicole strained her memory, trying to think of any sign that Tina had been sick. She hung her head. 'I don't know.'

'You haven't noticed anything?' the doctor asked impatiently.

'I haven't really seen her much recently,' Nicole found herself babbling. 'She's been so busy, working at the Vinnies and running the pub quiz night and, well, I've been travelling a lot with my partner. But we speak on the phone every week and she's never *sounded* sick.'

As she said it, she realised how evasive Tina had been over the last few months, always pulling out of social arrangements at the last minute. The few times they had caught up was at Tina's house, with the curtains drawn and the lighting low because Tina claimed she was hungover.

The doctor frowned and wrote on her clipboard, probably something about Nicole being a terrible daughter.

'Don't feel bad,' a nurse said to her, once the doctor had moved on, no doubt to be stern with someone else. 'People find all sorts of ways to hide the signs of their illness, like wearing big clothing to hide a swollen stomach, or using make-up to hide bruising or the yellow colour of their skin.'

'Bruising?'

'People with troubled livers bruise very easily.'

Nicole remembered the bruises on Tina's arms and legs that Tina had laughed off. 'Clumsy me,' she'd said.

As she and Jethro sat by Tina's side, Nicole thought of other ways Tina must have hidden the signs. She thought of the kaftans Tina had taken to wearing instead of her usual 1950s dresses, and all that foundation she'd started slapping on in the last year. She had joked that she was giving Celine a run for her money. 'Mwah!' she'd said.

But it had just been smoke and mirrors. Tricks she was using to hide a dying body.

After an hour of sitting and watching Tina, Jethro went to see if he could find them some food. He returned with sandwiches on a plate, cut into small triangles.

'The cafe and the kitchen are both shut, but the nurses gave us these,' he said, handing her the plate. 'It's your favourite: indeterminate meat and lettuce.'

'I'm not hungry,' Nicole replied, putting the sandwiches to the side. She picked up her phone to see if there were any messages from Samantha.

'Any word?' Jethro asked, sitting next to her. Nicole shook her head. 'We could think about going home, you know. They said Tina is unlikely to be awake until the morning and the nurses can fill Samantha in when she arrives.'

'I want to wait for Samantha,' Nicole replied. 'But you should go home and get some sleep. I know you've got that investors meeting tomorrow.'

'That's not important,' he replied, grabbing one of the sandwiches. 'I'm here for the long haul.'

Nicole smiled at him gratefully. 'Hopefully it's not too long. I'll try Sammy again to see if she's close.'

This time, however, her call went straight to voicemail. She left a quick message and then returned to watching Tina breathing in and out. She wanted more than anything for Tina to open her eyes and tell everyone to stop making a fuss.

'I honestly thought Tina would outlive us all,' she told Jethro. 'I thought she'd definitely outlive Dad, who's going to give himself a heart attack one of these days, worrying about the state of his car's upholstery.'

'She's not dead yet, Nic,' Jethro was quick to respond. 'I think we should move her to the Mount tomorrow. I'll find her the best specialist in Perth and we'll sort this out.'

But Nicole knew this situation wasn't something that they could buy themselves out of. The sternness of the doctor had left its mark.

*

THE NEXT MORNING, after Jethro left for his meeting, Nicole headed back to the Royal Perth where she found Tina awake, but weak. She was hooked up to oxygen, with tubes coming out of her nose.

'Where's the bar in this place?' Tina said when she saw her, but her voice wasn't her own. It was like one of those old lady cartoon voices, shaky and uncertain.

Nicole couldn't even smile at the joke. 'You've given us all such a big scare, Mum. Why didn't you tell us that you were sick?'

Tina just closed her eyes.

'Has Sam been in yet?' Nicole and Jethro had waited until almost midnight for Samantha to arrive before they'd finally left.

Tina shook her head, eyes still closed.

'Well, we're having you moved to a nicer hospital as soon as possible. Somewhere more comfortable. Sam will come and see you there.'

ANOTHER DAY PASSED and Samantha still hadn't come to see Tina, not at the Royal Perth, nor at the Mount after Tina had been moved.

'It's unlike Samantha to shy away from a crisis,' Nicole remarked to Jethro, after another failed attempt at contacting her. 'She usually thrives on this kind of thing.'

'Is it really that surprising?' Jethro responded. 'She's always had a complicated relationship with your mother.' Nicole couldn't argue with that. 'Have you had any luck with Trent?'

Nicole shook her head. 'I've messaged and rung him but you know how hopeless he is with his mobile. He probably only turns the thing on once a fortnight. And whenever I've tried the home phone, it just rings out.'

'Try calling him at work.'

'Good idea, Detective Anderson.' Nicole quickly googled the number.

'Nicky! Whassssssuppppp?' Trent said, after she was put through to him. 'It's been, what, six months since we last saw you?'

Nicole knew it had been longer, but she didn't correct him. 'I'm trying to get hold of Sam. Did she tell you about Mum?'

'She mentioned something about Tina tripping on the street and needing a bit of medical attention.'

Nicole's heart sank. 'It's more than that, Trent. It's really serious. Her liver is failing and she's dying. And Sam hasn't been to see her once.'

'Oh,' Trent said, after a short silence.

'I don't think Mum's going to be with us for much longer. I just don't want Sam to regret not seeing her. Can you please talk to her?'

'I'll do what I can,' Trent said. 'Leave it with me.'

Nicole sat and looked at her phone for a long while. Samantha, the unstoppable force, seemed to have become an immovable object.

Tina, in the meantime, wasn't getting any better, despite the fancy hospital and expensive specialists. Nicole spent a lot of time sitting by Tina's side while she slept.

'Sammy?' Tina asked, when she woke one time. She reached her hand out towards Nicole.

'No, it's me, Mum. It's Nicole.'

Nicole noticed how alarmingly yellow the whites of her eyes were.

'Where's Sammy?'

'I don't know.'

'She's a good girl. Not always the easiest girl, but a good girl.'

'Yes, Mum. We're both good girls.'

'Sammy is a good girl,' Tina repeated. 'I made sure of it.'

And with that, she fell back into sleep, beyond Nicole's reach.

THE SITUATION WAS hopeless. Nicole had been hoping to get Tina on the waiting list for a new liver, but was told Tina needed to stop drinking for six months to qualify. And even then, once she was on the list, the wait for a new liver was at least another nine months. The problem was, the doctor told Nicole, there was very little chance Tina would last long enough to even get on the list, at the rate she was deteriorating. It was as if her grasp on the world had loosened completely.

Nicole was crying silently by Tina's side when Jethro came in, holding a ridiculously huge bunch of red roses.

'I just spoke to the doctor. I'm so sorry,' he said.

'I know,' Nicole said, hanging her head.

'I'm so, so sorry,' he repeated, sitting in the chair next to her. He went to hug her but the roses were in the way. Nicole had to smile.

'Red roses are Tina's favourites,' she said. 'They must have cost you a fortune.'

'What's the point of having money if I can't spend it on the people I love?' he said, carefully placing the roses on the floor beside him. 'Listen, I've been ringing around this morning and I've found another specialist, a miracle-worker, based over in Sydney. Maybe I can fly him over. Maybe there's a private waiting list we can buy our way onto. Maybe—'

'No amount of money is going to save her now, Jethro.' Nicole felt the tears coming back.

Jethro didn't respond. He just wrapped her in his arms and for the briefest of moments she felt sheltered from her grief.

'Has Samantha been in?' he asked.

Nicole sighed. 'No. Trent texted me to say he'd tried to talk to her about it again last night. I think he's done his best. She's just not going to budge.'

'It's not your responsibility, Nic,' Jethro murmured into her hair. 'You've done your best, too. This is her decision. She's the one who needs to live with it, not you.'

'The last thing Tina said to me before she slipped under this time was about Samantha being a good girl,' Nicole said. 'I was the one who stayed, Jethro. I was the one who stayed with her, who looked after her, and yet *Samantha* is the good girl?' She started crying again.

'You need some more sleep.'

'I need to be here.'

Jethro pulled back and looked her in the eye. 'You're a mess, my love. You were here until late last night and back here at, what, seven this morning?'

Nicole had come in at five, before Jethro had even woken. 'I can't leave.'

'I know, I know. That's why I've got us a room at the hotel next door. The nurses will ring us if anything changes and we can come straight back.' He picked up the roses and stood up. 'Let's get these roses into a vase and then go to the hotel so you can have a nap. You need all the energy you can get to face what's ahead.'

Nicole nodded. She was too tired to disagree.

THE HOTEL WAS dark and quiet, but when she closed her eyes she imagined she could still hear the rasp of Tina's breathing. Still, she fell quickly into a dreamless sleep, her body heavy with fatigue and worry, while Jethro worked from his laptop beside her on the bed.

When she woke, three hours had passed.

'You said you wouldn't let me sleep too long,' she exclaimed, leaping out of the bed.

'The hospital hasn't rung,' Jethro replied. 'I thought it best to leave you.'

She hurried back to the hospital, but there was no real change in her mother's condition.

'Some more flowers arrived,' the nurse told her. She was trying to make space for them next to the roses and all the other bouquets. 'Your mum is very popular.'

'Yes, she's the life of every party, even the ones she's not invited to,' Nicole said. She noticed another bunch of flowers, small and slightly scrappy, that had been shoved into the same vase as Jethro's roses.

She pulled them. 'Can you please put these in their own vase?'

'Of course,' the nurse said, frowning at the flowers. 'Although we might be better just throwing them out. They're a bit past their expiry date.'

'Did anyone come and see my mum?' she asked.

'I just came on duty,' the nurse replied. 'But I can check with the desk.'

'Don't worry,' Nicole said. She knew Samantha wouldn't have come.

She sat next to Tina and took her hand. She was the real 'good girl'. She was going to have to see their mother through to the very end and she was going to have to do it alone.

Samantha

AFTER NICOLE FINALLY left, I lay on the couch and succumbed to sleep. In my dream, I saw Tina lying on her hospital bed, surrounded by a sea of red roses. I reached out to take her hand when she suddenly sat bolt upright and looked directly at me. As she opened her mouth, all the machines around her started beeping and the medical staff rushed in to help her, pushing me away, out of the room and into the cold, dark corridor.

I woke to realise the beeping was coming from the microwave, an indication that Rose was at home and awake. My mouth dry and my head thumping, I dragged myself up off the couch and into the kitchen.

'Rose, is your car back from Simon's?' I asked her, deciding to ignore the fact she was eating two-minute noodles from a mug. For breakfast, no less. I also ignored her T-shirt, which said 'HUNGOVER AS FUCK'.

Rosemary nodded. 'Yeah, it's fixed.'

'And have you got uni today?'

'Semester hasn't started yet. Why?'

'Can you help me get my car?' I asked.

'Where's your car?'

'Cottesloe.'

She frowned. 'Why is it there?'

'It just is.'

'But why?'

'I said, it just is.'

'What's that bruise on your arm?'

'I don't know.' Samantha had a vague memory of someone, maybe the bouncer at the OBH, pulling her back from the road after she'd bought more booze and then spilled all her change over the footpath. 'Look, can you help me or not?'

'Can I drive?'

'No.'

'But we'll be going in my car. I should be able to drive my own car.'

'You know I prefer to drive.'

'But you let taxis drive you.'

'You know how I feel.'

I held my breath and started to count to ten in my head in an attempt to push through the rising red mist. It was something I often had to do when faced with this fierce woman-child of mine, this beautiful bulldozer of a human being.

'Can you give me some money for petrol?'

I let the air out of my lungs. 'Yes.'

'Okay. Let's go.'

*

IT WAS ANOTHER clear, hot day. The air-conditioning in Rosemary's car was broken so we wound down all the windows. At the lights, I stuck my arm out of the car window to see if there was a sea breeze, but the air was still and heavy.

'No Doctor today, then,' I said. 'It's going to be a hot night. Are you working?'

'Not tonight. I was thinking of going down to Freo with some friends. There's a new club we want to try,' Rosemary said.

'What club?'

'Can't remember the name.'

'Which friends?'

'Friends from uni. You don't know them.'

'Will there be drugs there?'

'What is this, the Spanish Inquisition?' Rosemary said. She was her father's daughter through and through. 'I'm just going to Freo with some friends to a nightclub, okay? That's really all you need to know.'

I sighed as I changed lanes.

'I don't know why you're sighing like that,' Rosemary continued. 'After all, you won't tell me what you were doing in Cottesloe.'

'If you really need to know, Aunty Nic and I were meeting with our Aunt Meg, Tina's sister,' I explained.

'Oh, *her*. I met her at the wake. I didn't even know Tina had any siblings. She said she needed to tell you something important. For the record, she was being a bit creepy about it.'

I tried not to roll my eyes. Meg sure had been busy at the wake.

'So was it actually important?' Rosemary asked.

'Not really.' I wasn't ready to tell anyone else about what Meg had said. I was still too angry about it.

We drove in silence for a while. I could feel the sweat slowly sliding down my back. My headache was returning.

'Mum,' Rosemary said, her voice gentle now. 'Why didn't I see more of Tina when I was growing up?'

I remembered the conversation we'd had with Tina's cousin at the wake and how Rosemary's face had flushed with embarrassment. Now was my chance to set things straight.

'You should never feel guilty about that, Rosie. That was my choice,' I told her. 'Your grandmother wasn't a bad woman. Well, not really. She was a broken woman. And I needed to protect you.'

'She didn't look broken when we went to her flat for her birthday that time. In fact, she looked like she could be a lot of fun.'

'There's nothing fun about alcoholism,' I reminded her, and then regretted it when I turned to see her rolling her eyes.

'Yeah, yeah. Whatever,' she said. 'I was just saying.'

My head was now thumping. All this talking about drinking was making me feel queasy in the heat of the car, but I wanted to bring my daughter in close to me again. 'The real point was that we never really got on that well. Aunty Nic was much closer to her.'

'Do you think she was closer to her because you went to live with Grandpa?'

'Probably.'

'Why did you go to Grandpa's?'

'Talk about the Spanish Inquisition,' I tried to joke, but Rosemary was looking at me expectantly. She wanted an answer. 'Well, the thing is, I had a big fight with Tina when I was about thirteen. And I went to live with him after that.'

'Do you remember what the fight was about?'

'No,' I lied.

Even now, thirty years later, I still couldn't think about it without feeling that same shame and fear like a knot in my stomach – small and tight and impossible to untie.

'Did you ever regret it?'

'No,' I lied again.

'Because I would totally live with Dad if you guys split. We'd just eat takeaway pizza and watch reality TV.'

'God help the two of you if I ever die,' I said, laughing.

'Hey, is that your car?' Rosemary said, as we pulled into the small parking lot next to the Blue Duck.

My heart sank when I saw the parking ticket on the window. Combined with the cost of the vodka and the whisky and the taxi home, this was the most expensive night out I'd had in a long time.

THE NEXT MORNING I rose at seven, showered and got dressed for work.

'What are you doing?' Trent asked when he saw me come down for breakfast. 'I thought you were taking the whole week off.'

'I'm not like my sister,' I told him. 'I can't sit around doing nothing.'

'Nobody's saying you have to do nothing but you could at least do something that isn't work. If I had a week off, I'd spend it at the movies.'

'Well, maybe you'll get lucky and your mum will die.' The words fell out of my mouth before I could stop them. Trent's face fell and my heart contracted.

'I'm sorry,' I said, rushing to hug him. 'I'm really sorry. I don't mean to be such a bitch. People grieve—'

'—in different ways.' Trent nodded. 'I know. But please remember I'm on your team, Samantha.'

*

I KNEW THE minute I sat at my desk in my small office that coming back to work was the right decision. The tension that had been gathering around my neck the past few days immediately slipped away as I methodically made my way through my inbox. I then went all the way back through the emails I'd flagged but hadn't responded to before I went on leave. Among them was an email from Nicole, written two days before Tina had died, begging me to go into the hospital.

I took a deep breath and then deleted it.

'You look well . . . considering,' one of the women from Accounts Receivable remarked when she saw me in the break room. 'I'm so sorry for your loss.'

I wanted to say that there'd been not that much left for me to lose, but I didn't, of course.

'Thank you,' I said.

'If you need anything . . .' Her voice trailed off into that useless place most people end up when faced with other people's grief.

'Thank you,' I repeated. But this time, I knew there wasn't even a hint of gratitude in my voice.

I avoided the break room for the rest of the day, and by five o'clock, I almost felt like myself again – or, rather, the version of myself that I preferred to be. But then, when I got home and found the envelope in the mailbox, that façade immediately began to crumble.

The envelope was hastily scribbled to me with the following note in Nicole's loopy handwriting:

Read the entry marked with the Post-it note.

Inside the house, I threw the envelope down on the coffee table and ignored it for as long as I could. The evening was hot and airless and the air-conditioning was straining to keep up. I changed into a sarong and ate my supper on the couch, occasionally scowling at the unopened envelope on the coffee table, like it was an uninvited and incredibly unwelcome guest. Trent was playing tennis and god knew where Rosemary was. Probably in Fremantle again with her uni friends.

The more I looked at it, the more I found I wanted a drink. But I kept shovelling salad into my mouth, pretending to myself that it was really salad that I wanted and needed, and not booze.

When all the salad was gone, I opened the envelope. I would have preferred to have opened a bottle, but I knew Trent would be home any moment. Inside, I found a small pocket-sized diary with 1981 in gold embossed letters on the cover and knew instantly that it was Tina's. She had never been without one of these diaries, except perhaps at the very end in hospital. Once again, the regret rose up in my chest. I turned to the page with the yellow Post-it note and read Nicole's message: *See 31 Jan.*

The writing in the entry for the thirty-first of January was small and controlled.

My heart is broken.
The car is fucked.

I took a deep breath and rang Nicole.
'Okay,' I said. 'Let's talk to Dad.'

The Spill

1982

A N HOUR AFTER they left the motel in Hyden, they stopped for petrol. The sun was burning high and none of them could imagine ever feeling cool again.

Tina let the girls choose a soft drink from the petrol station's hardworking fridge. Nicole chose a Mello Yello and Samantha chose a Passiona. Tina didn't get a drink for herself. Instead, she took a big sip from Samantha's can and then from Nicole's.

'Mummy tax,' she explained to them.

She unfolded the large map and pretended to look at all the lines and dots but her mind kept going back to the phone call with Craig and the bottle of whisky she'd left behind in Hyden. She didn't want to know where she was going. She just wanted to drive. She shoved the map to the side and started the engine.

'We'll have lunch in Merredin,' she announced to the girls.

'Will we get to Nanna and Poppa's in time for *Young Talent Time?*' Nicole asked.

'Probably,' Tina replied, although she had no idea what time *Young Talent Time* was on.

Nicole quickly finished her Mello Yello and lay across the back seat, amidst the pile of pillows and doonas. She felt like she was being hugged by a cloud. She closed her eyes and thought about which song she would sing if she were a contestant on *Young Talent Time*. Probably 'He's My Number One' by Christie Allen, which was still her favourite song even though it wasn't in the charts any more.

In the front seat, Samantha sipped her Passiona slowly, but the can was growing warm in her hand, making its contents taste like passionfruit spit. The seatbelt was digging into her neck, and she was really too small to be able to see out of the windscreen properly. She wanted to ask her sister if she could have one of the pillows to sit on, but she was still upset with Nicole for pushing her off the swing back in Hyden.

Tina fiddled with the radio until she'd picked up a station playing music. It was 'Brass in Pocket' by The Pretenders and she began to sing along at the top of her voice.

As she drove along the dusty road, she hit a series of bends and she leant into them hard, approaching them at speed and then switching to the brake at the last minute. There was something about the pressure of the brakes followed by the release of the accelerator that made her feel in control of her life again.

In the back seat, Nicole had started sliding around. It was fun at first, but then her head banged hard against the door.

'Mum, can you slow down?' she shouted over the blare of the radio.

'It's fine. *We're* fine,' Tina said, more to herself than to anyone else. But then she leant too hard into the last corner and the world went into slow motion.

Tina turned to Samantha beside her, worried that she would slip out of the seatbelt. She reached out to hold Samantha back and shouted both girls' names in a desperate attempt to keep them in this world, to stop them from flying out of the car and away from her forever.

Nicole, in a tangle of doonas and pillows, felt her body bounce between the roof and the seat as the car spun and then flipped and rolled, but her mind was curiously calm as if she had remained perfectly still.

Samantha, with her mother's hand on her chest, felt like she was on the Mad Mouse at the Royal Perth Show. She closed her eyes and succumbed to the ride.

And then everything stopped. There was one last metallic groan as the car finished its slide along the hot gravel road and then there was silence, except for the final bars of 'Brass in Pocket' still playing on the radio.

Nicole's first thought was that she might be crying. She put her hand up to her eye, expecting to wipe away tears, but found blood instead.

Samantha's first thought was that she couldn't see the sky.

And Tina's first thought, after she'd seen that both her daughters were okay, was *I need a fucking drink.*

Nicole

I ARRIVED AT THE pub fifteen minutes ahead of time only to find Samantha already there, sitting at one of the tables out the front.

'The one time I'm actually early for a thing, you're even earlier,' I said to Samantha with a nervous laugh.

I didn't tell Samantha that the reason I'd arrived so early was because I wanted to give myself the opportunity to leave again before Samantha and Dad got there. Samantha already being there made that escape route impossible, not without a scene, not when I was the one who had pushed for all this. And, in any case, dramatic exits were more her thing than mine.

'I haven't been here for years,' I said, as I sat down. 'Not since Darren and I were still together. Or not together, as the case often was.'

'I've never been here at all,' Samantha replied. 'It's quite nice.'

I had been surprised when Samantha suggested we meet with Dad at The Queens, especially since I knew it was one of the places Trent liked to come on the nights he went out with his friends while Samantha stayed at home to be furious. She'd never actually spoken to me about how she felt about Trent occasionally drinking, but over the years she'd said volumes in eye rolls and pursed lips.

'How does Trent feel about you being on his turf?' I joked. 'Are you two going to have a dance-off in the carpark?'

'Trent doesn't know I'm here,' Samantha said. There was something about the offhandedness of her tone that worried me.

'Is everything okay with you two?' I asked before the words got swallowed.

'Yes. Why are you asking?' The sharpness of Samantha's response made me think I had touched a nerve.

'Because . . .' I started, but the words didn't come. 'I don't know.'

'Trent said he heard from Darren, by the way,' Samantha said. 'Apparently he's living in Osaka and getting married to some Japanese girl half his age.'

'Yeah, he emailed me, too.' I could tell he was pretending to do it out of courtesy, but really, he was gloating because he was getting married and I wasn't.

'Anyway, you're well shot of him. Remember how he didn't even come and see me in the hospital when Rosemary was born. Where was it that he went instead? Taekwondo?'

'He didn't do taekwondo. He did karate. But I don't think that was why he didn't go to the hospital.'

I thought it bold of Samantha to bitch about Darren's no-show at the hospital when she hadn't even visited her own mother on her deathbed, but I didn't mention it. I still couldn't talk to her about it and anyway, I needed to keep her onside.

'He was definitely at taekwondo,' she was still insisting.

'He didn't *do* taekwondo.'

'Whatever.' Samantha then changed the topic again by sliding Mum's diary back to me across the table. 'Here. You can have this back.'

'So, what did you think?'

'Not much.'

She obviously must have thought something if she'd agreed to meet with Dad, but I didn't challenge her. I just put the diary back in my bag.

'The diary entry might not be related to anything Dad actually did, you know,' Samantha informed me. 'Tina's heart might have been broken only because Dad was so angry at her for driving drunk.'

'We still don't know that for sure,' I said, immediately picking up the menu to try to block the old argument about whether or not Mum had been drunk. I didn't want to start fighting with Samantha before Dad even got here.

'I've ordered some polenta chips, by the way,' Samantha told me.

'Great. I'm going to the bar to get a drink,' I said, putting down the menu. 'Do you want anything?'

Samantha shook her head and took a sip of her soft drink through her straw, her lips pursed more than necessary.

Up at the bar, I decided to order a cocktail, something to sip slowly. I was worried that any other drink would go down too quickly and then I'd have to order a second drink and Samantha would ingest her lips altogether.

'Which cocktail do you recommend?' I asked the guy behind the bar.

'The Fourth of July is very popular,' he replied.

'So is dabbing,' I quipped and then regretted it. It was the kind of joke Mum would have made and it only deepened the Tina-shaped hole in my chest. The guy just looked at me blankly.

'I'll try one,' I added, quickly fumbling for my wallet.

'No wuckas,' he replied, as he rang up my order. 'Our mixologist will get right onto it and we'll bring it out to you.'

On the way back to the table, I passed Samantha, who was now on her way in.

'Just going to the loo,' she told me.

I sat at the table and looked around at the other patrons. Behind us was a large group of men in suits and loosened ties, chatting about the Australian cricket team's form over after-work drinks. At the table to my right, a couple were mid-argument. The woman was blowing her nose loudly into her paper napkin, while the man jabbed angrily at their shared bowl of nachos with his fork. I hoped the talk with Dad didn't end up in a public scene like that. Just the thought of it made my mouth go dry.

There was no water at our table so I quickly sneaked a sip of Samantha's soft drink and was surprised to taste the alcohol in it.

My first thought was that a mistake had been made. Samantha had got the wrong drink and hadn't realised it was alcoholic.

My second thought, however, was something darker and half-formed: booze-drenched lilies in a bin. But before the thought could properly crystallise, Dad arrived and Samantha returned from the bathroom.

'Sorry I'm late,' he said, kissing us both on the cheek. He sat next to Samantha and put his phone on the table, face up. 'I'm expecting a call from Cee-Cee,' he explained. 'She's just at the doctor's and might join us afterwards.'

'Is everything all right, Dad?' Samantha asked him.

'Yeah,' he replied, but he didn't offer any more information. Instead, he said, 'How are you both holding up?'

'Okay,' I replied at the very same time Samantha said, 'Great.'

I found myself bristling. 'Great' felt like a poor word choice so soon after losing our mother.

'So what's this big thing you need to talk to me about?' Dad asked.

Samantha gave me a look that at first I couldn't interpret. And then I realised that she was expecting me to start the conversation. My mouth had gone dry again. Where the fuck was my drink?

'Nic wants to ask you something,' Samantha eventually said.

Dad turned to look at me.

'Um, well . . .' I cleared my throat. 'The thing is, Dad, we caught up with Aunt Meg the day after Mum's funeral.'

'Oh.' His mouth formed a perfect round 'O' shape.

I forged on. 'She wanted to get something off her chest. Something she said that hap—'

'Did you guys order food?' One of the bar staff had arrived with a big basket of polenta chips.

'Yes, thanks,' Samantha said, clearing a space in the middle of the table.

'Too easy,' he replied, putting the basket down. He could not have been further away from describing the situation in front of him.

'Excuse me,' I said, touching the guy's arm lightly, as he went to leave. 'I ordered a cocktail and the bar guy said someone was going to bring it out?'

'I'll go check where's it at for you, champ,' the guy replied, flashing his too-white teeth.

Dad popped a polenta chip into his mouth and immediately took it out again. 'They're hot,' he remarked.

'Dip it in the sour cream,' Samantha told him.

'I'm trying to avoid dairy,' Dad replied. 'Cee-Cee says it makes my aura cloudy.'

'Aura?' I asked, glad for the digression but also genuinely curious why the very Christian Celine would be talking about auras.

'She's been taking me to her kinesiologist in Morley and apparently I have a hole in my aura,' Dad told us sheepishly. It wasn't clear whether he was feeling sheepish about the hole in his aura or the fact he was seeing a kinesiologist.

'What's a kinesiologist?' Samantha asked.

'I have no idea,' Dad admitted. 'All I know is that my aura is cloudy and holey and I can't eat cream.'

We all sat in silence for a moment, while Dad blew on his polenta chip. I had no idea how to steer everyone back into the conversation. Luckily, Samantha helped me out.

'Now, what were you saying about Aunt Meg?' she said, once Dad had finished his mouthful.

'Uh, yeah, Aunt Meg.' My stomach tightened. My heart was thumping and the blood was rushing around my ears, louder than the ocean. 'Aunt Meg said that there was more to your divorce than just Mum's alcohol abuse. She said, um . . . she said that you had an affair with her.'

'She said what?' I couldn't tell if he was questioning what Meg had said or if he genuinely hadn't heard me properly.

'She said—'

But Dad's phone was ringing. 'Sorry,' he said. 'I have to take this.'

He took his phone and moved away from the table, out onto the footpath in front of the pub.

'This is going well,' Samantha said. 'Do *you* know what kinesiology is? And how on earth does it fit in with Celine's Christian worldview?'

I ignored her. I was too busy watching Dad on the phone. He had his head down and his hand over his free ear, like he was listening to difficult news.

'I think something's happened with Celine,' I said to Samantha.

'Something's always happened with Celine,' Samantha replied. 'You could just say that *Celine* happened.'

'No, really,' I said.

Dad was approaching the table, his face grey with worry. 'I'm sorry, girls, I've got to go. Cee-Cee's on her way to the hospital. The doctor thinks she's having a miscarriage.'

We both rose from our seats.

'Is there anything we can do?' I asked, my heart suddenly aching. A fragment of memory: picking up a jar of cranberry sauce from the supermarket shelf, then feeling the blood between my legs. And then a second memory: sitting in the car with Jethro after the specialist's appointment.

'I'll text you both when I have more information. But for now, I've got to get over to the Charlie Gairdner.'

And then he was gone.

'I told you Celine was trying to get pregnant,' Samantha said matter-of-factly as we both sat back down.

Poor Celine. I imagined how frightened she must be feeling, and what she must have gone through to get pregnant in the first place. She had just turned forty-four. Pregnancies rarely 'just happened' to women in their mid-forties. I knew that from personal experience.

Not that Samantha was aware of any of that.

'Well, all I can say is Celine's timing is pretty lousy,' she said, as she picked up one of the polenta chips, scooped it through the sour cream and then popped it into her mouth. 'Now we'll have to do this all again.'

Wow, this is not all about you, I wanted to say. But, as I thought of having to ask Dad the question a second time, I realised she'd actually raised a fair point and I sighed.

'Here's your drink, champ.'

The waiter had finally arrived with my cocktail, complete with miniature umbrella and sparkler. Samantha looked at the drink and then at me. And in that moment, I remembered the alcohol in Samantha's own drink, but I didn't have the energy to speak. All I could do was wait for the sparkler to go out and then knock back the cocktail in one long gulp.

Piece #11: 1995

THREE WEEKS BEFORE their wedding, Samantha and Trent went through their to-do list over cups of tea and Tic Toc biscuits, as they did every Sunday morning.

'Have you paid the florist?' Samantha asked.

'Check.'

'Have you booked the PA for the ceremony?'

'Check,' Trent replied, taking two biscuits from the plate. 'Look, Sammy. A Tic Toc sandwich. I'm in two different time zones!'

'Stay on task,' Samantha said, but she was laughing.

'Okay, okay, my turn,' Trent said, showering crumbs every-where as he grabbed the list off her. 'Um, let me see . . . have you rung the venue about wheelchair access?'

'Check!'

'Have you spoken to your mum?'

Samantha's smile fell away. 'No, not yet.'

'Come on, Sammy. Just do it. The later you leave it, the worse it will be.'

'I know, I know,' Samantha said, taking back the list. She'd been putting off the phone call to Tina for a few weeks now. Every time she thought about it, she felt sick to her stomach. She frowned at the list, hoping to find something else to think about. 'What about the bucks' night?'

'Jacko's in charge of that. You don't need to worry about that. Next!'

'But I *am* worried, Trent,' Samantha replied. Karen in Marketing had told her some horror stories about her husband's bucks' night. 'I just want to you to promise me there's not going to be any strippers or too much booze.'

Trent sighed. 'Obviously, *I'm* not going to drink,' he said. 'But I can't stop other people from drinking. Or even stripping, for that matter. It's a bucks' night, after all.'

'Our twenty-firsts were alcohol-free,' Samantha argued. 'And the strongest thing at my hens' do was the tea. I don't see why your bucks' party can't be the same.'

'I'll talk to Briggsy at the footy this afternoon about keeping it calm.'

'Promise me?'

'If you promise to talk to your mum right now.'

'Okay,' Samantha sighed, picking up the phone. As much as she didn't want to do it, she knew it was a good time to call. 'I might still catch her before she goes to the pub.'

'Good.' Trent reached for another biscuit.

Samantha decided to make the call in the bedroom, away from Trent, just in case she changed her mind.

Predictably, Tina answered after about ten rings. Her lax attitude towards a ringing phone had always driven Samantha spare, but this time Samantha was grateful for the opportunity to focus on her breathing.

'Oh hello there, bridie,' Tina said when she heard it was Samantha on the phone. 'How is everything going? You got your to-do list under control?'

'Yes, it's all going well,' Samantha said, wanting to skip right past the pleasantries. 'I just wanted to ask you something. It's about the wedding.'

'Anything for you, my little love.'

Samantha's heart was beating violently now. 'Actually, it's about the reception. Obviously, Dad and Donna-Louise are coming and . . .' Samantha paused. The right words weren't coming to her.

'And what?' Tina's voice had a little bit of an edge now.

'And, well . . .' Samantha swallowed, and then opened her mouth to let all the wrong words come tumbling out. 'And I just need the day to be perfect and with you there and Dad and Donna-Louise there, well, I know how you feel about Donna-Louise and how Donna-Louise feels about you and—'

'I can behave myself,' Tina interrupted.

'But not when you're drinking,' Samantha burst out.

'Ah,' Tina replied.

There was a long silence after that. Eventually, Samantha had to check Tina was still on the line. 'Mum?'

'I'm still here,' Tina replied, all colour now gone from her voice. 'So let me get this straight: I can come to the reception if I promise not to drink and I behave myself. Is that right?'

'Basically, yes,' Samantha swallowed again.

'I see,' Tina said slowly. 'And what about Donna-Louise? What's to say that *she'll* behave? Are you phoning *her* to make the same request?' Tina's voice definitely had an edge now.

'Donna-Louise doesn't drink. And, well, you know how

you get, Mum,' Samantha's initial embarrassment was rapidly turning to exasperation.

'How do I get?'

'You know.' Samantha didn't want to say it.

'No, I don't know. Tell me, Sammy,' Tina persisted, each word a bullet. 'How do I get?'

'You get *drunk.*' The Other Samantha was taking over now. 'And embarrassing and sloppy and loud and showy and you ruin everything and this is my wedding day and I need it to be perfect.'

Tina was quiet now and so was Samantha, her sudden tsunami of rage subsiding.

They let the silence between them grow until finally Tina said with a sigh, 'Okay. I won't go if you feel that way.'

'That's not what I meant,' said Samantha, but she wasn't convincing anyone, not even herself. More than a few times she'd thought how much easier the wedding would be without Tina there at all. 'Just think about it.'

TWO WEEKS LATER when Briggsy and some other guy half-carried Trent through the front door wearing a pair of underpants on his head like a hat, Samantha saw immediately that Trent had not kept up his end of the bargain.

Trent fell onto the couch, where he lay on his back and smiled at the ceiling.

'Hello, ceiling,' he said.

'Yes, hello ceiling,' Briggsy repeated, as he slipped off Trent's shoes.

'He'll need some water and maybe a couple of aspros before bed,' the other guy said, obviously embarrassed by the situation. If he was drunk, he wasn't showing it. He spoke very clearly, like he was broadcasting for the BBC World Service.

'What the hell happened?' Samantha asked both of them, unable to hide her anger. 'What have you done to my fiancé?'

'Yeah, well, um, sorry about that,' Briggsy said, himself a little unsteady on his feet. 'When he said he'd never got drunk, I never thought in a million years he meant he'd never drunk *anything* full stop. Who gets to twenty-three years of age in this country without ever having had a drink? It's un-Australian.'

'He's only had three, maybe four beers,' the other guy jumped in to reassure her. 'Nothing too heavy.'

'Except for the vodka shots,' Briggsy interjected.

'What?' The other guy looked annoyed. 'I told you not to give him anything else.'

'He was up for it. Anyway, you're not his mother. He's a fully grown man.'

The other guy shook his head. Samantha felt like he was slightly more on her side, unlike Briggsy, whom she had never liked much and now liked even less.

'Did he embarrass himself?' Samantha wanted to know. The party had been full of people from work, maybe even Trent's boss, and some of her cousins.

'Did he ever!' Briggsy enthused.

'Not really,' the other guy assured her. 'I wouldn't worry about it. In Japan, people do all sorts of outrageous things at parties, and everyone just pretends the next day that none of it ever happened. I think bucks' parties in Australia are a little the same.'

'Well, thank you for getting him home,' she replied, ignoring any part Briggsy might have played in it. 'I'm Samantha.' She held out her hand.

'Darren,' the guy said, shaking her hand. 'I work with Trent.'

She walked over to the door and opened it wide, the smile

fixed on her face, like a screw that had been put on too tight. 'Well, thank you, Darren. I can deal with Trent now.'

As she closed the door behind them, she heard Trent say, 'Hello, ceiling,' again and the smile quickly disappeared from her face. She spun on her heel to face him.

'What the hell were you thinking?' she asked, but he was still grinning at the ceiling.

'I was thinking that the ceiling is my friend. And Briggsy is my friend. And Darren – even though he's an uptight prick half the time – he's my friend. And beer is my friend. And you, Sam. You are my best friend in the whole big fat world. I'm so lucky to have you and I can't wait for you to be my beautiful bride.'

He turned to her and held out his hand, but when she didn't take it, he let it drop and closed his eyes. Soon he was asleep.

Samantha sat in the armchair and watched him silently, unsure what to feel. She was furious with Briggsy (this had to be his fault) and furious with Trent (how could he have done this to her?). But mostly, she was furious with herself – she should never have agreed to the bucks' night in the first place. She was also envious. Trent seemed happier in this moment than she'd seen him for a long time.

But the worst of all the feelings was the uncertainty. She had no idea where this left her and Trent. They had been united by their commitment to not drinking and now that he had gone and got drunk – at a party that was supposed to celebrate their upcoming nuptials, no less – what did that mean for their future? For the first time since she'd met Trent, Samantha felt truly alone.

She stood up, hoping to step away from all these feelings. She picked up his shoes and socks and put them on the shoe rack. She peeled the underpants off his head and was relieved to see they at least belonged to a man. She found a blanket and gently laid it over him. Then she went over to the CD shelf and started sorting the CDs, changing them from alphabetical-by-band to alphabetical-by-title until she felt tired enough to sleep.

It was almost three by the time she lay her head back on the pillow.

THE NEXT MORNING, she woke to a completely silent flat. Usually, Trent watched TV on a Sunday morning, but instead, she found him sitting up on the couch, looking pretty sorry for himself.

'Turns out beer is not my friend,' he said when he saw her. 'At least, not when it's partnered with vodka.'

Samantha couldn't believe he was trying to make light of the situation. Instead of responding, she marched over to the kitchen and began putting away dishes as noisily as she could.

'Samantha, please talk to me,' Trent said, following her. 'I made a mistake.'

Samantha kept clanging dishes.

'Please,' he repeated as he put his hand on her shoulder. 'I'm sorry.'

Samantha stopped and, focusing on the warmth of his hand, counted to ten inside her head. She needed to keep the Other Samantha at bay.

'Talk to me, please,' Trent pleaded.

'I thought we didn't drink,' she said, louder than she intended. The Other Samantha was desperate to burst forth from her chest, like something from *Alien*.

'You're right. *We* don't drink,' Trent said, turning her to face him. 'But Sammy, this was about *me*. I've been lying out here on the couch trying to work out why I did it. I mean, I certainly didn't go out last night intending to get drunk. I want you to know that.'

'Well, you came home drunk all the same.' She freed herself of his hold and went back to the dishes.

'Please,' he said. 'Can you stop that and just listen to me a second?'

Samantha allowed him to lead her back to the lounge and sit her on the couch.

'Here's the thing,' he said, sitting beside her and taking her hand. 'I've spent the last few months doing so much for us and the wedding. I've licked stamps and booked the PA and tasted cake and looked at seating plans. I've done everything you've told me to do. Last night, I guess I just wanted to do something for myself. And you know what? I had a good time. Fuck it, Sam, I had a *great* time.'

Samantha's heart suddenly felt like it was being wrung out like a sponge. She pulled her hand away from him.

'Then go drink yourself into oblivion, if that's what you want to do,' she spat. 'Go on. Go join my drunken mother and the two of you can drink yourselves to death.' The Other Samantha was now fully unleashed. 'You know how I feel about my mother and her drinking. My whole life she has chosen alcohol over me. So how could you do it? How could you choose alcohol over me a week before my wedding? How could you break the promise you made me?'

'It's *our* wedding, remember? I'm in there too, you know.' Trent bristled a little. 'And anyway, all I promised you was that I would talk to Briggsy. And I *did* talk to Briggsy, so I didn't break any promises. Not exactly. But I want you to know I wasn't choosing alcohol over you, Sam. I was choosing myself. Just for one lousy fucking night.'

She couldn't believe that Trent, the one person she had always relied on to do what she needed to feel safe, was saying all this.

'But what if there's another night you want to do that?' she shouted, her face a mess of tears and snot now. 'And another night after that? What if you find out that you want to drink all the nights? Where will that leave me, Trent?'

But before he could answer, she had pushed past him, grabbed the car keys from the hook near the front door and run down to the car in her bare feet.

SHE KNEW SHE needed to talk this through with someone but it needed to be the right person. Not Tina, whom she hadn't spoken to since their last awkward phone call. Not Nicole, who didn't really know how to have a proper boyfriend. And not Craig; she didn't want him to know she was having any trouble. It was only when she was approaching Guildford Road that she finally thought about where she might be driving.

Donna-Louise. She needed to speak to Donna-Louise.

Samantha found Donna-Louise alone in the front garden of the Mount Lawley house, pruning the roses as she and Craig did every July. She was cutting the stems so far down Samantha thought she must be punishing the roses for something.

'One of these days, you're going to go too far with those secateurs,' Samantha said by way of greeting. She had cried the first time she'd seen her father attack the roses like that, certain the flowers would never come back. Even now, she wasn't entirely convinced.

'Pah!' Donna-Louise replied, looking up with a smile. 'It's impossible to over-prune a rose bush.'

'Where's Dad?' Samantha asked.

'Buying mulch. Where are your shoes?' Donna-Louise responded. 'It's a bit cold to be playing hippies.'

'I, uh, left the house in a hurry. I needed to talk to you.'

'Come inside,' Donna-Louise sighed, getting up from her gardening mat. 'It was about time I stopped for a cuppa.'

Inside the house, Donna-Louise gave Samantha a pair of Craig's explorer socks for her cold feet and then ushered her into the large, sunny kitchen.

'So what was worth rushing over here without shoes?' she asked, as she made them both tea.

Samantha silently counted to three before she spoke. She didn't want to cry in front of Donna-Louise. She suspected her stepmother secretly thought she was too young to be getting married and she wanted to prove she really was mature enough. She was twenty-three, after all.

'It's Trent. He got drunk at his bucks' party last night.'

'Did he now?' Donna-Louise's eyebrows arched up ever so slightly. 'I wouldn't have thought he'd be the first man to do that.'

Samantha was disappointed in Donna-Louise's lack of instant outrage, but she pushed on. 'It's just, well, I thought we were on the same page when it came to alcohol. I haven't drunk anything since that party I went to just before I came to live with you and Dad. Not even a single sip.'

She told Donna-Louise about the promise Trent had made and the fight they'd had and all the anger and confusion and loneliness she had felt. She left out the envy.

'If you ask me,' Donna-Louise said when Samantha had finally finished talking, 'it's a matter of regaining control of the situation.'

'But I did try to control the situation,' Samantha said, confused. 'I made him promise that the bucks' night wouldn't get out of hand, and he went and got drunk.'

'Ah, there's the problem right there,' Donna-Louise remarked. 'You *made* him promise. That's not how marriage works. You see, it's impossible to control another person, not a hundred percent. And even if you could, you would probably be like me: you would get bored quickly.' Donna-Louise took a careful sip of her tea. 'If he really wants to drink, let him drink. But just make sure he only does it according to a set of rules you've agreed on together.'

'Rules?' Samantha didn't understand. 'But aren't they the same as promises?'

'Promises are for children. Rules are for life,' Donna-Louise responded. 'However do you think I manage to be in a relationship with your father? We have *rules.*'

Samantha instantly thought of how Nicole always called the Mount Lawley place 'The House of No' precisely because it was held together by rules: no shoes inside the house, no feet on couches, no running inside, no clutter on the kitchen bench, no showers between 9pm and 7am, no outside voices inside. Neither of them had ever considered that the rules would extend to Craig and Donna-Louise's relationship as well.

'Think of the circumstances in which you could let Trent drink in the future – if he chooses to, that is,' Donna-Louise continued.

'I don't ever want to see it,' Samantha blurted out.

'There's your first rule: away from the house. He never drinks in the house or in front of you.'

'And I don't want to smell it.'

'There's another rule: he sleeps on the couch if he's been drinking.'

'But I don't want him to sleep on the couch every night.'

'Another rule: only once a week, or once a month. You can negotiate that with him, let him think he has some say in it.

Maybe even allow him to suggest a few rules for you. Ultimately, Trent needs to be allowed to be his own person from time to time, not just live life within your tight grasp. It will make him a better husband in the long run.'

Samantha nodded and sipped her tea. She'd been holding onto Trent so firmly for so long, the thought of letting him go, even just a little, was terrifying. But then she remembered him grinning at the ceiling and how happy he'd seemed. Maybe if she cut him back too much, he might never bloom again.

TRENT WAS WAITING for her on the couch when she got home. She could see that he had vacuumed and done the laundry while she was gone.

'You went without your shoes,' he said, jumping up.

'Donna-Louise gave me some socks,' she replied, busying herself with putting the car keys back on their hook and taking the socks off.

'I saw you re-arranged the CDs,' he said, pointing at the shelves awkwardly. 'You only do that when you're upset.'

'Yes. I did it last night while you were asleep on the couch.'

'I'm so sorry,' Trent said, rushing to hug her. 'I'm so very very sorry. I'll never do it again, I promise.'

'It's okay,' she said, hugging him back. 'We can work through this. We just need to set some rules.'

'Some rules?' Trent's brow knitted.

'Yes,' said Samantha, suddenly feeling stronger than she ever had before. 'Some rules.'

Piece #12: 1997

'ARE YOU EVER going to try to get a proper job?' Darren asked Nicole as she emerged from the bathroom, her hair wet.

I will, when you do, Nicole thought. Darren and Trent were on the same project team at the moment and Trent had confided that Darren spent most of his workday playing Minesweeper. Nicole, however, worked almost every second she was on the clock in her job as a kitchen hand and yet he was the one with the 'proper job'.

'You didn't even touch the paper I bought you yesterday,' Darren continued, when it became clear Nicole wasn't going to answer his question.

This was true. The copy of the *West Australian* remained unopened on the dining table. Nicole had meant to have a look, even just to put on a show for Darren, but she had ended up reading her book instead.

'I'll look at it after I've dried my hair,' she lied. 'Have you done the dishes?'

Darren groaned. 'Jesus, Nic, I'm exhausted. The last thing I want to do after a long week at work is more work.'

Nicole wanted to tell him that just because he got paid more didn't mean he worked harder but she didn't push it. The rent was due on Thursday and she needed him to sleep in the flat until then. If they had a fight, he might go stay at his parents' and deduct those nights' rent from his share, like he had in the past, and she was struggling to pay her half this month as it was.

Darren turned up the volume on the television, thus ending all talk about dishes and proper jobs, which suited them both. Nicole decided to make coffee.

'We're out of milk,' Darren shouted over an ad for Chicken Treat.

'I'll go get some,' she shouted back, but then realised she should probably stay near the phone. Samantha was past her due date and could have the baby at any moment. 'Actually, Sam might ring. Can you go?'

Darren made a single, emphatic gesture towards the television as if that explained exactly why he couldn't move. She had no idea what he was even watching.

'Okay, then,' she sighed. 'Can I at least take your mobile so you can ring me if Sam calls the landline?'

Darren finally turned the volume down and gave his own sigh. 'No, I might get a call from work.'

'But the baby is due any moment.'

'I'm on call, Nic. That comes with certain responsibilities.'

And the intranet going down on a Sunday morning when nobody is at work anyway is more important than my sister having a baby? Nicole wondered as she pulled her shoes on.

'Can you get me some Twisties?' Darren asked. He turned the volume back up without waiting for her answer.

AS NICOLE TRUDGED down to the milk bar, she looked at the other houses and wondered about the lives that were being lived inside them and if there were other people shouting at each other about the dishes over the drone of the television.

She passed a woman pushing a stroller with three small children dangling off it like Christmas ornaments.

'Good morning,' Nicole said.

'Is it?' the woman asked, but she was smiling.

Nicole thought of her sister and her hard-boiled-egg stomach, waiting for her life to change. Samantha's path had always been clear: career, husband, baby. Nicole's path felt as clear as Darren's reasons for not going to the shops to get milk.

Still, she reflected, things weren't too bad right now. While her current job wasn't exactly a career, the hours were reasonable and the people were nice. And while Darren wasn't her husband, she could at least call him her boyfriend – for the moment, anyway. It had been almost four months since he had last broken up with her – the longest stretch they'd had since they first got together – and he'd promised to take her for the smorgasbord at Miss Maude's when they got to six months. She'd already chosen what she was going to wear.

But as she went into the milk bar, she caught sight of her reflection in the glass of the door and was surprised to see how large she looked. In her mind's eye, she still had the lean frame of a hungry teen, but, in real life, there was padding on that frame in all the wrong places.

No wonder Darren kept telling her she was fat.

*

WHEN SHE RETURNED to the flat, Darren was in exactly the same position on the couch.

'Catch!' she said, throwing him the big bag of Twisties she'd bought him. He caught them, without thanks, and started eating them while she put the kettle on to boil.

'Do you want coffee?' she shouted out to him.

'Yeah. Can you bring a bowl for the Twisties?'

Nicole silently added the missing *thank you* and *please*.

As she handed him the bowl and his coffee, he turned the television on mute and, feeling his biceps, said, 'You know, I could get a younger girlfriend if I wanted. The girls at work think I look twenty-five.'

Nicole wasn't sure there was much to celebrate there. Darren's actual age was twenty-eight.

'I wonder how Sam's going,' she said, reaching for the phone. 'I might ring her.'

'Oh, yeah. Trent rang while you were out.'

'Why didn't you say?' Nicole jumped up onto her feet.

'You didn't ask,' Darren said, like he actually believed that was a valid reason. 'Anyway, they had the baby and blah blah blah. You can go visit it in the hospital later today. Visiting hours start at two. Or three. Actually, I can't remember what he said about that.'

Nicole dug her fingernails into the palm of her hand and spoke as calmly as she could. She needed to swallow her anger and avoid the fight. 'You said "it". Did he say it was a boy or a girl?'

'Don't think so.'

Jesus. 'Did he say *anything* else?'

'No. Except can you tell Tina. There was also something else about Tina visiting. Or not visiting.'

Double Jesus.

Darren had taken the television off mute so Nicole took the phone into the kitchenette to ring Tina.

'Mum,' she said, when Tina answered. 'Sam had the baby!'

'Oh, how wonderful!' Tina exclaimed. 'Is it a boy or a girl?'

'I don't know. Darren spoke to Trent . . .' She let the sentence dangle so that Tina could fill in the blanks. Even though he was watching the television, there was always a chance Darren could still be listening in.

Tina knew exactly what she was trying to say. 'That Darren has such attention to detail,' she said, with a sigh. She always called him 'That Darren', like he was more object than human.

'Yep,' Nicole nodded, glancing over at Darren, whose eyes were still on the television. 'So I was thinking of going into the hospital this afternoon. At two. Or maybe three. I have to ring to find out visiting hours. Do you, um, want to come with me?'

Thanks to Darren's meticulous message-taking, she still wasn't sure if Samantha wanted Tina there or not, but she was willing to take the risk. This was Tina's first grandchild, after all.

There was a pause on the other end of the phone. 'No, sweetheart. I'll wait until she's back in the comfort of her own home. That whole hospital scene can be pretty overwhelming.'

Nicole wasn't sure if Tina meant for herself or for Samantha.

'Send my love, though,' Tina said. 'Tell her my love for her and her son-slash-daughter is as solid as a Pritikin you-know-what.'

Nicole was still laughing when she hung up.

'What was your mother saying about me?' Darren demanded.

My sister just had a baby. The world doesn't revolve around you.
'Nothing.'

'Why are you laughing?'

'Just a private joke about scones,' she told him. 'I'm going to ring the hospital to check the visiting hours. Maybe we can pick up some flowers on the way?'

'Can't go, sorry. Got karate.'

Nicole swallowed. 'Well, can I use the car?'

'Sure. You can drop me at karate and then I'll stay at my parents' house tonight instead of catching the bus. The buses are shit on a Sunday.'

Nicole had a moment of panic. 'No, it's okay. You drop me off at the hospital and keep the car. I can catch the bus home.'

SHE RAN INTO Trent in the hallway of the maternity ward. He was carrying an empty champagne bottle and looking dazed, tired and happy all at the same time.

'How are they both doing?' she asked, after giving him a hug.

'Sammy's tired and a bit tender. The C-section wasn't quite what either of us had been expecting, but she's doing great. And so is little Rosemary.'

'Ah, so it's a girl,' Nicole said with a smile. 'Darren was a little scant on the details.'

'I'm not surprised. He didn't even turn down the volume on the TV when I rang. He didn't come with you?'

'He's on call this weekend,' she said, but then instantly knew she was telling the lie to the wrong person.

'Yeah, it must be hard to relax when there's all those mines to sweep,' Trent said with a wink.

Nicole nodded at the champagne bottle, keen to change the subject. 'Parenthood already driven you to drink?' she joked.

'Dad brought it in – you know, to wet the baby's head and stuff,' Trent replied, slipping the bottle into a nearby bin.

'I bet Sammy loved that,' Nicole said, as they began to walk down the corridor.

'Actually she had some. Two glasses, in fact.' Trent must have noticed the surprise on Nicole's face because he added,

'Maybe they accidentally swapped wives in the nursery. I should probably make sure I take the right one home.'

Nicole laughed. She always enjoyed Trent's company more when he wasn't standing in Samantha's shadow.

By now, they were outside Samantha's room. Trent took a dramatic deep breath. 'Are you ready to meet the fruit of my loins?' he asked.

Nicole paused. Samantha had always been the baby of the family and now that baby had had her own baby. Suddenly, Nicole felt very old. She took a deep breath. 'I'm as ready as I'll ever be,' she replied and they walked in together.

THE FIRST THING that Nicole noticed was not the baby but Samantha. Her long dark hair was messy and loose around her face and her eyes looked puffy, as if she'd been crying for hours, and yet she looked the most beautiful she had ever looked – serene and saintly with a sleeping baby in her arms.

'Look what I made,' she exclaimed when she saw Nicole. She held the baby out to her. 'Do you want a cuddle?'

Nicole nodded. She took Rosemary in her arms and looked down at her little face, her tiny nose, her delicate eyelashes. Her small perfection.

'Where's Darren?' Samantha asked.

'Karate,' Nicole replied, without thinking. She was too busy focusing on Rosemary's tiny fingers curling around her own index finger to be diplomatic about Darren's whereabouts.

'Karate? If Darren ever ends up in hospital, remind me to go get my nails done instead of visiting him.' Samantha pouted. 'I almost died, you know.'

But Nicole wasn't really listening. For the first time in forever, she felt a powerful surge, coming up from deep within her.

She knew she truly wanted something. She knew she wanted a baby of her own, with or without Darren.

And the knowledge that something could mean so much to her was absolutely terrifying.

Samantha

WHEN I ARRIVED at the Charlie Gairdner after work, I found Nicole already by Celine's side, holding her hand. It confused me. Having spent a decade rolling our eyes in unison at pretty much everything Celine did and said, I was fairly certain that Nicole had almost as little love for Celine as I did, and yet, there she was.

'Hi, Celine,' I said. 'I brought you some flowers.'

'Thank you,' Celine said, her voice a thin wisp. 'You can put them over there, next to Nicole's ones.'

I couldn't help but notice how small my flowers looked next to the huge bouquet Nicole had bought, no doubt using Jethro's spare change. I knew I had spent very little time, effort or money on my purchase but somehow, it still irked me to be outdone by Nicole again. I thought briefly of the big bunch of red roses next to Tina's hospital bed, but quickly pushed away the memory.

'How are you feeling?' I asked Celine as I sat on the other side of the bed from Nicole.

'I've felt better,' Celine said. Now that I was looking at her properly, I could see that she didn't have a hint of make-up on. It was the first time I'd ever seen her face naked that way and she looked so much younger than her forty-four years.

'I was so sorry to hear about your loss. How many weeks were you?'

'Fifteen. We thought . . . we thought we were in the clear.' Celine started crying, big fat tears rolling down her bare cheeks. 'My cervix started dilating too early. They say they'll have to sew me up when I get pregnant again. *If* I ever get pregnant again.'

Nicole was nodding and squeezing Celine's hand in support and I had no idea how to process that.

'Where's Dad?' I asked. I wondered if he was finding Nicole and Celine's newfound closeness as unsettling as I was.

'He went to the cafeteria to get some coffee,' Celine told me. 'But he's been gone a long time. Can you go find him?'

I stood up, glad to have been given something to do. 'Sure.'

I FOUND DAD alone in the ground floor cafe, stirring his coffee with a plastic spoon.

'There you are,' I said gently. 'How are you holding up?'

'Okay,' he said, but he looked so sad, sadder than I'd ever seen him. I sat down opposite him and put my hand on his arm.

'Why didn't you tell us Celine was pregnant?' I asked.

He sighed. 'It took us so long to get this far, we didn't want to jinx it.'

'I had no idea you were interested in being a father again.'

Craig looked surprised. 'I've always wanted to have more kids,' he said. 'Of course, DL wasn't interested. Too much mess. But Celine was up for it right from the start. When I first met her, one of the first things she told me was that she wanted to be a mother.'

I thought of Celine's perfectly manicured nails and fondness for all-white outfits and wondered if babies would be too much mess for her, too. But then I remembered how much attention and love she had always showered on Rosemary. There had been times when I'd been certain Rosemary loved her Aunty Celine more than she loved me.

Dad stared at his coffee as his plastic spoon went around and around, like he was hypnotising himself.

'This baby was an opportunity for me to be a better husband and a better father. It felt like I was being given a second chance. And now it's been taken away.'

I squeezed his arm. 'Oh Dad, you were a great father. You got that much right. And I know you're a good husband. Tina can't have been the easiest person to be a good husband for, but you managed it. And Donna-Louise . . . that was just bad luck.'

Dad just continued to stare at his coffee. I had really wanted him to look me in the eye and assure me he'd been a *great* husband to both his previous wives so that I could banish the uneasiness Meg had dredged up. But, I supposed, there was no point in him making such a statement without Nicole around to hear it. I needed her to hear the truth, too.

'Is Nicole still with Cee-Cee?' he asked.

'Yes.' I said. I thought again of that huge bunch of flowers.

'She's been there all afternoon. Yesterday, too. Jethro came as well.'

'Really?'

'Cee-Cee's so glad to talk to someone who understands what she's going through.'

'She is?' I was growing increasingly uneasy. I knew Nicole couldn't have children but I had never actually thought she had wanted them. Like, *really* wanted them. The first time she'd held Rosemary as a newborn baby, she'd acted like Rosemary was a bomb about to explode. Maybe I'd had it wrong all this time.

Dad stopped stirring the coffee and drank it all in one long gulp. I guessed he must have stirred the heat out of it completely. 'That Jethro is a good sort,' he said. 'I just hope Nicole agrees to marry him one day.'

'I'm not sure the ball is exactly in Nicole's court, Dad,' I said.

'*Au contraire.* Jethro asked my permission about eight years ago and I've heard nothing since.'

'Maybe he changed his mind,' I argued, half-heartedly. This conversation was starting to do my head in. One by one, all my assumptions were being turned upside down.

'Maybe.' Dad didn't look convinced. 'Let's go back.'

UP IN THE ward, we found Celine on her own.

'Where's Nicky?' Dad asked.

Celine frowned. 'You didn't see her? She said she'd try to find you both to say goodbye.'

I was about to comment that Nicole mustn't have looked very hard, but I chose to just shake my head instead. 'No, we missed her,' I said.

Dad sat by Celine's side, the same seat Nicole had been sitting in. Unsure of what to do, I started tidying a few things on Celine's bedside table and rearranging the flowers.

'Leave it,' Dad said and I felt stung. He was one of the few people who had always understood and supported my need for order. Him and Donna-Louise, who had taught me how to channel emotional uncertainty into physical order.

I sat down and then stood up again. 'Is there any laundry you would like me to do? I can take some with me now.'

'No, it's fine. They said I'll probably be discharged in the morning,' Celine said.

Dad was now holding Celine's hand in exactly the same way Nicole had done before. I quickly said my goodbyes and left, feeling as stirred up as Dad's coffee.

AS I STEPPED into the elevator, I checked my phone for the first time since I'd arrived at the hospital and found a text from Nicole from half an hour ago.

I'm on my way to Mum's to sort more stuff. Come by if you can.

I sighed and dropped my phone back into my bag. I knew I'd been putting off going to Tina's flat, a place I'd visited only a handful of times over the years. But I also knew that Nicole had been doing the lion's share of the work and it was time to step up.

Also, I needed something to do to settle myself and I knew that reordering our meagre CD collection wasn't going to cut it.

Leaving hospital now. There in 30.

AS I PULLED into the tenants' parking area at Tina's building, I immediately felt depressed. There was something about the dirty blond brick, the broken Venetian blinds and the weeds surrounding the block that made it feel post-apocalyptic. A haven for the living dead.

I'd made it to the first floor and had started along the walkway when I realised I couldn't remember which of the identical doors belonged to Tina's flat. I stopped and stood there, wondering what to do. I was too embarrassed to ring Nicole and admit that I didn't know, but also too embarrassed to go door-knocking until I found the right flat.

I remembered how, as a little girl, when we'd first moved to Bassendean, I was constantly going to the wrong door. The cookie-cutter sameness of the townhouses had been a bit of a shock after the grandness of the Mount Lawley house, with its double-fronted verandah and prize-winning rose garden.

Once, I'd asked Tina why she hadn't tried to keep that house, why she'd moved out so easily.

'That house was far too flashy for my tastes,' she'd replied. 'And that garden was a full-time job! In any case, you should know that there was nothing *easy* about moving out.'

I'd let that last comment slide at the time and I realised now that I would never know the full story. It had been buried with Tina.

One of the far doors opened and Nicole came out with a couple of bags of rubbish.

'Let me help you with those,' I said, stepping forward and hoping that Nicole hadn't noticed I had been just standing there.

'You couldn't remember which door was Mum's, right?' Nicole handed me a bag. 'Don't worry. I still get confused and I've been here way more than you.'

I couldn't help but feel a little judged by her remark, but I shook it off. It had been my choice to not visit Tina here very often and I knew I needed to stand by it.

'How was Dad when you found him?' Nicole asked, as we walked back down the stairs to the skip I'd hired.

'He was okay. Sad, but okay. How was Celine?' I asked, giving her a sideways glance.

'My heart really goes out to her,' Nicole replied. 'I had no idea they'd been trying so hard to have a baby. Did you know that was their third round of IVF?'

'No. I had no idea either.' I looked sideways at Nicole. 'Dad said you were being a "great comfort" to Celine. What did you talk to her about?'

'I didn't talk. I just listened,' Nicole said, as she flung the bag into the skip. 'You should try it sometime.'

'Are you saying I don't listen?' I said, flinging in my bag on top of hers. I could feel the blood rising up into my ears. 'If you ever said anything interesting, I'd be the first in line to listen to it.'

Nicole looked hurt. 'Jesus, Sam.'

I was ashamed of what I'd said, but I had no idea how to find my way back to her in that moment. So I turned and walked back up to the flat as fast as I could.

AS I STEPPED through Tina's front door, I was immediately hit by the ghost of Chanel No. 5, Tina's scent. I had to stand completely still, lest the surge of grief overtake me completely.

'The smell . . .' I turned to say to Nicole, standing behind me, but I couldn't put the rest into words.

'The flat's been shut up all this time. What did you expect?' Nicole replied tersely, as she pushed past me. She was clearly still upset with me.

'It smells like Tina,' I said, but Nicole was too busy banging cupboard doors to hear me.

I pressed my lips together and set to work.

Separately, we worked in silence. I went through the kitchen cupboards, dividing the crockery and cutlery into boxes labelled BIN and CHARITY on the small dining table, while Nicole went through Tina's books.

After a while, she brought an armful of them over to the table. I saw this as an invitation of sorts.

'So many Dan Brown books,' I remarked. 'I wouldn't have pegged Teensy as a fan.'

It had been years since I had called Tina 'Teensy', Dad's old nickname for her. When we were in high school, Nicole and I had sometimes joked it was because Tina was always a 'teensy bit drunk' or a 'teensy bit hungover' or a 'teensy bit negligent'. It had been one of those ha-ha-funny jokes we'd hid our pain behind.

Nicole shrugged, obviously not quite ready to forgive me. She began to pick through the charity box I had been adding to, separating out a few things.

'This platter belonged to Nanna, and this one too,' Nicole said. 'And this knife is the last remaining part of a set Mum and Dad got for their wedding.'

'How do you know all this?'

'I lived with Mum for much longer than you, remember.'

'As if you'd ever let me forget,' I muttered under my breath.

'What?' Nicole looked at me with a ferocity I hadn't seen in her for decades, not since she was a kid.

I backed off. 'Nothing,' I said.

We returned to our work in silence. I was now tending to an ancient wound, the one that Nicole always sought to re-open, given half a chance. She always treated me like I had abandoned Tina, as if me moving to Dad's house in Mount Lawley was something I had done on a whim and had nothing to do with Tina not wanting me in her home any longer.

I focused on the task at hand. Most of the crockery went into the bin box. It was either chipped or cracked. Nothing matched. Nothing was even particularly clean.

As I carried the box down to the skip, I found myself going over what Nicole had said about Celine needing someone just to listen. I'd never given Celine much consideration. All her make-up and hokey beliefs had got in the way, but perhaps there was more going on beneath the surface than I had allowed.

'Do you think Celine and Dad will go through another round of IVF?' I asked Nicole when I got back to the flat. She'd moved on to clearing greying frayed towels and torn bedsheets out of the small linen cupboard next to the bathroom.

'I don't know,' Nicole answered, her face hidden by the cupboard door. 'It's very invasive and expensive and extremely taxing. And the success rates aren't as high as everyone thinks. For most people it's just an expensive journey towards total heartbreak.'

'You seem to know a lot about this.' I wasn't used to Nicole speaking so authoritatively about anything.

'I couldn't have children, remember?' Nicole said with the kind of sigh that I usually gave.

'But you also never *wanted* children. Did you?'

Nicole closed the cupboard door and looked at me briefly, before scooping up an armful of rags for the skip.

'You know what, Sam?' she said as she started to walk out of the flat. 'You think you know everything about me. But you don't.'

I pressed my lips together and went back to work. But no amount of sorting could erase the feeling that I might not know my sister at all.

Piece #13: 2009

'WILL YOU LOOK at how cute our toothbrushes look together,' Jethro said, as he watched Nicole unpack her toiletries. He'd cleared one of the cabinets for her in the en suite. It was at least four times the size of the single cabinet she'd had in her flat.

'It's like they were meant to be together.' Nicole laughed, looking at the two toothbrushes. She'd had her toothbrush in Jethro's bathroom a hundred times but had never felt bold enough to put it in the fancy holder.

'You know, I thought you'd never move in. And yet, here you are,' Jethro said. 'Has it really taken three years for you to finally realise I'm the best thing that's ever happened to you?'

Nicole nodded. She'd given Jethro the impression that she'd finally made a decision, but the truth was that the lease on her flat hadn't been renewed and that had made the decision for her.

'Of course, had I known I'd get my own bathroom cabinet the size of a small warehouse three years ago, I might have moved in sooner. Like Suzette.'

The minute she mentioned his ex-wife's name, Jethro's smile disappeared. 'Please don't do a Suzette,' he said.

Legend had it that Suzette had turned up with a suitcase three weeks after she'd started dating Jethro and had stayed for a decade, before breaking his heart and making a considerable dent on his bank account.

'You know I won't do a Suzette,' she reassured him. 'As long as you don't do a Darren.'

'Yeah, nah. There's no risk of me running back to live with my mother. She'd never have me.' Jethro smiled.

WHILE JETHRO MADE dinner, Nicole started unpacking her clothes and stacking the usual pile of unread books next to the bed, the same unread pile that had sat next to her bed in Leederville. At the very bottom of the pile was the copy of *The Secret* that Samantha had given her for Christmas three years ago, just before she'd met Jethro. Nicole still had no idea why Samantha had bought it for her. Self-help books weren't really her thing. But every time she'd gone to get rid of it, she'd felt overwhelmed with guilt. Sometimes, Nicole thought that Samantha herself was like a book she felt she had to read, but perhaps didn't really want to.

She eased the book out from the bottom of the pile and, before she could change her mind, marched down the stairs to the bookshelves in Jethro's study – now also her study – where she quickly found a space for it. It felt good to free herself of that burden.

She'd used the move to free herself of other burdens, too, mostly Darren-related. The plastic trinkets from Japan he had given her, the Windows 95 sweatshirt he had forgotten to take the very last time he'd left her, the blanket they'd shared when they were watching TV together. The one thing she hadn't got rid of was the Cookie Monster jar, which she'd already put on display in the large modern kitchen, much to Jethro's amusement. Ever since her miscarriage, ten years ago, she'd kept it as a reminder that she should never want too much.

'Dinner's ready,' Jethro called from the dining room.

She wandered over to the dining room, noticing how it really was the kind of house that you could wander in, it was that large. It was hard to imagine that this was really her home, this fancy house with all its fancy rooms and furnishings. She wondered if she would ever feel as relaxed here as she had in her tiny three-room flat.

She stopped in the piano room, lifted the lid on the Steinway and played a few random notes.

'There you are.' Jethro slipped through the double doors that led through to the dining room.

'Here I am. And so is this piano,' Nicole said. 'Now that I've moved in, can you at last tell me the secret of how it got in here?'

The first time Nicole had come to the house, she'd quickly worked out that there was no way the piano could have fitted through any of the doorways or windows into the small room. But every time she'd asked Jethro about it, he'd made up another story. One had the piano grow slowly from a seedling. Another had him ordering the piano from IKEA and constructing it with a single allen key.

Jethro laughed. 'I've been building this up for so long, I'm afraid the answer is going to be quite disappointing.'

'Go on, then. Disappoint me.'

'As you've probably already worked out, we built the room around the piano. It was moved in here while the whole back of the house was still open. We'd have to completely pull this part of the house down to get it out.'

There was something about the story that made Nicole feel sad, like they had trapped the piano there against its will.

Jethro cleared his throat. 'If the lady would care to make her way through to the dining room . . .'

He opened both the double doors to reveal the dining table, decorated with candles and roses.

'Oh,' she said, touched. 'It's beautiful.'

'I thought we should make our first night officially living together special,' he said. 'I've made my legendary lasagne.'

'Well, that makes up for the disappointing story about the piano,' Nicole said with a smile, as she gently closed the lid. 'By the way, I just put some books on the shelves in the study, is that okay? I'm afraid there'll be a whole heap more in the boxes.'

'Of course! You should just put them wherever you want. I want our books to mingle, to really get to know each other, maybe even have little book babies together. Now, make yourself comfortable while I serve up dinner.'

Nicole sat down at the table, uncomfortable in her guilt. There was that word again. *Babies.* He dropped it every now and then. It was the only thing that made her uncomfortable about being with Jethro. She knew how much he wanted children and she knew that she should have told him the truth about her fucked-up womb before she agreed to move in. Not that she knew for certain that her womb was fucked up. She was supposed to have gone to a follow-up appointment after the miscarriage, but she never did. It felt easier not to know what the problem was.

'*Et voila!*' Jethro brought out a large silver platter with a lid and laid it on the table in front of Nicole. 'Will you do the honours?'

She lifted the cover and, instead of a lasagne, found a note with the words MARRY ME written in Sharpie.

Nicole was completely taken aback. 'But . . .' she stammered. 'But I thought you didn't want to do the marriage thing again.'

If Jethro had been expecting her to say 'Yes!' immediately, he didn't show it.

'I didn't think I would want to do "the marriage thing" again, either. And yet here I am, wanting it, and wanting to do it with you,' he admitted. 'And anyway, I never asked Suzette to marry me. She was the one who proposed.'

'I . . .' Nicole didn't know what to say. 'I don't know what to say.'

'Well, I do know what to say. I love you, Nicole. You've brought such gentle sunshine into my life. You've lit up corners that I thought would remain dark until I died.' He walked around the table and, taking a small velvet box out of his pocket, he knelt in front of her. 'Please, Nicole. Do me the honour of living with me for the rest of my life, putting up with my bad habits and even worse jokes, and maybe, just maybe, having a baby or two . . .'

As he opened the box to reveal a beautiful solitaire diamond ring, Nicole thought of her (potentially) barren womb and had a sudden impulse to run upstairs and repack her clothes. Most of her boxes were still untouched, she told herself. The truck could come back and this big mistake could be undone easily, quickly, without too much pain. Jethro would thank her in the end.

Jethro must have sensed her inner turmoil because, before she could run, he stood up and took her hand. 'I know I've done this all wrong. I've gone in too fast and hard. It's taken me so long to get you here and I thought . . .'

The room fell silent. Nicole watched the candle wax drip slowly down the candelabra onto the white embroidered tablecloth, her urge to flee now gone. Jethro had pulled her back from the brink.

'You don't need to give me a ring to keep me here,' she said, now looking at him. 'I *want* to be here.'

'And I want you to want to be here,' Jethro said. His cheeks were flushed and his eyes were wider than she'd ever seen them.

'And I want you to want me to . . . et cetera.'

They smiled shyly at each other, both eager to push past the awkwardness.

'It's just so great to finally have you here,' Jethro said, with a little shrug.

Nicole looked around the dining room with its elaborate light fixtures and fine art on the wall and realised she would never have to eat straight from a can in front of the television again. Unless she chose to, of course.

'Well, now that we know we're both happy, we may as well eat the lasagne. It's probably going dry in the oven,' Jethro said.

'Oh, so you're not serving me paper for dinner?' Nicole joked and then immediately regretted bringing up the note so soon.

'Nah, I tried that diet and it didn't work for me,' Jethro replied but he avoided her eyes.

'Let me get the lasagne. I'm not your guest anymore, I live here too, you know,' she said, trying hard to keep the mood light.

She stood in the kitchen and, for a few moments, concentrated on her breathing to calm herself down, a trick she'd seen Samantha use in her teens when she was trying to control her temper. It would be okay. She might not be actually barren. That miscarriage may have only been a blip, a minor aberration. She would book an appointment somewhere and get everything checked out. They would give her a certificate of fertility or something and she could frame it and mount it on the wall, next to the Cookie Monster jar, and she might even go on to have a dozen babies.

She looked at the Cookie Monster jar, staring at her with its huge googly eyes.

'I'm just going to try,' she said to it.

As she walked back into the dining room with the lasagne, Jethro was taking the ring from the centre of the platter and putting it back in his pocket. They both pretended she hadn't seen.

Piece #14: 1985

SAMANTHA HAD TOLD Tina she was going to stay over at Kerstin's house and Kerstin had told her mum she was staying over at Samantha's. Neither mum was the type to fuss or check. It was the perfect plan.

When they arrived at Danny's house, they were greeted by Danny and his friend Jamie, who went to another school.

'Our exclusive VIP party awaits you,' Danny said, with a sweeping gesture into a large peach-coloured bedroom at the front of the house. 'Just don't mess up the bed,' he added.

Danny's parents were away in Europe and his older brother, Gavin, had decided to throw a big party. He'd allowed Danny to invite a few friends of his own, as long as Danny didn't dob.

In the bedroom, a bunch of Year Eights that Samantha barely knew sat around on the shagpile carpet awkwardly, drinking cans of soft drink and listening to 96FM on Danny's boom box. Samantha helped herself to some Cheezels and sat with Kerstin against the far wall. With her mouth full, she didn't need to worry about not having anything interesting to say.

'Will you get a look at the little Year Eights.' Gavin was standing in the doorway, with a bottle of Jim Beam in one hand and a Year Eleven girl wearing too-high heels clutching the other.

'Aren't they cute?' the girl said, swaying a little on her stilts.

'Looks like they're having a Clayton's party to me. You know, the kind of party you're having when you're not having a party,' Gavin explained to the girl, as if he were the first person to ever make that joke.

'Leave us alone,' Danny said, shutting the door on them. He then turned back and surveyed the scene. 'You know what? Our party does look like a Clayton's party. Let's play a game or something. I know! Spin the bottle!'

As he went out to find a bottle, Kerstin shot Samantha a look. Samantha knew instantly what the look meant. Kerstin loved Danny more than anything. This could be her big chance. Samantha suddenly realised that if Kerstin got with Danny, she'd be left alone with all these kids she didn't really know, and her stomach tightened.

Danny returned with two bottles: an empty one and a full one.

'Let's make this extra fun. If the bottle lands on you, you have to have some of this.'

Now it was Samantha's turn to shoot Kerstin a look. She didn't feel comfortable with the drinking aspect, but Kerstin widened her eyes, pleading. *Don't ruin my chance.* So Samantha stayed put, although her heart was now pounding.

'What's the drink?' Kerstin asked.

Danny looked at the label. 'Koala,' he said. Samantha knew from Tina's own arsenal of alcohol that wasn't how you pronounced Kahlua, but she didn't correct him. She remained silent as everyone gathered on the floor in a circle and started spinning one bottle and passing the other one around. Samantha didn't know which prospect was making her more nervous: having to kiss someone or having to drink.

The first time the bottle landed on her, Jamie, the guy from the other school, had spun it. Danny handed her the Kahlua.

'Skol, skol, skol,' the kids all chanted. Samantha had no idea what 'skol' meant, and was pretty sure no one else did, either.

She took the bottle to her lips, thinking she could just pretend to take a sip, but was surprised to find how sweet and syrupy it was. She'd always thought all alcohol was bitter, like the smell on Tina's breath when she kissed her goodnight. She had no idea it might actually taste good.

'Kiss, kiss, kiss,' the kids now chanted. Jamie leant across the circle and brushed his lips against hers. Her first kiss. Without thinking, she took a second slug of the Kahlua, still in her hand.

'No fair!' Danny shouted and took the bottle off her, but he was smiling. He took another swig himself and passed it around the circle. 'Let's all have some. It will be more fun that way.'

The game went on and the Kahlua was passed around until it was empty. Another bottle of a different liquid, less sweet but still as warming, appeared at some point and that was passed around as well.

Samantha was feeling soft around the edges. The people in this circle all felt like her friends, even the ones whose names she didn't know.

Slowly, over time and with more alcohol, the game morphed into a spin-the-bottle version of truth, dare or torture.

'You should choose truth!' Samantha shouted, when the bottle landed on Kerstin. 'Tell Danny the truth!'

Kerstin elbowed Samantha firmly and then said, 'I choose dare.'

'Okay,' Danny said, pressing his fingertips together like a Bond villain. 'Run into the backyard and steal one of my brother's dickhead friends' beers.'

While Kerstin went on her mission, Samantha lay back on the carpet. She was aware that someone, maybe Jamie, was playing with her hair and it felt good.

Kerstin came back with a stubby of Emu Bitter and everyone cheered.

'Sam,' Kerstin leaned down to whisper in Samantha's ear. 'Your sister's here.'

'Let my sister be here,' she said, not caring.

'And she knows you're here.'

'Let her know I'm here.'

She closed her eyes and let the room spin around and her hair be stroked.

'Sammy?'

She opened her eyes again. Far above her was Nicole's face, looking down at her. She was frowning.

'Jesus, you're drunk,' Nicole said.

'I am. And it feels good, Nicky. You should try it.'

The awful spectre of Nicole melted away and the ceiling continued to gently rotate. Her insides were like honey, all warm and gooey. The bottle of the not-so-sweet liquid was passed to her and she sat up to take another swig before lying back down. She closed her eyes again.

'It's your turn, Sam,' Danny shouted at her, minutes, hours or days later. 'Truth, dare or torture?'

'Dare,' Samantha said, sitting up. She felt daring. Also a little woozy.

'Two minutes in the wardrobe with Jamie,' Danny proclaimed and all the kids cheered.

'Okey dokey,' Samantha said, trying to stand up and then falling back down again. 'Whoopsie!'

Jamie took her by the hand and pulled her up properly. 'This way, my lady,' he said. He looked a little like Matthew Broderick and the memory of that brief swish of his lips against hers made her feel excited.

They stumbled into the walk-in wardrobe and everyone cheered again as Danny closed the doors.

'What are we supposed to do?' Samantha whispered.

'I dunno. Can I touch your boob?'

'Okay.'

In the darkness, Jamie's hand felt around until it found her left breast. He squeezed it like it was a lump of playdough.

'Ouch,' Samantha said.

But now his hand was moving down towards her jeans. He fumbled with the button and then shoved his hand inside, like he was tucking in her shirt.

The wardrobe door flung open. 'Our time's not up!' Jamie protested, pulling his hand back out of Samantha's jeans as quickly as he could.

But it wasn't Danny standing there. It was Tina. Even through the veil of alcohol, Samantha could see that Tina was angry. Furious, even.

'Come with me, young lady,' she said, pulling Samantha out of the wardrobe. She sounded like she was trying to be one of those mothers on TV.

'And you,' she said, turning back to look at Jamie. 'Don't you ever take advantage of a drunk girl like that again, you little shit, or I will personally come around and cut off your little dick with the biggest, sharpest pair of scissors I can find.'

Jamie shrunk back. Samantha imagined him melting, like the Wicked Witch of the West, until only his tricolour deck shoes were left.

'Okay, we're going home,' Tina said, steering Samantha by her elbow out of the house and on to the footpath, where Nicole was waiting. 'You need the air.'

'*You* need the air,' Samantha said back.

'What do you mean?'

'You're probably drunker than me. You're always drunk.'

'Stop talking,' Nicole warned Samantha, trying to step in between her and Tina. '*Please.*'

'Come on, let's go,' Tina said, pulling on her elbow. Her mouth was a thin line.

'Wait,' Samantha said, digging in her heels. 'I don't have my bag. I need to go back inside.'

She didn't care about the bag. She just wanted to go back to the party and to Jamie.

'Can you please go and find her bag, Nic?' Tina asked. Samantha watched with envy as Nicole disappeared into the house.

'Can't I go back inside?' she pleaded with Tina. 'I was having so much fun.'

'I think you've had enough fun for tonight.'

'You can't stop me from having fun. And you can't stop me from drinking. I like it. I like being drunk. It makes me feel more like me.'

Tina grabbed her by the shoulders. 'Don't do this, Samantha. Don't end up like me.'

'I'm never going to end up like you, a sad old drunk,' Samantha spat out. 'Dad didn't want you. I don't want you either.'

Samantha felt the sting of the slap immediately, but it took a few moments for her mind to process what had happened.

'You hit me,' she said slowly, holding her hand to her face, although the real hurt went much deeper. She began to cry.

'I'm sorry, my little love. I'm sorry, I'm sorry,' Tina said, trying to hug her but Samantha pushed her away and ran into the darkness, still holding her face and crying.

She found a park and, after having a big vomit into one of the garden beds, she curled up inside the play equipment, a bright yellow plastic tunnel. The warmth the alcohol had given her had evaporated, leaving her feeling cold and sick. She wanted her bed. She wanted her dad. She even wanted her mum. Not the angry, furious version of her mum, but the smiling, laughing version, who danced to music and tucked her in.

She closed her eyes and let the sickness and drunkenness take her into sleep.

'SAMANTHA!'

She was woken to the sound of her father's distant voice shouting her name.

She pulled herself together and crawled out of the tunnel. The button on her jeans was still undone from when Jamie had shoved his hand down there. She did the button up, pulled her jacket around her and took a deep breath.

'Dad!' she called back weakly.

From the shadows, Craig came running. 'There you are. God, I've been so worried. I've been looking for you everywhere.'

'Why were you looking for me?'

'Your mother called me. She said you'd run off into the park. She said you were drunk.'

'She's the one who's drunk,' Samantha said, trying to muster more fury. But it was all spent.

'Let's get you home,' he said.

His car was parked around the corner, and they drove through the dark streets back to Mount Lawley, where Donna-Louise was waiting.

'Oh dear,' she said when she saw the state that Samantha was in.

She put a tentative arm around Samantha's shoulders and led her to the middle bedroom, where she tucked her in between cool cotton sheets. Samantha could hear Craig on the telephone in the hallway, but the alcohol still in her system made his voice feel far away, like it was being filtered through water.

Donna-Louise sat on the bed beside her. 'Here's a glass of water for you,' she said. 'And a bucket, too. Just in case.'

The bucket was on the floor, on top of a large sheet of plastic.

'I'm sorry,' Samantha moaned.

'It's okay. We all make mistakes,' Donna-Louise replied. 'The trick is not to repeat them.'

Craig appeared in the doorway, his phone call now over. 'How's my girl?'

'She'll be okay,' Donna-Louise said, before turning back to Samantha. 'Won't you?'

Samantha nodded.

'DL, can I talk to you a moment?' Craig asked.

The two of them stepped outside the room. Samantha could hear them whispering in the corridor and their voices felt like soft sand running through her brain. She closed her eyes and started to drift away into sleep.

Suddenly Craig was back by her side, taking her hand.

'I've talked it over with Tina and now with DL and we've all decided it's best for you to stay here with us for a while. For as long as you want.'

Samantha didn't have the energy to say anything. Instead, she just closed her eyes again and surrendered entirely to sleep.

And when she woke the next morning, her head fuzzy and her mouth dry, she had trouble remembering pretty much anything that happened.

Except the slap.

She would always remember that slap.

Nicole

'WE'RE GOING TO do another round of IVF,' Celine told me over the phone.

'Good for you,' I replied. 'Have you had any further thoughts about changing clinics? I can pass on the list that Jethro made, if you like. It's a bit out of date but it's a good place to start.'

'That would be great, thanks,' Celine said. 'You know, it's nice to be able to talk with you like this. It's the closest I've ever felt to having a sister.'

I thought of the way Samantha and I usually talked to each other and knew Celine was way off the mark. 'I'm really happy I'm able to help you, Celine. I know how hard it is.'

'Well, I appreciate it. I tried to talk to Samantha about it once, when she and Trent were over with Rosemary, but she just told me motherhood wasn't the gift everyone pretends it is.'

Samantha had used that line on me at least once, too. It bugged me, the way she treated motherhood like this big secret I would never be let in on.

'Can I ask you a favour?' Celine continued. 'Sister to sister?'

I did my best to push past the second 'sister' reference by taking a breath and saying, 'Sure.'

'Would you and Samantha take Craig out for lunch? I've been getting all the attention and he really only has colleagues, not friends. I think he'd like to talk to someone.'

Again, Celine was way off the mark. This wasn't a sister-to-sister favour, this was a stepmother favour. Real sisters didn't ask other sisters to take their husband, who was actually their other sister's father, out to lunch. Someone really needed to sit down and explain all that to Celine. However, it wasn't going to be me.

'Of course,' I said. 'I'll ring Sammy.'

'Great. I'd have asked Samantha myself but she can be a bit . . .'

'Scary?' I offered.

'Yeah. Thanks, *sis*.'

I winced.

I RANG SAMANTHA straight afterwards, before all my intentions dissolved. I'd been avoiding her since our fight at Mum's flat. And whatever was going on with her and Trent felt too big and too hard for me to tackle on my own. I wasn't even ready to talk to anyone about it yet, not even Jethro.

Samantha answered on the first ring. 'What's up?'

'I spoke to Celine just now and she's asked us to take Dad out to lunch. She says he's been feeling a bit down since the miscarriage.'

'I'm delighted to hear that you and Celine are taking your relationship to the next level. Are you officially going steady now?' Samantha's voice sounded strange, like she was trying very hard to keep her words completely separate from each other.

'We've been talking quite a bit,' I admitted. Celine had been ringing me every day since she had been discharged from the hospital and I was starting to worry how much she was depending on me. At some point, I knew I would disappoint her, just like I seemed to have disappointed everyone else. 'So will you come out for lunch on Saturday? I thought we could, you know, finish that unfinished business of ours.'

'Yes. Asking him prying questions will definitely cheer him up.'

'Don't be like that, Sam. Just say you'll come. *Please?*'

'Yes, I will. But only because you used your nice asking voice.'

'What?'

'Your nice asking voice. It's very nice that nice asking voice of yours.'

'Are you okay?'

'I am okay but I must go now,' she replied. 'Goodbye.'

I was left feeling unsettled. She'd sounded like a complete stranger just pretending to be Samantha.

I ARRIVED AT Mount Lawley just before noon the following Saturday. Celine greeted me at the door in her dressing gown but with a full face of make-up on.

'What do you think?' she said, fluttering her fake eyelashes. 'F'nelle brought me a new eyeshadow palette while I was in hospital and I've been having a play.'

'Um, the colours make your eyes really pop,' I said, pleased that I still remembered F'nelle's turn of phrase from the wedding day.

Celine beamed and opened the door wide. 'Come on through. Craig is just getting his jacket.'

We set off down the hall, but Celine paused outside the doorway of the room Samantha and I had once shared as children before Mum and Dad had broken up.

'We'd started to redo this room,' Celine said, and then lowered her voice. 'For the baby.'

She pushed the door open, like it was a reveal moment on one of those home makeover shows, except she was only revealing a shell of a room. The carpets had been ripped out, the walls had been stripped back to the bare plaster board and the ceiling fixtures had been removed.

'The ceiling rose . . .' I said, my own voice now almost a whisper. My childhood room had been destroyed. It hit me harder than anything Aunt Meg had said at the Blue Duck.

But then I saw Celine's face and I realised how selfish I was being. Her sadness was for a childhood that might never even touch this room. I put my hand on her arm and she gave me a small smile, before closing the door and leading me back down the corridor.

'Oh,' I exclaimed, as I stepped into the open living space out the back. It had been ages since I had last visited the house. Whereas it had once been filled with 1950s furniture in Tina's day, and fifty shades of beige during Donna-Louise's term in office, it was now awash with colour. The throw cushions were popping all over the place.

'I really like what you've done,' I told Celine, hoping to pull her away from her sadness. The compliment worked because her face lit up again, now brighter than all the throw cushions combined.

'Oh, thanks. I've changed the room's colourway. I think it's working, but Craig complains that it's too busy. He says it gives him a headache.'

'And so I've taken to wearing sunglasses indoors,' Dad said, as he walked into the room behind us. His hair was still wet from the shower and it made him look old and shrunken.

'Hello, darling,' he said, giving me a quick hug. 'Where are you girls taking me?'

'Jethro got us a reservation at Coco's. Sammy will meet us there.'

'Coco's? La-di-da!' Celine said, evidently impressed, and then she started to fuss over Dad. 'Maybe you should wear a tie?'

'It's not fancy.' I stepped in. 'What he's wearing is fine.'

I was now feeling a little anxious about the time. Samantha had never ever been late in her life and I knew if we didn't get there soon, she might burst a blood vessel.

'I THOUGHT WE said one,' was the first thing Samantha said when we met her outside the restaurant. It was only five minutes past. 'And however did you manage to get a reservation *here*?'

She spoke in hushed tones, like she was about to enter a church and I found myself getting annoyed.

'I rang and made a booking,' I said with a shrug. 'I don't understand all this fuss about Coco's. I've eaten in far fancier places, even in Perth.'

I was pretty sure I saw Samantha roll her eyes as she popped a peppermint into her mouth.

Inside, we were led by the maître d' to a table by the window.

'Nice spot,' Dad said, looking around.

Samantha was already scouring the menu. 'Bit pricey,' she remarked.

'I've got this covered. It's on me,' I said, thinking back to the number of times Samantha had bought me lunch when I was living by myself in Inglewood. It felt good to return the favour.

'You mean, it's on Jethro,' Samantha said, with a small laugh that grated my very soul.

'Well, whoever's paying,' I replied as breezily as I could, 'it's neither of you.'

'Thank you, darling.' Dad placed his hand on my arm and I smiled. At least he seemed grateful.

The waiter came over to take our orders. I ordered a pasta dish while Samantha and Dad continued to pore over the menu.

'I'll have the Atlantic salmon,' Samantha eventually said. Any issue she had with Jethro's money obviously didn't stop her from ordering the most expensive thing on the menu.

'I'll have the sirloin with mushroom sauce,' Dad said, before turning to me with a wink to add, 'Celine doesn't need to know about the cream.'

'And would you care to order some wine?' the waiter asked.

Before Dad and I had a chance to respond, Samantha jumped in. 'No, we'll just have some sparkling mineral water for the table.'

'Very good,' the waiter replied as he took the wine menu away.

Dad and I both stared at Samantha.

'What?' she said. 'It's daylight. You're not *winos*.'

And you're not the boss of me, I thought, somewhat sulkily.

A few tables over, a couple were sipping wine while their young child watched *Dora the Explorer* on an iPad, the volume turned up extra loud.

'Restaurants are no place for personal TVs,' Dad muttered.

'It's not a TV, Dad,' Samantha corrected him. 'It's an iPad.'

'Whatever it is, the kid shouldn't be on it.'

'Maybe it's the only way they can enjoy an uninterrupted meal.'

'If they have enough money to eat here, then they have enough money to hire a babysitter,' Dad observed.

'Maybe they want to enjoy the meal *with* their child,' Samantha argued. 'Give them a break. Some parents just have a hard time managing.'

Samantha's defensiveness didn't surprise me, considering how inseparable Rosemary had been from her various devices.

I had always put it down to Samantha and Trent's inability to say no to their child rather than them not managing.

Dad excused himself from the table and went off to the bathroom.

Samantha leaned forward. 'When are you going to ask him?'

'I thought you were going to ask him. I did it last time.'

'You're the one who organised this lunch. You're the one who's Team Meg. Why should I do it?'

I gave a small groan. She was right, of course, but this didn't make things any easier. This post-Tina version of Samantha that made me do everything was really starting to get me down. As the waiter came and poured out our sparkling mineral water, I wished I'd been allowed to order wine.

'This is a pretty nice spot to take a slash,' Dad said when he returned to the table. I had forgotten he used to call urinating 'taking a slash'. Donna-Louise absolutely hated it.

I went to open my mouth, ready to cut straight to the chase, but Dad reached out and put his hand on mine.

'Nicky, I've been thinking a lot about the conversation we started to have at the Queens and the question you asked me.'

I felt a brief moment of sweet relief at not having to repeat the question, but then I realised his reply was coming and I tensed up again.

'I'm sorry I didn't answer. Obviously, it was partly because of that phone call from Celine. But it was also partly because I've dreaded someone asking me that very same question for over three decades.'

I shot Samantha a glance but she was staring at Dad.

'You wanted to ask if it was true, if Meg and I had an affair,' he started and then paused to take a sip of his water. 'It's a funny word, "affair". When you apply it to politics or the news, it has a certain gravitas. Foreign *affair*. Current *affair*. A state *affair*. But when applied to the heart, it's all so sordid.'

As he took another sip of his water and gazed out at the view of the river and the city, I wondered if we were about to go to an ad break or something. He was drawing this out more than the finale of any reality TV show I had ever watched. And I'd watched plenty.

'And?' I eventually asked, now impatient.

'And, well, with this particular matter, the sordid undertones are completely appropriate.'

'Appropriate?' I was confused. His answer was wrapped up in too many words.

Dad looked down at his hands. 'Yes, I was unfaithful to Tina with Meg. And not just with Meg. I slept with other women, maybe eight,' he said quietly, his reality TV demeanour now gone. 'I'm not proud of what I did. And it's been hard not to feel like God has been punishing me for those things by taking away our baby.'

'God?' The only time I'd ever heard my father mention the word was when he was being led through the vows at his wedding to Celine.

'I've been going to church with Cee-Cee.'

'Christ,' I said, despite myself.

'I'm not proud of my behaviour,' Dad continued. 'Not at all. Tina was wonderful, but she was wild and unpredictable. I convinced her to marry me, hoping that it would contain her. But it didn't. So I ended up having little affairs on the side with women I thought I could control.'

'But Mum's *sister*?' I asked. Even though I had believed Meg, it was still hard to hear the truth.

'The two of them were so alike, they were almost like twins back then. But Meg was a little more biddable than Tina.

She had a track history of terrible boyfriends and was what you might consider "low-hanging fruit".' He sipped his mineral water. 'Of course, that's not what I thought at the time. I was just acting on instinct. The faith counsellor I've been seeing through the church has been helping me understand things better.'

I looked over again at Samantha in time to see her eyebrows shoot up at the mention of the 'faith counsellor'.

'And when I told him about the question you'd asked me, we prayed about it together and I realised that it was time to be honest. My biggest regret was that I was never honest with Tina and never really took full responsibility for my part in our separation. I told myself I only did those bad things because Tina was bad for me. And she *was* bad for me, in a way.'

'But how?' I asked.

'When I was a kid, I would get really upset when I accidentally coloured outside the lines. You were the same, weren't you, Sammy?' Samantha nodded. 'I convinced myself that Tina was the colour outside the lines – that she wasn't good for me because I really needed order. In fact, that's why you came to live with us, with DL and me. You needed order, too.'

'And me?' I wanted to know. 'What about me, Dad? Why was it okay to leave me behind?'

I realised, as the words fell out of my mouth, that I'd never expressed it that way, as being 'left behind'. I had only ever described it as Samantha leaving Mum and me.

'You always understood her,' Dad answered. 'She was good around you. Or rather, she was better having you with her than she would have been without you. Without you, she might have drunk herself to death much earlier.'

'And you never minded when you coloured outside the lines,' Samantha interjected, as if the whole fucking point of the conversation was about colouring in.

'Tina wasn't a colouring-in page or a Texta or anything else like that, she was a human and she was your wife,' I said. 'You slept with her *sister*, Dad.'

'I know, I know. Please forgive me,' he said, his head bowed as if in prayer.

'What about Donna-Louise?' Samantha asked. Her face was pale now. 'Did you cheat on Donna-Louise too?'

Craig picked up his napkin and started unfolding and refolding it. 'DL was the opposite of Tina. After years of feeling like I was careening out of control with Tina, DL was so . . . stabilising. But then I made a mistake. DL found out and she left me.'

'So that's why you broke up? Because you slept with someone else?' Samantha asked.

'It's complicated,' Dad said, eyes cast down. 'There was this one time—'

'I can't believe you did that to Donna-Louise, after all she did for you, after all she did for *us*.' Samantha's voice was rising and with it, I felt my own anger growing.

'What about Mum?' I asked. By this point, we were both being much louder than *Dora the Explorer*. 'You heard what Dad said: he slept with eight other women while he was with Mum, not just one. And one of them was her sister.'

'As if Tina would ever have noticed. In fact, if she hadn't been so drunk all the time, she might have paid more attention and he wouldn't have needed to sleep around.'

'Jesus Christ, Samantha! Nineteen fifty-two is calling and it wants its gender inequality back.'

'Girls, girls,' Dad said, touching both our arms in an attempt to calm us down.

'Don't touch me,' Samantha said, shaking off his hand and standing up. 'I'll never forgive you for doing that to Donna-Louise.'

'And not our mother?' I was seeing red now. After all these years, and Mum just buried, Samantha was still siding with Donna-Louise.

'She was only ever *your* mother,' she spat out.

As I watched her go, I wondered if I would ever be able to sit through a whole meal with my sister without her storming off. I turned to Dad, but he was standing now, too. Without even a glance in my direction, he grabbed his jacket and ran after Samantha.

'Sammy,' he was calling. 'Let me explain.'

I sat alone at our table and tried desperately to pretend half the restaurant wasn't staring at me as the waiter delivered our food.

'Can you please box up my companions' meals?' I asked him. 'And can I please see the wine menu?'

'Certainly, madam,' the waiter replied, and without missing a beat, he carried the steak and salmon away.

Over at the *Dora the Explorer* table, the iPad had been put away and the little girl was sleeping in her father's arms while he ate his meal with one hand. I found myself wishing Dad would come back, wishing Dad hadn't left me alone in the first place, hadn't chosen Samantha over me.

Again.

I took a forkful of my pasta and, chewing very slowly, I looked out at Perth and its river, both sparkling in the sunshine in spite of me.

Piece #15: 1999

THE 'BIG RED Car' video was playing for the fifth time that day and Dorothy the Dinosaur's voice was feeling like a chainsaw against Samantha's brain.

The feeling had been building for weeks. Weeks that were filled with seemingly endless days of the same: wake, breakfast, Wiggles, walk, Wiggles, lunch, Wiggles, nap, Wiggles, dinner, Wiggles, bath, bed. Then repeat.

But today had felt worse than ever. Rosemary had woken before six – on Trent's sleep-in day, no less – and had only had a forty-five-minute nap in the twelve hours that had passed since then. Samantha had spent most of those forty-five minutes putting away the lunch things and hanging out the washing and had only just put her head on her own pillow to try to get some sleep when she'd heard Rosemary shout for her. Samantha had shouted then, too, but into her pillow.

Now, Samantha looked at her daughter, this tiny ball of determination, who never did what Samantha wanted her to do, and never slept when Samantha wanted her to sleep, and never ate the things Samantha wanted her to eat. She wouldn't even wear the clothes Samantha chose for her, always choosing the same red velveteen leggings, pink ballet skirt and pirate top.

'She's headstrong, like her mother,' Trent would say to people, as if it were something to be admired. But Samantha was worried that Rosemary was headstrong like her grandmother. Like Tina.

As the hands on the wall clock approached six, Samantha finally started to relax. Trent would be walking through the door soon, just as the theme music for *Neighbours* came on, and he would whisk Rosemary away to the bath, leaving Samantha to watch the show as her reward for another long day alone with Rosemary. It wasn't much, but it was hers.

But then the phone rang.

The phone ringing at this time of day never brought good news. Still, she answered it, vaguely hoping it was Trent ringing from the shops, wondering what flavour ice cream he should buy.

'Hello?'

'Hi, Sammy,' Trent said. He sounded tired.

'You haven't left yet,' she said. Not as a question but as a note of extreme disappointment.

'No, I haven't. I have to wait until they've pushed the new fixes live,' Trent explained. 'I'm so sorry, Sammy.'

If he really was sorry, he wasn't anywhere near as sorry as Samantha was.

'Daddy is going to be late,' Samantha told Rosemary after she'd hung up. 'Let's watch Mummy's show together!'

Rosemary crossed her arms and pouted. 'No!' she said. 'Wiggles!'

'It's Mummy's turn now.'

'Wiggles!'

When Samantha switched over to TV mode, Rosemary put her hands over her ears and screeched loudly, harpy-style. 'Wiiiiiiiiiigglesssssssss!'

Samantha closed her eyes and counted to ten inside her head. Whenever she was faced with the full force of Rosemary's determination, the Other Samantha started to rise up inside her, like an ancient demon, ready for battle.

'Okay, darling,' she said, when the moment had passed and her eyes were back open. 'Let's watch more Wiggles, shall we?'

As she pressed play, she thought about how all the toddler books said you needed to be consistent and persistent. And here she was, feeling as consistent and persistent as wet toilet paper.

She lay on the carpet next to her dancing daughter and closed her eyes again. She thought back to the day Rosemary was born and wondered if things would be different if she'd managed to stick to her birth plan and birthed Rosemary the way she'd wanted to birth her, instead of being sliced into like a watermelon on a hot afternoon.

She remembered sitting in the hospital bed with everyone treating the arrival of the baby like it was something to celebrate and not the end of life as Samantha had known it. They'd brought champagne, for god's sake. She thought now of that glass of champagne and its taste of star-shine, a glimmer of light on a dark day and, for the second time in almost fifteen years, she felt like having a drink.

'Let's dance!' Rosemary exclaimed, jumping up and down. If Rosemary had been any older, Samantha would have sworn she was rubbing in the fact they were watching her show and not Samantha's.

'Let's drink!' Samantha exclaimed back. She got up from the floor and romp-bomp-a-stomped over to the small cupboard where Trent kept the spirits and liqueurs that had been left over from his twenty-fifth. At the time, she'd reluctantly agreed he could serve cocktails to his guests – as long as he didn't drink any himself, that was – but now, Samantha was incredibly glad about the decision, even if there was only an almost empty bottle of gin and an unopened bottle of blue Curacao to show for it.

She slugged back the gin. Even though it tasted like old flowers, it hit the spot. She quickly twisted the lid off the blue Curacao and held it to her nose. She grimaced. No chance. How something so blue could smell so orange was beyond her. But even as she poured it down the sink, she began to regret it. What could she drink now?

She looked up at the clock and then back at the TV. Captain Feathersword had almost finished singing 'Nicky Nacky Nocky Noo', which meant there was only 'Dorothy's Dance Party' and the titular 'Big Red Car' to go. If she waited until the end of the video, she'd have enough time to get Rosemary into the car and to drive to the bottle shop and back before Trent got home.

For the first time in months, she felt a little bit excited about life again.

SHE DIDN'T EVEN mind that Rosemary was asking her to play the Wiggles on the stereo before she'd even started the car. The tiny amount of alcohol in her system would surely soften Dorothy's screeching.

As she pulled into the drive-through bottle shop, she checked Rosemary in the rear-view mirror and saw that she had fallen asleep during the five-minute drive. Her heart sank. If Rosemary napped now, she'd be a nightmare to get to bed tonight. But then, she realised, that could be Trent's problem. After all, he owed her for being so late.

As the drive-through attendant walked over, she unwound her window.

'What can I do you for?' he asked.

As she scanned the rows of bottles, she realised she had no idea what to ask for. They all looked the same.

But then something caught her attention.

'What's that bottle with the little red hat?' she asked.

'Tequila,' he said. 'Personally speaking, I think more bottles should come with their own hats.'

Samantha found herself agreeing with him as she gently placed the bottle on the seat next to her, as if it were a passenger. There was something about its little red hat that seemed to promise happiness.

As she started the car, the stereo came back on, and even though Rosemary was still sleeping, Samantha turned the volume up. For the first time in forever, she wanted to sing along with the Wiggles. The road ahead no longer felt like it was leading her back to a domestic prison. She drove and she sang, and life felt so much lighter.

When she took the next corner, everything shifted. Something came loose, maybe in the car, maybe in her head, like a weak leg giving way under the weight of the rest of the body, and the car went into a spin, sending everything into slow motion. Samantha felt like she had slipped in between the minutes and the seconds into an infinite space where she would spin forever.

But then the car stopped.

She immediately turned to check on her daughter, but Rosemary was still sleeping, completely unaware of the danger they'd just been in. Samantha then looked around the car to see if anybody had seen the accident, and was relieved to find the street was empty.

As she got the car back into gear, she noticed her hands were shaking. At the first opportunity, she pulled over and rang Trent to tell him what had happened.

'Are you hurt?' Trent said in a low voice. It sounded like he was on the bus.

'No.' Samantha swallowed. She realised she had begun to cry.

'Is the car okay? Can you drive it?'

'There's no damage.'

'Then there's nothing to worry about.'

But Samantha couldn't stop crying. 'It's made me think of that accident, the one Nic and I had with Mum on the way back from Esperance. I can't remember if Mum cried afterwards, if she'd felt any shock from putting us at risk like that. I mean, we could have died. *I* could have died, if I had still been sitting in the back seat.'

'I'm sure she would have been upset,' Trent said, trying to soothe her.

'But I don't think she was. She was drunk, remember? She wouldn't have been thinking about anything except maybe where her next drink was coming from.'

As she said that, she looked at the bottle of tequila, still sitting there on the passenger seat, and she felt sickened by the fact she still wanted it. In fact, if she were to be completely honest with herself at that moment, she wanted to drink it more than ever. She grabbed it and shoved it onto the floor of the back seat, out of her sight and out of the way of temptation.

*

AS SHE PULLED into their small car space, she could see Trent coming up the street from the bus stop, his work bag slung over his shoulder. Rosemary was stirring in the back of the car, her cheeks rosy with sleep.

Samantha turned the ignition off and closed her eyes. She imagined the car was still spinning and she was trapped between the seconds, lost in time.

'How's my favourite girl?' Trent was opening the door on Rosemary's side of the car. Samantha kept her eyes closed. 'Did you have a little sleep?'

'Wake up, Jeff!' Rosemary shouted.

'Hey, what's this?'

Samantha opened her eyes and saw that Trent had picked up the bottle of tequila.

'It was on special,' Samantha said, thinking as quickly as she could. 'I bought it for you for New Year's. I thought I could make paella and we could invite Nicole and Darren. You know, have a bit of a party.'

Trent gave a nervous laugh. 'Who are you and what have you done with my wife?'

'I don't know. New millennium, new me?' Samantha said.

'Uh, okayyyyy . . .' Trent stretched the word out as he tucked the bottle away into his bag. 'Are there any more groceries for me to carry in?'

Thankfully Rosemary distracted him. 'Out!' she shouted, her arms opened wide. Trent unclipped her and lifted her out of the car onto his hip. Rosemary threw her arms around his neck, and shouted, 'I love Daddy!' She turned back to Samantha and gave her a knowing, defiant look. 'I love Daddy,' she repeated.

Samantha didn't respond. All she was thinking about was the seventeen days that remained until New Year's and that bottle.

Piece #16: 1982

NOTHING HAD BEEN the same since the accident at Bruce Rock. Whereas once, Tina and Craig used to fight behind closed doors, hissing like snakes, now they stormed around the house, each shouting at the top of their voice, and it was Nicole and Samantha's turn to hide behind closed doors and whisper to each other.

While they hid in their room, Nicole lay on her bed and stared at the ceiling rose, trying to find faces in the plasterwork, while Samantha dressed and undressed her doll. Occasionally, when there was a loud crash or the sound of something breaking into a thousand pieces against a wall, Samantha would look over at Nicole. But, Nicole would always avoid meeting her sister's eye, because it would mean acknowledging something that she didn't want to acknowledge: that their parents were splitting up.

Nicole preferred to stay in her own head and pretend it wasn't happening at all.

One Saturday, there was silence. Craig stayed in the bedroom while Tina grimly pruned the roses in the front yard with a large pair of garden shears. When neither of them noticed it was lunchtime, Nicole snuck into the kitchen to make some Vegemite sandwiches, which she and Samantha ate on the rug in their bedroom, like they were having a picnic.

'Do you think they'll get divorced?' Samantha asked her, after they'd finished eating.

'I don't know.'

'What does divorce even mean?'

'It means two people stop being married.'

'Davina's mum and dad are divorced.'

'Good for them,' Nicole said, and then regretted it. Samantha's eyes were filling with tears. 'I'm sure Mum and Dad won't get divorced. All couples fight.'

She thought of the fights in the comedies that she watched on TV; arguments with a laughter track in the background. But when Craig and Tina fought, Nicole and Samantha were their only audience and they didn't find any of it funny at all.

'Davina lives with her mum all the time and never sees her dad. I don't want to never see Dad.'

'I'm really sure it will be okay.'

Samantha bit her lip and picked the lint off the rug. 'She had to choose which parent she wanted to live with. I think if Mum and Dad get divorced, they should take one of us each.'

Nicole thought of school and how she was always being picked last for team sports, except basketball because she was so tall. She imagined Craig and Tina as team captains, standing at the front of the gym, fighting over who was going to take Samantha. Of course they'd both want Samantha because she was much neater than Nicole. She was also small and cute.

'I don't think it works that way,' she told Samantha, not wanting to think of it anymore.

Suddenly, voices erupted in the hall.

'I'll leave, shall I?' Craig was shouting. 'I mean, Kalgoorlie is too far for you to drink-drive to.'

'Jesus, Craig, I wasn't drunk when I crashed that car. I told you a billion times.'

'And I haven't believed you a trillion times.'

'You're the one lying!' Tina shouted. 'What about what you were up to while me and the kids were in Esperance?'

The shouting moved down the hallway to behind a closed door.

'They keep talking about the car accident,' Samantha whispered.

'I know.' Nicole felt sick to her stomach every time the topic came up. She knew it was her fault for rushing Tina, for wanting to be in Kalgoorlie in time for *Young Talent Time*. She kept waiting for Tina to tell Craig the truth.

'Dad thinks Mum was drunk. Do you think Mum was drunk?'

'No,' Nicole said.

'But what about the bottle at the motel you told me about?'

'I told you I wasn't sure about that.'

'Well, I told Dad,' Samantha said, crossing her arms.

Nicole frowned. She should never have told Samantha about the bottle. Ever since Craig had asked her if Tina had been drinking before the accident, the bottle had been weighing more and more heavily on her mind. She'd thought that talking about it with her sister would lighten the load. But now it was clear it had only made things worse. Yes, she'd seen Tina with the bottle and yes, she'd seen her go behind the building.

When she'd come back out, the bottle had been empty. But she hadn't seen Tina actually drink from the bottle, she kept telling herself. And now Samantha had gone and blabbed, and Tina and Craig were getting a divorce.

She climbed back onto her bed and picked up her book. She was reading *Flowers in the Attic* for the third time, and somehow, returning to its world of captivity, incest and arsenic poisoning felt comforting.

Back on the carpet, Samantha was sniffling in front of the bookcase, trying to hide the fact that she was crying. Nicole put her book back down and gazed at the ceiling, wondering what she could say to make her sister feel better. And then she realised that she was looking at the answer. 'Have you ever seen the faces in the ceiling rose, Sammy?'

Samantha lay back on the carpet and looked up. 'Kind of,' she said, her nose blocked from her tears.

'See the roses? That's their eyes. And the leaves are their ears and noses.'

'I can see them,' Samantha said.

'They're our friends. They're looking after us. They'll make sure we'll be okay. All of us. You. Me. Mum and Dad.'

Samantha smiled, happy for a moment, and it was like the sun had come out. But then they heard the bedroom door slam shut again and the smile disappeared.

AT AROUND TWO, Nicole ventured out to the garden to see what was happening.

Tina was sitting on the love seat, a drink in her hand and the pruning shears on her lap. Nicole looked around the garden. All the roses were lying on the ground, their red petals spilled, like blood, all over the grass.

'Tell your father I finished the gardening,' she told Nicole.

Nicole quickly beat a retreat back to her room. She didn't want to be around when Craig discovered what Tina had done to his roses.

'What's happening?' Samantha wanted to know. 'Can we come out?'

'I think we should stay here.'

'But I'm bored.'

This was starting to feel like the worst babysitting job in the world. Nicole imagined them being trapped in the bedroom forever, like the kids in *Flowers in the Attic*. She'd definitely have to take up a hobby like ballet or learning medicine from a book.

'I know, let's play Monopoly,' she said, fishing the game out from under her bed and lifting its lid off. She knew Samantha loved being the banker and the real estate agent. Maybe by the time they set up the game the fighting would be over and they could all have dinner and then watch a TV show together.

'I'm the iron,' said Samantha.

She picked up the wad of money and was carefully sorting it out into denominations when they heard Craig's voice booming from the garden, like a tenor delivering an aria on a large stage. 'Jesus, Tina. Not my fucking roses!'

And Tina's voice, like the soprano responding: 'Yes, your fucking roses, you fucking bastard!'

'Let's play,' Nicole said, focusing as hard as she could on the board before them.

AN HOUR OR so had passed. It had been so quiet outside, and the girls had been so consumed by their game that they'd almost forgotten that their parents were fighting. Samantha rolled the dice and landed on Trafalgar Square, now adorned with a hotel.

'GTBH!' she exclaimed.

Samantha had been using the expression all game, obviously dying for Nicole to ask her what it meant. So Nicole had decided to annoy her by not asking.

'Girls?' Craig opened the door. 'I just wanted to have a quick chat with you both.'

He came in and sat on the edge of Nicole's bed. His eyes were red, like he'd been crying. Nicole didn't know what to think. She'd never seen her father cry.

'You might have noticed your mother and I have been having a few, um, disagreements lately.'

Nicole knew that was putting it mildly, but she nodded nonetheless. So did Samantha.

'And so we've decided that it's probably best for me to go away for a little while.'

'Don't go, Daddy!' Samantha jumped up onto his lap and threw her arms around his neck. Nicole stood up but then hung back, unsure of whether they should make him stay or not. She didn't want her father to leave, but she also wanted the fighting to stop.

'It will just be for a little while. I need to think. Your mum needs to think.'

Nicole immediately thought of what Samantha had said and whether they might be deciding which child they were going to choose, but then she pushed the silly notion out of her head. Samantha was just a baby who still had baby thoughts. She didn't understand how the world worked.

But then it occurred to Nicole, neither did she.

Craig hugged Samantha, who was now sobbing.

'Be a brave girl. Mummy and Nicole will look after you until I get back.' Craig looked past at her at the board. 'Monopoly? I bet you're winning.'

'I have a hotel on Park Lane and on Trafalgar Square,' Samantha said, through her tears.

'That's my girl. You playing Free Parking rules?'

'Yes. Nicole landed there twice and she's still losing.'

Craig gave a little smile and then stood up. He turned to Nicole. 'Look after your sister, okay?' He paused for a moment, before adding, 'And your mum.'

Nicole nodded and watched as her father left their room, slowly closing the door behind him. Samantha remained in the same place, clearly unsure of what to do.

In the hallway, Tina and Craig started shouting again.

'Daddy?' Samantha said, her voice painfully small.

Nicole tried to distract her.

'Come and finish flogging me,' she said, sitting back down at the Monopoly board.

Samantha joined her reluctantly and threw the dice.

'GTBH,' she said again, sadly as she landed on one of her properties.

'Okay, okay, tell me what GTBH means.'

'Good to be home,' she replied, her eyes filling up with tears. 'GTBH.'

Outside in the hall, Craig shouted, 'You're going to die penniless and drunk in a ditch!' And then Tina responded, 'I hope your dick falls off!' And then the front door slammed.

Yep, thought Nicole. *GTBH.*

Samantha

AFTER I LEFT Coco's, I drove south to Donna-Louise's house in Busselton. The drive took two and a half hours and, a few times, I considered turning back and going home to my hidden stash of vodka. But then I would think of Donna-Louise and I would keep going.

Somewhere just outside Mandurah, my phone rang. It was Dad. I didn't want to talk to him. I didn't want to talk to Nicole or to Trent or to Rosemary. I just wanted to talk to Donna-Louise. I reached over and switched the phone to airplane mode and drove the rest of the way to Busselton in silence.

If Donna-Louise was surprised to see me standing on her doorstep, she didn't show it. Instead, she ushered me inside and offered me a cup of tea, like I was a neighbour dropping by and not some mad woman who had driven over two hundred kilometres on a whim.

'I was so sorry to hear the news about your mum,' Donna-Louise said, as she prepared the tea. 'I was going to drive up for the funeral but I thought it might be a bit awkward for everyone if your father was there with Celine.' She paused. 'I assume he *was* there with Celine.'

'Yes, they were both there.' I thought of Dad at the wake, hovering near Nicole's front door, like he'd already left before he'd even arrived. 'Actually, Celine has been in hospital. A miscarriage. She's fine, but I think it was disappointing for them both.'

'Ah,' Donna-Louise said, laying out lace doilies for the teacups. 'I thought Craig might try for fatherhood again. He certainly didn't have any luck persuading me.'

While the tea steeped, Donna-Louise asked how Rosemary was going in her third year of university.

'I've got no idea. She's out all the time,' I said. 'And the rare times that she is home, she's either asleep or in the bathroom taking selfies.'

I thought of Rosemary's Instagram account, full of photos taken in nightclub bathrooms, looking up at the camera with her lips pushed out so they looked like sausages. Of course, when I told her I wished she'd use her normal face, she blocked me.

'I see the apple doesn't fall far from the tree,' Donna-Louise remarked.

My face must have shown my confusion, because she quickly added, 'Oh, no, not you. You're not the tree. I was talking about Tina. Rosemary's always been so much like Tina.'

'You think so?' I said, trying to sound like I was disagreeing with her. But I knew in my heart, she was right. Despite all my efforts to keep them apart over the years, Rosemary had turned out just like Tina. A party girl.

'Of course, you had a touch of that wildness, too, when you first came to live with Craig and me. Do you remember how many times I had to get you to rearrange the bookcase?'

I nodded. It had been Donna-Louise's favourite task to give me whenever I lost my temper. At first it had felt like a punishment, but then, over time, it became a kind of meditation. I had tried the same with Rosemary but it hadn't worked.

'I wasn't that wild,' I said.

'No,' Donna-Louise reflected. 'But you certainly had the capacity for wildness, given half a chance.'

I briefly thought of all the vodka I'd recently had the capacity for and quickly changed the topic.

'How's the golf?'

'I'm president of the women's social team now,' she said, with a small laugh. 'I still miss the Mount Lawley Club, but some of the members still come down to play a few rounds with me every now and again.'

Donna-Louise poured the tea out through the strainer and I found myself wishing I could do the same with my life: pour it through something to make it pure again. 'How is Nicole? Has she finally got that rich boyfriend of hers to marry her?'

'I don't think Jethro will ever ask,' I said, choosing to ignore Dad's claim that Jethro had asked his permission years before. 'I think they pretty much live their lives in the shadow of his previous marriage.'

'Hmmm,' Donna-Louise said, tightening her lips. 'I always half-expected she would get herself knocked up to have some security.'

'I don't think she can have babies,' I replied. 'The only time she's ever talked to me about it was after some specialist appointment she'd had, but she didn't seem that upset about it. She's not really the maternal type.'

It was the standard response I gave whenever people asked me if my sister had children. But this time, as I spoke, all I could think about was Nicole holding Celine's hand.

Donna-Louise gently stirred some sugar into her tea. 'I suppose you'll eventually tell me why you've come here. Of course, it's a delight to see you. It's just that it's been a little while since you visited.'

'At least I'm wearing shoes this time,' I joked, suddenly remembering the time I'd turned up at the Mount Lawley house in my bare feet. I couldn't even remember why now, although I could still recall the feeling of the dew on their perfectly kept lawn against my soles.

'Shoes?' Donna-Louise glanced at my feet, her brow furrowed. Her memory was obviously even worse than mine.

'Anyway,' I began, 'the reason I'm here is because Nicole and I talked to Dad about his split with Tina and it spilled into some of the reasons you split with Dad.'

'Did it really?' Donna-Louise said, with one carefully plucked eyebrow arched.

'Yes, he admitted he was unfaithful to you.'

'Oh. Right.'

Donna-Louise looked away, back out the window into her immaculate garden. I was starting to wonder why I'd driven all this way if all it achieved was dredging up the painful past for poor Donna-Louise.

'Did he tell you who he slept with?' she asked, still looking outside.

'We, uh, didn't really drill down to that level of detail. But as I was driving here, I admit I did wonder. Was it someone at work? His secretary? That woman, Cheryl?' I shuddered. Cheryl had been all peroxide and cheap perfume and had a laugh like a hyena.

'Oh, a secretary would have been fine. We could have bounced back from that. We could have bounced back from a hundred secretaries.'

'Then who was it?' I began scouring my memory for other women Dad had known back then. 'Was it someone from the club?'

Donna-Louise lifted her chin and turned back to face me. 'It was your mother.'

I felt my stomach fall away, like I had just hit a dip on a rollercoaster. 'He slept with *Tina*?'

'When I found out, he told me some outlandish story to try to convince me it hadn't happened. He was always very good at telling stories, your father. But all his stories aside, the truth was I always knew that Tina was his real love.' She paused and straightened the lace doily underneath the teapot. 'You were talking about the shadow of the ex-wife that Nicole and her rich boyfriend live under? Well, let me tell you that Tina cast a very long shadow over every single day of the twenty years Craig and I were married.'

I had no words. That my father, who loved order as much as I loved it, could still love Tina, an agent of chaos – it just didn't make sense.

Donna-Louise poured us both some more tea. Her voice was as carefully measured as the sugar she spooned into her cup. 'I want you to know that I didn't leave him because he slept with his ex-wife. I left him because I finally accepted he had never really been mine.'

'But *he* left *her*. I don't understand.'

'I expect he left her for the very same reason as I left him: she was never really his. Tina was nobody's. I always admired her for that.'

I found it hard to believe that the cool, collected Donna-Louise could ever admire anything about my drunken whirlwind of a mother. This was a day full of surprises.

'The real question, of course, is why Tina slept with Craig. She never showed him anything other than joyous disdain. I suppose we'll never know now.'

'I guess we won't,' I said, sitting back in my chair. My head was a flurry of half-formed thoughts. One thing was for certain: I could no longer rely on the version of the past I had been carrying around all these years.

In the next room, a clock chimed. Donna-Louise stood up. 'It's getting late. Would you like to stay for dinner? I could even make up a bed for you in the spare room.'

I remembered the bed she had made for me the night my mother slapped me and how good the cool cotton sheets had felt. I found myself yearning for that kind of comfort again. But I knew I needed to get back to my husband and my child.

'No, I'd better get back to Perth. I have work in the morning,' I said, putting my cup very carefully down on its saucer. 'Thanks for the tea. And the chat.'

'Any time,' Donna-Louise said. 'Although, you could probably find a cuppa a little closer to home.'

I smiled, but I was aware that we were both now acting like the conversation about Dad and Tina had never taken place. I gathered my things and Donna-Louise walked with me to the door.

'Give my best to Trent and to Rosemary,' she said, embracing me quickly.

'I will.'

I nodded and went to go but then stopped myself. I turned back to face Donna-Louise. 'The real reason I came down here was I wanted to say I was sorry Dad hurt you like that. And actually, I don't care if Tina was the love of his life. The truth is you were the best thing that ever happened to him. You were the best thing that ever happened to *me.*'

'Oh Samantha,' Donna-Louise said, her grey eyes shining with almost-tears, but she didn't say anything else. She just gently shut the door.

I DROVE BACK to Perth, the long road ahead of me slipping under my car and into the past. As I drove by the turn-off for Mandurah, I remembered to turn my phone back on. A call instantly came through the car's Bluetooth system. It was Nicole. I accepted the call before I had time to think about it too much.

'Where are you?' Nicole sounded worried.

'I'm driving.'

'I can tell that much. Where are you going?'

'I'm driving back from Busselton. I went to see Donna-Louise.'

'What did The Iron Lady say?'

The use of the old nickname grated on me. 'She said a lot of things, actually.'

'And?'

I saw no reason to protect Nicole from the truth, not when she'd opened this can of worms with Dad in the first place. I took a big deep breath and let it all out. 'Remember how Dad said he was unfaithful to Donna-Louise? Well, it was with Tina. He slept with *Tina*.'

'What?' Nicole's voice was thick with confusion. 'I mean, why would he . . .'

'That bit's easy,' I replied, with a laugh that wasn't mine. Once again, the Other Samantha had taken charge. 'Tina was the love of his life and he never got over her. That's why he fucked her. The real question is why did *she* fuck *him*? Donna-Louise had no idea, but I know why.'

'Why?'

'Because Tina was a fucking bitch who just wanted to fuck everything up for everyone.'

'Oh Sammy, you know that's not true.'

She was right, of course. It wasn't true but I was saying it anyway. Tina felt like the obvious target for all this anger and grief I was feeling. And so I pushed on.

'Why else would she do it, Nicole, if not just to fuck up Dad and Donna-Louise's marriage? She was probably drunk and feeling mean. Or completely sober and even meaner. I remember her phoning from the pub, pretending to be sorry that Dad and DL were separating. She wasn't sorry. She was the fucking cause.'

'Don't do this. We just buried her.'

'No, Nicole. *You* buried her. She was never my mother to bury.'

And with that, I hung up and turned my phone back onto airplane mode, even though there was a part of me that wanted to ring back Nicole immediately and apologise. While Tina might have slept with Dad, there was no getting around the fact that *he* had also slept with *her*. Dad needed to take his share of the blame in all this. The problem was, I wasn't ready to give it to him.

Dad had been my saviour. He had pulled me out of the wreckage of my life with Tina. He had given me shelter and order. He had given me Donna-Louise. And yet, he'd valued none of it, instead yearning for the very thing he had saved me from.

In the silence of the car, all I could hear was my own rapid breathing above the hum of the motor. I pushed away all my thoughts and focused as hard as I could on each breath coming in and going out, until finally, my breathing slowed. Now there was only the hum and the lights of the drive-through bottle shop up ahead.

*

I ARRIVED BACK in Perth just after eight. The house was dark, save the glow of the television.

'Where have you been?' Trent asked. 'I called a thousand times.'

'My phone ran out of battery,' I lied.

'Well, your sister's been trying, too. And your dad. They've left messages on the answering machine if you want to listen to them.'

'Not really.'

I sat next to Trent on the couch and laid my head on his shoulder. My mind touched briefly on the bottle of vodka I'd just bought, now hidden in my handbag, but I pushed the thought aside. The vodka could wait until later, when Trent had gone to sleep. For the moment, I was happy to be sitting next to him.

He was watching a movie that involved a lot of alarming-looking blue people running around.

'What is this film? And why are those people so blue?' I asked.

'It's *Avatar*,' he replied. 'And the blue people are Smurfs gone rogue.'

'Smurfette looks well fierce,' I remarked. We continued watching in silence.

'But seriously,' Trent turned to me at the next ad break. 'You should ring your dad and your sister, Sam. They both sound really worried.'

'Let them worry. I'll ring them in the morning.'

But I knew I wouldn't ring them in the morning. Nor the next morning. I would keep ignoring their calls and texts. I imagined that in years to come I would tell Rosemary and maybe even my grandchildren that this was the summer that I lost them all: first my mother, then my father and then my sister. This, I'd tell them, was the summer that I chose to be an orphan.

Piece #17: 2013

AFTER THE APPOINTMENT with the specialist, Nicole and Jethro sat in the car in silence. Outside, people moved about living their lives. But inside their car, it felt as if everything had been put on pause.

'Nic—' Jethro finally began, but Nicole stopped him.

'It's okay. We don't have to talk about this yet. We need to let it sink in first. Can you just take me home?'

Jethro nodded and started the engine.

NICOLE'S FIRST IMPULSE, after Jethro had dropped her off and headed back to work, was to ring Tina.

'Sammy!' Tina answered the phone. There was lots of noise in the background.

'No, Mum, it's Nicole.'

'Nicole?'

'That's right.'

'Of course! It says it on the phone! Duh! Everyone, look, it says Nicole on the phone and I said Sammy.'

By now, Nicole's ears had adjusted to the laughter in the background and she knew that, even though it was barely midday, Tina was already at the pub. She found herself withdrawing.

'I can hear that you're busy. Don't worry about it, it's nothing urgent. I'll ring you back later.'

'What?'

'I'LL RING YOU BACK LATER.'

'Ta ta,' Tina said cheerfully.

After she hung up, Nicole sat and stared at her phone for a long time. She wanted to ring Jethro but she knew he would still be driving to work. But as she scrolled through her contacts, she knew there was nobody else she really wanted to talk to.

Her finger stopped on Samantha's name. It had been such a long time since they'd shared anything personal with each other. In recent times, they hadn't even shared the impersonal stuff. She decided to take the plunge and ring her. After all, they were sisters. They should be there for each other.

'Hi, Nic. What is it?' Samantha sounded distracted.

'Just thought I'd ring to say hi,' Nicole felt like a character from a sitcom, brimming with fake cheer.

'Okay . . .' Samantha sounded wary. It wasn't their practice to ring just to say hi.

'All right, okay, so I am ringing to say more than hi. I got some bad news today.'

'What's the matter?' Samantha sounded concerned enough for Nicole to continue.

'Well, Jethro and I have just been to see a fertility specialist.' Nicole took a deep breath before she said the next bit. 'And it turns out I have an incompetent cervix and it's unlikely that I'll ever be able to have children.'

'Oh,' Samantha said, her tone unreadable. 'I'm sorry to hear that.'

They fell into an uncomfortable silence and Nicole found herself trying to fill it.

'Of course, I'm forty-one,' she said. 'You could argue that most women over forty have incompetent cervixes to a certain degree. But mine, it turns out, is particularly incompetent.'

'Oh, well,' Samantha said, after another pause. 'At least the decision has been made for you.'

'What do you mean by that? What decision?'

'The decision about whether or not to have children. You've never been good with decisions.'

Nicole clenched the phone. Samantha had no clue about the decision she'd had to make back when she'd fallen pregnant to Darren, and how that had worked out for her.

'Yeah, I guess,' she said, pushing her feelings down with each word. They spoke for a few more minutes, mostly awkward chit-chat about what Rosemary was up to. And then Nicole made her excuses and hung up.

Ringing Samantha had been a mistake.

She thought again of ringing Jethro. He'd be at work by now. But she wanted to give him a little more time to digest the news. God knew that she, too, needed more time. The information was sitting high in her throat, like something she was having trouble swallowing.

She curled up on the couch and cocooned herself in the afghan blanket in the hope she might eventually emerge a different – maybe even fertile – person. She felt the same desperate loneliness she'd felt lying on that two-seater IKEA couch in Inglewood after her miscarriage.

Down the hall, she heard the key in the front door and her heart lifted. Jethro was home.

'I got halfway to work and I just couldn't do it. I've rung in sick,' he told her.

Jethro never rang in sick. He was so dedicated to his work that the one time he had gastro, he still led a two-hour conference call, pausing only to put his phone on mute and vomit into a bucket.

'I'd have rung in sick, too,' Nicole said. 'Except I've no one to ring.'

Jethro lifted her feet up so he could sit next to her on the couch. He held her feet in his soft, warm hands.

'I'm sorry,' Nicole said, eventually.

'What can you possibly be sorry about?'

'This is a problem with me. I'm the problem.'

'No, no, no, you're not the problem at all. You're my solution,' Jethro replied. 'Do you know how lonely I was before I met you? Even when I was married to Suzette, I was lonely.'

'That's because she wouldn't watch crap TV with you,' Nicole ventured.

'Yes, that. And many, many other reasons.' Jethro paused. 'Part of the reason I turned back and came home to you was that I couldn't stand the idea of you sitting with this sadness alone,' he said. 'So I came to sit with you.'

He began to rub Nicole's feet, gently and slowly, and she found herself falling into the rhythm of his hands.

'Also, I wanted to tell you this,' he said, choosing each word very carefully. 'Of course, I would love to have kids. But if it were a choice between having kids and being with you, I'd choose you every time.'

Nicole felt her whole body relax. 'I choose you back,' she said quietly.

'Then come up here and kiss me.'

She sat up slowly and turned towards him. He took her face in his hands and kissed her gently.

'Let's go on a holiday,' Jethro said, pulling back to look at her, his hands still cupping her face. 'Let's go somewhere beautiful and inaccessible, somewhere that it would be difficult to get to with a baby or a child. Let's go to lots of music festivals, or take up paragliding or climb Mount Everest. Let's buy a collection of extremely fragile and very expensive Fabergé eggs and put them on a display at knee height. Let's renovate this place or buy a new one, with glass walls and staircases without banisters. And let's buy a new couch, an impractical one, a white one. Made of suede or silk or even crepe paper.'

Nicole was laughing now through her tears. 'As long as we can watch crap TV on our white crepe-paper couch, I'll be happy with anything.'

'We can watch it with the volume up until 3 am every night.'

'Okay. You've got yourself a deal.'

Nicole realised then, that the thing she'd been bracing for was not the news about whether she could or couldn't have children, but whether Jethro would leave her if she couldn't. Every other important male in her life had left her. Her dad had done it twice: once when he left Tina, and then again when he'd taken Samantha to live with him. Darren had done it multiple times, but the worst was when he left her bleeding in a hospital all alone. Maybe finally, in Jethro, she had found someone who was going to stay with her despite all her imperfections.

But instead of feeling better, she felt worse. She wondered if Jethro, like the piano in that little room, was only staying with her because he had found himself trapped.

Piece #18: 2006

Now that she was back at work again, Samantha was almost beginning to enjoy being a mother. While other mothers complained about juggling work and parenting, Samantha could not get enough balls in the air. Every weeknight was filled with one activity or another, whether it was taking Rosemary to netball training or dance classes, or attending meetings for one of the many school and social committees she had joined, or baking late into the night for cake stalls or stuffing envelopes for mail-outs or sewing sequins on costumes.

It was only occasionally, usually on a Sunday, that the void would threaten to consume her again. She would wake to find nothing in the calendar, nowhere to be, nothing particularly urgent to do and her mind would turn to the bottle of vodka, still in its special hiding place in the wardrobe. But even then, she'd scrabble around to find something else to distract her from the thought of that bottle: a button on an old shirt of Trent's that needed replacing, or a scrapbooking project she'd been meaning to get around to. She'd give each of these tasks the same weight and urgency as saving the world from nuclear disaster.

The busier she became, the less often she thought of drinking. That had been Tina's problem, Samantha told herself. Tina hadn't kept herself busy enough.

AND THEN ONE day, Samantha got a call that changed everything.

She was in the middle of arguing with Rosemary about homework while trying to get dinner cooked when the phone rang. She answered it on speaker so she could keep chopping.

'Hello?' she said, hoping it wasn't Trent ringing to say he was late. She had a school council finance subcommittee at six-thirty.

'Hello, Samantha.' It was Donna-Louise.

Samantha's heart sank. Her immediate thought was that Donna-Louise was going to pull out of Rosemary's dance recital on the weekend. She and Craig had managed to miss three of the four recitals since Rose began dancing. And while Rose never seemed to notice or care, Samantha took each absence as a personal affront.

'Hi, DL. Are you still okay for Saturday?' she asked cautiously.

'There's been a complication,' Donna-Louise replied, her tone sharper than Samantha's knife. 'Your father and I are separating.'

Samantha's knife stopped mid-air. 'You're what?' she asked.

'Separating. I'm moving to the Busselton house this weekend.'

Samantha put the knife down. 'Go watch television,' she

told Rosemary, who gleefully threw her pencil down and ran off to the lounge room without question.

'Why? What's happened?' she asked, taking the phone off speaker and holding it tight against her ear.

'Samantha,' Donna-Louise replied, her voice thin and tight, 'people rarely separate for reasons that are easily explained over the phone.'

'Oh, okay.' Samantha felt smacked down. 'Do you need help with the move?'

'I'll be fine.'

'And Dad?'

'He'll be fine, too. He always is,' Donna-Louise replied in a way that wasn't comforting in the slightest.

Samantha finished the conversation feeling shaken.

Her first instinct was to ring Trent, but the call went straight to voicemail. She left a message and then rang Craig, only to have that call go to voicemail, too. So she phoned Nicole.

'Dad and Donna-Louise are splitting up!' She was surprised to feel the sting of tears as the words came tumbling out of her mouth.

'What? Why?' Nicole asked.

'What a ridiculous question. As if anyone could just answer it over the phone,' she told her.

'It's a reasonable question,' Nicole replied. 'At least, I think it is.'

'It's ridiculous,' Samantha insisted, blinking her eyes furiously in an attempt to fight back the tears.

'Sammy, are you okay?'

'I'm chopping onions.'

'Is Dad okay?'

'I don't know. His phone is off. But Donna-Louise sounds okay, in case you were wondering.' She knew Donna-Louise would be the last thing on Nicole's mind and somehow that made her tears fall faster. 'They've been together, what, twenty years? Donna-Louise has been like another parent to us.'

'To you, you mean. She never liked me because I only ever messed up her stuff.'

There was an awkward pause, while Samantha sniffled.

'Does Mum know?' Nicole eventually asked.

That stopped the tears. 'I don't think it's any of her business.'

'I'll tell her.'

'This isn't idle gossip, Nicole.'

'I'll tell her,' Nicole repeated.

SAMANTHA RETRIEVED THE vodka from its hiding place after she ended the call. She couldn't remember the last time she'd pulled it out or even got close to pulling it out, but tonight was different. She needed something to settle the unexpected maelstrom inside her.

She poured a large slug into a tall tumbler and filled the rest with lemonade and ice. As she went to take a sip, something about the clink of the ice cubes against the glass annoyed her, so she scooped them out with a spoon.

The vodka felt soothing, like a warm hand on her cold chest.

'Can I have some lemonade?' Rosemary was at the kitchen bench, eyeing off the bottle of lemonade, but not the vodka.

'With your dinner,' Samantha replied, whisking both bottles away.

'Why not now?'

'Because.'

'But why are you allowed to have lemonade now and I'm not?' Rosemary argued. 'It's not fair that the grown-ups get to have all the treats.'

'You get plenty of treats.'

'But not when I want them. And I want lemonade now.'

'Well, you're not having lemonade now.'

'But why not? You're having some.'

'You're just not.'

'Dad would let me have some.'

This last punch of Rosemary's landed hard. Samantha always envied Trent's easy relationship with their daughter. Even though he was a soft touch, Rosemary never quite dominated him in the way that she tried to dominate her mother.

'Okay,' Samantha said, giving in, and Rosemary smiled.

The will of that child, thought Samantha. It was a miracle she didn't drink every day just to deal with her.

She finished preparing the dinner, occasionally sipping her drink and trying not to think about Donna-Louise and Craig. Instead, she thought of how sophisticated it felt to be drinking and cooking at the same time, like she was in a movie.

She'd just slid the pasta bake into the oven when the phone rang again.

'Hello?' she answered.

'Darling! Nicky told me the news. Are you okay?' It was Tina, evidently ringing from the pub, judging by all the noise in the background.

'Why wouldn't I be okay?' Samantha bristled. 'It's not my relationship that's breaking up.'

'It's just . . .' Tina's voice trailed away for a moment before returning. 'It's just that Donna-Louise was always like a mother to you.'

Samantha drank the last dregs of her drink and threw the insult back. 'Well, someone had to be.'

If Tina heard the insult, Samantha couldn't be sure, because at that very moment, there was an explosion of shouts in the background.

'Sorry, darling! The game's on. I don't know which game or even which sport, but it's all terribly exciting.'

There was another shout. Samantha began wondering why Tina had even bothered to ring her with all that commotion going on.

'Anyway, Nicole didn't seem to know why they'd split up,' Tina continued, raising her voice in an attempt to compete with the shouting. 'Do you?'

'No.' There was no way Samantha was going to gossip with her mother about this.

'I expect it's down to another one of Craig's broken promises,' she said before she was drowned out by an almighty tsunami of roars. 'Oh! We seem to have scored a goal, or a wicket, or something. I'd better go. Kisses!'

And with that, Tina hung up, leaving Samantha with nothing but the urge for another drink.

BY THE TIME Trent came home from work, she was three vodka lemonades down and had more vodka hidden in a *Hannah Montana* drink bottle in her bag for the walk to the finance subcommittee meeting.

'I got your message,' Trent said, kissing her lightly on the cheek. 'What happened? Do you know why they're breaking up? Is Craig going to keep the house?'

'Donna-Louise said she's moving to Busselton, but I don't know if that's forever.'

'Yeah, that makes sense. She loves that house with all its white furniture. Of course, the real question is how they'll sort out the golf club memberships. My guess is that Craig will keep the Mount Lawley membership and DL will keep the Busselton one. The Busselton club is very prestigious, you know.'

'What are you, their property lawyer?' Samantha was annoyed now, mostly with herself because her eyes were filling with tears again. 'It's too soon to be talking like that.'

'Are you okay?' Trent asked, looking at her properly for the first time since he'd got home.

'No. Yes. I . . . It's just . . .'

'It's just what?'

'It's just that I thought they would grow old together,' she found herself wailing, like a three-year-old.

Trent was clearly taken aback by her tears. 'I'm sorry, Sammy. I'm being a dick about all this. Of course, you're upset.' He stepped in to hug her, but Samantha only momentarily surrendered before pushing him away, worried that he would smell the alcohol on her breath.

'I have to get to that finance meeting,' she said.

THE FINANCE SUBCOMMITTEE meeting was at Dawn's house, just near the school. Samantha paused outside to drain *Hannah Montana*'s remaining contents and then pop some chewing gum in her mouth.

'Sorry, I'm late,' Samantha said, her breath all minty-fresh, when Dawn greeted her at the door.

'Don't worry. We've only just started,' Dawn told her as she led her into the dining room.

'Sorry, I'm late,' Samantha repeated to the rest of the committee. 'We had some bad news. Family stuff.'

The table looked at her, obviously expecting her to elaborate on the bad news, but when Samantha didn't say anything more, their eyes turned back to the print-outs in front of them.

'Now, where were we?' a man in a shapeless grey suit said. Samantha could never remember his name. Maybe Stewart.

'We're just looking at the draft balance sheet for Q3,' Dawn whispered as she handed Samantha some papers.

Samantha looked down at the pages in front of her but it was like the figures were flailing around in a sea of vodka.

'I have to go to the bathroom,' Samantha announced, standing up again. She did it so quickly that her chair fell backwards, making an almighty noise, like a gunshot in the quiet room.

'Whoops,' she said.

'Those chairs are weighted strangely,' Dawn said, helping Samantha pick the chair up again. 'The kids are always knocking them over.'

Samantha apologised and quickly made her way to the bathroom, her cheeks flushed. She was sure that the entire finance subcommittee now knew she was drunk.

In the bathroom, she sat on the closed toilet lid and considered her options. She could make up an excuse to go home or she could stay and make even more of a fool of herself. Both felt like things that Tina would do.

Samantha's eye caught a book tucked into the magazine rack next to the toilet. She pulled it out and looked at the cover. *The Secret.* She closed one eye so she could focus on the blurb on the back.

'You will come to know the true magnificence that awaits you in life,' the book promised her.

Maybe the vodka is my true magnificence, she thought. *Maybe I can stay without being a fool.*

She stuffed the book into her handbag and re-joined the meeting, her head held high.

While the others murmured about liabilities and assets and accruals, Samantha picked up the quarterly report, and, closing one eye again, looked at the page until a couple of numbers swam briefly into focus.

'Why doesn't the posted surplus from the profit–loss match the figure on the balance sheet?' she asked, trying as hard as she could to stop her words colliding.

'That's a good question,' Maybe Stewart said and Samantha felt a huge wave of relief. Even if she was quiet for the rest of the meeting, she'd made a contribution and they couldn't ask any more of her than that.

'Would you like some wine?' Dawn offered.

'No, I'm good,' Samantha said, still looking at the papers, even though the figures had now swum away again.

'Samantha doesn't drink,' someone else said to Dawn.

'That's right. I don't drink,' Samantha said in a loud voice, looking up at them all as if daring them to contradict her.

Nicole

Mum had led such a small life in such a small flat and yet, after days of sorting and chucking, I was overwhelmed by how much stuff remained. Samantha still wasn't talking to me and it felt too hard to do it on my own. But the thought of paying strangers to throw out the final remnants of my mother's life felt harder still.

And so the flat sat there, uncleared and untouched, for over a month.

When the second rent bill came in, Jethro finally cornered me on the subject.

'You know I'm happy to keep paying the rent for as long as you need me to,' he said. 'But you also know I'm happy to help, right?'

'You'd help me?' I said, surprised. 'But you're so busy at work.'

'Work schmerk,' he replied with a grin.

We worked all day filling garbage bags with junk: unopened sugar sachets, Aldi catalogues, broken pencils, pen lids, odd socks and laddered stockings, single playing cards long since separated from their pack, and a large collection of almost-empty jars of night cream.

'It's like she wasn't ever able to see a night cream through to the very end,' Jethro remarked, but I was busy examining a piece of jigsaw puzzle I'd just found wedged under the skirting board. A piece of sky.

'I'm glad Sam's not here to see this,' I said. 'Mum's blatant disregard for keeping jigsaws as complete sets used to drive her nuts. Which reminds me . . .'

I pulled my phone out of my pocket and rang Samantha. Again. The phone went straight to voicemail. Again.

'Did it even ring this time?' Jethro asked. He'd watched me call Samantha and get no response so many times it had become a kind of spectator sport for him.

I shook my head.

'She'll speak to you when she's ready,' Jethro assured me. But he didn't understand Samantha the way I did. 'Hey, did your dad get back to you about whether he wanted the wedding album?'

'Not yet,' I replied.

The truth was I hadn't called Dad at all. Ever since Samantha had told me about him cheating on Donna-Louise with Mum, I'd been avoiding him. I told myself that he was probably too caught up with planning the next round of IVF with Celine to notice.

'Your family,' Jethro said, shaking his head.

'My family,' I echoed, although it didn't feel like I had much family left.

As I carried out the last item from the flat – a jar lid I'd found jammed behind the toilet cistern – I paused at the door and looked back into the empty space. I'd helped Mum move in here, just after I'd moved out into Inverness Crescent with Kim and Tom and she'd given up the lease on our old flat in Morley. I remembered opening and closing the cupboard doors, all loose on their hinges, and kicking at some unsightly staining on the carpet, while Mum had flitted about, full of plans for decorating. The chaise longue here, a standard lamp over there, the restored 1950s sideboard against the wall.

'I've never had my own space,' she'd told me. 'I moved straight from home into the house with Craig and then you girls came along.'

Now, stripped of all its chaise longues, lamps and sideboards, the place looked even emptier and bleaker than it did before she moved in.

Now the place wore the absence of Tina.

I closed the door.

WHEN WE WERE almost home, Jethro announced he was going to run me a bath and cook me dinner.

'And then maybe we can finally sit down and look at those architectural plans together,' he said. 'The real estate agent rang about a house that's come up on Jutland Parade, right on the water, so it's officially crunch time. We need to decide if we're going to move or we're going to reno—' He was interrupted by my ringing phone.

'Hold that important thought,' I said. 'It's Trent. He might be calling about Sam. Hello?'

'Um, Nicole?' Trent's voice sounded strange. 'I'm ringing from the Royal Perth. Sammy's had a car accident.'

'What?' I said, my throat suddenly tight. 'Is she okay?'

'Yes, yes, she's fine,' he quickly reassured me and I felt my throat unclench. 'A couple of scratches. Nothing broken, except the car. They're just keeping her in overnight for observation.'

'Thank God,' I said. 'I'll go see her in the morning. We've been cleaning out Mum's flat all day and we're just getting home now.'

'Um, could you come now? When they pulled her from the car, they thought she was unconscious but she was . . . look, can you just come in? Please?'

The strangeness in Trent's voice set off an alarm bell somewhere inside me. 'Okay, okay. I'll come,' I told him.

'Is everything all right?' Jethro asked, the minute I hung up.

'Sam's had a car accident. She's fine, but she's at the Royal Perth and Trent wants me to go.'

'We just came from near there,' Jethro said, a little sulkily.

I sighed. 'I know. But he was being pretty insistent. I think . . . I think they're having problems, although neither of them will admit it to me.'

'It can't be easy being married to your sister,' Jethro said.

'It's hard enough being her sister and I don't have to live with her,' I agreed. 'Look, I tell you what: let's drop you back home and then I'll go to the hospital. I won't be there long, and I'll be back in time for dinner. We can look at the things together then.' I reached over and squeezed his arm. 'I promise.'

Jethro kept his eyes ahead, but his jaw was tight. 'I'm trying to be patient, Nic,' he said, his voice low. 'But we really need to sit down and make a decision. This is for us. This is for *you*.'

This was as close to having an argument as we had ever got.

'We put everything on hold while your mother was sick,' he continued. 'And then there was the funeral preparations and the wake to plan and then Celine was in hospital and then we had to sort out Tina's flat. And now this. It's like you can never put yourself first. Ever. There's always someone else at the top of your list.'

I thought of all the times that I'd bent to Samantha's will, that I'd dropped everything for Tina or Dad, that I hadn't spoken up for myself. I had no idea what I wanted or needed because I had been too busy helping everyone around me get what *they* wanted and needed.

'You're right,' I said. He *was* right.

'Why is that, Nic?' Jethro asked. 'Your dad and your sister have no problem putting themselves first. Even Tina was pretty good at it. Why can't you?'

One memory in particular came into sharp relief.

'It's so silly,' I said, surprised by the sudden swell of tears in my eyes. 'It's because of *Young Talent Time.*'

'What?'

We had arrived home by now. Jethro pulled the car into the drive and turned off the engine.

'You remember that accident I told you about, when I was eleven?' I asked him.

'Yes, I remember.' His voice was quiet now.

'Well, just before the accident, I hassled Mum about getting to Kalgoorlie in time for *Young Talent Time.* It was my favourite show and I didn't want to miss it.'

He frowned. 'I don't get it. How is this related to the accident?'

'Well,' I started and then swallowed hard so the emotion in my throat didn't choke me. 'As I said, I hassled Mum and I'm pretty certain she was speeding to get us there on time.'

The tears started to spill from my eyes. I knew I really was being silly, but my shame in that moment was so great, I couldn't even look at him.

'Wait a minute,' he said. 'Do you think that's why Tina

crashed the car? Because she was trying to get to Kalgoorlie in time for a TV show?'

I nodded, my tears still falling.

Jethro breathed out. 'Well, even if that was true, even if Tina really was speeding because of *Young Talent Time*, it's still not your fault. It was *her* choice. *She* was the driver. *She* was the adult.'

He reached for my arm. I had never said any of this to anyone else and now that I had, now that I had pulled those words and thoughts out of the darkness and into the light, I could see how senseless it was to have blamed myself all this time. I found myself sobbing, releasing a great surge of emotion as Jethro gathered me into his arms.

'I *do* want to have a house that feels like ours, not some leftover from your previous marriage,' I told him. 'I really do. But it's like desire just sits in my throat, it's something I can't swallow or even spit out. The only time I can remember really trying to do something just for me was when I got pregnant when I was with Darren. And we know how that turned out.'

Jethro hugged me even tighter. 'You were alone then, but you're not alone now,' he told me. 'I'm here.'

I nodded and kept my head down, buried in the softness of his shirt.

I FOUND TRENT at the nurse's station. He was pacing back and forth, like a character in a movie. He looked angry.

He stopped pacing when he saw me. 'You're here,' he said. 'Good. I've got to pick up Rosemary but I didn't want to leave Sam alone in the hospital.'

'So why are you out here?' I said, looking around for Samantha. 'Is she ready to go home?'

'No, she's still in her room. I just can't bear to be in there with her.'

'What?' I was really confused now.

He looked at her, his face hard. 'Your sister crashed the car because she was *drunk*.' He spat out the word like it was something foul-tasting he'd put in his mouth by accident.

'Drunk?' I blinked.

'Yes, drunk. Off her face. She registered a reading almost twice the legal limit.'

I blinked again. 'But Samantha doesn't drink.'

Trent gave another angry laugh. 'I know, right? She certainly gives the rest of us a hard time about drinking, even when it's just a fucking light beer at a fucking picnic, and then she goes and does something as reckless as this. Thank God Rosemary wasn't in the car.'

'What?'

'Rose's car broke down again and she texted Sam to pick her up. Sam was on her way. The police reckon she was speeding and took a corner too fast, or something, because she lost control and slammed the car into a traffic light pole. The pole won.'

'And they're sure that Sam was really that drunk?'

'Yep.' Trent gave a sharp nod. 'I told them she didn't drink and they said they were surprised she'd been able to function at all with that much alcohol in her system. They said . . .' His voice faltered.

'What did they say?'

'They said they had assumed she was a regular drinker.'

In that moment, everything in that brightly lit corridor slid away. Memories, half-forgotten, half-repressed, began to rise to the surface of my mind, like something finally coming to the boil. I remembered Samantha lying on the floor at that high school party, looking the happiest and most relaxed I had ever seen her. I remembered the tequila bottle with the little red hat from that New Year's Eve. And the booze-soaked flowers in our bin and the taste of vodka in her drink at The Queens. I remembered other, tiny things, all enveloped in the overwhelming scent of peppermint that Samantha always had on her breath.

My own breath now caught in my throat with the full realisation that with all my worrying about Samantha and Trent's marriage, I had missed the real problem: my teetotal sister was an alcoholic.

'Jesus,' I said.

Trent just nodded, as if he knew exactly what I was thinking.

'Go get Rosemary,' I told him. 'I'll stay with Sam. I'll talk to her.'

EVEN THOUGH SAMANTHA'S room was on a different floor and in a different ward, it looked like the room Mum had been in when she'd first fallen sick. It wasn't helping that Samantha was lying on her back, eyes closed and chest rising and falling, just like Mum's. I began to panic that I was losing Samantha as well, by being inattentive, by letting things slip past me. By never opening my arms in time to catch anything.

I took a deep breath and reminded myself that Samantha wasn't Mum. It wasn't too late. Samantha could be saved.

After a few minutes of watching her, I began to suspect Samantha was faking sleep. There was something about the tension in her body and the exaggerated way she was breathing.

'You're awake,' I said.

Her eyes opened. 'How could you tell?'

'I remember how you used to fake being asleep on the couch when you were little so Mum would carry you to bed,' I said.

'Trent came in before and I managed to fool him.'

You've been fooling us all for years, I wanted to say. But instead, I just said, 'Tell me.'

Samantha sat up slowly. 'Tell you what?'

'Tell me everything.'

'Everything?' Samantha said and then gave a small, rueful laugh, like I'd asked her the impossible.

I stood my ground. 'Okay. Then start by telling me what happened today.'

'There's nothing to tell,' Samantha said, looking at me, daring me to push her further.

This was the point where I'd normally back down, make my excuses and leave, and she knew it. But not this time. I wasn't going to let this go. I wasn't going to lose her.

'That's bullshit and you know it,' I said.

Samantha held my gaze and, while we continued to stare at each other for what felt like years, I stuck my right thumbnail into the palm of my other hand. I needed some pain to focus on to stop me from walking away.

Eventually, to my surprise, Samantha caved. 'Fine,' she said. 'I'll tell you.'

I released my thumbnail from my palm. 'Okay,' I said. 'Thank you.'

Samantha took a deep breath. 'I was angry today about a lot of things,' she said. 'Little things. Silly things. But there were a lot of them. There was stuff at work—misfiled paperwork, computer problems, someone had taken my cup. And then I got home and Rosemary stormed out after a ridiculous fight about two-minute noodles stuck to the microwave door and then Trent rang me from the pub – he'd forgotten to tell me he had drinks after work – and the TV remote was missing and, well, I started drinking earlier than I . . .' She stopped herself. 'I drank a lot.

I drank so much that I don't remember getting Rosemary's text about her car. I don't remember texting her back or even leaving the house. I don't remember getting into the car or turning the key in the ignition or backing the car out of the driveway or driving down the road. Even the moment I hit that pole feels like it was something I watched in a movie a long time ago.'

I wanted so much to reach across and hug her but I was worried it might stop her from talking. I needed to know everything.

'So,' I said, trying to keep my voice as calm as possible. 'I'm guessing this isn't the first time.'

'It's the first time that I've driven when drunk, but no, it's not the first time I've been drunk.' She lifted her head and looked me square in the eye again, but this time without the defiance. 'I've been drinking for years, Nicole. At night, when nobody is watching. And during the day, when nobody is noticing. I drink and drink and drink and drink.'

'Does Trent know?'

Samantha shook her head. 'I don't think so. Nobody knows. Half the time, I pretend not to know as well.'

'Why didn't you tell anyone? Why didn't you let us help you?'

'I don't know,' Samantha said. She tensed her jaw for a moment and then relaxed. 'Actually, I *do* know. It was because I didn't want to admit I was like Tina.'

I thought of Mum, full of laughter and joy, dancing barefoot in the lounge room, a drink in one hand. Whatever Samantha was doing was nothing like Mum.

'I have all these rules that I stick to, that separate me from Tina. I even have a points system,' she said, and then gave that same rueful laugh again. 'Points! Like I'm on some kind of Weight Watchers program.'

Trust Samantha to be an organised alcoholic, I thought.

'And then when Tina died, I said fuck the points and fuck the rules. And I've gone and broken all of them. Including drink-driving, the one rule I swore I would never break. And now . . . what if Rose had been in the car? What if . . .'

Samantha put her hands over her face and started to cry. I felt like doing the same, but I held myself together. 'We'll get you the help you need,' I said. 'The best counselling.'

Samantha removed her hands and the fear on her face reminded me of her as a little girl, crying on her bed while our parents shouted in the hallway. I couldn't remember hugging her or comforting her back then. All I probably did was pick up another book and run away inside my head to another world.

'I should have been a better sister,' I told her. 'I knew there was something going on with you but I let myself believe it was a different problem altogether.'

'I'm not the easiest person to help,' Samantha admitted.

'And I haven't been the most helpful person,' I replied.

She looked at me again for the briefest of moments and then she shut her eyes.

'Trent has gone home,' I said quietly.

'I know. I'm not sure he'll be able to forgive me a second time.'

'A second time?'

Samantha didn't answer. We sat in silence and I thought of Mum's flat as it was now, cold and empty. I knew right then I couldn't leave my sister. I knew that I would have to ring Jethro and explain everything and I knew that he would be disappointed, maybe even angry again, but I hoped that he would come to understand. I knew, too, that he would be in bed and asleep by the time I got home, and that I'd crawl in next to him in the darkness and feel his warm body against mine. And I knew that tomorrow, he and I would wake together and we would finally make a decision about whether to move or renovate, and that we would be happy together wherever we lived for a very long time. I knew all this with a certainty that I had never felt before.

'Would you like me to sit with you for a while?' I asked Samantha.

'Yes,' Samantha said. 'I don't want to be alone.'

She still didn't open her eyes, but she held out her hand.

I took it and held it until she really was asleep.

Piece #19: 2001

THE MINUTE ROSEMARY started sleeping through the night, Trent started talking about having another baby and Samantha secretly went back on the pill.

At first she told herself that she was just creating a short-term (but necessary) buffer between Trent's enthusiasm for a second child and the reality of one. But by the end of the year, she had neither stopped taking the pill nor told Trent that she was taking it. She filed the guilt away in that dark space where all the other guilt lived.

'Look at the little angel's face,' Trent said, gazing at Rosemary asleep on the couch in front of *Hi-5*. He was conveniently overlooking the fact that she had just screamed herself to the point of exhaustion because she wasn't allowed to open the presents under the tree that weren't hers.

'She shouldn't be sleeping now. She's going to throw the whole schedule out,' Samantha observed as she carefully packed the contentious presents into two bags: one for the brunch at Trent's parents' house and one for lunch at Nicole's.

'Uh, she woke us up at four-thirty to see if Santa came. I think we can all agree there *is* no schedule today,' he replied. 'We should just let the little angel sleep while we get ready.'

He started helping her pack the bags. 'Seriously, Sammy, she's such a great kid,' he said. 'We're doing so well even though we've got no idea what we're doing. Imagine what perfection we'll be able to achieve the second time around!'

Samantha remembered with a jolt that she hadn't taken her pill that morning.

'Um, I think we're missing a couple of presents,' she told Trent. 'Can you go check the top of the wardrobe to see if I've left some there?'

'Sure. But *seriously*, Sammy,' he said as he headed up the stairs, 'we owe it to humanity to have another child.'

As she quickly fished out her contraceptive pills from the zipped compartment of her handbag, Samantha tried to imagine any perfection coming from having a second child but could only sense a deepening imperfection in herself.

She placed the pill on her tongue and swallowed it without water. There was something about feeling it travel down her throat that reassured her.

'Nah, there's nothing there.' Trent was already heading down the stairs so Samantha hastily shoved the pill packet into her bag.

'Did you look properly?' she asked him, annoyed that she hadn't been able to return the pills to their special compartment. It was another thing she'd need to remember to do later.

'Of course I did,' Trent replied. 'Are you sure you didn't hide any somewhere else? Like inside our wardrobe?'

Samantha tensed up. 'No, I would have asked you to check there if I had,' she replied sharply.

'They'll turn up eventually,' Trent shrugged. 'Shall we start loading the car?'

Samantha nodded, but her mind was now on the vodka bottle stashed under the false floor of the wardrobe. Since the previous New Year's, she had been drinking maybe once or twice a week, on the nights Trent was out or working late. She would sit in the dark lounge room, enjoying the silence and the physical freedom that came from not having Rosemary's small hands pulling at her. And she would drink – vodka, mostly, as it left hardly any trace on her breath and she could mix it with a bit of orange juice, in case Trent came home early. Not that he ever did. She was always in bed before he got back and then up again with Rosemary at shit o'clock to watch ABC Kids and drink black coffee. By the time Trent woke up, she felt almost human again, albeit a human filled with regret and self-loathing.

To offset the regret, Samantha kept to some very clear rules:
1. She didn't drink every night.
2. She never drank before Rosemary was in bed asleep.
3. She never mixed spirits.
4. She never let the drink get in the way of a tidy and well-run house.
5. She never ever drank and drove.
6. She didn't interact with anyone else while she was drinking, unless she absolutely couldn't avoid it.

The last two rules were particularly important. She'd always regarded drink-driving as one of the worst things a person could do. And she didn't like the way her voice came out of her mouth when she was drunk, all thick and syrupy.

It sounded too much like Tina's voice when she used to tuck Samantha and Nicole into bed at night, the voice she still used whenever Samantha rang her after midday any day of the week.

Samantha knew that if she kept to her rules, she would not be like Tina. And she was managing to keep to the rules. Just. Another baby, however, might push her over some edge. Another baby might turn her into Tina completely.

WHEN THEY ARRIVED at Trent's parents' house, it didn't take long for his mother, Barb, to corner Samantha and echo Trent's call for a second child.

'I've been thinking that Rosemary could do with a little friend,' Barb said, following Samantha into the kitchen, a drink in her hand. Everyone was drinking Moët in tall flutes as they opened their presents. Everyone except Samantha, who was drinking tea out of a mug that said *Don't let the turkeys get you down.*

'Someone she can moan about you to when she's older,' Barb continued, even though Samantha had barely acknowledged what she'd said. 'Trent says he doesn't talk to his brothers about us, about me, but I don't believe him. The only time I ever talk to my siblings is to moan about my parents, and they've both been dead for five years.'

Samantha poured herself some more tea. 'We have time,' she told Barb. 'I'm still young.'

'You don't want too many years in between them. And you won't be young forever,' Barb warned. 'Nobody likes an old mother.'

Samantha sipped her tea and pretended it had a huge slug of gin in it. Her relationship with Barb had always been polite, friendly even. But since she'd had Rosemary, it had felt like Barb had been suddenly promoted to line manager, constantly reviewing her work and giving her tips on how she could do better.

'Let's get back to the others,' Samantha suggested.

'Yes, let's. I'm just going to grab another bottle of bubbly,' she said, wrenching the fridge open. 'Also, I've been thinking . . . isn't it time Rose stopped wearing nappies at night?'

'YOUR MOTHER IS even pushier with her advice when she's drunk,' Samantha observed, as they pulled the car out onto the road. They were already half an hour late for lunch at Nicole's house. Not that it mattered. Nicole would probably still be peeling the potatoes when they arrived.

'You shouldn't let her bother you,' Trent replied from the back seat, where he was sitting to amuse Rosemary. 'I've mastered the art of switching my brain to a mode that makes her mostly sound like white noise. Or like the teacher in *Peanuts*, all *wah-wah-wah-wah*.'

Rosemary clapped her hands with delight. 'Wah-wah-wah!' she echoed.

Samantha ignored her. 'Well, now she's hassling me about having another baby.'

'Did you tell her we've been trying? Speaking of which, perhaps we could leave Rose with Nicole after lunch and go home to try a bit harder . . .'

He reached out to touch her shoulder but she shrugged him off.

'Don't be ridiculous,' she said. 'It's Christmas.'

'Chrissmasss!' Rosemary exclaimed. 'I'm getting more presssennntttsss!'

'Yes, baby girl, you sure are going to get some more presents,' Trent told her, before turning back to Samantha. 'Do you think it might be time to make an appointment with someone? To check everything is, um, okay?'

'What do you mean?'

'Maybe that emergency caesarean stuffed up your, um, how do you say, plumbing?'

'My complex reproductive system is just plumbing to you?'

'You know what I mean.'

'I suppose I do,' she said. She was feeling tetchy now. 'Well, in answer to your rather badly put question, I think it's just time. We don't need help.' She rubbed her temple.

'Are you having one of your headaches?'

'I'm okay.'

'You should take something.'

'I don't have anything.'

'You always have something,' he laughed, as he reached forward and plunged his hand deep into her handbag on the passenger seat.

'Don't go through my bag,' she said, now panicked.

But it was too late. Trent's hand emerged from her bag holding the foil packet, its little coloured pills all round and intact, except for one empty row that she'd already taken.

'What. The. Fuck,' Trent said, each word falling like a ten-tonne weight onto the car.

'Trent—'

'Faahk!' Rosemary shouted, now clapping her hands with demonic glee. 'Daddy said faahk!'

'Rose! That's a bad word,' Samantha said, trying to catch Rosemary's eye in the rear-view mirror.

'Faahk! Faahk!'

'No, seriously, Samantha, what the actual fuck?' Trent

repeated, over the din. 'When were you going to tell me about this? I thought we were trying to have another baby!'

'I meant to . . .' She couldn't even finish the sentence. She hadn't meant anything other than to never get pregnant again.

'Pull over,' he said loudly, while Rosemary continued to clap and say *faahk*.

'We're almost at Nic's.'

'Pull over!' He was shouting now. 'I'm not going to Nicole's, I'm going home.'

'Daddy?' Rosemary said, and went quiet.

'Daddy's going for a long walk,' Trent told her.

Samantha stopped at the kerb and Trent got out without another word, slamming the door behind him.

'Trent, stop!' She wrenched her door open and ran after him.

'How long?' Trent turned to look at her, his face twisted with anger. 'How long have you been taking them?'

'Since February,' she admitted.

'The whole fucking time?'

Samantha nodded. She was on the very edge of the precipice now and it was time to jump. 'I don't want another baby, Trent.'

There. She finally said it. The relief of finally shedding one of the terrible secrets she'd been carrying around was so overwhelming, she felt giddy.

'So why didn't you just say so? You've had, what, ten months to tell me? But instead, you let me believe that we wanted the same thing.'

'I—'

'That's fucked up, Samantha. We're married. We're meant to be on the same team, not working against each other. What else have you been hiding from me?'

Samantha opened her mouth, ready to jump again, ready to tell him about the tequila bottle with the little red hat and the vodka and all the nights of self-erasure, but then Rosemary started crying from the car. Samantha closed her mouth. Instead, she put her hand on Trent's arm. She needed to feel his skin, she needed to regain control of the situation. 'Come back to the car, come to Christmas lunch. We can talk about this properly later.'

'I don't want to be around you right now,' Trent said. It was his turn to shrug her hand off.

Samantha watched him go and then slowly returned to the car and her screaming child. She sat in the driver's seat, clutching the steering wheel, wondering what to do. She was too tired to go after Trent. She was also too tired to face Tina at Nicole's house without Trent by her side. But if she went home and Rosemary refused to have a nap while Trent was still AWOL, she wasn't sure if she could cope. At least at Nicole's, she might be able to sneak in her own nap while her sister looked after Rose.

'Let's go see Aunty Nic and Grammy Tina,' she said, once Rosemary had calmed down enough to hear her. 'Won't that be fun?'

'I want Daddy,' Rosemary said tearfully.

'I want . . .' Samantha had no idea how to end that sentence. She clenched her jaw and started the car up again, revving the engine a little to drown out Rosemary's sniffling. 'Let's go have ourselves some Christmas!'

At the mention of the word 'Christmas', Rosemary's tears instantly dried up.

'Did Santa go to Aunty Nic's house?' she asked.

'Yes, Santa went to Aunty Nic's house,' Samantha replied, hoping to God that Nicole had pulled her finger out and made an effort.

But at Nicole's, there was no sign of Christmas. No decorations, not even a tree. Not even a sign of Nicole. Just Tina, in the lounge room, looking like the Ghost of Christmas

Past, her make-up already smudged a little, with the inevitable drink in her hand.

'Hello!' Tina said brightly.

Rosemary lingered warily at the front door. 'Where's Christmas?'

'Where's Nic?' Samantha asked. The chance of a nap felt even further away than ever and she felt so very, very tired.

'In bed.'

'In bed?' Nicole didn't have children. She had no excuse to be in bed.

'Lucky I came early and put the ham in the oven,' Tina said. 'I'm hoping it's not still frozen in the middle. Where's Troy?'

'Trent.'

'Where's Trent?'

'We . . . we had a fight,' Samantha said and before she could stop herself, she added, 'I think we might be breaking up.'

As she said it, she realised it might be true, and she burst into tears. When Tina put her drink down – *actually* put it down – to give her a hug, the tears came even harder.

Piece #20: 2001

ABOUT SIX WEEKS after her last break-up with Darren, Nicole bought a pregnancy test. Her period, which usually arrived every twenty-eight days without fail and was the only part of her life that could be relied upon, was about three weeks late.

While she waited for the result, she imagined what it might be like to have a baby and whether it would be easier with or without Darren around. She thought of the times she'd babysat Rosemary and how Rosemary had cried and cried and how utterly helpless she'd felt, and then she imagined feeling like that twenty-four hours a day, 365 days a year, across the lifetime of a child. It would be hard to do it on her own. But then she thought about Darren and the way he jutted out his jaw whenever she failed to do something the way he liked it, which was more often than either of them was comfortable with, and she wondered if it might actually be easier without him.

She picked up the stick and saw the blue line and she knew, Darren or no Darren, that nothing would ever be easy again.

WHEN SHE WENT to Tina's place for Sunday dinner three weeks – and four more pregnancy tests – later, she was still pregnant. She hadn't told anyone. Not Darren. Not Tina. Not any of her friends at the bar she worked at, mostly because they were all a decade younger than she was and were likely to freak out. And certainly not Samantha. In the last conversation they'd had, before Nicole knew she was pregnant, Samantha had been talking about motherhood like it was something you needed an advanced degree in. Nicole didn't want Samantha to make her feel like she couldn't do it.

While the roast finished cooking, they sat down in front of Tina's current jigsaw. It was a European streetscape from the 1970s featuring lolly-coloured buildings and men standing around in flares.

'I haven't seen you in a few weeks,' Tina said. 'Is everything okay?'

'I've been busy,' Nicole replied. Hiding in her flat and taking pregnancy tests had certainly taken up a lot of her time.

'It's a busy time of year,' Tina said. 'I'm organising the Kris Kringle at the pub this year. Every year, I swear I'll never do it again, but by the time November comes around, I've forgotten the pain.' She poured herself some wine. 'A bit like childbirth.'

'I'll stick with water,' Nicole said, as Tina went to pour some into her glass. 'I've . . . got a headache.'

Tina raised an eyebrow but said nothing. Instead, she asked, 'How's That Darren?'

'I wouldn't know. It's been over two months since we broke up. This time it might stick.'

'Oh, well,' Tina said, sitting back in her seat. 'It's probably for the best. Although I'll miss having him around at parties. It's been nice not always being the worst-behaved person in the room.'

Nicole gave a small smile. Tina had once said Darren had the social delicacy of a Pritikin scone. Darren himself blamed it on his time in Japan, but that was now over six years ago, and Nicole had started to suspect he had always been that way.

She started rummaging through the puzzle box while Tina connected pieces of sky. Most people left the sky until the very end, but Tina always liked to tackle it first.

'Mum,' she said, as she fished a blue piece out of the box and placed it on the board. 'Do you ever wish you'd broken up with Dad earlier? You know, before you had kids?'

'And not have had you and Sammy? No. Never.'

'Okay, pretend for a moment that you were able to have had both of us, but without Dad knowing, without him in the picture.'

'I couldn't have done that to your father,' Tina said, as she held her wine glass up to the light and swirled the red liquid around. 'While he and I disappointed each other terribly, you two have never disappointed us. Not at all. You two are the best of both of us and I couldn't have denied him that.' She took a sip from her glass and then set it down on the table. 'Why do you ask?'

'I was just wondering.'

Tina looked at her for a moment and then turned back to the jigsaw.

'Ooh, these two bits of cloud fit together,' she said, suddenly delighted.

*

THAT NIGHT, NICOLE sat in her small unit in Inglewood and treated herself to a latest release video, *Bridget Jones's Diary*. She watched it from the two-seater IKEA couch she and Darren had put together during one of their happier periods, when it looked like he might be moving in for good. She remembered how she had made sure not to drop the allen key, not even once, and, as a result, Darren hadn't shouted at her at all.

As she watched the final scene of the film where Bridget Jones runs out in the snow in her underwear, Nicole realised she was the same age as Bridget, and yet Nicole had never been close to making a grand gesture like that. She'd let Darren come and go like he was a cat, not the love of her life. Maybe, she thought, the reason he had never really given himself to her is that she had never asked anything of him.

So she decided to tell him about the pregnancy.

After a few attempts to reach him on his mobile, she rang his parents' house.

'I'll get him for you,' Darren's mother said, reluctantly. She put her hand over the phone, but Nicole could still hear her say, 'It's Whatsherface.'

Whatsherface. She and Darren had been dating on and off for almost six years and she was still Whatsherface. She wondered if being pregnant with Darren's child would finally elevate her to something more.

'Hello?' Darren said. He sounded pissed off.

'Darren, can we meet?'

'We've broken up.'

'Yes, I know we've broken up. There's just something I need to tell you.'

'I don't need any of the stuff I left behind. Give it to charity. Like you did last time.' He still hadn't forgiven her for the time she'd given his Steely Dan and Phil Collins-era Genesis records to the Salvos, even though she'd rung him five times to collect them.

'This is another thing. Something a bit more complicated,' she told him. 'I'm pregnant. We're having a baby.'

In her mind, she was running after him wearing her underwear in the snow, making that grand gesture.

There was a long pause on the other end of the phone, followed by the sound of Darren clearing his throat, like he was about to make his own big announcement.

'How do you know it's mine?' he finally said.

Her heart sank. 'You know it's yours.'

Darren knew perfectly well that he was only the third person she'd ever slept with.

'I need to think about this,' he said.

'Thinking about it does nothing. It won't make me less pregnant. I want to be with you. I want us to do this together.'

'I need to think about this,' he repeated. 'I'll ring you back.'

And with that, he hung up, leaving Nicole to listen to the dial tone for so long that it turned into beeps.

DARREN NEVER RANG her back. After a few days of tears, Nicole told herself she didn't care. She had done the right thing by letting him know. The rest was up to him.

Instead, she focused on being happy about the pregnancy. She stopped thinking of her babysitting disasters with Rosemary and instead remembered happier times, like taking Rosemary to the park and how people had smiled at the two of them, thinking that Rosemary was hers. In those moments, she'd felt like she belonged to something and to somebody. And so she began to feel excited about the baby that was growing inside her and the sense of belonging that baby would bring. Maybe having this child was her grand gesture for herself.

More and more, she found herself looking at baby clothes and baby things in children's shops, turning their delicate wonder around in her large hands. But she never bought any of them, out of some vague sense of superstition. Her only transgression was the impulse purchase of a ceramic cookie jar in the shape of Cookie Monster's head. The minute she saw it, she imagined her future self, doling out cookies and comfort to a small child, who looked up at her as if she were the whole world.

While the woman behind the counter wrapped the cookie jar up in newspaper, she found herself saying, 'It's for my child.'

'That's nice,' the woman said. She obviously sold a lot of things for people's children.

THE BLEEDING STARTED early on Christmas Eve. She was at the supermarket, trying to choose cranberry sauce for lunch the next day, when she felt a wetness between her legs. She surreptitiously touched the crotch of her shorts and found a pink metallic-smelling stickiness that sent her heart plummeting. On the way to the hospital, the taxi driver ranted about asylum seekers and property prices while she sat quietly in the back seat, her thighs pressed together. She'd forgotten to recharge her phone overnight and she wondered if she should call someone, probably Darren, before it died completely. He was the only person who knew she was pregnant.

On the footpath outside emergency, she dialled his number.

'Darren, I think I'm miscarrying,' she told his voicemail. 'I'm at Charlie Gairdner and my phone's almost out of battery. Come if you can. Please.'

By the end of the message, she couldn't hide her tears or her panic.

Inside the hospital, there were questions to answer and forms to fill. 'Are you here with anyone?' the admissions clerk asked.

'No,' she replied, clutching her phone, now completely dead, tightly in her hand.

She was entirely on her own.

AS SHE WAS prepped for surgery a few hours later, there was still no sign of Darren. Hospital staff came and went with forms for her to sign and talk of curettes and incompetent cervixes. She couldn't focus on what they were saying. All she could think about was her happiness seeping out of her, along with all that blood.

'Is there someone we can call?' one nurse asked. 'You'll need someone to collect you after the procedure and stay with you at home for the first twelve hours.'

Nicole started to give Darren's number, but then paused. She thought of him jutting out his chin when he saw her or, worse yet, not coming at all.

'No, you should ring my mum,' she said. 'But there's no point ringing her at home. Try the Ambassador's Tavern in Bassendean.'

As the anaesthetic started to take effect, she embraced its nothingness.

AFTERWARDS, IT TOOK a while to work out where she was and why she was there. She felt as fragile as one of those eggshells she used to paint with Tina at Easter, the ones with all the insides blown out of them. She tried to stay as still as she possibly could so that she didn't collapse in on herself and become dust.

Tina arrived just before six, stinking of the pub, but with a change of clothes and a small bunch of red roses.

'My baby,' she said when she saw Nicole.

My baby, Nicole thought, and she burst into tears.

'It's going to be all right,' Tina said, rushing in to hug her, and Nicole accepted the embrace and the platitude. 'They said I'm allowed to take you home after the doctor checks you. Shall we get Sam to pick us up?'

Nicole shook her head. She didn't want to see her sister just yet. Like Darren, Samantha might say something that would make Nicole feel like the miscarriage was all her fault.

IT WAS ONLY as she and Tina were in the taxi home, watching the Christmas lights and decorations in shop windows go by, that Nicole remembered her abandoned shopping list.

'What time do the shops shut?' she asked the taxi driver.

'There's a supermarket on Guildford Road that might still be open,' the driver said. 'Otherwise, I could take you over to Karrinyup. I think the shops are open until midnight there.'

Nicole thought of all the people who would be at Karrinyup, all the babies crying in their prams, and she knew she couldn't do it.

'Let's try Guildford Road,' she said.

They pulled up outside the supermarket just as it was about to close.

'I'll go in for you,' Tina suggested.

'I said I would host,' Nicole replied firmly, as she pulled herself gingerly out of the cab. She wanted to get at least one thing right.

'Do you have any hams?' she shouted at the first staff member she saw when she stepped through the automatic doors. She felt like she was in one of those movies where the world was ending.

The guy shrugged. 'Maybe in the freezer section.'

There was one left. Black and Gold brand. She snatched it up and, then, as an afterthought, grabbed a packet of potato gems and a bag of frozen peas.

'You got something special planned for Chrissie?' the checkout chick said, with a sideways glance at the hospital tag still around her wrist.

'Very special,' Nicole replied, dumping the frozen goods on the conveyor belt. It wasn't the Christmas feast she had planned, but it would have to do.

Back in the taxi, Tina was waiting patiently.

'Did you get what you need?' she asked.

'Not really,' Nicole replied, now exhausted. She thought of Tina fussing over her back in her small flat, asking her questions or, worse yet, not asking her questions and trying to pretend nothing had happened, and she realised she needed to be alone.

'Mum, I think we should drop you back home,' she said.

'But the nurses said—'

'I don't care what the nurses said. I just need to sleep.'

'Okay,' Tina said. 'But I'll come over first thing in the morning.'

'Okay,' Nicole echoed. She gave the driver Tina's address and then leant her head against the car window and let the world fall away behind her.

BACK AT HOME, Nicole put the ham in the sink to defrost. Samantha was going to flip if she found out it was Black and Gold brand, but she would just have to deal with it. At least, Nicole thought, Rosemary would be thrilled with the potato gems.

She caught sight of her reflection in the kitchen window and stopped. Her own little Rosemary was gone. Those walks to the park would never happen. And she felt foolish to have thought they ever would.

She picked up her mobile phone, now charging, and stared at its message-less screen. Darren was probably out somewhere celebrating the fact he didn't have to have a baby with her. She placed her phone face down and turned her attention to the wine sitting on the kitchen counter. It was the nice bottle she'd been given at work that she'd saved for Tina and Trent to drink at Christmas lunch, while she did the right thing with Samantha and abstained. But now she wanted to do the wrong thing and drink the entire bottle to rid herself of her foolish dreams.

With the Christmas lights from the house across the road flashing gently, she poured some wine into the largest glass she could find. All the while Cookie Monster's head watched her from the top shelf, admonishing her for her greed.

Samantha

A T MY THIRD therapy session, I asked if I could lie on the couch. This seemed to please Linda, my therapist.

'Of course,' she replied, with the kind of small smile that promised something and yet gave nothing away.

I liked Linda a lot. She had a severe silver bob, just like Donna-Louise, but her face was softer. She exuded a kind of warmth and openness that I'd always wished Donna-Louise had.

'Do you like it when people ask if they can lie on the couch?' I asked her, as I slipped off my shoes.

'Are you asking to lie on the couch because you think it will please me?'

I shrugged and stretched out along the couch. It felt good.

'How are you feeling today?' Linda asked.

'Okay. I wanted to drink last night but I didn't. Partly

because my cover has been blown. When nobody knew I drank, I could fly under the radar, but now Rosemary is watching me like a hawk. No matter what I'm doing, she's watching. I'm not sure she'll ever trust me again. I know Trent will never trust me again.'

'Will *you* ever trust yourself again?'

'I don't know.'

'Have you seen Trent?'

After a week or so of Trent sleeping in the spare room, he'd finally packed up his things and gone to his parents' house the previous week. Although I hadn't admitted it to anyone, our townhouse no longer felt like home. Without him, it was just a place to eat and sleep.

'We've spoken on the phone a few times and exchanged messages. He says maybe we'll catch up for dinner next week.'

I'd hated it when Trent had used the term 'catch up' because it made me feel like a work colleague, not his wife.

'What was the other reason for not drinking?'

'What do you mean?'

'You said before that everyone knowing was only partly the reason.'

'Oh. Um, I guess, because my drinking problem isn't a secret anymore, I can't pretend to myself it's not a problem. If you know what I mean.'

'Hm,' was all Linda said as she wrote something on her notepad. 'Have you told your father about your drinking yet?'

'No. I haven't spoken to him at all.' Dad had rung me a few times since the accident, but hadn't left a message.

Linda wrote more things on her notepad.

'You've been able to tell your husband and your daughter and your sister, but not your father. Why do you think that is?' she asked me.

I shrugged again. 'I guess I'm still angry at him for cheating on Donna-Louise with Tina. Tina! Of all people!'

'And you're not angry at your mother?'

'Yes, but not just about that.' There was a well of unlabelled emotion in my chest reserved for Tina.

Linda looked back through her notes. 'You told me last week that you always thought your father left your mother because of her alcoholism. Do you think there's a part of you that thinks he might reject you if he knows about yours?'

I started to disagree but stopped myself. This was a new way of looking at my determination not to be like Tina that I hadn't considered before. I closed my mouth and focused on the ceiling rose instead.

'You know, Nicole used to say that she could see faces in the ceiling rose in the bedroom we shared, that they were our friends looking down on us, protecting us,' I told Linda. 'I don't know why she said that. It's just plaster.'

I knew I was trying to change the subject. It was a tactic that usually worked, but not in this room. Linda didn't say anything. She just let the silence grow.

'You think I should talk to Dad, don't you?' I finally said. Something in me felt like a surly teenager being asked to fold laundry.

'And why do you think I would think that?'

'You always answer my questions with another question, don't you?'

'Not always.' Linda smiled that smile of hers again. She knew she was right. It was time for me to talk to my father.

AS I WALKED up the path to the Mount Lawley house, I could see Dad waiting for me. He was sitting on the love seat that used to be in the backyard, but now took pride of place on the front porch, all freshly re-painted and adorned with bright orange cushions.

'You got here fast,' he said, standing up to greet me. 'The tea hasn't brewed properly yet.'

'The bus came quickly,' I lied. When I'd phoned him to say I was coming over, I pretended I was about to catch the bus. In truth, I had been sitting just around the corner, debating with myself about whether or not I was ready to face him.

We waited for the tea and made small talk about the weather and the garden, about Dad's work and Rosemary's studies. All the words flowed over and away from me like clear mountain water over a dark riverbed.

'Shall I be Mother?' Dad finally said, picking up the teapot.

I nodded, but the turn of phrase threw me. I suddenly imagined Tina sitting in front of me, pouring out pure gin instead of tea and I wanted a drink more than anything. But before the thought consumed me, I challenged it, in the way that Linda had been teaching me. *Really, Samantha? You need a drink in order to be able to tell your father about your drinking?* I asked myself, and the thought lost its power. At least, for the moment.

I looked around. 'Where's Celine?' Another of Linda's strategies: distraction.

'She's doing a make-up party for a group of eleven-year-olds,' Craig replied. 'She pretended that she's only doing it as favour for a client, but I think she was really looking forward to it. You know how much she likes kids.' Dad gave a small smile.

'How is she doing?' I realised that I hadn't seen or spoken to Celine since she was in hospital, almost three months ago. It was a relief to talk about someone else's problems for a moment.

'Better. We've decided to give IVF one more try a bit later in the year, and then, if that doesn't work, we'll look into adopting, maybe from China or Korea. Our church has offered to help.'

'Let me know if I can help, too,' I said, and I actually meant it. Something in me had shifted towards Celine. All this time, I'd treated her like she was one of Dad's accessories, but I'd finally come to understand that she was family and I needed to take more time to get to know her.

Dad nodded and we sipped our tea. I imagined Linda's voice telling me to get on with it. My stomach still in knots, I took a deep breath and began.

'Dad, I need to tell you something that's quite difficult for me to talk about.'

'I'm listening,' he said, folding his hands on his lap. In that gesture, I caught a glimpse of what he must have been like as an open-faced and open-hearted boy, and I took the plunge.

'I had to catch the bus here because I've lost my licence.'

Dad looked confused. 'Where did you lose it?'

'I didn't misplace it, Dad. It was taken away from me because I was drunk when I had that accident. And now I'll have to go to court.'

'Drunk?' Now Dad looked even more confused. 'But I've never seen you have a single drink in your life. Not since that high school party.'

'Nobody has. But I've been drinking all the same.'

And I told him my story – starting right back at that high school party and then on to Rosemary's birth and the Wiggles years through to the days following Tina's funeral, right up to the moment I started sobering up after the accident. Dad listened carefully, his hands still folded.

'And now I've lost my licence and maybe even my husband. Trent's put up with so much from me over the years. I think this might be the final straw,' I told my father. 'Basically, I've stuffed up in all the ways a person can stuff up.'

Dad reached over and took my hand. I felt so grateful for the human contact I almost cried.

'You can't have stuffed up more than I have,' he told me. 'I've failed you, Samantha. All these years, I thought you were doing okay. You were organised and capable and, to be honest, fearsome. And yet, you were carrying this burden around the entire time.' He squeezed my hand. 'My poor girl. Why did you hide it from all of us?'

'That's something I've been talking over with this therapist I've been seeing, and I think the main reason is that I didn't want anyone to think I was like Tina.' I took a deep breath and then continued. 'More specifically, I didn't want *you* to think I was like Tina. I think I was afraid you'd stop loving me too.'

'What?' Dad blinked, genuinely surprised. 'You really think I stopped loving your mother because she was a drunk?'

'That's why you left her, right?' I asked.

'I might have pretended it was the reason, but it wasn't. Not at all. In fact, the truth is I never stopped loving her.'

'Then why did you leave her?'

'I left her because I thought she was going to leave me and I was too proud to let that happen,' he admitted. 'I should have stayed and tried to work things out. She was the love of my life, Sammy. Even after I married DL, I still missed her like mad. I never stopped loving her. Not for a moment.'

'And is that why you slept with her when you were married to DL?' I said it not as an accusation – I knew I was in no position to be casting stones – but as a genuine question. I wanted to know.

'Ah,' Dad said, taking his hand away from mine and folding them in his lap again. 'That.'

'Yes. *That*. Donna-Louise told me what happened.'

'It's not what you think. It's not even what Donna-Louise thinks.'

I frowned. 'Then what is it, Dad?'

'It's a big stuff-up. That's what it is. This is where I stuffed up the most. Even more than I did by sleeping with Meg.'

'Okay. So tell me about it.' I had the urge to tell Dad to lie down on the love seat, while I took notes, like Linda. 'When did it happen?'

'The night of Nicole's twenty-first.'

'Oh god,' I said, my hand automatically flying up to my mouth, but then dropping away. 'Hang on. You and Donna-Louise didn't separate until, what, a decade after that?'

'It was almost twelve years later that DL found the letter Tina wrote me at the time, begging me to keep it a secret.'

'Jesus, Dad. Why did you keep the letter?'

'To convince myself it had happened.'

'What do you mean "convince"?'

Dad looked down, embarrassed.

'It's so embarrassing to admit this, Sammy. The thing is, we didn't *actually* sleep together,' he said quietly. 'I'd only had a few light beers that night because DL and I were driving the people who didn't fit onto that awful Gobbles bus into the city. When we got back, DL went straight to bed with one of her headaches and I found Tina and your sister in the backyard. I drove them both home – Nicole first and then your mother. Tina was so drunk. Drunker than I'd seen her in years. But friendly. We laughed and chatted, like we had when we first got together. And then, when we got to her flat, I didn't want the evening to end and for us to resume hostilities. So I invited myself in.'

He stopped to watch a brightly coloured bird land on one of the rose bushes.

'That's a Western Rosella,' he explained, although I hadn't asked. 'They usually travel in pairs, so it's quite rare to see one on its own. DL used to hate them because they ate her fruit trees, but I've always loved them. All that colour . . .'

'Dad?' I said tentatively. I needed him to return to the story. I needed to understand what had happened.

'Ah, yes. Now, where was I?' Dad said, as if waking himself from a dream. He turned back to face me. 'I invited myself in. I guess I thought we might share a few more drinks and chat more, but she just went straight to her bed and fell asleep. I waited for a while in the lounge room and then – and this is the part I'm not proud of – I went into her room and lay down next to her. I didn't touch her, I swear. I just wanted to be close to her. And then, when she woke up an hour later and saw me there and assumed that she and I had . . . so I let her think . . .'

'Why would you let her think that?' None of this made sense to me.

'I've been exploring this with my own counsellor and I'm still not sure. I think I thought she might get back together with me if she believed we'd slept together. That she would think the door between us that had been firmly shut had somehow been opened again and she might decide to step through it and come back to me. But then she wrote me that letter and I realised how horrified and full of regret she was. The truth is that my lie just made her slam that door shut for good.

'And then years later, when DL found the letter, I tried to tell her that it hadn't actually happened, but she didn't believe me.' He unfolded his hands and turned them, palms up as if he was hoping to catch the sky. 'But why should she have believed me? I'm not a good man, Samantha. I'm weak. My counsellor says that's why I surround myself with strong women.'

'But Tina wasn't strong. She was a drunk.'

'You think she wasn't strong because she drank?' Dad seemed genuinely confounded. 'She was strong, Sammy. Strong enough to know when to hold on and when to let go. I've always held on to the wrong things for much longer than I ought to and let go of the right things at the wrong time.'

We sat in silence. I thought of Donna-Louise, straight-backed and proud, and how she had deserved so much more than feeling like someone's leftovers. I wondered if Celine felt the same way.

'Have you told Celine any of this?'

'Yes. She's come along to a couple of my sessions with my counsellor and we've all prayed together,' Dad said, as if that answered the question.

'And?'

'Cee-Cee understands, like I do, that you can't change the past. You can only change the way you behave in the future. And she knows and trusts that I'm trying hard to be a better person.'

I realised in that moment that the past was like one of Rosemary's slinky toys when it got all twisted and bent. Even if I managed to untangle all the lies and resentment, I could never fix it. So why shouldn't I try to be like Dad and leave it behind?

'I'm going to try to be a better person, too,' I said.

'That's why Tina sent you to live with me, you know,' Dad said, looking out at the garden that he and Tina had planted together, and the roses she tried to destroy. 'She was worried you were too much like her. She wanted you to have a chance to be a better person than she thought she was.'

My jaw dropped. 'But I thought it was because she didn't want to deal with me anymore. I know I'm not . . . easy.'

In fact, I was a pain in the arse. Therapy had been showing me that. I had been so busy stamping my foot and demanding what I wanted from the world that I had never stopped to listen to anyone around me.

'No, it wasn't that at all. She wanted to protect you. And then, when you were hovering between the two houses for a while, she made that decision to move to a smaller place that didn't have room for you.'

'She did that on purpose?'

'She did that out of love.'

I bowed my head. All those years, I had thought Tina hadn't wanted or cared for me.

'I wish I'd known all this before she . . .'

'Before she died?' Dad put his arm around me. 'Nicole told me you didn't go see her in the hospital. That must be a hard thing to sit with.'

I started to cry. 'Nicole doesn't know, but I did go and see her. Too late, though. I left it too late.'

Dad gently squeezed my shoulder. 'Let that one go, darling. Tina had her faults, but, as I said, she knew when to hold on and when to let go. We could all learn something from her.'

Piece #21: 1986

IT WAS THE kind of day when even the sky seemed defeated by the heat. When Nicole went into Tina's room and suggested they go to the beach, she was surprised that Tina said yes. Tina's hangovers had been a little worse in the six months since Samantha had gone to live with Craig and that morning's had been even more severe than usual.

'We can pick up your sister on the way,' Tina said, from underneath the wheat pack on her forehead.

'No need. She's already here.'

'Again?'

'Yes, again.'

Samantha might have been officially living in Mount Lawley, but she had been constantly turning up unannounced in Bassendean, like a moth flitting uncertainly between two flames.

Most Saturday mornings, Nicole would get up to make coffee for her and Tina and find Samantha sitting at the dining room table doing her homework or quietly rearranging the books on the bookshelf so they were back in alphabetical order. One time, she'd admitted to Nicole that she came to Bassendean because she had no idea where to stand in the Mount Lawley house on Saturday mornings without feeling like she was in Donna-Louise's way.

'Mum said yes,' Nicole told Samantha when she got back out to the living room.

'I'll have to stay here tonight,' Samantha replied. 'Donna-Louise doesn't like sand in the house, not after she's cleaned all the floors.'

'Another rule of The House of No,' Nicole said, picking up a book and pretending to make a note inside it. '*No sand.*'

'Don't call it that,' Samantha protested. 'It's not really like that. Not when you live there.'

'Sorry, Sammy, but you can't sleep here,' Tina shouted from her room. 'There's a couple of bicycles on your bed. It's kind of a long story.'

Samantha frowned and leapt up, muttering, 'It's still my room,' as she stormed off down the hall.

Nicole returned to her copy of *The Accidental Tourist*, but she couldn't concentrate on the story. For one thing, Samantha was making way too much noise trying to remove one of the bicycles from her room. And for another thing, it was bugging her that she still didn't understand why Samantha had gone to live in Mount Lawley. No number of questions, direct or indirect, to Tina, Craig or even Samantha herself, would reveal the reason. Nicole figured it had something to do with Samantha getting drunk at that party, but she thought there must be more to it than that.

Whenever she asked her sister, all Samantha would say is, 'It's between me and Tina,' in a voice she seemed to have borrowed from a soap opera. Nicole wasn't used to things being between Tina and Samantha that didn't involve her. She wondered if Samantha wasn't telling Nicole because she was still angry that Nicole had dobbed her in to Tina. But even that didn't make sense. It was entirely the kind of thing Samantha herself would have done. Surely, she could see that.

Samantha was still wrestling with one of the bicycles in the corridor when Tina emerged from her room.

'Leave it in there,' Tina told her. 'We'll deal with it later.'

'But I want to change the sheets.'

'You'll have to wash some sheets first,' Tina laughed.

'There's always clean sheets at Dad's.'

'Well, maybe you should sleep there,' Tina said, her tone a little pointy. 'Actually, that reminds me. I need to talk to you.'

She made a wide sweeping 'step into my office' gesture back in through her door. Samantha gave up on the bicycle, leaving it so it was half in her room and half in the corridor, and stomped into Tina's bedroom.

'What about me? I'm part of this family too,' Nicole shouted after them.

'This is between me and Samantha,' Tina replied in her own soap opera voice, as she closed the door.

Nicole strained to hear what they were talking about, but she couldn't make out any words, just a low rumble. She put her book down and edged her way down the corridor, past the bicycle, and was almost there when the door was flung open again. Tina's smile was brighter than the sun, but Samantha's face was flushed with an emotion Nicole couldn't quite name.

'Grab your bathers, Nicole,' Tina said. 'We've got a date with the Indian Ocean.'

*

NICOLE TOLD SAMANTHA that she could sit in the front seat. Normally, she'd assert her front seat rights as the elder sister but today, she just wanted Samantha's face to go back to normal.

'I'm happy to sit in the back,' Samantha said, her voice quiet.

The car remained silent as they drove along the highway. Nicole was thankful that they'd had to wind all the windows down because of the heat. The rush of air in her ears drowned out the weirdness between Tina and Samantha.

A few times she twisted around to look at Samantha in the back seat, leaning over to flick her gently on her bare leg. But Samantha remained still and quiet, like a zombie version of herself.

As they got closer to the beach, Nicole had an idea on how to perk her sister up. 'Mum, can we drive past the Jetson house?'

'Of course.' Tina laughed as she turned down the West Coast Highway, past the huge square monstrosity with multiple levels and seafront views that Tina had always joked she would buy when she won Lotto.

'See our house, Sam?' Nicole turned around in her seat to look at Samantha, but she was looking the other way.

'There's probably no room for me in that house either,' Samantha muttered.

TINA PULLED INTO the BP, but not in front of the petrol bowsers.

'Go in and get yourselves an ice cream. Anything you want,' she told them, which finally snapped Samantha out of whatever dark spell she was under.

'Can we really choose anything?' Samantha said, like Christmas had suddenly arrived early and offered her an ice cream.

'Yes, you can really choose anything.'

'So we can choose any ice cream we want, even the expensive ones?' Nicole had to double check. Sometimes when Tina said 'anything you want' it meant nothing over fifty cents.

'Anything. Now go in and choose before I change my mind,' Tina said, handing them a five dollar note. 'And get me a Heart.'

Inside the BP, Samantha was loving the fact she could choose anything she wanted. 'I can't decide between a Gaytime or a Bubble O' Bill,' she was saying. 'Or maybe I should get a Funny Feet? Although, shouldn't it be "Funny Foot"? There's only one of them.'

Nicole was having trouble concentrating on the ice creams. 'What did Mum want to talk to you about?'

'Nothing,' Samantha said sharply, before adding 'Maybe I'll get a Vienna Chocolate! They're mintox.'

'She must have said something.'

'I said *nothing*.' Samantha was looking fierce again, like her normal self, which was an improvement on the hollow version of Samantha she'd been in the car. Nicole backed off and returned to the freezer, trying to convince herself it really was nothing. She ended up choosing a Heart. It felt easier to copy Tina's choice than to make one of her own.

THEY ENDED UP eating their ice creams in the beach carpark, still sitting in the car with all the windows down. Out on the horizon, dark clouds were rolling in from the far west.

'Looks like a storm is coming,' Tina said, as she fished her diary from her bag. 'What ice cream did you eat again, Sam?'

Samantha, still sitting in the back seat, had gobbled up her ice cream and was now on to the bubblegum nose, making loud cracking noises as she chewed.

Nicole answered for her. 'A Bubble O' Bill. I had a Heart like you.'

'Samantha has a heart like me, too,' Tina said to nobody in particular, noting something in her diary.

'I reckon I'm ready for a swim,' Nicole said.

'You'd better get in quick before the storm hits,' Tina replied. 'Those clouds are looking very Pritikin.'

Nicole turned around just in time to see Samantha grimace in the back seat. She then looked at her mum, hoping a swim would do what seeing the Jetson house hadn't, that it would bring them all back together. 'Aren't you coming?'

'No, I'm going to stay up here to watch Mother Nature's show,' Tina replied.

Down on the beach, Nicole threw off her sundress, ready to run into the water, but Samantha hung back.

'I forgot to put my bathers on.'

'Then swim in your T-shirt and undies. They'll dry soon enough.'

Samantha looked around, no doubt checking that no one from school was nearby, and then primly took off her shorts, folding them next to Nicole's abandoned dress.

The two girls bobbed up and over the breaking waves, not saying much to each other. Nicole could see Tina, now sitting on top of the dunes. She waved but Tina didn't see her.

'Mum told me you were moving,' Samantha said suddenly.

'You mean *we* are moving. You, too. You still kind of live with us. Sometimes.'

'No, just you and her. She's getting a two-bedroom place. She said I won't have my own room anymore, but I can still sleep on the fold-out sofa.'

Nicole remembered the last time they'd opened the fold-out sofa, and how even Tina had been alarmed by the amount of debris and dust that had gathered on the thin grey mattress. She knew Tina wanted to get a cheaper place now that Craig wasn't paying child support for Samantha, but Nicole had assumed it would be a cheaper place with room for all of them.

'You can share my room,' Nicole offered, but Samantha had duck-dived under the water and didn't hear her.

The waves were getting choppier and a couple of times they almost got dumped so they headed back to shore. As she towelled herself off, Nicole regarded the incoming storm. The clouds were now almost black and there was lightning sparking up the horizon. The whole world was starting to shake.

'Let's go back to the car,' she shouted to Samantha. The two girls grabbed their things and ran back up through the dunes past Tina and into the car, where they huddled, clutching their towels around them, as the rain started to hit.

Tina was now standing up on top of the highest dune. Nicole hung out the passenger window and shouted for her to come to the car, but she stayed where she was.

'What's she doing?' Samantha asked. She sounded frightened.

'What are you doing?' Nicole shouted to Tina.

Tina turned and looked at the girls. 'I'm greeting my demons!' she shouted back to them. Nicole couldn't be sure, but Tina looked like she had been crying. Or maybe she'd just got sand in her eyes. Or rain.

The girls watched as Tina turned back to the storm and held her arms out, as if to embrace it.

Piece #22: 2018

WHEN SAMANTHA GOT the call from Nicole saying Tina had been admitted to the Royal Perth, she drove straight to the hospital. But when it came to getting out of the car and walking into the hospital, she couldn't do it. Instead, she sat in the car for an hour, listening to the cricket on the radio, despite the fact that she didn't even like cricket.

As she listened, she imagined the ball being hit around the cricket ground. With each hit, the ball created a line in her mind and the lines grew and grew, creating a pattern, like a web. Or a safety net of sorts.

And then she found herself starting the engine and driving home. Via the bottle shop.

Nicole could deal with the doctors, she told herself. It was about time she stepped up, anyway.

At first, Nicole left Samantha long, chatty voice mail messages with updates about Tina's health and suggestions about when might be a good time for Samantha to visit.

'Come in the morning, before the doctors do their rounds and piss her off,' she'd said. 'She's good in the mornings. She makes all the nurses laugh.'

But as the week passed by and Samantha still hadn't gone to the hospital, the messages grew shorter. And the most recent message was the shortest of all.

'Please, Samantha.'

But Samantha didn't go. Couldn't go.

Instead, she did other things. She did her work. She did the laundry and the shopping and the cleaning. She cooked dinner and washed dishes, she organised and re-organised the books and the CDs and the video games, and then, when everything that could be done was done, she sat down next to Trent to watch TV before retreating to the spare bedroom and her secret stash of vodka.

After three nights in a row of joining him to watch the test cricket highlights, Trent was finally onto her.

'Don't get me wrong,' he said. 'I love having you next to me here on the couch, I really do, but I think you need to go and see your mum.'

'I know,' she said, putting her head on his shoulder.

'Nicole rang me at work. She said it was serious, that Tina wasn't going to last much longer.'

'I know.'

'This isn't like you, avoiding things like this. You're being like Nicole.'

'I know.' She was whispering now.

They watched as the red ball was whacked about on a sea of green and white. The lines began to grow in Samantha's mind again, one on top of another. Trent put his arm around her and pulled her in tight.

'I could go with you,' he said, turning the sound down at the next ad break. 'If that makes it easier.'

Samantha didn't say anything. She knew that nothing would make it easier. Not even drinking was making it easier.

THAT NIGHT, AS the vodka carried her off into sleep, she felt her body relax into the mattress of the spare bed and it took her back to an early memory. It was late at night, at the end of a long car trip, maybe coming back from Esperance. She and Nicole were lying on the back seat and she could hear her parents talking in low voices in the front, laughing together over some story, and their laughter sounded like music. When she felt the car pull into the driveway, Samantha closed her eyes and pretended to be asleep, so she could be carried into bed. She felt Nicole being lifted away from her and then Tina's arms around her, lifting her up so that her face was nestled in against Tina's hair, which smelt like exotic flowers and coconut.

As Samantha remembered this, she realised that she would never experience that feeling of being carried by her mother again. Her parents, she realised, were going to die. Tina first, any day now, and then later, Craig. And then Donna-Louise. After that, there would be nobody left to carry her, not even for part of her journey.

WHEN SHE WOKE in the morning, she knew it was time. She called in sick at work and headed into the Mount, where Jethro's millions had transferred Tina. She didn't tell Trent she was going; she didn't tell Nicole either. She just went.

In her expensive private room in the palliative care unit, Tina looked like a small, broken puppet on the bed, her wires all tangled up with machines. Her skin was yellow and her breathing was laboured, despite the tubes leading from her nose to a tank of oxygen. Her arms were as thin as fingers, but her stomach, even under the bedding, looked bloated.

'Mum, it's me, Sammy. I'm here,' she said tentatively, as she approached Tina's bed, but she may as well have been talking to a cloudless sky. Tina's eyes stayed shut and she remained perfectly still, except for the slow rise and fall of her chest.

She remembered watching Tina asleep on the couch when she was younger, the little *ptttht* noises the air made as it had escaped her mouth, slack with sleep and booze. Back then, she knew Tina would eventually wake up and ask Samantha to make her coffee; three heaped spoons each of International Roast and sugar with a splash of milk.

Now, there would be no instant coffee. There may not even be any more waking up.

Samantha looked around at the flowers and cards that surrounded Tina's bed. The biggest bunch – an explosion of red roses – was from Nicole and Jethro. She felt the usual sting of jealousy, imagining Nicole walking into a florist and choosing the largest bunch without having to even look at the price tag. She tucked the small bunch of flowers she'd bought from the hospital florist into the same vase as Nicole's extravagance and sat down on the chair by the bed.

As she took her mother's hand in her own, it felt small and fragile, like it was made of tiny bird bones.

'Mum,' she said. 'I'm sorry I didn't come sooner. I . . .'

But she didn't know what to say. There were no clear words for her to grasp on to. She felt that ancient rage rise up inside her, the rage of the Other Samantha. Rage at her mother for not loving her, for not choosing her, for always putting drink ahead of her. Rage at her mother for giving her the same disease and then rage at herself for succumbing to that disease. And then sadness for Tina's life, spent in the company of the bottle at the exclusion of everyone else, even her daughters. A life pissed away. And then she remembered to breathe.

She breathed in time with Tina, in and out, holding Tina's hand in hers and listening to the hum of the machines until a nurse came in to usher her out.

'We'll be ten minutes,' the nurse told her kindly. 'We just need to take some blood and change her sheets. Go get yourself a coffee and by the time you come back, we'll be gone.'

Samantha headed towards the cafeteria on the ground floor but found it was easier to keep walking out to the carpark, get in the car and drive away without having to say goodbye. A part of her felt that Tina would understand. Another part of her felt like a lost child, separated from her mother in a crowd, wanting to cry, but the tears wouldn't come, as much as she might have wanted them to.

SHE ENDED UP driving around for hours, visiting the landmarks of her childhood, places that she regularly drove past but never stopped and thought about. She drove up to Kings Park and walked around the clock made of flowers. She looked out over the river and the Narrows Bridge and the windmill in South Perth that she had once thought to be so exotic. She got back in the car and she drove over to Rokeby Road, past the old Subi markets, where Tina would sometimes take them to have stuffed baked potatoes for lunch if she wasn't too hungover, and then she cut across towards the coast, to City Beach.

When she reached the Indian Ocean, she paused for a moment and considered turning left, towards Cottesloe and back to the Ocean Beach Hotel. But instead, she turned right and drove all the way up the coast, past the monstrous blue units that had once been the Jetson house that Tina had always said she would buy when she won the Lotto.

At Observation City, she cut inland and started heading down Scarborough Beach Road and, before she really knew it, she was in Dog Swamp, where that semi-boyfriend of Nicole's had once worked at the video store. Finally, she headed east towards Bassendean, to the little townhouse she had lived in with Tina and Nicole all those years ago. And she knew that this was where she had been heading all along.

She parked outside and looked at its curtained windows and thought of the many nights she had slept there: Tina drinking and doing jigsaws in front of the television in the small lounge room; Nicole reading her books under the covers with a torch; and Samantha lying in her bed, dreaming of a better life, with a valance and clean sheets. Of course, she'd eventually found that better life, living with Craig and Donna-Louise. But a little part of her had always remained in Bassendean, yearning for something else.

Her phone rang and broke her thoughts. It was Nicole. This time, she took the call.

'Hello?'

There was a long pause on the other end of the phone and Samantha knew what Nicole was going to say. But she let her say it anyway.

'Mum's gone.'

She said more but Samantha didn't really process any of it. She thought of Tina in that hospital room, finally still, her chest no longer rising and falling with the effort of living, with the effort of staying sober and the effort of getting drunk.

And she found herself yearning for that same relief, whatever shape it took.

Nicole

W<small>E FLEW ALONG</small> the State 40 highway, stirring up the red dirt and all our secrets. It was much easier to talk to each other honestly while we drove, our eyes forward and Perth fading behind us. I told Samantha my secrets and she told me hers, our conversation underlined by an '80s compilation CD on the car stereo: 'Don't You Forget About Me', 'We Built This City', 'Total Eclipse of the Heart'. The soundtrack of our youth.

'And all that time I gave you shit about the frozen ham, you never thought to tell me about your miscarriage?' Samantha asked. She sounded hurt, but not in the petulant way she used to as a kid. I recognised it as the kind of hurt you feel when you realise how much pain you've caused someone you love. I knew that feeling well.

'I wish you'd told me you went to see Mum,' I told her. 'I've been so furious with you. If I'd known you went, maybe I might have been kinder to you instead of behaving like I was the only person entitled to grieve.'

'Well, I should have seen her earlier. I should have told you how I was feeling, I should have . . .'

I shot a glance at her but her face was turned towards the passenger window.

'You should have what?' I asked.

'I should have done a lot of things,' she said, turning back to me. 'But the point is, I can't do anything about all that. It's what I do *now* that matters. At least that's what Dad told me. And look at us both: I'm here talking to you and you are here talking to me. We got there in the end.'

'Amen to that,' I said, cranking up 'Everybody Wants to Rule the World' on the stereo. Perhaps our secrets could ultimately cancel each other out, leaving us both feeling as clear as the road ahead.

AS WE HIT the first bend in the road outside Narembeen on the way up towards Bruce Rock, Samantha turned to me.

'Is this it?'

'No. Maybe. I don't know,' I replied. 'I feel like we'd driven around a few bends before we crashed.'

I took the corners slowly, a lot more carefully than I guessed Tina would have taken them. At the fourth bend in the road, I pulled over.

'This is it,' I said. 'I remember the gravel road here, off to the side.'

We slowly climbed out of the car. The air was heavy with flies and memories.

'Or maybe I'm wrong.' I was doubting my memory now. 'I remember a tree. There's no tree here.'

'It's been thirty-six years. Maybe the tree got chopped down?'

We took in the expanse of the wide, brown land around us while the flies tried to crawl up our noses and into our mouths.

'I wonder what would have happened if she hadn't flipped the car here,' I said.

'What do you mean?' Samantha asked, swatting a fly away.

'With the divorce and everything.'

Samantha squinted at the sky for a moment. 'I think things would have turned out the same,' she eventually said, looking back down at me. 'Especially now we know why Mum was driving this way.'

'Yeah, maybe,' I replied. 'But maybe they would have separated under different terms where it didn't look and feel like it was all Mum's fault.'

Samantha shrugged. 'It's hard to know.'

We stood for a while longer. I remembered the couple who had stopped and pulled blankets out of their station wagon. I remembered the nurse's kind face when she offered me that lollipop. I remembered the dogs who sat at our feet while we waited for Dad. It was funny how people tended to remember the aftermath more than the disaster itself.

AT THE BRUCE Rock pub, we walked into the same front bar where Mum had sat and drank with the locals so many years ago.

I ordered two lemonades and a packet of salt and vinegar chips.

'For old times' sake,' I said to Samantha.

'You can get a beer, you know,' Samantha told me. 'I won't mind.'

'Nah,' I said. 'I'm not in the mood.'

Samantha went to pull her purse out.

'Don't worry,' I told her. 'I've got this.'

Even in the dawn of this new era between us, I sensed that she wanted to give her usual answer: *You mean, Jethro's got this.* But she put her purse away, nonetheless.

Still, I decided not to let it go this time. As we waited for our drinks, I asked her, 'Why does Jethro's money bother you so much?'

'Ha,' Samantha replied. 'My therapist asked me the very same question the other day.'

'And what did you tell her?'

Samantha started straightening the stack of coasters on the bar. 'Even though I know you've worked in shitty jobs most of your life, it kills me that you now never have to worry about work or money or where to live. It's like you've been drifting along out at sea for years and yet have somehow managed to wash up on the shore in exactly the right spot. Meanwhile, I've felt like I've been slogging away, never getting anywhere. I certainly haven't landed in the same beautiful spot as you.'

'But then, you're a much richer person than I'll ever be,' I replied. 'You have Rosemary. All I have is that awful Cookie Monster jar to remind me of my incompetent cervix.'

'We should have some kind of ceremony where we smash it together,' Samantha suggested. 'To remind you that you are much more than your cervix.'

I smiled. It wasn't a bad idea.

We took our drinks to a table in the corner. Samantha watched me as I took a sip of my lemonade.

'I've always envied you for that, you know,' she said instead.

'For what?'

'Just now you didn't order a beer because you didn't feel like it. You can have one drink or a hundred drinks or none at all. It never seems to bother you or hold you captive the way it does for me. You even spent a whole year stoned and then one day, you just stopped. Just like that.'

'I've never really thought about it that way.'

'Because you've never had to think about it. Every day is a struggle for me not to drink. Every hour, every minute. Every second. Even now that I've decided I don't want to drink anymore, I still think about it all the time.'

'Oh, Sam,' I said. 'I had no idea.'

'Of course, you didn't. Because I never told you. I never told you a lot of things.'

'Like why you didn't ask me to be a bridesmaid at your wedding?' The words surprised me by falling out of my mouth. Sure, it had bothered me at the time, but I honestly hadn't thought of it for years.

'Oh, yes. That.' Samantha shifted uncomfortably in her seat. 'Since we're spilling all our secrets, I may as well tell you the real, horrible truth. I know I pretended at the time it was because Trent wanted to matchmake you with Darren—'

'But wasn't it you?'

'Wasn't it me what?'

'That wanted to matchmake me with Darren? That's how I remember it,' I said.

Samantha looked surprised. 'Really?' she said. 'I don't remember ever liking Darren enough to wish him upon my beloved sister. But if I did, I'm truly sorry. Anyway, the truth is even worse. The real reason I didn't make you a bridesmaid was because you were too tall.'

I felt my jaw drop. 'What?'

'Trent's groomsmen were all so short and I just didn't want

the wedding photos ruined with you towering over everyone,' Samantha admitted sheepishly.

'Really?' I started laughing. 'I knew you went a bit bridezilla, but I had no idea about the extent of it.'

'I know, right? I was even worse to Mum. I basically told her not to come to the reception. Or rather, I told her she could only come if she didn't drink.'

'Oh.' I stopped laughing. I remembered Mum at the church, making her flimsy excuses and disappearing.

'For years, I told myself she chose alcohol over me by not coming,' Samantha continued. 'But the truth was, I didn't want her to come. And I'm ashamed of that. She probably told you all about it.'

I shook my head. 'No, she just said she had a headache.'

Samantha looked legitimately surprised. 'God, she was even better at keeping secrets than we were.'

I looked down at the carpet, faded with age and spilled beer, and I thought of Mum and the things she never told us, all now buried with her in Karrakatta Cemetery. They were like the missing pieces of a puzzle.

And then I remembered the present I had for Samantha. 'I was going to give this to you when we got back to Perth,' I said, reaching into my bag. 'But it feels the right time to give it to you now.'

I handed her a gift box. Samantha looked surprised.

'Jethro and I found these when we were tidying up Mum's flat,' I explained. 'And I got them framed.'

Samantha opened the gift box to find a glass frame holding a photo of us both, nestled in between layers of pink tissue paper. The photo had been taken when we were eleven and nine. In the corner of the photo was the piece of puzzle I'd found wedged in the skirting board.

'Oh god,' Samantha laughed when she saw the piece of puzzle. 'One of Tina's missing pieces. You've put that there to taunt me.'

'No, no,' I assured her. 'It's there as a reminder that we don't need all the pieces to get an idea of the larger picture.'

'Except in the case of this one, where we'll never know what the larger picture is,' Samantha joked. 'I expect the rest of the pieces are in the bin.'

'That's where the photo comes in.'

Samantha took a closer look at the photo. The two of us were wearing matching sundresses, arms around each other, arms, legs and faces bronzed by summer.

'The photo is from that summer in Esperance. Just before the accident,' I told her.

'Oh!' Samantha exclaimed. 'I remember we got those dresses for Christmas. Aunty Meg gave them to us.'

'Now turn it over.'

Samantha flipped it over. The transparent frame allowed her to see what was written on the back of the photograph in Mum's writing:

These are the two things that we did best in this world.

'"We"? She must mean her and Dad,' Samantha wondered. 'Do you think she was planning to give this photo to him?'

'Maybe. Although, I also wondered if it was just a reminder for her. Anyway, we'll never know. But now it's a reminder for you. And for me.'

Samantha smiled, and I liked seeing her smile.

Before the spill

1982

THE WEEK IN Esperance staying with friends had been a happy one, but then Tina surprised everyone by packing up the car a day early.

'We'll surprise Daddy,' Tina told the girls. 'We'll drive as far as we can tonight and we'll stay at a motel. And in the morning, we'll ring and pretend we're only just leaving Esperance, but then we'll get to Perth and we'll surprise him.'

Neither of the girls understood why Tina had come up with this elaborate plan but they both liked surprises and assumed their dad liked them too.

THEY ARRIVED AT the Wave Rock Motel in Hyden just before 10 pm and had a good night's sleep. Breakfast arrived in the morning on three trays, each with its own stainless-steel cover that made the toast sweat.

After they'd eaten, the girls played on the swing set in the motel's garden while Tina went to reception to pay the bill and to call Craig from the public phone.

As she fed the twenty cent coins into the slot, she could hear the girls laughing outside and she felt as much hope as she'd dared to feel in months, maybe years. The promise she had made to Craig had been a hard one, but she'd stuck to it so far: she hadn't had a single drink in over three weeks. She just hoped he'd kept his promise too.

After maybe ten rings, the phone was picked up. Tina could hear music faintly, but still distinct, in the background. Rod Stewart, 'Tonight's the Night'. She could also hear a man shouting.

'Hello?' a familiar woman's voice said.

Tina, surprised, felt her voice rise in pitch. 'Meg?'

There was a scuffling noise that swallowed Rod Stewart completely. Tina realised Meg had covered the mouthpiece, but she could still hear Meg's voice and then the man's voice again, distant as thunder. She strained to hear what they were saying, but she couldn't make the words out.

'Hello?' Tina said again, when the phone was uncovered and she could hear Rod Stewart in the background again.

'Sorry, Teens. I have a friend over and he, um, wanted to know where the bathroom was,' Meg replied. There was something giddy about her voice that made Tina think she might be high.

'Why are you and your friend at my house?' Tina wanted to know.

'What? But I'm at my house.' Meg laughed. 'You must have rung my number by mistake. Again.'

Tina laughed, too. It was a mistake she made often enough because Meg's number was the one she rang the most.

'Who's the man friend?' she asked.

'Oh, no one,' Meg replied, coyly.

'Right. Well, I don't have many coins and I've still got to ring Craig, so I'll have to interrogate you later.' Tina hung up and rang home, this time paying attention to each number as she dialled it. This time, the phone rang three times before Craig answered.

'Hello?' he said. 'Craig speaking.'

'Craig?'

'Teensy!' Craig's voice was bright. He sounded pleased to hear from her. 'Are you coming back today?'

Tina bit her bottom lip. 'No,' she found herself saying. 'I'm just ringing to say that the kids and I are going to stay in Esperance a couple more days.'

She was surprised by how easily the lie came to her.

'It will do you good,' Craig said. 'Give me a call when you plan to head home.'

Tina stared at the brown swirls on the motel reception wallpaper and felt herself falling into them.

'Are you still there, Teensy?' Craig asked.

'Yes,' Tina said. 'I better go. The girls want to go to the beach.'

'Okay. I love you.'

Tina gently replaced the phone in its cradle.

Neither Craig nor Meg had realised that they'd left Rod Stewart playing in the background.

TINA WENT STRAIGHT out to the boot of the car, where she'd shoved the bottle-shaped package her father had given her for her birthday. 'You can still drink on special occasions, right?' he'd said when she'd tried to refuse it, and she'd felt like dropping it then and there on the parquet floor just to make a point to everyone that she didn't need it. Not on special occasions. Not ever.

But now she really did need it. Her mind felt like a snow globe, shaken up with a thousand thoughts. How long had this been going on? How could Meg be so foolish? How could Craig be so selfish?

She ripped off the wrapping to find a bottle of Teacher's whisky, the kind her parents used to have when she was younger that she would swig from when nobody was looking. She glanced across to where the girls were playing. She could have a quick swig now and get away with it. Nobody would know. It was the only thing she could think of that would loosen the grip that the phone call had on her heart.

She turned away from the girls and brought the bottle quickly to her lips.

Just a sip, she told herself.

NICOLE WAS PUSHING Samantha on the swing.

'Harder!' Samantha shouted. 'Higher!'

She leant back in the swing, stretched her legs out in front of her and aimed for the sky.

'Mummy!' she shouted, as she pulled her legs back in and anticipated the weight of Nicole's hands on her back. 'Look at me fly!'

Back at the car, Tina turned around just in time to see Nicole give Samantha an almighty shove out of the swing and onto the grass. Before she knew it, Tina was running towards them.

'Why did you do that?' Samantha was wailing at her sister from her crumpled position.

'What?' Nicole was confused. 'But you told me to push you hard!'

'Not *that* hard!' Samantha's face was a tight ball held together with snot and outrage.

'I was only doing what you told me to do.'

'Nicole, you need to be more careful!' Tina ran over to where the girls were. 'You need to look after your little sister.'

But as Tina bent down to comfort her crying daughter, she realised she was still holding the open whisky bottle. She immediately put it down on the grass behind her.

'Are you hurt?'

'No,' Samantha replied, before glaring back at Nicole. 'But I could have been. Very, *very* hurt.'

Nicole rolled her eyes.

'Well, that's lucky. Let's get you into the car, my little love,' Tina said. 'I tell you what, you can sit in the front.'

'But Mum!' Nicole protested.

'But nothing. It's Sam's turn.'

And with that, Tina scooped Samantha up and carried her over to the car.

Nicole stayed behind. She was staring at the bottle.

'Come on, Nic,' Tina shouted at her.

And Nicole ran to the car, leaving the bottle behind.

AS TINA PUSHED the key into the ignition, she thought of the long drive ahead, back to Craig and his lies and his empty promises.

'Who wants to go to Kalgoorlie to see Nanna and Poppa?'

'What about surprising Daddy?' Samantha asked.

'He's busy with work,' Tina replied.

'But it's a Saturday.'

Tina ignored this. She turned the key but the engine just made a clicking sound.

'What about school on Monday?' Nicole asked.

Tina ignored this, too. She turned the key again and this time, the car briefly shuddered but then fell silent.

'How long is it to Kalgoorlie?'

'I don't know. Maybe five hours?'

One more turn of the key.

'What about *Young Talent Time*? We'll miss it,' Nicole moaned. It was her favourite show.

But Tina wasn't listening. The engine had finally roared to life and in any case, she was too busy wondering what the hell Craig was up to with her sister. She wanted to be furious at Meg, but all she felt was pity. Craig would finish with Meg soon enough, like he had with all the other women. Tina and Meg, however, were sisters. And in that moment, Tina realised that Meg didn't need to know that she knew. What had she just told Nicole? *You need to look after your little sister.*

She would look after her little sister.

In the back seat, Nicole stretched out along the mountain of pillows and doonas. She hadn't realised that Samantha had had it so sweet back there all this time.

'You can keep the front seat, Sam,' she said, but nobody heard her over the sound of Tina revving the engine.

Tina started to put the car into reverse but then remembered the bottle of whisky, still there on the grass.

'Wait one moment,' she said.

Leaving the engine running, she got out of the car and ran over to get the bottle. She took it around to the back of the motel, out of sight of the road and the reception and the girls waiting for her in the car, and she emptied its entire contents onto the ground.

The smell of the whisky as it hit the earth was the smell of failure.

'What were you doing?' Nicole asked her, as she climbed back into the car.

'Trying to keep a promise to myself.'

Putting the car in gear and pressing her foot hard on the accelerator, Tina pulled out onto the road and they were off.

Acknowledgements

THANK YOU TO:

The team at Penguin Random House Australia, particularly my publisher, Meredith Curnow, for her passion and care; my editor, Genevieve Buzo, for her keen eye and gentle hand (and for continuing the creative collaboration of our fathers, Alex and Aarne); Claire de Medici, for her forensic proofreading; and Alex Ross, for the beautiful cover.

My agent, Jane Novak, for patiently answering all my questions (so many questions!) and for championing my work.

The judges of the 2019 Penguin Literary Prize, for choosing my manuscript above 490 others (I'm still pinching myself!). Also Leading Edge Books, for supporting the prize and for all the great work they do.

My beta readers, Silvia Ercole, Rachelle Walsh, Kali Napier, Victoria Carless, Clive Wansbrough and Julie Hudspeth, for their invaluable feedback (especially Kali Napier, who read the first and fifth drafts and always managed to see something worthwhile in *The Spill*, even at those times when I could not).

My writing group, Deborah Crabtree, Troy Hunter, Karen McKnight and Clive Wansbrough, for reading random chapters and weathering lengthy explanations of the book's structure and encouraging me nonetheless. May this be the first of many publications for The Prologues.

Emilie Collyer, Jenny Green and Jane Rawson, for the writerly brunches and loving support. Also for being ace human beings.

Antoni Jach and Alison Goodman, for their timely insights into structure.

Anjanette Fennell and Ailsa Piper, for their support and guidance along the long road to getting published.

The Eleanor Dark Foundation and the Henry Handel Richardson Society, for giving me two weeks of writing in Varuna at a critical point in this book's development. And Tracy Farr, Lisa Siberry, Helen Meany, Stef Johnstone and Heather Collins, for their fine company and jigsaw-related enthusiasm during my residency.

Jacie Anderson, Chelsea Cruse, Phil Jeng Kane, Mel May and Chrissy Wilson, for helping me remember 1980s Perth.

Glynis Traill-Nash, for her knowledge of 1990s fashion.

Jo-Anne Zappia, for her help when I was writing about Tina's final days.

My mother, Helen, for patiently waiting until this was a real book.

The elders past, present and emerging of the Wurundjeri people of the Kulin nation, upon whose land I wrote this book. And of the Noongar people, upon whose land the book is set.

And very special thanks to:

My late grandfather, the artist and writer Gunnar Neeme, for teaching me about dedication and perseverance.

The five beautiful young people in my life, Hal, Luke, Evie, Orla and Leo, for being patient and good-humoured while I wrote and wrote and wrote.

And my husband, Derek, for being the best reason for everything I do.